Tim Wilson was born ... ... borough on the edge of the Fens. He was a student on the University of East Anglia MA Course in Creative Writing under Malcolm Bradbury and Angela Carter. He and his partner Mary-Anne live in Peterborough with two cats.

His first two psychological thrillers, PURGATORY and CLOSE TO YOU, are also available from Headline Feature:

'A tightly written debut by Mr Wilson who commands attention to the end' *Cardiff Western Mail*

'Another superb psychological thriller from Wilson's pen. It grips from the start, takes the reader on a nerve-wracking roller-coaster and holds a strict pace' *Peterborough Evening Telegraph*

Also by Tim Wilson from Headline Feature

Purgatory
Close To You

Freezing Point

Tim Wilson

KNIGHT

Copyright © 1995 Tim Wilson

The right of Tim Wilson to be identified as the Author of the Work has been asserted by him in accordance with the Copyright, Designs and Patents Act 1988.

First published in 1995
by HEADLINE BOOK PUBLISHING

First published in paperback in 1996
by HEADLINE BOOK PUBLISHING

A HEADLINE FEATURE paperback

This edition published 2001 by
Knight an imprint of Caxton Publishing Group

10 9 8 7 6 5 4 3 2 1

All rights reserved. No part of this publication may be reproduced, stored in a retrieval system, or transmitted, in any form or by any means without the prior written permission of the publisher, nor be otherwise circulated in any form of binding or cover other than that in which it is published and without a similar condition being imposed on the subsequent purchaser.

All characters in this publication are fictitious and any resemblance to real persons, living or dead, is purely coincidental.

ISBN 1 84067 378 8

Printed and bound in Great Britain by
The Guernsey Press Co. Ltd, Guernsey, C.I.

Caxton Publishing Group
20 Bloomsbury Street
London
WC1B 3JH

Freezing Point

ONE

1

Maybe it was the colour of the girl's hair that first caught Sarah's attention.

A glimpse of red hair. A record request. And her habit of piling every conceivable piece of junk into the glove compartment of her car. Not much, all things considered. Trivial things. But enough.

After all, it only took a morsel of cheese to start a nightmare.

2

Sarah liked doing the disco at the Ice Arena. One or two of her colleagues – the sort who liked to call themselves broadcasters rather than DJs – affected to shudder at the very idea. For Sarah, the fortnightly Thursdays were fun. It wasn't as if you had to prove your hip credentials with an unbroken string of the latest, fiercest dance tracks. Nor did you have to wrap up the evening with a few smoochies and a blast of 'Hi-Ho Silver Lining' to send the rugby boys home happy. You just kept the music moving – anything from rock'n'roll chestnuts to this week's chart – and created the right party atmosphere to encourage people on to the ice.

'Punters,' as the manager said. 'It's all about geeing up punters to get out on the ice instead of gawping from the stands.' He was an intolerably young man in a dickie and tux with an impressive facial resemblance to a pig. Every now and then he would interrupt being shitty to the underlings picking litter from the stands and serving Slush Puppy at the cafeteria hatch to approach the disco dais and favour Sarah with a few words about punters. 'It's a good night tonight. Going good. This weather, you can't be sure of the punters.' He was obsessed with the word. Meanwhile he thrust his little porky hands into his trouser pockets to redistribute his balls. It amazed Sarah how obvious some men could be about that. Thinking their movements were undetectable, they did everything but flop the damned things out and scratch them right in front of you.

He was right, though. It was going good tonight. The rink was full. From the dais where Sarah operated she could see everything: the silhouettes of drinkers in the windows of the upper-level bar, excited kids cramming burgers and fries in the cafeteria directly below it, the queue for skates outside the hire shop at the other end, the ranks of spectators in the stands. And immediately below her, the milling skaters, producing a noise that was part squeal and part growl. The squeal was their voices, which all seemed to blend into one high-pitched tone that was neither infant nor adult, neither female nor male. The growl was the skates on the ice. Sarah had the amplification up because of the rink's size, not least the height of the hangar-like roof that dissipated the bass, but that growl of skates always came through. It suggested something frantic, intense; yet the impression of the moving skaters on the eye was slow and almost languorous. Dream-like. She used no strobes at these events because the disorientation effect might jeopardize safety on the ice, but sometimes when she looked up from the decks it was just as if a strobe were playing over the figures below, arresting them in vivid postures, faces flushed, uplifted, caught in a laugh or a grimace. Creatures frozen in headlights, eyes glinting.

'OK, while you get your breath back and count your bruises, let me just mention my show on Tudor . . . Yes, you knew I was going to get round to that sooner or later . . . Every weekday, eleven till two, not only the best sounds around but the best in local news . . . So whatever you're doing, why not tune us in on Tudor Radio – *your* station . . . What do you mean, you listen to Radio East? OK, here's something we're all pretty used to in this weather. It's Tina Turner with those "Steamy Windows" . . .'

Of course, the discos were an unashamed piece of mutual back-scratching by the Ice Arena and Tudor Radio. The station flourished its logo all over the rink for the night; the Ice Arena got a free plug over the airwaves. There had even been some talk of Tudor sponsoring the Arena's resident ice hockey team, the Corsairs, but the station controller was a confirmed penny-pincher, and he figured the discos were publicity enough. On a good Thursday a couple of hundred people passed through the Arena's turnstiles: families, groups of teens, groups of thirtysomethings, even coach parties from as far as fifty miles away.

They came to skate, or try to. Sarah had been hosting the disco nights for a year now, and had never seen anyone with more than a modicum of ability take to the ice. But these Thursday nights were about coaxing beginners on to the ice in a good-natured, swirling free-for-all, where they needn't fear making fools of themselves. Sarah had seen a few sobersides trying Torvill and Dean moves in the midst of the mêlée, but on the whole she guessed that the serious skaters strutted their stuff on the other weekday nights, when an endless loop of shopping-mall muzak trickled from the Tannoys.

'You want a Coke, Sarah?'

'Any chance of a double shot of rum in it?'

'Sorry. Can't take alcoholic drinks out of the bar.' Rob, the sound engineer and station dogsbody, paused from shouting in her ear to examine the snarl of cables hanging from the decks. 'Look at that. This is one crap system, you know. You could go up like a torch one of these days.' Rob was a blond, beardless, blue-eyed stripling with the manner of a grouchy old man. 'Coke, then? It's warm, mind you. Warm as piss. You'd think you'd be able to get a cold drink in an ice rink, wouldn't you? But oh no.'

It was true that the system wasn't up to much. Tudor's roadshow equipment was always passed over in the annual budgeting: higher priorities, like new carpets in the controller's suite, took precedence. But that was part of its charm for Sarah. When she got behind the old mesh-headed mikes and the big coffin-like speakers she was living out with peculiar exactness the dream of her childhood. The ten-year-old Sarah Winter, granted a view of this scene in a crystal ball, would have been thrilled to bits. If the thirty-year-old Sarah was not quite so thrilled, well, that was life. But she could still feel pleased for that lost ten-year-old, introducing records to an audience of

Snoopys in her bedroom with the Christmas tree lights flashing round the dingy chrome of a third-hand hi-fi.

Rob was back with the Coke. It *was* warm, but not unwelcome, as it happened, because if her hands had got any colder she would have had no more finesse at the decks than a gloved-up boxer. It wasn't just the refrigerated atmosphere of the rink. Outside it was three below zero, and it had been that way, it seemed, for ever. It was January now, and if she had ever once been thoroughly warm since November, she couldn't remember it.

'... That's Kool and the Gang there ... not the only ones who are cool just lately, but I think things are warming up nicely here ... so let's keep it going with Janet Jackson ...'

The crazy thing was, after two months of this unrelenting bitter weather people still commented on it. She was doing it herself. You'd think there would be nothing left to say, yet everywhere people met, the topic of the weather came up. It had almost created a Blitz spirit. Total strangers swapped bad-winter stories, and there was camaraderie in lifts and on trains. Even bank clerks had attained a semblance of humanity. And to add to the Churchillian atmosphere, people coughed into mufflers and wore hats. Chilblains were making a comeback. Radio listening figures were up, as commuters tuned in for the weather reports.

And the Ice Arena did brisk business, even though every street in the city was a rink. 'You'd think people would have had enough of ice,' Sarah had said, conversationally, to the manager earlier that evening. Mistake. The porky one rose up full-armed. Ice was his business, and he would not hear it impugned.

'Hey, no one can have enough of ice. The punters love

it. Visitor throughput's up twenty per cent this fiscal year. The profile of ice recreation's never been higher. No, take it from me, ice is going to play as big a part in leisure in this country as it does in the States . . .' So much for conversational.

'Big Country there . . . Let me welcome you to Thursday night at the Arena if you've just come in. I'm Sarah Winter bringing you the Tudor Radio roadshow . . . music all the way to keep you gliding, waltzing, salchowing – or just plain staying upright on the ice. And let me just remind you that the bar is open until eleven o'clock, and the cafeteria will be serving burgers, fries, shakes and lots more goodies until half-past ten tonight. And don't forget to keep those requests coming. Now here's a track to get you moving – Bryan Adams and "The Best Years of My Life" . . .'

The girl with red hair was standing a few yards to her left, leaning on the crash barrier, when Sarah first noticed her.

It wasn't that the shade of red was unusual. It was just that it was exactly the shade of deep auburn – mahogany, you might call it – that Sarah had always longed for. Her own hair was jet black, and it was years now since she had last hung over the sink in a polythene cape, half asphyxiated with ammonia, only to find that her raven locks were still raven – or crow, if you liked. Her hair wouldn't take colour, no way, no how, and she had called it quits – but just occasionally, as when she happened to notice the girl leaning on the barrier, a grip of mild envy would still go through her.

So it was the colour of that hair, absently glimpsed as she waited out the fade of 'When Doves Cry' and tried to control the reverb with the system's somewhat primitive equalizer, which first engaged a mere snippet of Sarah's attention. But that attention was just enough for her to notice something else. The girl was alone. It was plain from the way she was leaning on the barrier, her chin on her hands, watching the skaters with a faint, shy half-smile.

Unusual. The Ice Arena on a Thursday night was not a place for solitaries. Couples, families, groups of friends, gaggles of teens eyeing each other up, were the rule. Then Sarah cued Wet Wet Wet to follow Prince, and forgot about the girl with red hair as she became involved in a protracted discussion with two pubescents who came up to the dais to request a jungle track.

'You're kidding me, man. You got to have some jungle. Play one track. Just play one track, yeah?'

They were dressed authentically as New York street urchins, and had the hyper-speed speech patterns and gestures down to a T. Only the Midland vowels spoiled the effect. Sarah could at least acquit herself of not knowing what they were talking about. Hip-hop, acid, ragga, grunge, new new wave – she had managed to keep abreast of them all. But Tudor Radio's playlist stopped at the charts, and explaining this over the amplification to a brace of kids who made the Muppets look restful was not easy.

'They think it's you who chooses the stuff,' said Rob. A dedicated mistruster of his fellow man, he had just returned from checking the equipment van for the tenth time. 'Got you tagged as a crumbly now. Or whatever term they use. Watch 'em, though. Won't stop 'em nicking whatever they can get their hands on.'

'What's it like out there?'

'Freezing harder and harder,' said Rob with gloomy

relish. 'I tell you, it's the new Ice Age. All that global warming was bullshit to throw us off the scent. Sort these sleeves for you?'

'Thanks. Uh-oh, here comes Baby Doc himself.'

The manager was back, and asking her to give a mention to the gift shop. 'Adjacent to the hire shop,' he said, assessing the front of Sarah's pullover and juggling the contents of his groin. 'You can get your souvenir T-shirts, sweatshirts, mugs and car stickers, plus genuine Corsairs merchandising. Just give it a mensh, could you? Punters love that stuff.'

'They won't when they see the prices,' said Rob when he had waddled off.

A group of polite young people had gathered at the front of the dais. Student teachers or nurses, Sarah thought. They wanted a request for one of their number – Geoff. It was his birthday. Shoulder-slaps and cuffs for Geoff, who looked to be having less than the time of his life. There came a point where falling over on your butt just ceased to be funny. Geoff looked as if he had passed that point. He was crimson with exertion and could hardly speak. His friends requested Level 42 for him, and then dragged him away to torture him some more.

'OK, had a request for some Level 42 for Geoff. He's twenty-two today. So many happy returns to you, Geoff, and here's some "Lessons in Love" for you . . . beats lessons in ice-skating anyway . . . And a reminder about the gift shop at the Arena . . .'

Half-past nine: the rink was filled to capacity now, and that massed squealing and growling was at its peak. Soon the ice would clear a little as the families with younger children made a move and the weary-legged adjourned upstairs to the bar.

'Oh, by the way, your friend called in at reception again today.' Rob looked morosely devilish. 'Fire-Mark Fred.'

'Oh no. What did they say?'

'Well. Janet was on the desk, and she was just about to fob him off. But as I happened to be there I told him you'd be in early tomorrow to do recording and that you'd *love* to see him then.'

'Wonderful, Rob. Thanks a bunch.'

'Don't mensh, as Porky would say.'

Sarah lined up a Tears for Fears medley, a hollow groan inside her. Not Fire-Mark Fred. The trouble was, he was such a sweet old man. You could no more snub him than you could punch out Santa Claus. But he kept coming back. God, he kept coming back.

It had started with an item on her show about fire-marks. Not the most gripping of items, but what the hell, you had to fill the schedules. A clutch of ancient buildings in the cathedral close were getting a facelift, and fire-mark plates had been discovered on their façades. A local history boffin had come into the studio for a quickie interview on what they were all about. Old-time fire insurance policies, written in stone. So far, so mildly interesting.

Not to Fire-Mark Fred. Sarah was used to getting audience feedback on the most unlikely items, but the possibility that her listeners might include an amateur enthusiast of fire-marks would never have occurred to her. Nor that Fred would not only phone in to tell her of his consuming interest, but proceed to haunt the studios of Tudor Radio with fire-mark lore. Photographs of fire-marks. Books about fire-marks. There were even fire-mark jokes: Fred had told them to her.

How to tell the poor old guy that just because you ran

a little feature on fire-marks, didn't mean you had a real thing about them? Well, if you were Sarah you didn't tell him. You just tiptoed through reception every morning hoping he wouldn't be there this time. And waited to see who weakened first.

Maybe it would be her. Maybe this time next year she would be telling fire-mark jokes at parties . . .

'Excuse me . . .'

Someone had come to the front of the dais with a request. After a moment Sarah recognized her as the girl with red hair. Yes, dammit, that was the exact shade. Looked natural too. Lucky cow.

'Have you got "I Can't Stand Up For Falling Down" by Elvis Costello?' the girl said.

Sarah laughed. 'Yes, I think I have. That's a good choice.'

'Yeah.' The girl laughed a little too, looking over her shoulder at the skaters, chewing a fingernail.

'I'll just let this run and see if I can find it,' said Sarah, reaching behind her to the case of eighties discs. 'Who shall I say it's for?'

But when she turned back the girl had already moved away, and was lost in the crowd.

Sarah played the song anyhow. Would she have forgotten her if she had never seen the girl again? Probably. So she concluded long afterwards, when the question had become momentous. And again she did forget, for a while. She cued more records. She played more requests. She plugged Tudor Radio at regular intervals. She had a good-humoured dispute with Rob, who put forward his view that the young of the nineties had undergone a complete breakdown of moral sense. It was an argument they had had before, but it was fun to hear Rob go at it.

He had a theory that humanity went through lemming-like phases of mass irresponsibility in which it hovered on the edge of self-destruction. The fourteenth century was one: Hundred Years' War, Black Death, fanatics scourging themselves in the streets. The First World War was another: a whole generation electing to butcher itself for no reason at all. And now, now. 'Mark my words,' said Rob, and went off to check the van again. He was the only person under sixty Sarah had ever heard say that phrase.

Meanwhile the number of skaters lessened as usual. Cross, tired children were borne away to be appeased with a burger before home: bruised novices limped off the ice laughing distressfully. The security guard, with the fat-necked mania of his tribe, collared two boys who had added an obscene appendage to the Arena's cartoon penguin logo on the crash barrier. The skating coach, who on Thursday nights did little but gracefully patrol the ice displaying his globular buttocks like a Tom of Finland drawing, homed in on a couple of impressionable teenage girls who needed coaching, and copped a feel with his usual brazenness.

And meanwhile Sarah wondered what Murray was doing. Had he worked late again tonight? Was he on his way home now, perhaps? She hoped he'd take care on the roads. He was a reasonably careful driver, but a long day subbing spreads for *Golfing Today* might throw his judgement and make him want to get away from Mid Anglia Pursuit Publishing as fast as possible. ('Oh, *Golfing Today*'s one of our more mainstream titles,' he'd told her. 'You want to try leafing through *Pond-Keeper's Monthly*.')

Give him a ring when she got home. They had a date

tomorrow for this new Malaysian place that had opened. Murray loved mouth-searing chilli. She had seen him sitting before a plate of incendiary curry with tears running down his face, blissful. Funny how she still thought in terms of 'dates', when they had been together over a year. The question that perplexed them both, really, was how to proceed. Yes, it was serious, but what did they do? Get engaged? That had a faintly adolescent ring. Ring, geddit? Live together? In whose place? Maybe their reluctance to address these questions was a warning sign, and yet it didn't feel that way. Oh, well . . .

Yes, her thoughts were straightforward, untroubled, that night. Flowing over a reasonably smooth bed of normality. No depths, no jagged rocks. No hint of the rapids ahead.

'Well, the time's not too far off now when I say ta-ta and trundle off home for my Ovaltine, but we've got a little while yet, so keep the requests coming, and if you've enjoyed yourself tonight – you have, haven't you? – remember we're here with the Tudor Radio roadshow every second Thursday. This one's for Carol and her mates – it's Queen and "I Want To Break Free" . . .'

Bodies gliding, swaying, swerving. An impromptu conga line. A couple managing some heavy smooching as they skated, really making with the old lips. A boy skating head down, steadfastly refusing to hear his parents calling time on him from the stands.

And there, in the midst of the skaters, the girl with red hair. Sarah, looking up from the mixing desk, was mildly surprised, and pleased. Good to see that she'd ventured on to the ice. And no longer alone, either. Three young guys were with her. They were helping her stay upright – she was obviously the completest beginner – with a lot of laughing gallantry. She was laughing too. The shy look was gone.

Well, that was good to see. Met up with friends, maybe: or perhaps a new friendship, formed in the comradely chaos of the ice. Sarah's last glimpse before she returned her attention to the decks was a lock of red hair being pushed back to reveal a laughing face, of a young fair man holding the girl's elbow, of the other two guys crouching beside her with exaggerated we'll-catch-you gestures.

Soon, time to wrap up. Sarah played out with a Simply Red sequence whilst Rob carted the cases of discs out to the van. The manager, chewing on a burger, mounted the dais to treat Sarah to a few last thoughts on punters and trends in the leisure industry. Breathing onion over her, he asked her what she did on the alternate Thursday nights. Sarah told him she attended the meetings of the local Fire-Mark Society. He nodded blankly, gave his wedding tackle a last shuffle, and strutted away to scarify the helots who were waiting on the sidelines with vacuum cleaners.

The last stragglers left the ice: amongst them, the girl with red hair and her companions. Rob and his assistant, a youth whom Tudor had taken on as part of a work-for-dole scheme and who had very sensibly spent the evening trying to chat up a waitress in the cafeteria, dismantled the sound system and carried it out to the van through the service doors behind the dais. Muzak resumed its droning from the in-house PA, interrupted once by the adenoidal tones of the manager informing patrons that the Arena was closing shortly. A curious vehicle like a cross between a tractor and a hovercraft puttered down a ramp on to the ice, driven by a maintenance man who was defiantly fat and defiantly smoking. That was nice to see. The emphasis on good clean healthy fun could be a little wearing. I'll polish this damned ice, he seemed to say, but don't expect me to ponce around on it like bloody Sonja Henie.

Sarah assisted with the last removals, overriding Rob's protests. Along with the millenarian gloom he had a thing about women never lifting anything heavier than a handbag. It was possible to find it unbearably sexist or rather sweet, depending what mood you were in. Outside the air was like nerve gas. It numbed you as soon as you breathed in. The tarmac surface of the staff car park was like evil glass. Rob slipped and fell, with dour unsurprise. 'It'll get worse before it gets better,' he said, picking himself up. 'You mark my words.'

Sarah waited to make sure the Tudor van started before heading for her own car. The combustion engine had become an unfaithful servant in the recent weather. For some minutes the van's engine would only whinny like a dying horse, but at last it caught. A thumbs-up from Rob, and then the van moved away at a steady creep, the ice licking at the tyres like poisoned sugar.

Sarah stirred, shivering inside her coat. Even a few minutes' standing out here had left her feet bloodless, and when she moved it was with the blocky gait of Herman Munster. Cute of her to have left her car right over the other side of the car park. And to have left her gloves in it. Digging her hands into her pockets, she clumped her way over to her Sierra, praying that it hadn't been frozen to the spot.

Inside the car felt colder, if anything, than the air outside. There was ice on the windscreen, both sides. She keyed the ignition, murmured a thank you to the gods when it caught on the third attempt, turned on the heater, and then pulled out the can of de-icer from under the driver's seat. The can was so cold it stuck to her hand. Hastily she sprayed the windscreen, cursing at the pain in her fingers and wondering how people in Russia could stand it. Maybe that was where the gloomy music and doomy novels came from. She used a scraper on the worst of the ice and then plumped herself back in the car, slamming the door and willing the heater to take effect.

Her teeth were chattering. She concentrated on a beguiling vision of her house, radiators gurgling and banging companionably, curtains drawn against the night, Charlie and Penny sleeping the sleep of the feline on mountainous cushions. Fifteen minutes, and it would be a reality.

Right. She turned on the windscreen wipers. The screen was reasonably de-iced, but now condensation had formed on the inside. Sarah wiped at it impatiently with her bare hand. God, it felt like she had a hoof there instead of fingers. Where the hell were her gloves?

Glove compartment: that made sense. She fumbled it open, and an avalanche of junk tumbled out on to the floor.

Groaning, Sarah leaned over horizontally, her cheek against the cold musty leather of the passenger seat, and began scooping the stuff up in her numbed hands. What *was* all this? Road maps, bills, sweet wrappers, receipts, filling-station freebies... Some of it she didn't even recognize. And no gloves. A pair of sunglasses, of all the most absurdly inappropriate things... wait – had she not, in fact, very sensibly and conveniently tucked them into the pocket on the inside of the driver's door?

Sarah straightened up. The sudden swoop back to the

perpendicular sent her woozy for a moment. She blinked through the cleared windscreen. The harsh glitter of frozen tarmac under sodium lights presented a stark scene when the four figures came into view.

The staff car park was separated from the patrons' car park by a chain-link fence, and Sarah's car was parked right next to it, with the cafeteria kitchens behind. The view through her windscreen was of almost complete emptiness: a few solitary remaining vehicles, stark verticals of lampposts, and a background of the high grass banks and functional shrubs which surrounded the Arena site, out in the new-town suburbs. The four figures moving across this emptiness looked densely black against the bleached sparkle of arc-lit frost; but then a faint flash of colour caught Sarah's attention.

Red. One of the figures was the girl with red hair. She was walking across the patrons' car park alongside the three men she had been skating with. Sarah recognized the fair-haired one. Walking slowly, as if they were chatting and laughing, towards a van parked on the far side, close to the grass banks.

Walking together, though not entirely together. The girl kept the faintest of distances from her companions, as if to say that she was not really part of their group. And when they were a few yards short of the van, she stopped. The others stopped too.

Four dark figures, communing amongst the cold glitter. No other movement in all that emptiness. No sound reached Sarah, inside her car. The girl with red hair lifting her hand now, as if in farewell, hesitated as if about to move away. Come on, stop being nosy. Sarah reached down in the door pocket for her gloves. Pulled them on. Lifted her eyes again.

It all happened in a few seconds. And her perception of those few seconds was jangled, obscured by frost-glitter and weariness, and by her own utter unpreparedness for seeing anything important. But out of that jangle she was left with a clear visual impression of sudden and violent movement. Between her retinas and her brain there flashed an image of the static tableau of one girl and three men dramatically rearranging itself. An image of the men taking the girl by the arms, but grabbing, not as they had done on the ice, of the door of the van being flung open, and the girl being bundled inside.

And then, before her brain could interpret the image, the van's engine was revving. There was a twist of blue fumes in the crystalline air, and the vehicle shot away, chunky tyres dismissing the icy surface. It had been reverse-parked. For a getaway . . .?

Sarah blinked and blinked again at the place where the four figures and the van had been and where now there was nothing. Her eyes hurt. It felt as if the moisture on her eyeballs was freezing.

There was a half-empty pack of cigarettes amongst the rubbish that had fallen out of the glove compartment. Hiding them from herself was a moderately successful aid to quitting completely. Now she took one, her fingers trembling slightly. She lit it with the car lighter.

Then she opened the car door and got out. Layers of embedded ice scrunched beneath her shoes. She stood by the car, smoking, gazing at the place across the other side of the sparkling tarmac.

Her mind groped at the images that her eyes had thrust upon it: red hair, four figures. The space between the figures suddenly closed up: a swift huddle: door slamming.

Had she heard anything? A shout, a cry?

The silence of the car park was so complete – a rigorous, iron-bound silence. A frozen silence, that seemed never to have been broken in paralysed ages.

And yet she had heard the van's engine revving. Had she heard a cry too? Her brain felt as numb as her fingers. She hadn't been *expecting* to hear a cry, so . . .

She hadn't been expecting to see anything untoward, either.

Sarah turned around. Not a soul in sight. There were lights in the kitchens of the cafeteria: a Jag drawn up near the staff entrance. Probably Porky's. The dancing penguin logo atop the Arena building, seen from the reverse in silhouette, looked like some sinister crucifix. She was the only person in the car park.

She ground her half-smoked cigarette underfoot and got back in her car. It was warming up a little. She tried to picture that van. A sturdy thing, new-looking. What colour? Maybe blue, maybe grey: the sodium lights made nonsense of colours. As for the registration number, forget it. Not a clue.

Sarah found she was gripping the steering-wheel as if to break it in two.

The girl had lifted a hand. She hesitated, started moving away. And then . . . then she was in the van and it was speeding away.

A new coldness struck Sarah. A coldness in her guts.

She rubbed her eyes, and when she opened them again two figures were crossing the patrons' car park. Dark figures against the ice, just like before. A man and a woman. They crossed to a car parked nearer to the chain-link fence and paused beside it. The man's arm came out, grabbing. A huddled confusion of figures, struggling . . .

Laughter on their faces. Shenanigans. Horseplay. Innocent.

The couple got in their car and drove away.

Do the same, Sarah.

Condensation was thickening on the windscreen again. She wound down the window a little, then ground at the gears and drove slowly out of the car park.

She did see something, she *did*, but it wasn't as simple as that. Not for Sarah.

There was little traffic on the parkways leading back to the city centre, and what there was moved slowly. Though the roads had been gritted that morning, the bonds of ice had begun tightening again soon after dark, and the road surface was like black Cellophane. Along the verges heaped-up slush had frozen and thawed and refrozen again, until it resembled weird ruins. The bare trees were half beauty, half cruelty, as if cake icing had been applied to barbed wire.

No sign of that chunky-wheeled van. But then, what if there was? What would she do? Force it to pull over? 'I have reason to believe that a girl with red hair entered that van against her will...' Reason to believe. Did she really have a reason? It had all been so quick, so unlikely.

She had noticed the girl at the rink because of the colour of her hair, and because she was alone. Then she wasn't alone any more: she was skating with three young men. Having a good time like everybody else. And then she had left the rink in company with the three men, and paused near the van as if to say goodbye, and then...

Images, slippery, jagged, melting like icicles in her hand.

The city centre was a frozen film set cleared for action. Sarah waited out a red light at a junction, no other vehicle in sight. The red persisted and persisted, as if the lights too had been caught under the arresting spell of ice. Amber at last: Sarah gunned the engine, only to find four figures conjured in her headlights, directly in front of the car.

Sounding the horn was a reflex, done before she knew she had done it. The figures turned their faces to her. Three men and a woman – no, two men and two women...

'UP YOURS...!'

She lipread the words, inaudible inside the car. The hulking man who spoke them rapped on the bonnet as the foursome crossed, straggling, lurching, pissed. One of the women looked a little embarrassed, and grabbed Hulk's arm to hurry him to the kerb.

Pubgoers, staggering home. A lesson, Sarah. Normality was the rule in any given situation, unless there were clear indications to the contrary.

Clear indications.

Go home, Sarah. Home is where the normality is.

Home was in a curving street of Edwardian redbricks overlooking the old municipal park. Her car was a solitary stop-out: all the others were sleepers, draped in blankets like stabled horses. A wise precaution, but it was a wise precaution she wasn't going to take, not tonight. She just wanted to be indoors, right now. She hurried up the frozen steps to her front door, opened it, plunged into heat.

Normality.

Her cheeks burned, and she gave a gasp of stinging pleasure. She closed the door behind her, locked and bolted it. Next, heat inside. The vodka bottle was in the kitchen, next to a box of cornflakes. Slutsville, she thought, pouring a glass. But where *did* people put their bottles of spirits? It was a choice between upfront sleaze, or an antique-globe cocktail cabinet.

The vodka's burning finger hit the spot, or several spots. Her tabby cat, Charlie, came sashaying in from the living room and wiped his nose on her legs for a minute before approaching his food bowl with that air of fastidious resignation. Suppose I'd better eat this muck, rather than offend you. Penny, the black and white fluffball, stayed upstairs. It would take a silver salver of rainbow trout to get a welcome out of her.

Sarah took her drink into the living room, sinking into the sofa and waking the TV with the remote. The disco amps had left a faint ringing in her ears.

On the subject of ringing, Sarah, there's the phone over there. Now why the hell don't you pick the damn thing up, call the police, and tell them what you saw in that car park?

Sarah gulped her vodka.

Tell them . . . and that would be the end of it.

The end of it? Or the exhumation of something else? Something that she thought she had left behind for good? Something that she feared, feared like death?

Just call them.

She finished the drink, stood up, took a step towards the phone.

But what could she say? What she had seen didn't exactly add up to much, did it?

No. But her gut feeling did. Her gut feeling was an entirely different matter. And if her gut feeling was right, she might be making things worse with every moment's delay . . .

She reached out for the phone, and almost leaped into the air when it rang.

'Hello?'

She had snatched up the receiver, and her tone must have had the same snatch in it, because Murray gave a puzzled laugh as he said, 'Sarah? You OK?'

'Oh hi, Murray. Sorry – phone made me jump. I – I was just going to ring you.'

'Great minds. How you doing, sweetheart? Good night at the Arena?'

She caught sight of her reflection, shadowy, ghostly, in the glass of a picture frame opposite her. Where were her eyes? All she could see was dark sockets.

'Sarah . . .?'

'Sorry – uh. Charlie wanted the door opening. Yes, it went OK. Busy night again. I just got in. How about you?'

Charlie moseyed into the room, looking his reproach at her fib.

'Yeah, working late again. The computer was down this morning. It was quite fun doing paste-ups with real paste. Bit like infants' school. How was Porky?'

'Hm? Oh . . . you know, his usual self.' Porky. The Arena. Skaters. The girl with red hair. 'I Can't Stand Up For Falling Down.' Three men. The girl with red hair. The van . . .

Oh God, I wish I'd never seen it.

'Sarah? You sure you're OK?'

'Fine. Fine.' She injected breeziness into her tone. 'Just a bit knackered, you know. Bit of a headache too. I think it's this damn cold.'

'You've got a cold?'

'No, no, I mean . . .' This was some communications breakdown. 'The weather, you know. Cold weather. Gives me a headache sometimes. I think it's something to do with your ears getting cold. Maybe I should wear a balaclava helmet.'

'Get arrested as a terrorist... Have you got anything for it? Aspirin or whatever?'

'Oh... I think I'll feel better after a good sleep...' *Will I?* 'So, are we still on for tomorrow night? This Indonesian place?'

'Malaysian. Or is that the same? You bet, anyway. Shall I meet you in town?'

'No – why not come to my place straight after work?'

'Sounds good to me.' Pause, and she knew she couldn't fill it. 'Listen, Sarah – do you want me to come over now?'

Yes. No. 'No, it's OK, Murray. I'm just a bit tired and dopey, you know? Must be that disco. Too much for me in my old age. A good sleep should set me up.'

'Well, if you're sure...'

'Really. You keep warm. How's that boiler holding up, by the way?'

'Well, either there's somebody trapped inside it hammering to be let out, or it's going to conk out quite soon. But the radiators are hot, so who cares? You sure you're OK? I hope you're not coming down with something.'

Tell him. Tell Murray. 'No. Right as rain tomorrow, you'll see. I'll match you chilli for chilli. And we'll have a... a really great weekend.'

'You're on. Well, I'd better let you get to bed.'

'You too. Thanks for ringing, Murray. Love you.'

'Love you too.'

The receiver clicked softly into its cradle. Sarah let it go, stood with her hand suspended a few inches above it.

OK, so you couldn't tell Murray. So tell the police.

Tell them what? Tell them that she saw that girl – whom she didn't know from Adam – being forced into a van – which she couldn't really identify – by those three men – whom she couldn't really identify either. And that no one else had been there to witness it.

And while you're at it, try telling the marines.

She bent to give Charlie a perfunctory stroke and headed back to the kitchen. Her nerves were like twanging wires. Murray was the calmest and most patient person she had ever met, and normally the sound of his voice acted on her like the caress of a cool hand. But not tonight.

Not tonight.

OK. One more shot of vodka, and then she'd . . .

She'd decide.

Except there shouldn't be any question of decision. Anyone else would have reported what they'd seen to the police, wouldn't they? Even if there was a fair chance that they'd been mistaken in what they'd seen, they wouldn't hesitate.

Sarah swallowed vodka and, to her own astonishment, swallowed a sob of wretchedness and fear down with it. It was not doubt that made her hesitate.

3

She dreamed of the one-eyed man. She knew she would.

At four thirty in the morning she woke drenched in sweat, though the air in her bedroom was chill and there were ice ferns on the window. Her mouth was dry. She switched on the lamp and drank from the glass of water on the bedside table. It was cold as spring water and made her gasp.

Had she been crying out? Penny, a globe of white fluff on the end of the bed, was giving her a displeased look.

Bedside telephone. Why persecute thou me, bedside telephone?

Because you haven't used me.

No. But then maybe it was all a dream. Maybe the girl with red hair and the three men and the van and the sudden flurry of dark movement amidst the blinding glitter were all simply fragments of a dream, meaningless and blessedly forgettable, and when dawn came she could shower and dress and have breakfast in the serene knowledge that it was just another day, a day with its fleeting shadows like all days but no darkness, no fearful pits of darkness ready to swallow her up.

But she knew, with a certainty as cold and clammy as the sweat drying on her body, that it could not be so. She had dreamed, but not of the events at the Arena. The phantom that had stalked her sleeping brain was the one-eyed man.

She still thought of him as the one-eyed man, though she had learned his name in the end. Foley: Mr Peter Foley. It was a name she had forced herself to repeat mentally, when she was recovering from the bad time. Her counselling therapist had encouraged her to do so.

'Think of it like a jigsaw, Sarah. The jigsaw of normality. And then try and fit that missing piece in.' The therapist had had a soft Lowland Scots accent, and she had made the word 'jigsaw' sound specially pleasant and soothing and innocuous. It made Sarah think of sitting on a carpeted floor as a child, clicking the worn cardboard pieces into place, seeing the dancing figures of Snow White and the Dwarfs taking shape before her eyes as they had taken shape a dozen times before. Safe. So safe.

And she had finally convinced the therapist, and convinced herself, that the jigsaw of normality was complete.

Indeed, she had based her life for the last five years on that very conviction. And yet she lived with a lie too – just a little one. She still thought of him as the one-eyed man – or even The One-Eyed Man – rather than Mr Foley. If she thought of him at all.

She couldn't honestly say that she never thought of him. The human brain just didn't work that way. But the memory of that nightmare time five years ago had become quiescent. She might randomly access it: it never thrust itself upon her. Certainly it never infiltrated her dreams.

And now it was back. Now here she was starting awake with the bedsheet twisted and damp and that flavour in her mouth like cold pennies and that sensation of spinning down long howling corridors where she would be lost for ever more.

And no possibility of assuring herself that this was just a chance relapse, the twinge of an old war wound. The one-eyed man was back for a reason.

She sat up in bed and lifted the telephone in her lap, her fingers playing nervously with the cord, making little nooses.

Officer, I'm being menaced by a one-eyed man.

Officer, I saw an abduction in the Arena car park.

Spot the difference.

Penny scowled as Sarah banged the telephone back on to the table and swung herself out of bed.

It was strangely reminiscent of Christmas, going downstairs at five in the morning with wintry darkness at the windows. She filled the kettle for tea, peering through the kitchen window at the leafless garden. The frozen clothesline looked like spun glass. On the roofs of neighbouring houses frost had ruled delicate staves. There was one lit window, an intensely warm orange amidst the steely dark, like a view into a furnace.

Cold hard world, and she had shelter.

Hope that girl's all right.

She scalded a teabag. Homely odour. True Brit, making tea with the walls coming down.

The walls are not coming down. You've got to get a grip on this situation. You've really got to get a grip.

But supposing she did report it? She had only the vaguest of descriptions. Her information was not going to be of any use. How could it be?

Well, it might. You've seen those police appeals on TV. Anyone with any information whatsoever, please contact us . . .

Sarah sipped her tea, hunched at the kitchen table. A magazine lay there, the vacuous face of a supermodel looking out. Desperately contemporary, and doomed to look as dated as a Gaiety Girl in about five minutes' time.

But it wasn't that smooth, character-free face that Sarah was seeing as she sat there warming her hands on her mug and sipping at phoney comfort. Sarah was seeing the face of the girl with red hair.

And that face, she knew, was not going to go away.

TWO

1

They took Sarah seriously: that was something. Perhaps the city police were used to receiving incoherent calls from very nervy-sounding women at five thirty in the morning.

They took her seriously, because it wasn't just a matter of the duty officer at the station noting down the details. They sent someone to interview her early next day, before she went to work. And not a uniform either.

Detective Sergeant Routh was a slight man, no more than five-nine. Certain aspects of him reminded Sarah of a teenager who has yet to finish growing: a bony, high-strung look, black hair growing thick and low on his brow, a fullness about the lips unusual in a man in his thirties. But he wore the dowdiest mud-coloured suit, and his shoes looked as if they had been chosen for him by an elderly mother: no designer copper he. And he had a stinking cold, for which he kept apologizing.

'I've got some Beechams Powders if that'd help,' Sarah offered, as he sat down at the kitchen table and unwrapped a fresh packet of tissues.

'Thanks, but I'm rattling with paracetamol as it is, so

I'd better not.' His voice was dry-stone-wall Yorkshire, fogged with catarrh. He saw her looking at the clock. 'This won't take long.'

'No, I . . . Just worried about getting to work.' Was she? She didn't know what she was feeling. She knew what she was doing, though. Flitting about the kitchen like, as her mother would say, a fart in a colander, rearranging, wiping, fiddling with things to no purpose. She made herself stop it, sit down at the table opposite him. Calm down.

'What is it you do?'

'DJ. On Tudor.'

'Sarah Winter – I *thought* I'd heard the name. Tu-dor Ra-di-ooo, one oh three eff-emmm . . .' Sergeant Routh sang the station jingle under his breath, then looked slightly abashed. 'Of course, that's it. When are you on?'

'Eleven. But I need to be in around ten, and I'd been hoping to do a little recording this morning. We do this Sunday arts show, we host it alternately – it's my turn next week and I've got this interview with a local artist on tape, I wanted to do an intro and a follow-on . . .' She was doing it again: she could hear her voice babbling, high and fragile. She made herself take a deep breath. Sergeant Routh's eyes observed her above his tissue, not missing much. 'Anyway,' she said, avoiding his look, 'plenty of time yet.'

'OK.' He was brisk. 'I've got the details of the call you made early this morning, but obviously there are several things we need to follow up with you.'

She did not like that *obviously*. Its implications revived the fears that daylight had eased.

'You mean,' she said, defensive, rocking back on her chair like a sulky schoolchild, 'why didn't I call earlier?'

'The call was logged at five thirty-five today,' Routh said, consulting a spiral notebook. Cheapo item from a corner shop, she noticed randomly: somehow you expected more gloss from the CID. 'And you apparently placed the time of the incident at about ten past eleven last night. Do you want to revise the estimate of that time at all?'

'You see,' Sarah said sharply, getting up and running the taps at the sink for no reason, 'this is precisely what puts people off reporting anything to the police, this – this accusing way they have, as if it's you who's the criminal, it's really no wonder that people are reluctant to help...'

The outburst was ungovernable: as soon as it was over, she was ashamed. She came back and sat down. Routh was looking surprised. He blew his nose again, and said nothing, but she had a sense of something being stored away.

'No,' she said, 'that was definitely the time I saw it. I mean, I can be that sure because that's around the time the Arena closes, and that's when I went to my car. But I didn't report it straight away because I just...' The hesitation was fractional, but Sarah seemed to inhabit the pause for hours, 'there's so little I can give you to go on.'

'Yep. That's fair enough. The main thing is establishing exactly what happened, when it happened, who was there. OK?'

And establishing whether I'm simply one of these hysterical sad cases who starts reporting prowlers when she hears a cat climbing the garden fence.

'So...' Sergeant Routh sneezed. 'Bugger. Just can't shake it off.'

Sarah was momentarily amused. That was very male:

illness as a failure of the will. 'How about some tea? You should take plenty of fluids.'

She made tea, and she went through with him what she had seen from the beginning.

He took some notes, and drank thirstily of the tea; but mostly he just listened, eyes fixed on her. Accustomed to doing interviews on her show with people who ranged from the tongue-tied to the unstoppably prolix, Sarah expected nods and supporting questions. Attentiveness like this, complete and unsullied by response, was unnerving.

Sarah finished as Penny swaggered into the kitchen, tail aloft. Routh bent to stroke her: Penny, as always when men were around, went into her floozie number, wrapping herself round his legs.

'Well, that's it,' Sarah said, sitting back. The curious feeling of oppression that overcame her was rather like the post-coital blues. 'That's everything I can remember.'

'Right . . .' Routh was abstracted. 'May need you to make a formal statement, if . . .' He drained his tea.

If an offence has been committed, she thought. And for a terrible moment she hoped it was so. Because at least she would be proved right, and the police would know she had not invented the whole thing like some neurotic weirdo.

Terrible indeed. Terrible to think that you were depending on the commission of some awful act. This thing had turned her into a mental vampire.

'Never tried ice-skating myself,' Routh said, putting away his notebook. 'I think it looks bloody dangerous.'

'Yes, I know what you mean.' What was this? Was she being fobbed off? Had he simply written the word 'Nutcase' in that notebook and put a line under it? 'For God's sake,' she said uncontrollably, 'what do you suppose has happened? I mean, what can you do, what can I do—'

'You can go over to the Ice Arena with me,' Routh said, 'if you would. Show me where it all happened, go through it step by step. We'll see what we can find out. Staff'll be there, I suppose?'

'I suppose . . . some, anyway. The place doesn't really get moving until the afternoon, when the kids are out of school.'

He was on his feet. 'It won't take long. I'll make sure you're in time for work.' He extinguished his face in a tissue, already sodden, then frowning patted his pockets.

'Here.' She handed him a box of Kleenex. 'Take them.'

'Oh, thanks, you're a lifesaver.'

Chance remark: if he was alert to the overtones of it he gave no sign. But then, for all the sneezes and the casualness and reassuring salesman-like ordinariness, Detective Sergeant Routh was giving nothing away: he was as opaque as he was transparent.

He gave no sign, for example, of whether he believed her.

2

'It was here. I was parked right here.'

Sarah hoped she sounded more convinced than she felt. The car park of the Ice Arena had scarcely been out of her mind for the last ten hours: she had pictured it obsessively, it had been the continual backdrop to the rehearsals of her mind's eye. But now that she was actually here again, damn it all if it didn't look completely different.

Of course, then it had been night. A cruel wasp of a

night: black and yellow, bitter darkness intersected with sodium glare. Now it was morning, a chromium-bright morning as they often were this winter, filled with an intense witchy light. The chief landmarks were the same – the landscaped perimeter, the chain-link fence, the rear of the catering block. There were about the same number of parked cars – that is, not many. The tarmac was still sheathed in knobbly ice. But the whole place looked bigger. Measuring the distance with her eye to where that van had been parked she found it was much further than she had supposed.

And then there were the harsh lights that sapped colour and detail. And that headachey glitter from the ice. In fact . . .

In fact nothing. Somehow the very dubiousness of the circumstantial evidence threw into stronger relief that one, cryptic, inexpressibly disturbing image: the girl with red hair disappearing into that van just when it had seemed certain that she was not going to get into it.

I saw it, and I know that it wasn't right.

When Routh spoke the face she turned to him was grim and tight with conviction.

'Miss Winter, do you wear glasses at all, contact lenses . . .?'

'No. There's nothing wrong with my eyesight. But if you think it's that, why are we here at all? If you think I was mistaken, why not just say so?'

'Because,' he sighed, seeming to feel it hardly worthwhile getting tough with her, 'witnesses are often mistaken, and we have to be careful. That doesn't mean no witness is to be trusted. And I asked you about your eyesight because the question is relevant. If you were short-sighted, we would naturally take that into account. It turns out your vision is good, so we'll take that into account, too, on the other side. All right?'

'Sorry,' she said, mutinously.

'Don't be.' He was wondering why she was being so defensive, she could tell. Maybe she should say. Maybe she should come out with it – all about the one-eyed man, the bad time, the way the brakes on her mind had failed and left her careering. *But this isn't like that. I'm not like that now. It was a one-off. They mended me. So you can trust what I'm telling you.*

Yes, say it. Saying it out loud might help her to believe it herself.

No, can't say it.

'So they came out to the car park this way. You were parked here, you were sitting in your car – directly facing them?'

'Yes.'

'And the van was over by the verge there. Can you give me a clearer idea of the van?'

The freezing air was causing moisture to collect at the corners of her eyes. She blinked it away, staring at the spot, trying to conjure the van, exact lines, dimensions, features . . .

'A closed panel van, for example, or a leisure van?'

'Closed panel sort, I think. It was reverse-parked, so I mainly saw the front. Big chunky tyres, big grille . . . I don't know. It was a newer sort, I mean not like an old plumber's van or anything like that. Blue or grey, it was hard to tell with the artificial light.'

'Any signwriting on it? A business name, a logo?'

She shook her head.

'OK. So the girl came out with these three guys – '

'Not really with them. I mean, yes, I'd seen her with these three inside the rink, they were skating together, horsing around, you know. And the four of them crossed the car park. But it wasn't really in a group, do you see what I mean? There was this little distance. The three guys were heading for the van, and she was walking with them because they were still chatting, I suppose, but she kept on this side of the van. And then she stopped as if she were ready to go.'

'To her own car, do you think?'

'I don't know. There weren't many left. She was young, eighteen or so. Teenage sort of clothes – old coat, those boots they wear. I don't see her as a car owner, but maybe . . .'

'Well, we can check if any cars were left here overnight. Go on.'

Sarah sucked in a breath of the blade-like air and said without knowing she was going to say it, 'Oh God, I hope nothing's happened to her.'

Routh gave a short cough into his scarf, as if in place of a comment.

'And then . . . it all happened so quickly. One second she was standing there as if to say goodbye, the next second she was . . . in amongst them, getting into that van . . .' Sarah squeezed her eyes shut, blocking out the now, trying to see the past in its stead. 'She got in that van . . . she was *bundled* in. Just like – just like on the news pictures where they – they put some criminal into a police van with a blanket over his head . . .'

She found she was speaking in little gasps. Distress, rising in her throat: she was angry with herself. Routh didn't seem to notice anything, but then that fog of catarrh made a damned good disguise.

'You said horsing around,' he said. 'When the four of them were skating. Can you be more precise?'

She looked at him. Two eyeblinks.

'Physical contact?' he said, dry and precise. 'Touching each other? Arms round the shoulder, that sort of thing?'

'That sort of thing. She was a beginner, it was obvious, she was wobbly. People do that at the rink, they hold each other up – '

'Strangers? Would strangers do that? Or only friends?'

'I don't know. Friends, really, but strangers too. I mean they *make* friends there, it's part of the fun.'

'Sure. What I'm getting at – '

'I know what you're getting at. Young people, an evening out, a lot of horseplay. And no, I don't know whether they were friends of hers or whether she'd met them that night and I don't see that it matters. When that girl got in that van it was against her will, I'm sure of it.'

'And yet you didn't report it immediately.' No change in his tone, still mild and level.

'It was so sudden, I wasn't expecting to see anything like that ... But I'm sure now. Look, OK, that was my fault. For some stupid reason I hovered about before I called the police. Blame me for that. But that shouldn't affect what happened. I mean, what are you saying, the girl was asking for it?'

Oh shit, she thought, now I'm turning into Millie Tant. Routh gave her a disdainful look, the first deviation from his general blandness.

'I'm just really worried,' she said quietly.

'That's why people turn a blind eye,' he said. 'They don't want to be worried. You didn't do that.'

Some sort of gesture had been made. Sarah accepted it.

'And then the van drove away, right? Really fast?'

'Fast for these conditions. Like I say, it had these really sturdy tyres.' She shrugged. 'And it went thataway.'

'You'd be able to identify this girl if you saw her again? Let's go inside, by the way.'

'Yes. Yes, I would.'

'The three men?'

'This one with fair hair . . . I'm sure I'd know his face. Maybe the others too.'

Three young men. The trouble was that, although they would hate to think so, all young men looked alike. Slippery shards of memory, melting when she grasped them too hard. But she thought she had a fix on the fair-haired one. He had been the one holding on to the girl's hand while they skated. Not tall. Boyish looks, one of those switch-on smiles. Bit of a heartbreaker.

Clothes . . . ? No. The icicles of memory slipped through her fingers.

Routh was doing a good job of not watching her too closely. 'Who do I ask for, by the way?' he said, holding open the glass door. 'Who's in charge?'

She had to think for a minute. 'Oh! His name's Ellis.' Not Porky.

The Corsairs were playing the Durham Wasps tonight. In the carpeted lobby an old jobsworth was pinning up posters advertising the fact. There was a grille drawn down over the ticket window. The place had the smell of theatres and cinemas out of hours – stale popcorn and floor polish and lavatory disinfectant.

Sarah didn't know what Sergeant Routh said to the manager in his glass-windowed office upstairs, overlooking the ice, but he was back in five minutes. 'Hundred and twenty tickets sold last night,' was all he said, leading the way into the rink.

The Corsairs were taking a practice session on the ice. Several of them were Canadian, and their nasal accents rang out from behind the grotesque hockey masks, echoing round the vast space.

'Well, this is where we were set up,' Sarah said as they mounted the dais.

'Your colleagues who were here last night, I can get in touch with them at your workplace?'

'Yes. But I don't think they saw anything.'

Well, there's a coincidence, because I'm not so sure you saw anything either. She almost wished the policeman would say these things. At least then it would be out in the open. Better than these mental flea-bites.

'Do you have to bring your own skates?'

'No, no. A few do. Most people hire them. From the hire shop, down there.'

'Need ID for that, sign something?'

'Don't think so. It's a pretty hefty deposit. And there's security – they'd spot you if you tried to run out with them.'

She gazed out across the ice, trying to conjure memory. Nothing useful. It looked like a different place. Last night, eager swarms of people and surges of sound. Now there were just these few hulking trolls, with a few curt commands and the crack of duelling hockey sticks.

'She was just along there when I first saw her,' Sarah said. 'Watching. And then later I looked up and she was on the ice with these three men.' Up above the awning of the cafeteria Sarah noticed Porky observing them from his office window. Routh, however, was looking in the opposite direction.

'Is that a licensed bar up there?'

'Yes,' she said. 'I've never been in it though.' Defensive again: but still Routh only rubbernecked, dull-eyed and catarrhal.

'You didn't see them go up there?'

'No. I mean, a lot of the time my attention was on the decks.'

'Didn't see them leave the ice?'

'No. But I remember they were among the last ones still skating . . . Shit.'

'What's that?'

One of the hockey players, standing on the sidelines, was giving them a good eyeballing: the sight of that bizarre masked face, eyes blinking steadily in the leather holes, had made her jump.

'Sorry,' she said, 'just him. Like Hannibal the Cannibal.'

Inappropriate, perhaps, in the context: one of the awful things about this experience was that she didn't know, didn't know how serious anything was. She just knew how serious it felt to her.

Routh, however, only grunted and nodded, and then putting away his notebook said, 'Well, thanks for coming down here with me, Miss Winter. I won't keep you any more, you'll be wanting to get to work.'

She stared.

'Enquiries to make with the staff,' he said. 'See if anyone saw anything.'

'I saw something.'

It was hard to tell whether his sharp intake of breath was impatience or just pathology. Randomly she remembered a rhyme that had been scandalously bandied about the playgrounds of her childhood. 'I'll sing you a song and it won't take long, ALL COPPERS ARE BASTARDS.'

'You believe you saw something highly suspicious and potentially very alarming,' Routh said. 'Very rightly you reported it, and we're grateful. Wish everybody did the same.'

She couldn't leave it, she just couldn't leave it like that. 'I want to know what happens.'

'You can rest assured we'll follow up every line of enquiry.'

'I can easily find out. We're hooked up to the ILR news at Tudor. And the newsdesk monitors the local police radio.'

Pulling rank, of a sort. Maybe unwise, what with the paper tissues and the Just William grooming.

'We enjoy a very good relationship with the local media,' Routh said drearily. 'We give full and regular briefings to BBC East, Tudor Radio and all the local press. As far as I can remember the only complaints we've had are that we swamp them with too much information.'

'I want to make a statement.'

'That's fine. Just contact Croft Wood station and they'll make all the arrangements.' He looked at her, seemed to relent. 'Look, this came through to us on the off chance. I had a bad feeling about it and my boss let me pick it up, otherwise you'd have had a uniform about twelve years old fitting you in between a ram raid and a lost dog. It may seem to you that the whole thing's just being jotted down on the back of a brown envelope but believe me, that's not true. If anything comes in that ties up with what you've told us, we'll be on to it like a shot.'

She knew what he was saying to her. He was saying that he investigated crimes. Unless a crime had been committed, he couldn't investigate it.

'A lot of rapes aren't reported,' she said.

Didn't know why she said it. Maybe because she felt he had her tagged as a meddling pinko trendy with a cushy job – something about the spin he had put on that word *media*.

He was prompt. 'A lot of rapists get put in jail,' he said. 'And you know what? I enjoy sending them there. Thanks for your help.'

3

There wasn't too much chilli in the food at Lelia's, the new Malaysian place in town – enough to raise your eyebrows and moisten your brow, but not enough to contract your radial muscles so that your hands turned into claws. There were other flavours besides, some wonderfully delicate, and there was Tiger beer and a warm relaxed atmosphere. And, thank God, there was Murray, the world's champion listener.

'Well, if anything has happened to that girl,' he said judiciously towards the end of the evening, 'you've got to remember that you did your best and you couldn't have done any more.'

'It's just the time-lag that bothers me. The way I waited before reporting it. But I didn't want the police to think I was wasting their time.'

A nod from Murray in the moment's silence: it was all that was needed. Murray knew about the one-eyed man. In the emotional backwash of their only major row, some time ago, she had found herself telling him that whole story, hectically, spewing it out. She didn't know why: maybe somewhere amongst the confusion a gauntlet was being thrown down. In return Murray had tortuously confessed to a hopeless crush on a male work colleague that had destroyed his first job and apparently brought him within hailing distance of suicide. A quid pro quo:

you thought you were nuts, I thought I was queer. The unburdening splurge had done good things for them as a couple, but they didn't harp on it. You could only open the box once.

'Well, the police were OK about that, anyway,' she said. 'It happens, apparently. People hesitate. Think they were mistaken. Then it gets to them and they call.' She gave up on the vivid ice cream. 'I just keep thinking, maybe if I'd reported it straight away – '

'No. Maybe if you'd had the reg number of that van, but even then it's doubtful. Patrol cars screeching in pursuit at a moment's notice? They'd probably still be asking you to spell your name. But all you had was a glimpse. And what you did see, you've made sure they've put on the record. So if anything bad has happened, your statement's there to corroborate it.'

'If she reports it.'

'If she reports it,' Murray agreed. 'God, what an awful thing . . . I know the statistics. Date rape and all that. But surely she would . . .?'

'I hope so.'

Sarah wanted more than reassurance. She wanted absolution. She wanted to eradicate the image of that girl's face.

Murray could do much. His own face, across the little table from hers in a well of candlelight, could do much in itself. A long lean face with a widow's peak, cool blue eyes speckled with grey, lots of humour in the mouth. An age-of-reason face, no moody-broody in it.

Just the face you needed in a situation, across the table, on the pillow beside you. But Murray could only do so much, and she wondered whether he knew that.

At work today she had been, she felt, a fair imitation

of herself. Her show had gone smoothly enough. She had managed to conceal her distaste through the lunchtime interview with a local concert promoter and nightclub person named Steve Jordan, whom she had known at school when he had been plain Steven Smithwick and slightly less of a conceited airhead than he was now. Steve referred to women as 'Ladies', and did not think they made good DJs. In your face, Steve. Just after the one o'clock news she cued a commercial cartridge when it should have been the waveband jingle and Midshires Motors got one more plug than they'd paid for, but that was the only distraction she showed.

She even managed to refer on air to last night at the Arena, thanking everyone for coming and saying what a great night it was. Managed not to wonder too hard whether the girl with red hair was listening, or able to.

And after work, she had made a statement at Croft Wood police station, the sleek new HQ on the city's greener outskirts. It hadn't been built at the time of the one-eyed man . . . Managed not to think of that either, as she told her story once more in an atmosphere of over-dry heating and pattering keyboards and white shirt-sleeves. She had felt different there, closer to the dark facts of crime, than with Routh and his salesman flannel.

So, got through the day. Managed.

Didn't quite manage to stop thinking of the day as the first day of something, something fearful.

'You did all you could,' Murray said again.

'I just wish I knew the girl's name. Or that I'd seen the registration on that van. Or something I could get hold of.'

'What did this plain-clothes chap say to you in the end?'

'Said he'd be in touch if he needed me again. Presumably that's if . . . anything happens. I told him everything I could remember.'

'Well, I'm sure if anything had happened it would have come out by now. And it hasn't has it?'

She shook her head. At the radio station today she had haunted Ravinder, who manned the news computer, craning over his shoulder, scanning everything that came in with a local byline. 'What's up, they found you out at last?' he'd said. Continued controversy over proposed closure of memorial hospital. Break-in at city pharmaceuticals company. Road deaths on A1, all too common this winter. United to sign Czech striker. She hovered, feeling like a vulture. Nothing.

'How long,' she said now, carefully, 'before someone becomes a missing person?'

The bill came. Murray put down his Visa, coughed.

'Forty-eight hours, I think. But look, that's just torturing yourself – '

'I know it is.' And then, differently, softer, 'I know it is.'

The cold outside was unthinkable, blasphemous, after the warmth of the restaurant. Lelia's occupied a townhouse that had survived, stripped and solitary, in an old street cleared for redevelopment, and to get to Murray's car they had to cross a blasted landscape. It was as if a bomb had gone off here, a bomb of cold, destroying ice.

Sarah was chatty on the drive home. All light bright stuff, like the conversation of someone on the phone who fears those magnified silences. Meanwhile her eyes took in the city, darting. Her head turned at each new perspective of twinkling streets. When Murray pulled up in front of her house and turned off the engine and then moved to face her she knew he wasn't fooled.

'This thing's still bugging you.'

'Can't shake it off,' she said with an awkward laugh.

He found her hands. His were warm.

'That copper didn't seem to take you seriously. I am taking you seriously. But I seriously, honestly believe that what you saw wasn't anything... anything bad. I don't mean it didn't *look* bad: I know it did from what you've told me. You were dead right in what you did. It's like when you hear a lot of screaming at night, down the street. Is it someone arsing around on the way home from the pub, shoving snowballs down each other's collars, or is it something else? Be sure: ring the police. And it nearly always is innocent, and I'm sure the same applies to what you saw. But you've got to be sure.'

He was trying so hard not to sound patronizing, trying his damnedest: the effort at least was commendable.

'I know,' she said; and then, she couldn't help it, 'But if it was innocent, I'll never know. And if it wasn't...'

'You might know. What about the next disco at the Arena? You might see the girl there again. The whole thing will probably just clear itself up.'

A little too loftily soothing, that: she extricated her hands. And then Sarah caught herself in the act of marking Murray's consolations out of ten and remembered she was a grown-up woman and not an adolescent playing the game of You-Don't-Love-Me. She offered a smile.

'My dad's got ulcers. Ulcers in his gut from worrying whether he left the trowel in the garden or put it away in the shed. Wonder if I take after him?'

Murray picked up the smile, but hesitated. He would be glad to seize the opportunity of dropping the subject, she knew, but he didn't like taking the easy way out. 'I suppose,' he said, 'there's nothing against you getting in touch with this Routh chap. You're concerned, you want to know what's happening, surely they can understand that.'

Trouble was, she'd got off on the wrong foot with Detective Sergeant Routh, though she hadn't really said as much to Murray. Perhaps that was why she had this feeling that it was just her and the red-haired girl, in it together, no allies. A strange bond.

'I'll do that,' she said. 'Maybe. Come on, let's go in.'

Well, there was warmth in her house, to set against the outward chill and the inward chill, and presently more warmth. It had been a long time: the weather tended to make you a shivering prude, medieval, sewn into your clothes. Warmth, love like a garment that had passion in its rich folds. It was good, it was real. Penny, snoozing by the bed, gave a little sneeze at a critical moment, but their laughter did not disable them.

And then peace, the long breaths of a long day being put quietly away in darkness. Sarah Winter lay in the crook of her lover's arm and parleyed with shadows. It was going to be all right. The police would deal with it, somehow, and she had done all she could.

She slept. But it was a different sleep from that of Murray, lying angular beside her, or of the two cats in their tail-wrapped oblivion; and the waking that lay on the far side of it was different too. She knew it even in her dreams.

THREE

1

Ian Christopher Elderkin, I. C. Elderkin as the signboard above his market stall styles him, Chill as he is known to his friends on account not only of his initials but of his coolness of temperament, sometimes jokes that he is a sort of honorary Asian brother.

This is because he sells clothing from his market stall. Jeans, chinos, bomber jackets, denim shirts, check workshirts, T-shirts, sweatshirts. Cheap and cheerful, but not the sort of sad catalogue gear that has Social Security written all over it. Stuff for your average guy and girl who wants to look good without getting a fixation about it, that's how he sees it. He wears the same sort of gear himself, though Trend curls his lip at it on those rare occasions when he helps out on the stall. Trend would.

But Ian Christopher Elderkin, a.k.a. I. C. Elderkin, a.k.a. Chill, is a rarity in selling these goods because he is white. Most of the other clothing stalls in the city's large covered market are run by Pakistanis and Bangladeshis and Sikhs, and the same goes for the wholesalers with whom he deals on his buying trips to

Birmingham, Leicester and Nottingham.

Don't ask him why: they've just got a flair for it, he says. Ian Christopher Elderkin is on good terms with all his fellow traders at the market, and that includes his direct rivals, Pete Singh and the Siddiqis and all the rest. He'll undersell them if he can and they'll undersell him if they can, but that's free enterprise, in which Ian Christopher Elderkin is a firm believer. It doesn't stop them being good mates. Hence his joke about being an honorary Asian brother.

Not just a joke, either. Saturday afternoon, busiest time of the week, he hears of a bit of trouble over at Rashid's pitch and though there's only Sean to mind the stall and Sean, bless his cottons, is not the brightest spark in the world, Ian Christopher Elderkin doesn't hesitate. He's over there.

It's as he thought. A couple of football supporters of the suedehead persuasion trying to rip Rashid off and then coming out with the neo-Nazi lip when he reams them out. It's only the verbals that are threatening just yet but Rashid is only a slip of a guy and his brother's off sick today. So Ian Christopher Elderkin, a.k.a. Chill, wades in.

A more thoroughly dislikeable pair of individuals he has never seen. And as he squares up to them, Chill finds he knows all about them: it's just all there, if you've got eyes and ears. The housing estate with the chippie that won't open after ten and the video shop that doesn't stock anything newer than *Porky's*, the foxy-smelling bedroom with the team photos sellotaped to the wallpaper, the festering memory of Cheryl at the youth club disco who wouldn't and laughed and since then it's been nothing but monosyllables in the job centre and the single tin of

Special Brew passed from mouth to scabby mouth on street corners.

It's all there for Chill, and it may be that the knowledge is in his eyes as he places his forefinger on a suedehead chest and cheerfully invites the gruesome twosome to back off. There is something about Chill that discourages challenge. He is not particularly tall, and no more than averagely built: he has fair hair and a fair complexion: when he grins he looks boyish, very boyish for thirty. Nothing about him suggests the nasty piece of work. Even the tattoo on his right forearm – Chill rolls his sleeves despite the weather – manages to avoid the brutishness such things usually suggest. 'CHEEKY MONKEY', it reads, and the picture accompanying it is all innocence, a cartoon simian with no harm in him.

And yet there is something about Chill and one of the two bonebrains knows it at once. His companion is a little slower to know it and suffers accordingly. Not much: all that happens is that Chill steps closer and smiles right in his face and with a quick deft movement mashes his balls in one hand so that the suedehead goes scurrying away at an agonized crouch like Quasimodo.

Sad cases, in the opinion of Ian Christopher Elderkin, a.k.a. Chill. He has rather a soft spot for sad cases, but not of that sort. He considers that sort to be well out of order. He says as much to Rashid, and they shake hands, and then Chill has to get back to his stall in case Sean has been tendered a ten-pound note for a nine ninety-nine shirt and can't work out the change. Sean is a sketch all right, but Chill can't help liking him.

Harsh music of traders' voices, raw and throaty from the sandpaper air; the high iron roof they built over the market keeps rain off, just, otherwise you might as well be in the open. Thirty pence a pound. Two for a fiver. Your very last chance, ladies. Vegetables with the cold peat still caked on them. Batteries from Taiwan guaranteed to last three minutes. Secondhand books, old dears rummaging in the Mills & Boons, red-eared men pausing and pausing again before the erotica, not daring. Stall for the heads, tarot cards and hookahs and ethnic jewellery, sold by lace-mittened henna girl who never looks as she takes the money. Smell of fish like a belch from the sea, carcase smell from the meat market, blood on sawdust.

For Chill, a buzz from all of it. It does not exhilarate him, because mild exhilaration is his normal state of mind: it simply tunes him up a little higher. Chill's firm opinion is that it's a good life if you don't weaken. He finds the world endlessly interesting: not conventionally religious, he nevertheless feels gratitude to whoever's-up-there for turning him loose in this world, turning him out to play.

Interesting, for example, are these two girls hesitating over and ultimately buying a pair of stonewashed jeans each. One of them has a love-bite on her neck, a real gnasher, and at some point she becomes aware that he has seen it and tries to cover it with her scarf. But the scarf keeps slipping. Couldn't draw more attention to it if she tried! Fascinating. And if she's a day over fourteen then he is a banana. Still, he was a bit of a devil at that age.

'Will they shrink? I don't want 'em tight. I don't want 'em too tight.'

'Course you want them tight, duck. You don't want that grungy baggy look now, do you? That's had it. That's yesterday's news. What music you into?'

Unanimously, 'Indie.'

Freezing Point

'There you are then.' Chill hitches his leather change-bag, mock-cowboy style. Gets grins. He sees them. Sees it all. Nice parents who forked out for the Doc Martens and the good haircuts, toy Garfields still on the bed, and if the boyfriend's got to fingers and tops that's as far as he's going to get. 'Straight leg, tight round the doodah, that's how they're wearing them. What, you want to look like Coco the clown?'

'I dunno.'

'I dunno, she says. How much are they selling them for in C & A? How much do you reckon they're charging for jeans exactly like this in C & A?'

'Dunno.'

'Dunno, she says. You're a right little chatterbox, you are, aren't you? Thirty quid. You go and look if you don't believe me. Cheeky monkey, that's right –' they've spotted his tattoo, 'cheeky monkey, that's me. I was born cheeky – I came out arse first. Eh? You might well laugh . . .'

Home with their purchases to agonize in front of Mum's mirror, and then down to McDonald's all togged up. Boyfriend with a new haircut, walking stiff as if he's balancing it on his head. Chill sees it all.

Another sale. Another Saturday, all too short, turning blue and thin about four, cage lamps coming on above the stalls. Another day.

And then Chill remembers that it's not just another day and this time he really does feel exhilarated. Bouncing to the sky.

He sends Sean to the greasy spoon in the arcade for two mugs of tea. He has to specify the mugs because otherwise Sean brings paper cups and burns himself something chronic. Poor old Sean.

'Picking up?'

Lou, on the stall adjoining his, poking her headscarf round the back with her friendly bashed-in mug all purple from the cold, also from the flask of Scotch she keeps in her change-bag. Dilutes it with Panda Pops that she fetches from The Kandy Man across the way. 'I'm getting addicted to these,' she'll say, all innocent. Poor old Lou.

'Not so bad,' says Chill. Business is always slow after Christmas. 'Yourself, Lou?'

'Well, there's some buggers got some money left, don't know how.'

'Some buggers' is Lou's version of 'somebody'. She does the same with 'anybody'. If Lou went to a karaoke evening she'd probably sing 'Some Bugger To Watch Over Me'. She's a sketch, old Lou.

'Here. Don't let me forget. Before you go.' Lou struggles for breath, and lights up a Piccadilly. Lou can't manage air, can only inhale properly if it's got tobacco smoke in it. 'Nice bit of tripes, I been saving it. You take it home with you when you go. For that pup of yours.'

Pet supplies, Lou. Her stall smells of offal, cat litter, dog biscuit, rabbit pellets, and hay; so does she.

'I know he's a young 'un, but it won't hurt him, if you chop it up fine. It's good for 'em, good for their bones. Now don't let me forget.'

'Ah, bless you, Lou,' says Chill. 'But you'd better keep it, love. I haven't got my dog any more. He ran away.'

'Oh, he didn't. Oh, you're kidding me. Really? What a shame. Can't you find him? Can't you do an advert?'

'I've tried. He hadn't got his collar yet, that's the trouble. And there's a lot of traffic round our way.'

'Shame.' Lou clucks her tongue and croons her sympathy, her eyes searching Chill's face. Lizard eyes, red-rimmed and rheumy, mottled with blood vessels. There is fascination in Chill's disgust. 'Dear, what a shame. You never know, some bugger's perhaps picked him up and took him in for a stray.'

'Well, I hope so. Rather than . . . you know. It's funny, I don't seem to have much luck with pets,' says Chill, and suddenly he is a bouncing ball again, springing into the sky, while he keeps the sad smile going and gently receives the clucks and croonings of Lou.

'Dear. Perhaps he'll turn up. Find his way home. You never know.'

'You never know.'

The market officially closes at five, but most traders start packing up between four and four-thirty. Who makes the first move and why is a mystery like the migration of birds. But the shutters on the stall of I. C. Elderkin are usually among the last to go up. Chill's firm opinion is that nobody ever went bust from working too hard. Work hard, play hard, that's his motto.

Not tonight though.

'What, we going already?' Not protest from Sean: just that wide-eyed, empty-vessel look, waiting to be told what to do. Jump off that cliff, Sean. OK, cheers, will do. Bless him.

'Yes, my old fruit. Home. Take me home country roads.' Something about Sean's baby bogtrotter innocence just makes Chill want to knock his hat off his head (Sean and that hat, what a sketch) and start a bit of horseplay. They romp about like a couple of schoolboys for a minute, old Lou tut-tutting and laughing. But Chill calls a halt when he sees a look coming into Sean's eyes not unlike the look in the eyes of those suedeheads when he showed them he meant business. Chill isn't one of these people who doesn't know his own strength. He knows it very well. So he ruffles Sean's hair and they set about the packing up.

Not too difficult a task, with the stock Chill deals in. Knick-knack merchants are the ones he feels sorry for – poor old Maureen, the fag hag with the bracelets, having to pack away all those itsy-bitsy china toadstools with cute mice living in them and what have you, now *there's* a chore. As it is, Chill quite enjoys the shifting of his gear, as he enjoys most things physical and purposeful. He enjoys clambering up on the stall to take the jackets off the top rail, feeling his engineer boots gripping the boards, delighting in balance, conscious of presenting an admirable denimed arse to his public. And he has the capacity of performing mechanical tasks whilst keeping his mind separate from them.

It is a bright, smooth, shiny mind, this mind of Ian Christopher Elderkin's, self-regarding but not incurious. It can penetrate, though it cannot receive. It is a mind very much at ease with itself, though eager and energetic in pursuit of things it wants. A cheerful mind. If it could have a colour, it would be sunshine yellow.

'I say.' Here's Lou again. Paper bag in her stiff, puffed, nearly-useless hand. 'You want to take this anyway? Tripes. Like I say, you never know. He might be sitting on your doorstep when you get home. Take it anyway.'

Chill hesitates. Something flitters upward in the emotional ether that surrounds Ian Christopher Elderkin: high glee, yammering up to the iron rafters.

'OK,' he says. 'Like you say, Lou, you never know. Good on you. You're a princess.'

He takes the bag of tripe, and when he glances into it the bat of glee makes another ascent.

Only momentary: there's work to be done. 'Well,' says Chill, 'no rest for the wicked,' and tipping Lou the wink he begins piling stock on to a hand trolley, ready to be loaded into his van.

2

'Eric Clapton there, and "Wonderful Tonight". Well, I'm sure you've seen the posters round about the city announcing the coming of something called God On My Side, and if like me you've been wondering just what it's all about, then my guest this lunchtime should be able to shed some light on the subject. John Shirebrook is one of the organizers of God On My Side, which he describes as the city's very own Festival of Light, and I'll be talking to him right after this from Neneh Cherry.'

He seemed a nice enough man. Phone-ins had given Sarah a mistrust of religious flakes – she had come in for the worst verbal abuse of her life from a pro-lifer who had described herself as a fiancée of Christ – but Mr Shirebrook seemed like a normal human being. He was chubby and genial, like a friendly grocer. At least the festival was called God On my Side and not Jesus On My Side. In her experience the more they emphasized Jesus the flakier they were.

'Excuse me. I'm a lay preacher. Could you mention that, please?'

'A lay preacher. Certainly. I'll bring it in when I introduce you.' Sarah checked the running time on the CD track. One minute.

'Only I don't want people to think I'm ordained.' Mr Shirebrook shifted in his chair, too small for his outsized rump. 'I could have been, you know. I could have followed that course. I just didn't need some old whore of a bishop to tell me I was fit for the ministry of Christ.'

Sarah's smile felt like crumbs on her face. Uh-oh. She checked the time, glanced through the glass at the adjoining studio where Jackie was preparing the one o'clock news. Rob's teenage gofer was handing Jackie a flimsy from Ravinder. New running order, new item?

New headline?

Sarah recovered herself, took up the headset, came in on the fade. 'Well, my guest this morning is John Shirebrook, who's a lay preacher and one of the organizers of God On My Side. John, welcome . . .'

This was issue-led broadcasting. The controller of Tudor had picked the phrase up from public service broadcasting, had a rush of blood to the head, and started circulating memos. Here was a new credential in establishing station identity. Popular music radio must cross over with talk radio: it was in the wind. Issue-led meant, as far as Sarah could see, a Sunday broadsheet mentality. Nothing could be simply interesting in itself any more. No more fire-marks, probably, unless you could tie them down to heritage and conservation or some such flummery.

As for God On My Side, she had a memo about that. New Age spirituality, reaction to eighties materialism, or maybe return to traditional values. Discuss.

She discussed. Mr Shirebrook bellied up to the microphone.

'God On My Side is a non-denominational gathering of all those who believe and all those who want to believe. It's an opportunity for everyone who's felt the lack of that something important in their life to come along and share the experience. I'm sure, in fact I know, that there are many, many people today who feel that way. And the thing that's lacking is faith and the redeeming love of Christ and if people will come along and join us in Harmon Park on Saturday then I can guarantee them the opportunity of laying hold of that faith and sharing in it.'

Mr Shirebrook was booming, and Sarah had to adjust the sound balance. She saw his eyes dart suspiciously over to her hand on the equalizer. What, did he think she was switching him off?

'So why now? What's the special impetus, if you like, behind God On My Side?'

As she spoke she was running the scanner over the barcode sheet that listed each CD played, and cocking an eye at the schedule sheet for the next commercial slot. Standard practice: but Mr Shirebrook, watching, didn't seem to like it.

'I think my answer to that question would be simply this: Look around you.'

He stopped, smiled. Air silence, fill it quick.

'There's . . . So it's a response to a situation? A world situation, a social situation?' Situation, situation, yuck.

'There's no such thing as a social situation. There are only spiritual and moral situations.' Mr Shirebrook had his fat hands clasped between his thighs. 'This is precisely what has brought the world to the sorry state it's in. Looking for remedies in a lot of social and political tinkering instead of going straight to the heart of the matter. Yes, God On My Side is about changing the world, if you like. But only through changing people's souls, because that's the only way it can be done. All the rest is futile.'

'But with the world in such a sorry state, as you say, aren't there other questions to be addressed? If people are starving or homeless, for example, aren't they crying out for food and shelter, not religion?'

'I would reverse that question, and ask you this.' Smiling, smiling. 'If, as recently happened, two college students decide to accost a passing motorist, an innocent father of two children, and brutally murder him just for kicks, what does that say about our world? What were they crying out for? Certainly not food and shelter. Same with the teenagers who blare out loud music and take drugs and scrounge and steal to finance their habits. Aids, satanic abuse, abortion, pornography – we're not talking about deprivation here. Whatever's amiss, I don't think it's something the do-gooders and social workers can do anything about.'

'But can religious revivalism? There has after all been plenty of it and it doesn't seem to have worked so far.'

Sarah was ignoring the golden rule and being adversarial in her questions. God On My Side sounded like a season in hell to her, but she should keep that out of it. She knew it. He knew it.

'Faith isn't a quick fix,' he said. 'We're simply seeking to show the world an example of what it can do. We're saying to people, come along and see what you're missing.'

Change tack. 'So tell us a little bit more about the events at the festival.'

'Well, we have several speakers, including one from America whose name is Jerry Peasgood and I think he's going to be very exciting. We'll have lots of stalls selling books and greetings cards and so on and crèche facilities and games for children. We have a choir also visiting from America and we have two musical groups, quite modern I think, who express their Christian beliefs directly through their songs. But let me emphasize that it's all about participation, it's about making a joyful noise unto the Lord, and I hope everyone will do just that.'

'Right, sounds great, but if I can just play devil's advocate for a moment – you mentioned loud music and drugs and so on earlier. Now Harmon Park's in quite a built-up area. I mean wouldn't it be fair to say that if a pop concert were held there, there would be complaints of noise and disruption, probably from the very people who would attend God On My Side?'

In the next studio Jackie raised an eyebrow over her coffee cup. Sarah wasn't playing devil's advocate: she was getting on his back.

'That's a rather strange idea of what Christians are like. Christianity is all about understanding and forgiveness, not judging. Christianity seeks to foster moral responsibility, no more, no less. People nowadays like to pretend they don't have a choice. It gets them off the hook. They do wrong, and then pretend they had no choice but to do wrong.'

'So you've never done wrong, then, never been morally irresponsible, never shirked or compromised or turned a blind eye—'

'Not at all. Not at all. But I wouldn't lie to myself about it.' He looked at her closely. 'That's what I mean by moral responsibility. You know, Sarah, the proper response to the question "Am I my brother's keeper?" is "Yes." '

Air silence again, several long seconds of it. This time it was her.

Through the glass Jackie, eyes wide, made a talk-talk hand signal.

'Well, John, it's a . . . challenging subject, and I'm sure

you're used to locking horns, as it were, over it . . .' She needed help here, but she didn't think he would give it. 'But God On My Side, as you say, is non-denominational, so I'd imagine that there'll be a broad spectrum of opinion represented there?'

'There's room for everyone. God isn't exclusive. All we ask is that you bring an open mind and an open heart.' He took another look at her down at the bottom of the well. 'Don't ask yourself, what can God offer me? Just come along and feel the atmosphere. I think a lot of people are going to be pleasantly surprised. Perhaps we'll even see you there, Sarah.'

Cute. She thanked him and signed him off. He was still smiling as Rachel, her researcher, ushered him out of the studio.

Two tracks and a local events round-up took her through to the news. Rob came in bearing coffee as the red light winked off.

'That was the worst since those bloody snakes,' Sarah said, throwing down her headset.

Last year she had interviewed an off-the-wall couple who kept a houseful of pet snakes. They had brought a small selection of the creatures into the studio for the occasion, draping them round their necks as they talked. The controller's idea: 'hands-on' broadcasting had been the bee in his bonnet back then. Listeners couldn't see the damned snakes, of course. Just hear the tremble of terror in Sarah's voice.

'Why?' Rob said. 'Sounded OK to me. Expect a bit of controversy with religion.'

'I needled him. Unprofessional.'

'Balls to him.' Rob, tinkering with the sound mixer, slid his eyes round to her. 'You all right? Want an aspirin?'

She shook her head, no thanks. There was something nasty lurking between her brows, but she didn't want to acknowledge it.

She wondered, though, what she looked like to make him ask. Stressed out, anxious, haunted?

She sipped coffee and cocked an ear to Jackie on the relay. Jackie was a seamless operator, splicing in the syndicated ILR reports without a jolt. Her voice was creamy, mellow, even with horrendous headlines. The closure of the memorial hospital still led. A family had had a miracle escape from a house fire. Mideast Water were shedding a hundred jobs: streamlining, said a vox from the surely unstreamlined Customer Services Director. Part of our ongoing commitment to burble snarfle a higher quality of gibble gabble to our rhubarb rhubarb in the nineties and beyond.

'In other words, bring a bucket to the standpipe and get the sucker yourself,' said Rob, drifting through again.

No horrors in the local news today. No one had been reported raped, kidnapped or murdered. Nothing of that sort had been going on, except in Sarah Winter's dreams.

And now the weather. Jackie had given up on being facetious with this now. There was nothing to do but trot it out again: cold, hard frost, top temp three below.

The one-to-two slot was fine. Sarah talked down the line to an old comedy pro who was appearing at the city panto and had just landed a part in a TV soap, previewed a schoolkids' phone-in at five, got anecdotal about school dinners. Stuff she was good at. It gave her satisfaction, this job. It was good to feel that she did it well and that people liked what she did. When the harsh winds blew, this stayed standing.

Except today she felt like crud and nothing could change it.

Sure, she disliked Shirebrook and all his oily kind. But not enough to make her feel like this. What she really disliked was what had happened to her as she interviewed him. The sensation of losing it. Of being prey to something inside herself, outside herself, whatever.

She wondered if she would be ticked off for hostile interviewing. No way of saying that hostile was just how it had come out. As it so often did when you were on the defensive.

Three minutes to two, and Sarah traded some handing-over banter with Mark Malone, the young motormouth who made antic hay of the two-to-five slot and received indecent proposals by the sackload from besotted jailbait. Then she signed off and tried, failing, not to listen to the news again before tidying up and moving out.

In the studio office Rachel, a misty young woman who looked like Ophelia drowning, handed her a garishly coloured leaflet. It felt tacky to the touch.

'Mr Shirebrook left this for you.'

The thing was fairly typical of its kind. Like porn flyers, religious leaflets always seemed to be printed on bad colour offset so that your eyes crossed when you looked at them. The matter too was standard. 'WHOSE SIDE ARE YOU ON?' screamed the cover, over a Cecil B. de Mille crucifixion.

Sarah did not take the trouble to read it. But she took the trouble to screw it up into a ball and toss it into the waste bin.

3

It would help if she knew where she was.

Now there was some book she had read where some amazing Sherlock Holmes type, maybe it was Sherlock Holmes, pinpointed where he was through a distant sound of trains, he knew the timetable off by heart or something and he calculated it like that, or maybe it was subway trains which would rule Sherlock Holmes out as she didn't think they had them then, or did they, that was an interesting question. But now, what about those films where the psycho made taunting phone calls to the police from phone boxes and they recorded them and listened to the background noises to work out where he was, airport noises and factory whistles and streetcars, no, that was American stuff, they must have more noises in America because here she heard *nothing* she just heard *nothing* except her own heart beating. No don't think of that, think again, ways and means, wasn't there another book she had read where some kid worked out where he was through the changes of temperature, sea breezes or something, oh great help, WHAT THEN, traffic, traffic noises how about them. Yes, some, she was sure she heard some, felt some rather, faintly vibrating through the bed, but then what did that mean, nothing nothing, she knew she hadn't been in the van long enough to have left the city, only ten or fifteen minutes though it was hard to tell with the terror and the blanket choking her thrust in her mouth and the knees pinning her down, her arms and legs in the soft places between the joints felt the bruises still NO DON'T THINK OF THAT. So. Somewhere in the city yes big deal but where north south east west if only she were a bird wasn't it birds who knew which way to go when you released them into a planetarium but that was the stars she had no stars, cats and dogs then, always knew their way home, what was that Walt Disney film about two dogs and a cat going home right across America or was it two cats and a dog went to see it at the Odeon with her best friend when she was nine or ten . . .

Thus Alison Holdenby rummaged among memories, digging frantically and uselessly down into them like a trapped animal digging the earth around the snare. And when she came across that one, a trip to the cinema with her best friend when she was a girl, a far, sweet memory, round and pure like an apple, Alison went away.

The going away was not good, she knew that. It was all she had done at first. There was no telling day from night here and she had no watch, so time had no shape; but she reckoned she had spent at least the first two days just going away in her head, when they allowed her to. No, the going away was not good. It cut off what was happening to her, but at the expense of life itself. She could see that now. When she curled up in a ball, squeezed her eyes shut and went away in her head, Alison was also going towards something – towards death. Willing the world to cease: willing the breath to be taken from her lungs for ever. Just like a sick animal giving up and hiding under a bush and letting the milky film form over its eyes. Just like that.

And it was so tempting and sometimes she couldn't help herself. If you really got yourself into a tight ball with your chin on your chest and your eyes *really* shut then you could almost feel your soul leave your body. And Alison's body was not a good place to be any more.

Soul? Yes – whatever. Not something she'd given a lot

of thought to, and in an argument over religion – sort of argument Martin used to delight in – she'd have come down on the sceptical side. All pie in the sky.

But soul – yes. At least, there was something here, in this place, that was Alison but wasn't Alison's body. Whatever it was, it was all she had.

Didn't know if she could keep it though, intact and recognizable. Didn't know at all.

The terror that revisited Alison at this thought was special. It was a terror that steamrollered her every now and then – in so far as there was any such thing as now or then in this new timeless shapeless world – and when it did there was no resisting it. No mental bracing, no psychological strategies, no inner pep-talks could do anything with it. Fear was her constant condition, but the fear contained certain impurities – anger, indignation, hatred, sometimes hope. When the true terror came, it was unmixed and elemental. After it passed over her she was able to assess it, describe it to herself; and the one and only apt comparison was with films she had seen of the explosion of nuclear weapons. Stillness: then the flash, whiteness and power beyond bearing, devouring the world in long moments of killing brilliance. That was how she saw the terror afterwards. When she was in it, there was no seeing it. She was in it and it was in her, bone of her bone.

Alison Holdenby, nineteen years old and alone, gasped and sweated in the blast of absolute terror.

It lasted an age, perhaps two minutes. As usual something external brought her out of it and back on to the relatively steady ground of hateful fear. It was a tear that had escaped her eye and ran tickling down her creased cheek. A surprise: she had thought they were all gone.

She put up a finger to wipe it and then put the finger in her mouth, tasting warmth and salt. The finger in her mouth felt nice, nice with ancient association. She sucked.

Tempting, tempting. She could go away like this: body coiled, finger in mouth, eyes tuned to the fantastic dancing darkness behind her lids. It was easy.

No. Her mind, staggering around, tried to assert itself. It had been doing some work a little while ago, before the terror-blast. Come on. Get back to it.

It would help, it would help a lot, if she knew where she was. And never mind *Why?* Never mind *What difference will it make?* Thinking of that would just set the terror off again. Stick to the task. Make the task an end in itself.

OK, the traffic noises. Off and on, not constant. What did that tell her? Couldn't be a main road – too little. Nor, on the other hand, could it be one of those new town suburbs that were all pedestrian precincts and cul-de-sacs – too much. But then she already knew she must be in an old part of the city, because of this room. This room was a cellar and only old houses had cellars.

Time for another look at this cellar, Ali.

She whimpered.

The fact of being in a cellar had fairly established itself in her mind by now. She did not like having that fact in there, but she made room for it somehow. Opening her eyes and looking round her at the cellar was a different matter.

She had done a lot of that at first, when they had put her in here. Along with the yelling and screaming and threatening and begging Alison had done plenty of looking around her. But she had seen only as a pig sees the walls of an abattoir. And since then she had kept her eyes closed as much as possible. Even when the ceiling light was on – and whether that meant day or night she couldn't tell – Alison had preferred the darkness behind her eyelids.

She didn't like to look at the room. Maybe that was more the anger than the fear. This room was nothing to do with her: she shouldn't *have* to see it. Least of all should she have to be *interested* in it.

But it was either that, or continuing to hide her face like a lost child among strangers. It was either that, or going away in her head, perhaps for ever.

Do you want to do that, Ali?

Maybe. Maybe not.

Alison Holdenby, curled up like an embryo on the bed with her fists clenched, took a deep breath and then slowly, slowly lifted her head.

Stick to the task. Make the task an end in itself.

The light was on: she could tell that even with her eyes closed. When it was off, the darkness was beyond everything. It was like black sand.

She felt no warmth on her face, so the heater must be off. It was a fan heater, somewhere over the other side of the room. She knew that not so much from the wild whirling looks she had given her prison as from the sounds it made. Little thermostat clickings as it adjusted its temperature. Her only companion.

Smell: fusty as usual, but not foul. The bucket and the litter tray had been taken away and cleaned, she remembered now: the boy with the hat had done it. It seemed to be his job, now that she used them. At first she had fouled herself. Fear, perhaps, also protest. Dirty protest. The smiler had stopped her doing that. The weasel one had watched, snickering.

She knew their names. They had told her their names, that night at the Arena. The weasel one was Derek, but he was known as Trend because of that trendy gear he wore. The boy with the hat was Sean: Irish. And the smiler . . . she didn't know what his proper name was. He just called himself Chill.

Trend, Sean, Chill. Chill, Sean, Trend. She tried the names over in her mind, but she felt the resistance. She didn't want those names in her head. Better her own names: boy with the hat, weasel one, smiler, names that had hate and disdain in them. Names that did not acknowledge them as human beings.

And yet Alison Holdenby knew – way down inside of her she knew – that she was going to have to acknowledge them if she was going to survive.

She remembered another book she had read – she had read a great deal, in spite of her mother's pinched, hopeless discouragement, her sighing refrain of, 'What good are those books going to do you?' It was a book by an Australian recalling his childhood. The post offices in Australia all had posters up illustrating which snakes and spiders were poisonous. It was a thing you had to know if you lived there, because snakes and spiders were all over. Alison could outstare a Rottweiler but snakes and spiders terrified her: she hated even to see pictures of them. But it had occurred to her on reading that book, and it occurred to her again now, that if she lived in Australia she would not be able to close her eyes to their existence in that way. She would have to study those posters. She would have to learn about the creatures she loathed. Simply out of self-preservation, she would have to take an interest.

Just like with this room, this cellar.

Alison opened her eyes and, after a few moments' squinting pain as her pupils contracted, let them roam.

Oh God, the bar.

She fought the impulse to close her eyes again.

That bar. She remembered it from when they had first put her in here. It stood in the opposite corner. An uncle of hers had had a similar thing in his front room. A tacky home bar with a melamine top and a front panel covered with some sort of copper-effect material and a set of fake beer pumps. Her uncle's had been all adorned with knick-knacks and a plastic ice-bucket in the shape of a pineapple, but there was nothing on this bar but a layer of dust. Dumped down here out of the way? No: there were optics fixed to the wall behind it. It had been set up down here and then abandoned. Alison had to force herself to think in these deductive terms, to keep her eyes on the thing, to see it for what it was. Because somehow that bar appalled her. The conjunction of it with her situation was an obscenity. The bar was hideous because it was jolly, crudely jolly and cheerful.

Somehow she knew that that bar was the smiler's idea, but the idea had been abandoned. And adjacent to the bar, against the right-hand wall, was another abandoned idea: a small pool table propped up on its end, one leg broken. There was a dartboard too, the cheap sort made of cardboard rings, which had warped from damp.

Ideas. They had this cellar, and they had tried to do things with it. Rigged it up with electricity – at least, one ceiling light bulb and one socket. A cellar bar, a games room. Those ideas hadn't worked out.

Alison had to close her eyes again at the knowledge that the latest idea was her.

No. The only knowledge she was concerned with right

now was knowledge of this room. And what it could do for her.

She sat up on the bed, making herself ignore the clinking of chain.

It was a big room, maybe twenty feet by fifteen. Low ceiling: a man over six feet would bump his head. The walls had been painted some sort of beige colour, but it hadn't taken well and in places the rough plaster showed through. There was a bricked-up square on the wall behind her: originally, surely a coal chute. Definitely an old house then. Victorian or something. The sort that were often carved up into flats and bedsits. There were lots of them in the old city.

The floor was bare – what, concrete, cement? – except for a square of old floral carpet, granny carpet she would call it, just in front of the bed. The stairs were in the far left-hand corner. They turned at the top so she couldn't see the door directly from here. It had a lock and a latch: she knew that from the sounds when they came down to her.

She had a feeling, from the way the stairs turned like that, that the door to the cellar was under the main stairs of the house. And above her . . .? No telling. She could just catch the sound of footsteps sometimes, occasionally the faint beat of a hi-fi.

Well, there was the fan heater, near the foot of the stairs, plugged into the dodgy-looking wall socket. Safety standard kitemark still attached, brown discoloration around the grille: well used.

And then there was this bed, parallel with the wall. The bed was familiar to her. It was an old type of folding bed called a Z-bed. Very old. It had an iron frame and clangy springs and a harsh industrial look. Her grandmother had had one: it had weighed about twice as much as an ordinary bed. In the first wild hours Alison had tried shifting it, as if that might help her. She had rubbed her wrists raw and exhausted herself and budged it precisely an inch.

So. The task. Did the room contain anything else?

Well, there was the food tray by the bed, but that was just a thing that was brought in here, not a fixture, and besides she didn't like to think about that, no, shut it out shut it out...

Too late, it was there. The memory of the time – what would it be yesterday? – when the smiler had brought the tray down. Usually it was the boy in the hat: she should have known something was up.

The smiler's cheeky grin danced in her head and she thought of it and tried not to think of it and swallowed a scream as she remembered the dog bowl being thrust towards her with its pile of stinking white stuff and his grin, his cheeky grin...

'Tripes, gel. Good for you. Lots of iron. Give you a nice shiny nose...'

No.

No. The task.

Alison's eyes roamed again. She could feel them moving in the sockets, heavy as ball bearings. They seemed to grind as they turned.

One more thing. Away to her right, a few feet from the dartboard. A mousetrap. No occupant. Though that didn't mean to say –

No, don't think of that either.

Floor, walls, stairs. Bar, pool table, dartboard. Carpet, fan heater. Mousetrap. Bed. Bare bulb hanging from frayed flex, showing it all to her in a light at once garish and dismal, like a public lavatory.

And Alison.

So, what could she learn from it all, what could she...

Oh Jesus what is this what is all this Sherlock Holmes shit it's useless they've got you chained up in a cellar and there's nothing you can do about it, nothing, and nobody knows you're here...

Alison Holdenby writhed and raved. When she got control of herself, some time later that might have been a minute or half an hour, her hair was caught in a web about her face and her tongue was bleeding where she had bitten it.

She lay back, panting. The hair in her face had a stale odour. She knew she didn't smell good. However long she had been here – three days, four days? – she had gone unwashed. The boy with the hat had brought a bowl of soapy water once and tried to get her to submit to a blanket bath, but she had fought him so much he had given it up. He must have told the smiler about it, because the smiler came down later and gave her a lecture about cleanliness, which she terminated by spitting at him and calling him a cocksucker. Then the smiler had gone and fetched a bottle of washing-up liquid and squirted it in her mouth, holding her down, until she gagged and nearby choked.

And said, grinning: 'You'll learn.'

Alison Holdenby, nineteen years old and in mortal terror, lay back and tasted her own blood, and gazing at the cracks in the low ceiling above her silently cried out *Why?*

She thought about mistakes. She thought about leaving school at sixteen when her English teacher had all but begged her to stay on and try for college. She thought about moving down here from Tyneside just to be with Martin when she didn't know another soul in the whole city and was very likely to be left high and dry if the relationship finished. She thought about how the relationship *had* finished and how she had added hurt to hurt by throwing cruel untruths, recriminations, accusations, creating hate. Mistakes, plenty of them. More than most people made? Maybe. But there had been some sort of proportion between mistake and consequence.

And then there was that one small mistake. She had decided to celebrate her own birthday by blowing half her fortnightly Giro on a night out at the Arena: just to remind herself she was young, just to break the monotony and loneliness of her YMCA flat and the fruitless search for work. And out of that same loneliness she had allowed herself to get friendly with three young guys who got talking to her at the rink and helped her to skate and they had clowned around and generally had a good time until the end of the evening.

When she had walked out to the car park with them, still chatting away about nothing in particular – *except yourself, Ali, the smiler kept asking you lots of questions about yourself because he was pumping you sussing you out* and then they had offered her a lift home in their van and she had refused with thanks, saying she would get the late bus.

Except – and maybe here was the nugget of the mistake – she had hesitated. Just for a moment, she had thought about accepting. And then the moment passed, and she knew it wouldn't be sensible to get in a van with three guys she hardly knew at eleven o'clock at night, nice enough guys though they seemed. You never knew and you couldn't be too careful and all the rest of it. But the hesitating moment had brought her a step closer to the van. It had prevented her saying goodbye and turning smartly and walking away.

And so the rest had followed.

A small mistake. A small carelessness, born out of being lonely on her own birthday and enjoying herself too much and not wanting the good time to end. Surely the consequences of such a mistake should have been small also.

Surely *this* should not have happened.

Alison could sense the approach of another blast-wave of terror and she had to get out of its path. Another would shatter her, she felt, like a girl of crystal glass. And the Sherlock Holmes crap might not get her anywhere but it might at least get her out of the path of that terror, so. *Think*.

In a cellar, in a house, an old house that must be somewhere near the city centre rather than the outskirts. Yes: here was another memory, and it fitted. The journey in the van with the blanket over her head and the hard knees and the chuckles hadn't been smooth. It had been jerky, quick-quick slow: she had been thrown from side to side by the motion of the van. Turnings, then, a lot of them. No long straight stretches of road. That meant the old city with its narrow streets and junctions and awkward bends.

There. The simple piece of deduction gave her a feeling of almost absurd satisfaction. Keep it up. Old house. Whose?

Well, the smiler and the weasel one and the boy with the hat were the only people who lived here, she was pretty sure of that. The screaming proved it, if nothing else. When they had first put her in here she had screamed all the time: then she had restricted her screams to whenever they opened the door to the cellar. It hadn't seemed to bother them – *except maybe the boy with the hat. Not pity there, but perhaps alarm. Not so sure. Squirrel that thought away. Might come in handy* – and that indicated that there was no one else to hear.

More. That the sounds of screams in that house wouldn't communicate anywhere else. No paper-thin walls and neighbours two feet away beyond the partition.

All right, so that only confirmed that it was an old house, solidly built as old houses tended to be. She was just going in circles –

No, she mustn't think of it that way. It was good. It was solid evidence, it was order in chaos. Big solid old house . . .

Now why big? How did she know that?

Cellar, of course. The sheer space taken up by this cellar showed there must be a reasonable-sized house above it. Plus: the sort of old city houses that had cellars weren't poky railwaymen's cottages. They were originally built for the sort of people who kept a lot of coal and maybe had a servant girl pushing the pram or whatever. Roomy.

She tried to back that up with the memory of being bundled, blind and blanketed, into the house. Once she had heard the door closing behind her, how far had she been dragged before entering the musty chill of the cellar? A long hall or passage? No, impossible to remember. But she did recall one thing. The distance between the van and the doorstep had been short. She had been out in the air for only a few seconds.

Thus, on-street parking. Thus, no long front garden. And thus again: quiet area, keeping to itself, and no passers-by to see a girl being dragged into a house by three men. Off the main thoroughfare, then. Near town, but tucked away.

And in this house it was just the three of them. Maybe renting and sharing. In that thought there was a bright paring of hope – *a landlord, a landlord inspection, what's going on in that cellar* – but it quickly blew away. Because she recalled something the smiler had said at the ice rink: something about 'my place'. Just casual chat about the miserable weather, and the smiler had said, 'My place is as cold as a witch's tit.'

His place. Add to that the way the other two deferred to him, even when they came down the stairs to have a look at her. He was older too. She was almost sure that this house belonged to the smiler. As for the others, they must live here with him: they were around all the time.

And while we're at it, take hold of that: *cold as a witch's tit*. Difficult to heat, in other words. That fitted too.

His place. He had let that slip at the rink, but very little else. She saw now, but damn her for a fool she hadn't seen then, that none of them had offered much about themselves. It had all been about her, and she had been so lonely and flattered and simply unused to people taking an interest in her that she hadn't noticed. She had given everything away and they had given nothing away.

Wait, though. The smiler had let something slip about himself that she hadn't taken much notice of, perhaps because it was fairly unsurprising. He was a market trader. As they skated he said something about all work and no play and she asked him what it was he did and he had answered, 'Market trader'. And had looked so every inch a market trader that she had thought no more about it.

Alison currently had no job. She had found a job on

first moving down to the city, but her employer had thought it would be a good wheeze to reduce her working hours to ten, perhaps so that she would have lots of leisure to forage in dustbins, and that had been the end of that. She was nineteen, unqualified, from a poor background, and marooned at the latter end of the twentieth century: steady employment was as remote from her experience as Lloyd George and the foxtrot. And so the ins and outs of economic sufficiency were somewhat shadowy to her. But she was pretty certain that market traders didn't rake it in. If a market trader had a big Victorian house with a cellar, it wouldn't be one of the chichi ones on the west side of the city where you saw women in sculptured earrings driving pink-cheeked children to school in Volvos: that was another league altogether. No, to be affordable it would have to be on the other side, the land of Bangladeshi corner shops and old shoe factories. It would just have to be.

Alison drew in deep, shuddering breaths as if she had just completed some taxing physical exercise.

Damn it, she could almost *see* this house.

Before she could push it away, she was touched by a corpse caress of despair. What difference would it make if she *could* see it? What difference if she knew the name of the street and the number and even the bloody postcode?

Because one thing was for sure: they had her fast. And they were . . . *cool* about it. At least the smiler certainly was; and the others seemed to take his lead. When she had been doing the screaming he had ordered the boy with the hat to gag her; but she had a feeling that this was more for fun than anything. The smiler had seemed to enjoy looking at her with the gag on: he had crouched down by the bed and studied her with the gentle amusement of someone peeking at a kitten in a shoebox. And when later they had taken the gag off to pour water down her throat, they hadn't replaced it. Really, she could scream all she wanted. The screaming was a thing to be disregarded, just like – and here she could feel the onrush of that terror again – just like the howling of a new puppy left downstairs at night.

Alison Holdenby, nineteen, alone in a way that no one could ever reasonably expect to be alone, turned herself about on the bed so that she was in a squatting position and gave a tug at the handcuffs that bound her.

She was hardly aware of doing this, so habitual had the movement become. She supposed that all prisoners had hopeless little routines like this. They tried to dig a tunnel with a teaspoon or whatever. Lacking even that freedom, Alison applied herself, at intervals that seemed to be decided by some inner clock of which she had not previously been aware, to the only instrument of her captivity within reach.

There had been something fastening her legs to the bed at first; but that had been the time of the screaming and spitting and thrashing, when she might have killed herself if she hadn't been restrained, and she guessed that the leg-bonds were impromptu. Not so with these handcuffs. These had been prepared. These were ready and waiting.

That question *Why?* rang in her head again and Alison seemed to hear the answer booming up from a pit of madness.

It said: *Because you were there, Ali. Because they were looking for a pair of wrists to put in these handcuffs, and they picked yours. Why? Might as well ask why you pick a T-shirt off the rack. Because you want one, and that one suits.*

Alison gave the handcuffs a last tug, then stopped and bowed her head. She knew they wouldn't break or loosen because they had been carefully prepared. God only knew where they had come from. Maybe some sleazy supplier of adult goods, bondage gear a speciality. It was heavy-duty stuff, if so. And the length of the links had been judged to a nicety. The cuffs had each been locked around the steel frame below the bed-head, just where a triangle was formed with the legs and the struts supporting them: they would move sideways along the frame maybe an inch and a half. Then came the links of steel chain joined to the cuffs at her wrists: each just long enough for her to be able to sit up against the bed-head, to put either hand up to her face, to use either hand to shuck her jeans down and manage a piss in the bucket, but not long enough or closely spaced enough for her to get her hands together.

She would never have believed how effectively hampered you were by not being able to get your hands together. Your fingers became like a monkey's, awkwardly clever, quaintly limited. As for fighting, she had done a lot of scrabbling and clawing whenever they came near her, but it was all baby stuff. No swing, no power. And she tried to banish the light-headed visions that sometimes came to her of grabbing something in both hands and smashing in their skulls with it, because the visions were just too sad, like the flying dreams of a crippled child.

Grab what, anyway? She could just manage, with her arms behind her, to sit on the edge of the bed, and she had tried feeling around with an outstretched foot for something she could hook towards her. But she knew there was nothing. The bucket and the litter tray, sometimes, but they were no damned use. She suspected that the boy with the hat was pretty dumb, and that there was a chance he wouldn't notice if the bucket wasn't there when he came down. But where to hide it? She might shuffle it under the bed, but it was unlikely, with the cuffs, that she would be able to reach it out again. And it would be so obvious as to be laughable. What are you fumbling at down there? The bucket, you know. I was going to hit you with it.

Besides, it was plastic.

As was the food tray. Alison had an ambiguous relationship with the food tray. She had refused to contemplate it at first. They had forced water into her throat and her epiglottis had done the rest; but the food could be spat out and spit it she did. In the nature of things, she got a few direct hits in their faces, and the slapping around that had followed this did not discourage her from doing it again. Eating the food was acceptance. Eating the food was acquiescing in what they had done to her. Eating the food was acknowledging their common humanity, when they were nothing but reptiles.

The body was treacherous. No enemy could be as subtly destructive as your own body. Look at the guy before Martin. (Two: there had only been two for Alison, though to hear her mother talk you would think she was nothing less than the village bicycle of the north-east.) Mick his name was, though she wouldn't have been entirely surprised if even that was a fake. Specialized in floods of self-accusing tears, as the shortest route into her knickers. And God help her, she still let him in long after she had spotted that he was as genuine as a bowl of wax fruit. Her mind saw all through him, smart and sharp, while her body acted like a drivelling doormat with a peroxide scrunch cut and a readers'-wives smile. She could remember feeling mistrust, contempt, weariness and his penis inside her all at the same time.

No trusting the body. After a while in the cellar the body didn't care about hatred and fear and indignation and making the only stand left to a powerless prisoner. The body turned into a slobbering, gluttonous, red-cheeked Fat Boy, looking at the plate of cold spaghetti with winking button eyes. The body said that accepting food from the hands of torturers was better than starving. The body was a liar, but Alison believed it, just as she had believed it when it had droned in a lubricious whisper that Mick wasn't such a bad guy.

Remorse and self-hatred – and here the comparison still held – came immediately after. Eating, keeping herself alive in their hands, was collusion. But sooner or later she would give in again: even such pranks as the tripe in the dog bowl did not stop her for long.

She could always tell herself, of course, that she was keeping herself alive for a reason. Keeping herself alive for the moment of her release. Keeping herself alive so as to have the rest of her life, outside of this cellar, away from the reptiles. Keeping herself alive so that Alison Holdenby could exist in the world again.

But telling herself these things involved her in a darkness more profound even than the physical darkness of the cellar when the light was off. It involved her in a renewed struggle with the old question *Why?*

At the time of the screaming and fighting she recalled the words *What do you want?* echoing round the bare puce walls, and she supposed they had come from her mouth; but it was a reflex more than a question. They had taken her to gang-rape her. From the moment they had hustled her into the van she had known that she was on course to becoming a sex-attack statistic, and some strong part of her mind had already been readying itself to bear, to brace, to recover, to have a future when it was over.

But there were other statistics. There were the statistics of victims who did not live to tell the tale: of those who had been treated as entirely, purely disposable. And the strong part of her mind couldn't be strong against that. These men hadn't hidden their identities from her: they hadn't jumped her in a dark alley leaving a blurred impression of eager faces. She could identify them with ease, and they didn't care . . .

But the house. They hadn't let her see the house. There was hope in that, surely. Hope that she would be released when they were finished, driven away and dumped maybe, maybe, maybe . . .

Then why was she still here?

Because they just love having you to stay, Ali.

It was no use playing the statistics game. Rape was terribly familiar, a presence in the air any woman breathed: abduction and kidnap were part of another world. You had to be embroiled in something significant to start with, for those things to have any meaning: tug-of-love, politics, wealthy family, the keys to the bank safe, these were the reasons people were spirited away. None of them applied to Alison Holdenby. Her mother's total assets came to a few pounds in a Post Office savings account and a glass case full of crystal Bambis, and her father was God knew where just as he had been since she was three years old. She knew no one in this city except the ex-boyfriend she had come here to be with and who had disappeared from her life with finality. She hoped she had as much pride and self-respect as the next person, but she could not deny that objectively speaking she was one obscure individual, alone, impoverished, and rootless except for a flatlet in a YMCA block full of corridors and loud strangers.

But isn't that precisely why they took you? Because someone like you can be taken? Someone like you can be made to disappear, and no one will ever know about it?

No one would know. The smiler had winkled all the relevant facts out of her that night at the rink; and the defiant threats she had made in amongst the screaming had carried no conviction even to herself. 'Someone will come and find me,' she'd cried, and: 'They'll be on to you.' It was crap. She might as well have gone the whole B-movie hog and said, 'You'll never get away with this.' There was no one. It was six months since she had last seen Martin, and that had been when she was still living in the mouldy bedsit: he didn't even know she'd got the YMCA flat, and it was highly unlikely that he cared one way or another after the way they had parted. Except for him, there was no one in the whole city of two hundred thousand people whom she could count as more than a casual acquaintance. That was the trouble with these heavy romances: the two of them had been so wrapped up in each other they'd thought they didn't need anyone else. Which was easier for Martin, as he'd lived in this city as a boy and had moved down here a good six months before she followed.

No, she wouldn't be missed. Maybe that fact was written all over her: maybe the smiler had hardly needed to get it all out of her with his matey tell-me-about-yourself spiel at the rink. But no, that route lay self-pity, and she rejected that as another way of giving in, of saying that she was the sort of pitiable creature this thing would happen to. As the reptiles no doubt thought when they singled her out.

Well, no way. Maybe it was as much choice as circumstance that had brought her to penniless loneliness in a city of strangers, but she would abide by that choice, and she would never believe that there was anything about her or the things she had done that marked her down for such a fate. That was victim thinking, and somehow she knew that nothing the reptiles could do to her could confirm their power over her as much as that.

No self-pity. Just facts. No one would notice that she was not around. She knew a few of her neighbours at the YMCA to pass the time of day with, but the population of that place was naturally a transient one: here today and gone tomorrow. No one knew she had been headed for the Arena that night; it had been a snap decision. As for her mother, Alison sent a postcard now and then to remind her she was alive, but that was as close as they got, and if the postcards stopped coming it was doubtful that Mrs Holdenby would be sufficiently troubled to get out of her chair and turn off the afternoon soaps.

There was one fact that was a little more hopeful, and that fact was the Department of Social Security, not a place normally associated with hope. If she failed to turn up to sign on for her fortnightly income support, it would be no big deal: they just wouldn't send her Giro. If it happened again they might send a snotty letter saying they presumed she had signed off and if so could they have their plastic card back, but that would be about it. The hope lay in the fact that claiming income support automatically entitled her to housing benefit, and when she stopped claiming income support the housing benefit automatically stopped too. And when the housing benefit stopped, the rent on the flat wasn't paid.

The block of flats was run jointly by the YMCA and a local housing association, both registered charities: but she knew they wouldn't be *that* charitable. Sooner or later they would cut up rough about the fact that no rent was being paid for Flat 14, Lyle House. Tenant, Ms A. Holdenby. There would be, surely, enquiries. Officialdom wasn't a fair-weather friend who lost your address and stopped writing. Officialdom was the class dork who buttonholed you in the street and kept sending tacky Christmas cards. Officialdom never let you go.

There must be hope, then. The world of brown envelopes and acid receptionists and national insurance numbers would miss her, if no one else did. But that thought did not lift her. It slid into her like a dentist's syringe, numbing her. Because everything hung on a thin thread of time. It would take time for the housing benefit to stop, for her landlords to start proceedings. Since losing her job Alison was used to dealing with time, measuring it out, dicing and spicing it, making it work for her instead of against her. But she didn't know about time now, here. It was a pit of mystery, because she didn't know what they were going to do with her.

Just what they're doing already, Ali. Keeping you here. Keeping you as a prisoner, and enjoying it.

That was the darkness that yawned at her: timescale. This wasn't gang-bang-thank-you-ma'am. (She had to think thus coarsely: it put a bouncer on the door where madness might come in.) They were playing the long game. She had not been raped, not yet, though she had little doubt she would be. Instead the familiarities had been teasing, tweaking stuff. From the smiler, at any rate.

He was the leader, no doubt of it, and he was the one who visited her to – play with her.

No other term would fit. She let the thought of that dog bowl filled with tripe slip under her defences momentarily before slapping it away.

The long game. When the smiler walked all round her, touching her hair, flicking the tips of her breasts, he knew what he was doing and so did she. He was denying her the knowledge that was shared, in different ways, by rape victims and by bored tired wives: that male lust was short-lived. That it was over quickly.

The long game. And he loved the game, the smiler: it was written all over him. His game. The boy with the hat was allowed to look, allowed to laugh; but not to touch, not in that way, not yet. And as for the weasel one, he kept in the background – at least, when the three of them visited her in the cellar. He had paid her one visit on his own, and she knew in her gut that that had been secret, maybe when the others were out. He hadn't said anything. Just come slowly down the stairs, all trendy rave gear and Jesus-of-Nazareth haircut, and walked slowly over to the bed.

He had looked pale and sick: not right. And Alison had dared a few seconds of dangerous hope: he was going to let her go. And then she saw what was behind the paleness and sickness and she knew it for hate just an instant before he spat all over her face.

Something else was going on there, something that was not exclusively to do with her. A reminder: the reptiles were creatures who came into her prison to look and to torment, but that was not all they did. They had lives, and she had come into their lives, willy-nilly. And surely not without effect.

Maybe there was hope in that, maybe not. Everything hung on that thin thread of time. The smiler knew it was safe to play the long game because no one was going to miss her, not yet. But even a long game did not last for ever. Even a long game had an end.

Alison curled up on her left side in a ball, drawing her legs tight under her, squeezing her eyes shut. In this position her right arm was cocked like a chicken wing, the chain that held it at its full extent. But her left arm was freer, and soon her left thumb began to move of its own accord towards her mouth and after a brief struggle she let it in. This was a thing she hadn't even done in childhood, but in the cellar she let it happen, just now and then, because it felt good. A treat, if you liked. Not to be indulged too often, because it tended to encourage going away, and going away was not good. But she wouldn't go away. Just rest a bit. Let the soreness in her wrists, from the ritual tugging, throb with her pulsebeat and gradually subside. Let her mind rest from its labours. Maybe even sleep. Sleep was good: sleep didn't count as going away.

They never let her sleep for long, anyway.

Alison Holdenby, nineteen years old, abducted, imprisoned, plucked from society like a single hair from a head, fighting despair with a courage that was like a knife without a handle, curled up in a ball and waited for sleep as a trauma patient might wait for anaesthetic.

Twenty feet away, an old man paused on the frozen pavement outside 43 Grenville Street to relight his rollup. He sucked in smoke that had the extra rawness of winter air in it, tossed the spent match in the gutter, and went on his careful way down the quiet street.

4

The weekend had been fine.

The weekend had been awful.

On Saturday Sarah and Murray had driven over to Stamford, a Georgian time-capsule just off the motorway, spent the day pottering about the catty-cornered town, had lunch at a coaching inn and appeared in the background of a hundred tourist snapshots. Sunday had been warm rooms and lassitude and newspapers and slow-cooking smells.

All that had been fine. Life strolling along on confident feet. Awful had been the undercurrent: the wondering, the remembering, the washes of cold fear. Life turning dark corners with a madman's scuttle.

Murray had known, but had not pressed. Concern and reassurance had been there, but at a graceful distance, like the passes of a conjuror round a levitating body.

It wasn't like the time of the one-eyed man. After all, that had completely screwed her up in the head so that work or play she couldn't think of anything else. Whereas this was just . . .

Just screwing up her work and play so she drifted round Stamford seeing nothing and wondering what the police were doing and got bitchy on air with some perfectly ordinary Soapy Sam just because some of his platitudes rubbed against sore places. Hell, that was all this was doing. Nothing much at all.

Sarah came to a conclusion, or a conclusion came to Sarah, as she walked down the corridor to her producer's office.

Radio East dispensed its homely fare from a sidestreet redbrick that had once been the city's labour exchange.

Tudor Radio paid an unthinkable rent for a site right on the mezzanine of the city's premier shopping mall, with its glass-and-girders entrance fronting the footbridge that crossed the inner city ring road to the railway station. The interior picked up the same theme: smoked glass, chrome rails, charcoal carpeting, dwarf trees in terracotta pots. In a few years it was going to look hilarious, and in a few more it would have the retro-chic of Art Deco cocktail cabinets and mosaic coffee tables. Sarah's producer, David, was a broadcaster of the old school who had tried to take the sleekness off his office with dog-eared posters and pots of scruffy pencils and kept the blind drawn over the megalomaniac window overlooking the city. He wanted to discuss some ideas for the Sunday arts show, which was his baby. Sarah was afraid he didn't get much out of her today except mechanical agreement, which must have sounded like disinterest. Perhaps he thought she had been got at by the controller, who thoughtfully fingered a paper-knife whenever the arts show was mentioned.

Sarah couldn't help it. She couldn't concentrate on what David was saying: her mind was on her conclusion. And she knew she was going to be this useless, this unreliable, this removed from herself until she had acted on it.

She used the studio office phone.

'I'm afraid I can't help you with that, madam.' Croft Wood police station seemed to sing twenty variations on that, now switchboard soprano, now desk-sergeant baritone, until someone referred her to CID. By then her knuckles were white on the receiver and she tried leap-frogging. She wasn't Sarah Winter calling, she was Tudor Radio.

A little more response to that. What exactly was it about? But she only had fudge, and they weren't buying. No, Detective Sergeant Routh wasn't available. Had an interview been arranged with DS Routh? No, she said, thinking too late she should have said yes. Well, there would be the usual release of information to the media, valued co-operation, this was DC Martindale, what exactly was she—

Routh, she wanted to talk to Routh. She hardly understood her own insistence on this. Detective Sergeant Routh had seemed to regard her report as little more serious than one of those tales of phantom hitchhikers. She had certainly not, anyhow, found him simpatico. Any copper would have done, really, any copper who could put out a hand and lift the burden from her.

Except for one thing. Somehow she knew Routh wouldn't be slick about anything. He was the boy who laboured inkily through his sums without peeking at the answers in the back of the book. He was the apprentice who diligently went to fetch a left-handed spanner. He hoovered in the corners. She didn't know how she knew this. It was a certainty and in that certainty was another – that he was her best hope, in spite of a personal feeling that was all edge and no ease.

But Detective Sergeant Routh was not available. Detective sergeants, it was plain, did not just come to the phone when you called in. They were not, madam, as DC Martindale so obviously refrained from saying, bloody takeaway pizza merchants. But he would make sure that Detective Sergeant Routh got whatever message she wished to leave.

'Sarah Winter at Tudor Radio needs to speak to him urgently. That's all . . . It's important.'

Voice cracking just a little on that *important*. Rachel interrupted her hunt-and-peck at the word processor to put back her drowning hair and give Sarah a look of limpid Pre-Raphaelite alarm. What was important?

DC Martindale soothed. He would pass the message on. Beyond the hum of the wire Sarah sensed the large ritualized complexity of the law, self-contained and inaccessible. Would Routh get back to her? DC Martindale would pass the message on. Now if he could help her in any way . . .

Sarah rapped the phone down. She caught another look of alarm from Rachel, who turned her head and went into a typing flurry. Qwertyuiop.

'Rachel, if there are any messages for me from – from the police, could you let me know on my home number, please? It's important.'

Pursuing her as as she left the studio, the question: *What was important?*

The answer, many-faceted, sharp like a dark diamond: *Not knowing.*

5

At first the very idea of shopping together had made Sarah and Murray laugh. What? *What?* Place the kiss of death on the brow of romance by mooching round a supermarket with a mutual trolley? Next it would be winceyette pyjamas. No way.

Then they accidentally did it, and found it good, and inaugurated a Wednesday evening habit. The weekly shopping trip was a pain when you made it alone, much nicer in loving company. You bought more booze and goodies, and swore unison vengeance on the pushy who

came to the store just to break shins. You got smug too.
All around couples were quarrelling viciously over cuts of
meat. Unbearable men loaded groceries on to the conveyor belt with absurdist precision, tins first, eggs last.
Fleshless women gave tomatoes a forensic once-over. We,
thank God, are not like that. We can be routine and still
have fun.

Two days had gone by since she had made that call,
and Sarah had had no word from Detective Sergeant
Routh. What had happened in the Arena car park was
nearly a week away now. Time was taking it further and
further from her, disposing of it, moving towards the day
when she would helplessly have to shrug the whole business off. Whatever she had seen, she was powerless to
prove alone. She was waiting, mentally pacing, for the
next move to be made.

Sarah felt she was hanging tough right up until the
moment she stood at the supermarket checkout with
Murray and looked behind her and saw the girl with red
hair.

Murray was hefting cat litter on to the conveyor belt.
He didn't see Sarah go, didn't know she had run until a
minute later, and by then she was tearing down the aisles,
skidding on the tiled floor, making less progress the more
she tried to hurry. Exactly as in a dream.

Except this wasn't a dream, she had *seen* her. She had
looked round from the checkout and there, there was the
red-haired girl just turning a corner of the aisle behind
her. In sight for a moment and then gone but *there*,
goddammit, *there*.

The store was crowded: sprinting through a dense
forest would have been easier. Shoppers stared or, thinking she was pursuing an errant child, chose not to stare.

Sarah collided with a trolley. Her feet slid wildly from under her like a novice skater's, but she picked herself up with dusty hands and bruised hip, ran down another aisle between homely things, sauces and pickles and preserves, and could not find the girl with red hair.

She was *there*, she was *there* . . .

She was there. Waiting at the delicatessen counter, holding her ticket, looking up at the display for her number. Her head was back and the bob of auburn hair fell over her collar.

It was the little boy beside her who first saw Sarah's approach, and gave a mute tug at the skirt of the girl with red hair.

Woman with red hair. Woman of thirty with red hair, about to ask Sarah what the hell she thought she was doing grabbing her shoulder and whirling her round like that, but held back by something. Maybe the normality jigsaw. Strangers didn't just grab you in the supermarket and stare into your face for no reason at all.

'Sorry,' Sarah burbled, 'sorry, I'm really so sorry, I thought you were – I thought you were someone else, I made a mistake, I'm so sorry . . .'

The woman was giving Sarah one hell of a look. Not because of the mistake – they happened – but because Sarah was still staring into her face, still staring and could not stop, disappointment hammering into her guts and disbelief lifting her till she felt dizzy and light-headed. She had been so sure, so sure . . . and yet this woman was thirty and looked it, the hair a similar shade and the build much the same but really not much of a resemblance. Not much of a resemblance at all.

I can't believe my eyes . . .

The bell was ringing at the deli counter for the next

customer but no one was paying any attention. They had a sideshow and it was Sarah. She came awake to their goggling faces, but still it was several moments before she came awake to how she must look. She made an abrupt about-turn and almost collided with Murray. He'd come to look for her.

'What's going on?'

She didn't answer, and they said nothing more, except an apology to the impatient queue at their checkout, until they were paid up and on their way out.

'I thought I saw someone I knew,' Sarah said then, and felt like laughing hysterically.

Two Securicor men were steering a trolley full of cashbags in through the doors. People stood aside with a curious hushed respect, as if for a stretcher case.

'Who?' Murray said.

Again she didn't answer, and didn't need to. In silence they loaded the groceries into Murray's car, got in. Murray put the key in the ignition, then let it be. Sarah stared forward through the misted windscreen. Another out-of-town car park sheathed in ice.

'I thought it was the girl,' she said, and the sound of her own voice made her jump.

'And it wasn't?'

'No. Somebody ... somebody else.'

'You know you've got to get that stupid business out of your system, don't you?'

When Murray was pissed off his voice turned oddly flat and colourless. Perhaps it was because he was normally so calm and temperate: anger robbed him of his personality.

'Tell me how, then.'

Murray fumbled irritably at the heater switch. 'I wish

FREEZING POINT

I could. I don't know. Try, just try to put it out of your mind.'

'You think I haven't tried?' Now her voice was loud. Quarrel volume. 'You think I'm enjoying this? Do you really think I'm enjoying this?'

More than a few men would have picked that one up and run with it. Murray was at least beyond such cheap shots. He grumped something and fished for his cigarettes.

'If I could get it out of my mind I would,' she said. 'But what I saw—'

'What you saw, come on, Sarah, think about what you're saying.' Murray whipped round to face her. 'Just think about it, for God's sake. This girl. This girl with the auburn hair and all the rest of it. You don't really even know what she looks like.'

Cliché, of course, about blue-grey eyes being cold and remote, but Murray's certainly seemed so at this moment.

'I do,' she said. 'I do know.'

'Do you? How can you be so sure, after what happened in there? You've just got this girl on the brain. What are you going to do, chase after every redhead you ever see?'

'I'd know her if I saw her.' Quietly now: there was misery within, not all of it caused by Murray. 'I wish I could see her. But I'm right this time, I'm certain of it . . .'

'Shit. You bastard,' Murray said to his reflection in the rear-view mirror. 'I'm sorry, Sarah. That was a lousy thing to say. Jesus.' Slow to lose his rag, Murray was swift to recover it. 'You make a simple mistake. Murray jumps down your throat. Hmm.'

'I'm not cracking up.' Sarah let the words lightly out, and they buzzed round the car and came back to her,

wild hornets, and then she was sobbing. 'I know what I saw. Murray, don't say you don't believe me either . . .'
Murray, not saying it, held her and stroked her hair.

FOUR

1

It hadn't been much of a quarrel, after all, but Murray was punctilious about such things and the making-up had been very thorough. It wasn't her, he assured her any number of times, it was him. He had been nervy himself, that night at the supermarket: a tin alarm clock ready to go off.

It was hearing about Soapy Shirebrook and God On My Side that had done it. Murray had been brought up in the sort of hyper-religious household that Sarah had thought only existed in comic novels. There were framed texts on the walls – yes, sir, framed texts. His elderly parents had responded to teenage tantrums by falling down on their knees and offering up a prayer for their straying son. Apart from the sash-window-raising sessions, as Murray called their prayer meetings, they never went out: they played Scrabble instead to the accompaniment of the radio, and if a programme came on that featured swearwords or other unpleasantnesses one or other of them would say, straight-faced, 'Shall we have it off, dear?' When he went away to university they sent him a weekly mail-shot of tracts, calling on him to remember Jesus.

Murray had broken with it, but it hadn't been easy. He was in the middle. His elder sister had taken the whole thing on board, married another sash-window-raiser, and begotten a rash of children with biblical names. His younger brother, viewing his parents as no more than amusing curiosities and their religion as a faintly pitiable infirmity, had cheerfully got on with a God-free life as a professional musician and drug-taker. Meanwhile Murray swapped faith for guilt. The Jesus jive was hogwash but to reject it was at least in part to reject his parents, since they had nothing else but the Scrabble. So Murray came up in psychological hives whenever religion was mentioned, and got scratchy – especially when there was a little extra guilt attached, as there was just now. 'I haven't been in touch with them lately,' he told Sarah. 'And so when I heard about God Up My Arse or whatever it's called I started thinking about them and when I started thinking about them I started thinking about how I haven't phoned them lately and what a rotten son I am and then . . . you know the rest.'

The sensible thing to do, of course, was to ring them, and she prodded him to it when she was over at his place the next evening. She had heard many more easeful phone calls, but it seemed to do the trick. 'The funny thing is,' he said afterwards, flushed and chatty like a child leaving the dentist's, 'that they're such nice people. Wouldn't hurt a fly. In a way I couldn't have had nicer parents. Work *that* one out.'

So that was all right. Murray was good at making things all right. Maybe too good. Two days after the incident at the supermarket Sarah found herself virtually believing that nothing had happened there at all, that any emotional backflips had been performed by Murray not by her, that

Freezing Point

she was cruising. And so she was all the more devastatingly unprepared for what came her way on Friday morning.

She had just entered the studio office when there was a buzz through from reception. Rachel was off sick – patchouli poisoning maybe – and Sarah took it herself, with a rueful certainty that it was Fire-Mark Fred out there. This time she really ought to talk to him, she had plenty of time, it wouldn't hurt her to listen to a few more anecdotes from the wonderful world of fire-marks...

Not Fred. Somebody called Paul Routh. It took her a moment to catch on, and another moment to juggle a few guesses as to why he hadn't mentioned that he was a copper.

'Thanks, Janet. Ask him to come through.' She was so eager that she was shaking, but she had the broadcaster's voice that gave nothing away.

Routh seemed more awkward than ever in here. He walked in with exaggerated care, as if afraid that the sound of his footsteps would come over on air. His cold was still intact: you could almost see it like a seedy cloud round his head.

'Is this an OK time? I won't be long. Only—'

'Of course, of course. Have a seat. I've been trying to get in touch with you...'

'I know.'

That didn't come out too friendly, and he looked sour as he sat down and gave the office a cursory look. But Sarah's eagerness let that go.

'Have you found out anything? Is there anything I can do, make another statement...?'

He was shaking his head. He wasn't looking at her. She

became aware of her eagerness, like a slipped bra strap.

'No, we haven't found out anything. That's why I wanted to come and see you. To let you know and . . . With respect, Miss Winter, this shouldn't be necessary. I understand your concern, but we're very busy just now and it doesn't help when we keep getting these calls supposedly from Tudor Radio and supposedly urgent.'

Yes. She had called again yesterday.

'My boss got a bit jumpy and wanted to know why Tudor Radio were on our backs and what did they want that the Press Officer wasn't giving them. Stuff like that.' Routh picked up a cartridge from a new batch of commercials piled on the desk, studied the spine for a moment. 'Obviously it wasn't Tudor Radio, it was you.'

'All right, fair cop,' she said impatiently, 'but what else was I supposed to do? It's impossible getting straight answers out of you lot.'

'The progress of any ongoing investigations, unless there are particular reasons for secrecy, is routinely made public through our liaison with the county Press Officer. You of all people should know that.'

'OK, OK, it was out of order what I did, but really I can't rest until I know what's happening. Surely you can understand that?'

'Yes, Miss Winter, I do understand.'

Maybe he did: but Sarah sure as hell didn't understand that sudden transition from constabulary snottiness to soft soap.

'Anyway, while I'm here let me thank you for your cooperation. It's not very trendy to talk about good citizenship, but some of us still believe in it. I've seen a lot of nasty things happen all because someone decided it was none of their business.'

The soap was getting softer. But he was at least looking at her now.

'Anyway,' he said again – his speech seemed to be all wrong turnings – 'obviously you're concerned, and I thought it was only fair to put your mind at rest on this one.' He fumbled for tissues. 'We've checked up with all the staff at the Arena. Now nobody remembers the individuals you gave a description of, but then that's hardly surprising as there were well over a hundred people there that night. Main thing is, nobody saw anything dodgy—'

'They wouldn't. There was only me in the car park when it happened. I was the only one who—'

He held up a hand. 'Bear with me. Now there were no cars left in the car park overnight. Reports of assaults – plenty in the past week, just like any week, but nothing that ties in. Believe me,' he said as she tried to speak, 'I've personally checked through them all and there's nothing. Same with Missing Persons. I didn't get back to you before because obviously you have to allow that time. No. Nothing from Missing Persons.'

'Are you sure?'

'I can tell you what missing persons reports we've had this week, if you like. Old guy with Alzheimer's wandered off in his pyjamas and turned up at the dog track. Fifteen-year-old got pissed off with mum and dad and popped over to Leicester for a couple of days. Husband with tattoos everywhere except his teeth cleared off again and his wife contacted us instead of clapping her hands—'

'Maybe they killed her.'

She silenced him for a moment. He honked into a tissue.

'In that case she would have been reported missing,'

he said muddily, and then, brisk again, 'look, Miss Winter, there's nothing. If a crime occurs, especially if it's a crime against the person, the police get to hear about it. That's their job. And as far as we're concerned . . . well, I say again, there's nothing. And before you hit me with some statistics about how many sexual assaults don't get reported, let me say this force has got an excellent record as far as that goes. And we've mounted a drive the last couple of years to improve it, we held a very productive seminar with the Rape Crisis Helpline to tackle the negative image of police response to rape reports . . .'

Funny to hear workman-like, catarrhal Sergeant Routh coming out with this career-copper spiel. Actually she had a feeling he believed in it. Random thoughts: Sarah was shaking again, and not from eagerness.

'But I've told you what I saw. Doesn't that count for anything?'

'If it didn't count for anything, we wouldn't have been following it up for the past week. What you saw needed checking out in case there was something nasty at the bottom of it, and there isn't.' He hunted impatiently for a clean tissue, and then the impatience swung over to her. 'Look, I think you saw an innocent piece of horseplay. These people were young and young people arse about. They don't act like responsible adults because they're not. I think the girl knew these guys and she was getting a lift home with them or they were all going on to a club or whatever. They'd probably had a drink in the bar. It was a youngsters' night out. And with absolutely no evidence to the contrary I don't see in what way we can be further involved. I mean, your statement will be kept on file, and as I say we're grateful for your co-operation—'

'You mean you're going to leave it at that? Just drop it?'

Perhaps it was her – something about her he didn't like: perhaps it was being here on her ground. Combination of the two maybe. Whatever: that last question had needled him, and when he spoke there were catty-claws in his voice. 'Well, I thought I knew my job, but I'm open to suggestions. What do you think – an all-points bulletin for a girl in her late teens with auburn hair and a van that might be blue and might be grey?'

'Maybe I should have said the guys were black. Then you'd all be galloping around like the cavalry.'

Routh gave her a look as if she had cracked a joke about a cripple.

'All right, forget I said that. It just seems so . . . I mean, supposing the girl was here on a day trip? People come from fifty miles away to the Arena, I've even done requests for parties from Norwich. You're not telling me you've been through every missing persons report throughout the whole country?'

'No, I'm not. I'm CID, not Missing Persons. But I can tell you that Missing Persons at Croft Wood are not entirely useless and if they got a report of someone who went on a day trip to the Ice Arena and never went back to Norwich or wherever, they would pick up on it. Now give us a break, will you?'

'So you think I . . .' She swallowed an obstruction in her throat. 'You think I was mistaken.'

'Yes,' he said promptly. 'You were mistaken. No big deal. No big deal at all. Down in the south of the county we've got one of these big cats, pumas or panthers or whatever, wandering round the fens. It's there all right, there's even a video of it: some prat who fancied exotic pets and then couldn't handle it is my guess. The local officers get reports of it and sometimes they're mistaken. No big deal: just mistakes.'

So what she had seen was down there with sightings of the Loch Ness Monster and all the other fruitcake mythology. He couldn't know how ill chosen those words were. Could he . . . ?

'A mistake,' she said. 'Fair enough.'

She saw the close look he gave her, though he kept it subtle. 'I'd better be going,' he said. 'Sorry, I haven't put this very well. I really did want to thank you for being – what is it? – public-spirited, and I do appreciate that you were worried. I know, you can start imagining all sorts of things in these situations. But I'm here to tell you: put it out of your mind.'

She felt vague and light-headed, and it came out in the way she murmured, 'Easier said than done.'

No big deal. That was what he was saying. So why the hell *was* it such a big deal to her? That was what he was thinking, surely, in his dry suspicious copper way.

Except he wasn't thinking that, not if the look on his face was anything to go by. Once again Sarah detected the odour of soft soap. The odour reminded her of something, something from the past.

'I mean,' he said, after a few moments' silence, 'if you really find it difficult to, you know, put this thing out of your mind, then maybe you could get some sort of help with it. I mean, I can categorically assure you that there isn't a thing to worry about, but obviously you are worried, and so . . .'

He shrugged, but the shrug was awkward not dismissive. A subject was not being broached. Sarah could feel its shadow falling across her.

'What sort of help?' she said. He was floundering, but she wouldn't rescue him. 'Don't tell me there's a helpline for people who've witnessed something disturbing but nobody believes them?'

She wasn't like this. This wasn't her. But the situation brought it out of her. Routh brought it out of her. And if smart-arsed needling was the only thing that would make him say what he was refraining from saying—

'Look,' he said, 'I'm trying to help here. I don't have to be doing this at all. You happen to have that bit of clout from working in the media and you knew that when you made those phone calls and OK, it worked and I'm here. As it happened it's probably a good thing you did phone again because a colleague of mine picked up on your name.'

An eyelash-beat of silence.

'Did he now.'

'She. Moved up to CID a couple of years ago. When she was a WPC she was involved in a case of, er, harassment and so on, against a Miss Sarah Winter, which turned out to be—'

'Mistaken.' Here it was. Sarah grasped at a passing truth, that nothing ever, ever died. 'Yes. Five years ago. No secret about that. I thought I was being . . . harassed, as you say, by this man. But it turned out I was mistaken. It was all sorted out. I was mistaken. It was all sorted out. I was under a lot of pressure at the time.' She nearly said, *It was no big deal*. 'I don't see what that's got to do with anything. I mean, was I supposed to tell you this, or what? It never occurred to me.' Words in the wind, thrown back at her emptily. She was really shaking now, and he couldn't miss it.

'Apparently, Miss Winter, there was rather more to

it than that.' His tone flattened and in that flatness there was all the bleakness of officialdom, the doubts of the taxman and the dentist discovering a cavity and the teacher spotting the cheated homework. 'It seems there was a possibility of prosecution at one point – against you, that is. Criminal damage – a phone box. But it was decided to let the matter drop. You were, as you say, under a lot of pressure, and it seemed to be a matter for—'

'A matter for the doctors, yes. Don't tell me you've never been under stress, with the job you have to do? Come on, you know how it is. You get so stressed out that you're not yourself any more, and so you get help for it, you see your doctor and if he's no good he just feeds you tranquillizers and if he's any good he gets you specialized help. A therapist.'

She was gabbling. But Routh didn't get caught in her slipstream. He moved on his own slow track. 'A therapist,' he said. 'That would be, what, a psychiatrist?'

'Oh, I don't think we talk about psychiatrists any more, that's all a bit 1950s, we have therapists nowadays, everybody has them, they have them in offices and schools . . .' Whoa. If she was trying to demonstrate to him that she wasn't a crazy lady, then this fast-forward flippancy was one hell of a way to do it.

'Sure. Even the fuddy-duddy old police force has them. They help us if we get upset over trivial things like seeing mangled kids pulled out of crashed cars.' It was his turn to look immediately regretful: that was pulling rank and he knew it. 'All I'm saying is, there's help available if you've found this thing . . . disturbing.'

'What happened to me,' she said tightly, ignoring this, 'what happened to me five years ago shouldn't have any bearing on this. Surely to God it shouldn't. I mean even a criminal up in court isn't supposed to have his case prejudiced by previous convictions. Because I made a mistake once before, that makes me a completely unreliable witness, does it?'

Routh paused for a second before answering, and the pause was a hole down which Sarah fell, wailing. 'Nothing of the sort. We don't act that way. I only brought it up because . . . well, to remind you that these things can be upsetting, you know that from your own experience, and that there's ways of dealing with them. That's all.'

'I see. Well. Thank you for the thought, anyway.'

She had withdrawn from him. Not in anger: she was seeing something. Seeing the wood for the trees, maybe. Seeing what Routh, and the authorities he represented, really suspected, now that the one-eyed man had popped up out of the filing cabinets. It was no longer a matter of her being mistaken in what she had witnessed. In Detective Sergeant Routh's heavy eyes she saw a strong doubt whether she had witnessed anything at all.

Maybe that was why he had come here to the studio. Maybe there was goodwill in it: to see her on her high-powered home ground, broadcaster, sort of public figure, to convince her and himself that he recognized her as such, and not as some addle-brained bag lady with a tale of Martians landing behind the Co-op. Pity, then, that she had done nothing to allay the doubt. Pity about the gabbling and the shaking and all the other evidence that she was just a hysterical obsessive with a brand-new bee in her bonnet – it's that Winter woman again, Sarge. What is it this time? Oh, just non-existent girls with non-existent red hair getting spirited away in non-existent vans . . .

He was on his feet: relieved, seemingly, that she had clammed up and let it drop. 'Sorry to take up so much of your time,' he said.

'No, no. Sorry I've wasted yours.'

She didn't say it with any edge: no point.

Still he hung back a moment. She had been right about him in one respect: he was conscientious. He wouldn't take an easy way out even if it was offered him, as she was offering it to him now. Reminiscent of Murray in that.

'That other business,' he said. 'I honestly wouldn't have brought it up. I mean, I haven't been checking up on you or anything.'

'It's OK.'

'I just wanted to set your mind at rest.'

She showed him the way back to reception: more than one studio guest had got lost and ended up blundering into the newsroom, and besides it was common courtesy.

Which she owed him, surely. She had some indignation, because he had patronized her in spite of his best efforts; but it didn't go far. He had reason on his side, after all. He had the one-eyed man on his side. And once the one-eyed man entered the fray, she had lost.

I just wanted to set your mind at rest.

Yes: he probably believed that that was what he was doing. There was no way of conveying to him, or to anyone, that he had done precisely the opposite.

2

At the time of the one-eyed man, Sarah had been living in a small block of flats called Chadwick Court. They had been built on a tiny corner of vacant land in the old city centre, at the height of the flight to the urban. Forget suburbs, trees, and cycleways. The new des res was as close to the gasworks as possible. Pubs took down the dayglo signs proclaiming them Charlie's Bar & Grill or Top Nobs and reverted to Nag's Head and Shunter's Arms. Every second house of a terrace sported a skip in its front garden. Chadwick Court was all boxy lines and slate and brick. They hadn't found a way of making the brick look blackened with a hundred years of coal smoke, but they were probably working on it.

Sarah hadn't been entirely proof against this curious fantasy, and had felt pretty pleased with herself on moving into Chadwick Court. Traffic racket, drunks pissing in the wheelie bins and the impossibility of swinging a cat – or, more importantly, keeping one as a pet – had emerged later as reasons for moving on. But at the time she had been happy enough.

That was the strange thing, in retrospect: the frightening thing also. She had been in a state of reasonable contentment just before things had suddenly fallen apart. An unexciting relationship had recently died a mercifully peaceful death, her bank balance was just the right side of red. She was enjoying her work as a hospital DJ, as well as contributing what she now saw as an unbearably smart-arsed record review column to the local rag.

And there had been a death in the family. Not the sort of circumstance you normally added to the total when you were counting your blessings. But then this wasn't a blood relation of Sarah's who had died. Or a normal relation, come to that.

The late unlamented was her stepfather. An economy-size, industrial-strength, one hundred per cent pure bastard named Graham.

Sarah's parents had divorced when she was twelve. Her father, a building contractor, had moved to Ireland, whence she still received biannual letters precisely two pages long and, on her birthday and Christmas Day, phone calls which were like oral versions of the letters. He was a gaunt man with the costive correctness of a Prussian officer. Kind, Sarah suspected; but he had never learned to express kindness. And so it was only possible to miss him so much and no more.

Especially when most – perhaps all – of the warmth of the family emanated from her mother. Sarah was old enough by now to know that there was no mismatch of personalities so blatant that it hadn't been solemnized in a church some time, somewhere; but still, the disparity between her austere father and her vivacious mother was striking. Her father's face said No Entry. Her mother had all the lights on, the door wide open, and a kettle boiling on the hob.

Graham, the poison dwarf, saw the welcome mat and walked in when Sarah was fourteen.

He was the life and soul in the way that Sarah's father could never have been, and Sarah's mother thought the sun shone out of his backside, low to the ground though it was. Her second marriage was a hit: she was like a kid again.

Graham wanted to be loved. He wanted to win everybody over: usually he did. Sarah, impervious to his bonhomie, was a challenge to him, and a challenge he couldn't leave alone. Whatever she did, he was there with a comment, the footnote on every page of her teenage life. And when the rebellion genes kicked in, Graham was the one whose wagging finger awaited her when she got home late, pissed and lovebitten.

And here he turned nasty. The mutual dislike became precisely that – mutual, a matter between the two of them. But Graham brought Sarah's mother into the equation. As Sarah grew up, looked outward, began to spread her wings, Graham portrayed each and every natural step as a slap in the face to her mother. And, God help her, Sarah's mother ended up believing it. Having driven Sarah away, Graham cried out at her perfidy in leaving. He was all puzzled reproach at Sarah's neglect of her mother, meanwhile carefully positioning himself so that she could not get near her.

And then, five years ago, Graham suffered a heart attack when he was playing squash, and was dead before he hit the floor. The poison dwarf had kicked the bucket at last. Sarah knew she shouldn't have phrased it like that, even to herself, for her mother's sake. Her mother's grief was great, and the task of consolation that fell to Sarah was made harder by the fact that the dwarf's legacy to his widow included an abiding mistrust of her own daughter. Still, Sarah tried; and a little lost ground was painfully made up. She hoped she managed to conceal from her mother what she could not conceal from herself: her sheer relief that the bastard was no longer around.

So that was how she stood, five years ago, when the bad time began. Her stepfather had been dead some six months, her mother was beginning to bounce back, and Sarah, doing what she thought then were tasteful things to her overpriced flat in Chadwick Court, was at peace with her world.

And along came the one-eyed man.

It was spring when it began, an unusually warm spring, so warm that – as with this winter – people just couldn't stop remarking on it. Sarah had thought that someone ought to market a series of placards that you could just hold up at the bus stop or in the lift whenever you didn't feel like making the appropriate comment. 'WARM AGAIN TODAY', or 'ISN'T IT GORGEOUS?' or 'IF IT STAYS LIKE THIS I SHAN'T COMPLAIN'.

But the one-eyed man never said anything. Perhaps that was what brought him to her attention.

He was a tall man with a neat pointed beard. Forty or forty-five, conservatively dressed in white shirt and tie, rather craggy-looking. The missing eye was the left. For whatever reason, he wore no artificial eye in the socket; there was just a pouchy seam between the lids, so that he looked as if he were continually wincing in pain.

Through those bright spring days, Sarah became aware that the one-eyed man was following her.

She was always seeing him. She would be picking up a few groceries at the local store, and she would catch sight of him in the security mirror, pretending to choose biscuits. She would leave the hospital at lunchtime, taking a side exit by the maternity wing, and she would see him from the corner of her eye crossing the road with studied casualness. She would turn the corner of her own street, and she would see him walking fifty yards behind her.

And when her car was in dock for a week and she had to take the bus to work, the one-eyed man was at the bus stop in the morning. He got on the same bus as her, always sitting a few seats away, and he got off at the same stop. Come the afternoon, the same thing.

As spring progressed, Sarah found herself a prisoner of her own fear.

The fear was like the invasion of health by sickness. Unless you were an outright hypochondriac, you generally thought of yourself as a healthy person; and when the signs of illness began to appear, your impulse was to ignore them, dismiss them until there came the morning when you woke and knew. *I'm ill . . . oh God, I'm so ill . . .*

Sarah didn't know how long she lived alone with her fear, precisely because it was so difficult to pinpoint when it began. Less than two months, probably, but it felt like a lifetime. The one-eyed man could not have exerted a more dreadful and inescapable power over her if he had been a malign spirit who had entered her body and possessed her. And the ultimate nightmare touch was that she had to, and did, carry on with her normal life. All the time that she was being menaced by him, she continued to work, to eat and sleep, to act as if nothing was wrong.

At least, if you put a very loose construction on those words. She worked in the sense that she turned up for work and went through certain motions reminiscent of her job – all the time wondering if the one-eyed man would be waiting to follow her home when she was finished. She ate in the sense that she contrived to cook meals in the intervals of going to the door to check it was locked and bolted, and then sat down at the table and looked at them for a while before scraping them into the bin. She slept in the sense that she got into bed and sometimes lay still for as long as half an hour before running to the window and parting the curtains with a trembling hand, certain that she had heard footsteps and expecting to see the one-eyed man standing in the courtyard below, looking up.

And she carried on as normal, too, in as much as no one knew otherwise. Sarah told no one what was happening to her. There was hell inside her, but somehow she felt it was better to keep it there than let it out. If she let it out, it would take over the whole world.

She might have kept it there for ever, perhaps – if her tormentor had not decided to turn up the heat. She might lock and bolt her door against him, but there was still the telephone.

When did *that* begin? Again, impossible to say. It was not frequent enough to be completely obvious – that was not his style: after all, there were some days in which she didn't see him at all, just enough to make the torture more exquisite. And so it was with those single sharp rings that her telephone gave, and which terrified her so much that sometimes she whimpered and cowered at the sound, pressing herself into the corner of the settee and covering her eyes like a helpless child.

Once or twice she managed to pick up the receiver within a couple of seconds of that solitary ring. No one spoke – at least, not audibly. There was a sort of distant murmuring, and then the softest of clicks, as if a phone cradle were being pressed down with dreadful gentleness.

Sarah had known even then, for all her denials, that there was an edge and she was coming close to it. What she did not know was what lay on the other side of the edge; or what would finally take her to it. All she could do was scream silently inside her prison of fear, the screams sometimes forming into the despairing articulation *Why me?*

There were no dates in her memory of that time, no landmarks in the amorphous waste of terror; only of the climax did she have some circumstantial recollection. It had been a Friday afternoon: she had been home from the hospital for about half an hour, and she had checked the locks a fairly modest three times, and she was just wondering what culinary futility to concoct this evening when her ears, sensitive as a nervous dog's, caught the sound of rapid footsteps approaching her front door.

Another sound: something being pushed through her letterbox.

It was strange – strange then, and strange in retrospect – that Sarah had still managed to cover the seething surface of her mind with a layer of denial. It must be the local evening paper being delivered. Never mind the fact that the evening paper always, without fail, plopped on to her doormat at six-fifteen, and it was now only five. The voice of reason had its own special irrationality. Thus, knowing and pretending not to know, Sarah walked like a zombie out to the hall.

A pornographic magazine lay on the doormat. A tattered, well-thumbed pornographic magazine: it had fallen open as it hit the floor. Sarah bent and picked it up, just as it lay.

The centrefold was the usual gynaecological shot with the sensual allure of a cold kebab. It was the sort of thing she would have dismissed with a disdainful shrug – if it had not been posted through her door for her to see. And if she were not being harassed by the man who had put it there. And if it had not been so grotesquely embellished with violent strokes of a ballpoint pen.

The phallus was as crude as anything drawn on a public toilet wall: a peeled banana dribbling cartoon droplets, superimposed on that Technicolor crotch. The same slashing pen had added an arrow, pointing; and a word, a word that had then been crossed out so viciously that the glossy paper was scored through, ripped, mutilated.

And then Sarah was over the edge. Ran out of her flat screaming, yelling. *Where are you, you bastard, where are you?* The doctors told her later she was in a fugue state, but she couldn't connect that decorous, baroque term with what she went through that afternoon – in so far as she could remember what she went through. There was a lot more screaming, she knew that, some of it obscene. At one point she was on the old town bridge, gripping the iron balustrade and threatening to throw herself into the river, though she was sure she hadn't meant it. There was a lot of running. And there were two passers-by who took charge of her at last and helped her home. One was an old lady with her hair lacquered into a crest like a cockatoo's, the other a young man of nineteen or so with a sweet face and long fingers: Sarah, or whatever skewed version of Sarah existed that wild afternoon, had found herself briefly and intensely wanting to screw him blind.

And then she was back in her flat and in a righteous haze was calling the police. As it happened, someone had already called them about her: they had seen her smashing the receiver of a callbox phone that she had found out of order, though she had only a vague recollection of that part herself.

They took her seriously. For a while she blessed their constabulary hearts, wished to drop grateful tears on the hands of the WPC who made her a cup of umber tea. They filled out a detailed report. They gave her a number to ring when she saw this man again. They also suggested she see her doctor, get something to calm her down, but that was fair enough.

It was the humiliation of the finale that brought her low, so low she had felt she would never climb up to the light again.

Hunter became hunted, and Sarah, made bold by the

massed weight of the law she imagined at her back, had staked out the one-eyed man. She followed him one lunchtime, and saw him go into a secondary school that was just round the corner from the hospital. Then she rang the police, mentally preparing herself for the witness box.

The one-eyed man – no, Mr Foley – must have been a decent sort, because he never held any sort of grudge afterwards. He was wholly understanding, in fact: for the next couple of years Sarah even got a Christmas card from him and his wife. The therapist was pleased with that: it helped fit him into the normality jigsaw.

Mr Foley, the one-eyed man, was a neighbour of hers. He and his wife lived in Chadwick Court – over the other side of the block, on the top floor. The community that such places were supposed to foster was entirely spurious: you didn't know your neighbours, you just saw them around a lot.

Mr Foley was a geography teacher at the secondary school round the corner from the hospital where Sarah worked. He went there to teach. Monday to Friday: on the bus, as his vision prevented him driving. At lunchtimes he walked across the road to a coffee shop or, occasionally, a pub nearby. And, being unable to drive, he was a regular user of the local grocery store near Chadwick Court.

Mr Foley had been having problems with his telephone: it kept giving a single ring and then stopping, and when he had picked it up there had been only a murmurous interference on the line. He had reported this to the telephone company on several occasions, as had one or two other residents of Chadwick Court who experienced the same problem; he had got quite angry about it, and consulted the Citizens' Advice Bureau. The fault was eventually repaired.

Mr Foley, in fact, was quite a crusader. He had come down hard on some of his pupils for possessing dirty magazines. The revenge of those pupils would have been more effective if they had got the right flat.

The police, Sarah had to admit, had been pretty good about it. Having established that Sarah's nemesis was a harmless schoolteacher who happened to live and work in the same geographical orbit as Sarah and had only the vaguest idea of what she looked like, they did not follow up the closure of the file with a caution for wasting police time. Not a single reproach came her way. But there was a simple reason for that. They had concluded that she was as nutty as a fruitcake.

Or having a nervous breakdown, if you preferred, though she gathered from the doctors she saw in the following months that there was really no such thing and the term was a flag of convenience for a range of psychological and emotional afflictions. But then, comforting flannel seemed to be the order of the day. 'So that's normal, is it?' Sarah would say, as the trick-cyclists delved into her psyche in various bland offices filled with areca palms. 'Who's to say what's normal?' they would reply, spreading their hands. Nothing was more or less normal than anything else, they seemed to say.

She didn't want to be a citizen of this twilight zone where everything was relative, where there was no such thing as sane or mad. Where what had happened to her was apparently treated as some perfectly natural development in a person's life, rather than an appalling aberration to be stamped on and got rid of.

But they had helped her, in the end. Sessions with a

counselling therapist were prescribed, and Jane, as Sarah was to call her, had devoted what seemed a humbling amount of effort to convincing her that her weird emotional and mental state was not a sign that she was going to end up picking spots of light off the wall and putting them in a basket. There were bumpy moments. Jane's flourishing of those statistics which proved that practically everybody in the United Kingdom except one old lady in Penzance suffered a psychological illness at sometime in their lives did not have a comforting effect on Sarah. She didn't want to be told that looney tunes were everywhere: she wanted to be told it was a chance in a million. But gradually they got there.

Accepting that she had gone through a period of anxiety neurosis which had focused on a harmless source and then magnified it to the nth degree wasn't too difficult. The tough hurdles to get over were *Why?* and *Why now?*

Jane had answers, and Sarah, sitting among the areca palms longing to be normal, was more than ready to be handed some tablets of stone. Down they came, and they had one word written on them: *Graham.*

Revenge of the poison dwarf from beyond the grave – that was the gist of it. Sarah's feelings after his death, as she had freely admitted, had chiefly included relief. The little toerag was out of her life at last, hot diggety. But there was guilt mixed up with those feelings too: because it wasn't very nice to rejoice over anyone's death, and it was even less nice when it was her own mother who was bereft and grieving. So, though Sarah had *thought* she was coasting in the time leading up to her breakdown, in truth her emotions were all shot to hell. Add to this what the death of her stepfather meant to her everyday life. It meant something unpleasant and oppressive was suddenly removed. That nosy, censorious, spiteful attention was lifted. At last no one was watching her.

But because of her guilt, some part of her mind had felt that she didn't deserve to have that threat lifted. And so it had created another threat, a replica in its place: it had invented the persecution of the one-eyed man to restore the status quo.

QED. There was the lion's share of the therapy – digging down to these simple roots. The rest was a matter of putting the normality jigsaw together again, and simple exercises aimed at restoring her confidence. Confidence, mainly, in her ability to step out of her front door without immediately making a complete arsehole out of herself. And the day came when Jane smilingly informed her that she didn't need to come and see her any more. Successful extraction of essence of fruitcake.

Sarah *was* better: she hadn't doubted it. Better, in that she knew for a fact, the solidest fact on God's earth, that the menace of the one-eyed man had been a creation of her overwrought imagination, put together out of odds and ends of coincidence. There had never been anything to fear from that quarter: she knew that still.

As for those lucidly explained reasons for her breakdown . . . she swallowed them. She swallowed them down, and said thank you very much. And just occasionally, they repeated on her. Now and then – only now and then – they left a taste, which suggested that she found them indigestible.

3

Sarah went on air as usual at eleven.

Radio broadcasting was all about conjuring the illusion of presence out of a disembodied voice. It would be a pretty smart trick if she could manage that today, because the disembodied voice was all she had. The rest of her was a million miles away.

Nothing ever died. That included your past selves: they remained inside you, one on top of another, like a set of Russian dolls. Ditto, then, with her self of five years ago. It was still there, and the police had dragged it back into the light, leaving her powerless and alone with the knowledge of what she had seen at the Arena.

She realized she'd been half hoping for a scenario straight out of a movie script, a detective rasping cheerfully down the phone: 'We got the three guys, miss. That van was the giveaway. They're down at the station right now and looking at the wrong end of thirty years inside. And the girl's gonna be just fine. Thanks a million, Miss Winter.'

Not to be. Not in the script, just as it hadn't been in the script that two brawny coppers would drag the one-eyed man away cursing and looking maniacally guilty.

She alone had to prove to Detective Sergeant Routh that she had seen something real and bad. It was important and urgent, maybe a matter of life and death.

At eleven twenty Sarah muffed a voice-over, badly enough for her to notice at least. At eleven forty-five, doing a local events plug, she stumbled repeatedly over the words 'Aristocrats Nightclub' in a way she hadn't done since her novice days as a hospital DJ and then dried for a good five seconds afterwards. During the twelve o'clock news she took deep breaths and made herself bear down. At twelve ten reinforcements arrived.

Michael Malinowski was the manager of a city bookshop and came in to Tudor every fortnight to do a new books review. He was a nerveless man with the coltish looks of an undergraduate and a radio natural who could talk in rounded soundbites. He chose the three books, and it was forgiveable if now and then he puffed a real turkey that he had over-ordered, such as the royal kiss-and-tell they talked about first.

Sarah hadn't read it. She hadn't read any of the three, which was a first for her. Always she made sure she had at least one of them under her belt. It wasn't necessary: Rachel always gave her a typed rundown, and Michael Malinowski could carry the whole thing himself with ease; but the unprofessionalism of it pricked her. Why hadn't she found the time to read at least one?

Well, she knew why. Same reason her dustbin was overflowing: same reason she hadn't replaced Penny's flea-collar: same reason there was a dead light bulb in her downstairs loo so she peed in the dark. There was no room in her mind.

No room in there, since this thing had moved in. And it was making her claustrophobic.

'Michael, welcome again. Well, now that Christmas is behind us and with it, presumably, all those cookbooks and TV spin-offs and diaries of Edwardian ladies, what's being served up in the bookshops to beguile these long winter evenings?'

Michael gave the royal kiss-and-tell the thumbs-up, using the words 'fascinating' and 'irresistible' while signalling to Sarah with his eyebrows that it was all bullshit. Next up was a horror novel. Sarah was at least familiar with the writer, who was much commended for his literary subtlety. He had an irritating habit, which a glance at the front of the book showed he had not given up, of writing long pretentious prefaces and forewords, as if his stuff were already classic texts.

'But is it really frightening?'

Michael had just given an admirable précis of the novel's plot – something about an entity that slipped over from the other side through hypnotic subjects – and Sarah's abrupt question left him, unusually, a little fazed.

'It aims,' he said, recovering after a moment, 'for a creepy, unnerving effect, rather than just hitting you with blood and guts, and it does succeed in that, I think. Makes you look over your shoulder rather than putting you off your supper. I suppose it's a debatable point with horror fiction whether this sort of subtlety can go a little too far, so that it stops being horror and just becomes a sort of literary exercise, and I think that danger does exist, though in this case—'

'But entities,' Sarah said, cutting him off. 'I mean, do we really believe in things like that? All that old supernatural paraphernalia. The really frightening things are around us. Inside us. Entities and vampires and phantoms and ghosties and ghoulies – can anyone really truly be frightened by that stuff, when we're so likely to meet... fear, real fear, in our everyday lives?'

Michael gave her a puzzled look, as if to say *he* didn't write this damned stuff; but he responded sturdily. 'I think it's really a question of what horror as a genre is trying to do. This is the paradox, I suppose, that all fiction has to work as entertainment, at least on some level, and so how can we be entertained by really horrible, ghastly things happening? There has to be a sort of distance, a make-believe element to make it palatable.'

'So really these books don't frighten us at all. They comfort us. They comfort us because we know far worse things are going on all around us.'

Michael added to his look of puzzlement a glance at the wall clock. *Weekday lunchtime commercial radio, bit heavy, isn't it?* But Sarah didn't soften or modify.

'Yes,' he said after a moment. 'They comfort us. But, as you say, there are enough horrors in real life, and I suppose it's quite natural not to want to read about them.'

'Doesn't make them go away though.'

She was being weird. She knew it afterwards, if not at the time, and it was fortunate she had such a relaxed interviewee as Michael Malinowski, who never even sat forward to the mike but reclined in his chair as if by a fireside.

'No indeed,' he said. 'And this whole question of escapism brings us on to the next book, which presents an insider's view, a worm's-eye view you might say, of Hollywood and has apparently had a few writs thrown its way . . .'

He was doing her job for her: the realization was like a slap in the face to Sarah. The slap made her bear down again, and she was smooth all the way to the news.

'Well, might shift a few more of this royal dud, anyway,' Michael said when the red light went off, gathering up his books. His imperturbable expression did not change as he added, 'Don't know about the horror, mind you.'

'Sorry,' Sarah said. She massaged the bridge of her nose. 'Haven't even read it. I didn't mean to slag it, really.'

'Issue-led broadcasting?'

'Something like that.'

Bad broadcasting, more like. Broadcasting of someone whose approach to her work was becoming compromised by outside thoughts. Broadcasting of someone who was riding a hobbyhorse just as surely as old Fire-Mark Fred. Except this was a much more skittish and dangerous beast.

A call came through from her producer while she waited out the news. David wanted to see her straight after the show. He was too mild a man to tick her off, but he would be puzzled. Tudor already had a resident curmudgeon, an old BBC hand who conducted cantankerous phone-ins on Sunday nights. That wasn't what the Sarah Winter programme was about. Sarah Winter the radio personality was the voice of sweet reason, a cool, gentle breeze in the middle of the fume and fug of the working day. She occasionally received letters from timid sad male listeners who thought she was so nice she might even like them. She had an identity and it was what earned her salary: without it she was just an operator who knew her way around the mixing desk.

An item on a local lottery winner featured in the news. Sarah made a note of it for a pick-up when she came back on air.

Look, Miss Winter. There's nothing.

Putting aside the schedule sheet and keeping an eye on the clock, Sarah allowed herself for the first time to think about her encounter with Routh, rather than simply feeling it like a monkey on her back. The way he had sat with his elbows on his knees and his hands pressed together – significant body language, like a doctor giving it to you straight. Restless fiddling with the cartridges on the desk. All this to give her what should, after all, have been good news. But of course, he had known that it wasn't that simple, not for her. Some damnably efficient policewoman – had it been the one who had made her cups of tea and assured her that they would deal with the creep? – had remembered the farrago of the one-eyed man, dug it up, and laid the suspicious remains before the forensic eye of Detective Sergeant Routh. And though Sarah had protested – protested too much, in fact – that it shouldn't make any difference, it was written in Routh's every look and gesture that it did make a difference.

Hell, of course it did. Look what a difference it made to her.

Sarah lined up the first CD track, listened to Jackie trot out the weather. Very cold, chance of a snow shower later, take care on the roads.

Nothing had happened to the girl with red hair. Detective Sergeant Routh had assured her of that. And he was not Madame Zeta peering into the tealeaves, he was an officer of the CID whose exclusive business was the investigation of serious crimes. So why couldn't she accept that and let it go?

Well, simply on the rational level, it was unsatisfactory because it was negative evidence. Nothing had been *reported*, that was all. And in spite of his assurances, Sarah had seen enough of the don't-worry-your-pretty-little-head-about-it school of policing to know that women weren't being entirely unreasonable when they hesitated to report something suffered at the hand of men.

But it was more than that. It was more than a Madame Zeta gut feeling that something terrible had happened. It was more complicated than that and it was less complicated than that. It was a matter of Sarah's mind, the mind he had tried to set at rest. If you had a gammy ankle and couldn't trust it, then you just favoured the other one and didn't attempt the hundred-metre hurdles. But if you couldn't trust your mind, you were sunk.

No, she couldn't allow the past to weigh her down, to retreat into the inertia of fear because the police had found nothing. She must concentrate on what she knew – what she had seen, and she must do something about it.

'... Thank you, Jackie ... You know, I think if I won seven hundred thousand on the lottery I don't think I'd know quite what to do with it either. And if you believe that, as they say, you'll believe anything. My thanks again to Michael Malinowski ... he'll be joining us again in a fortnight's time. And if you fancy getting your nose stuck into any of the books featured on today's programme, then pop along to Waterman's in Cathedral Square. Coming up in a moment we've got the new single from 4 Non Blondes, but first let me just mention that I'll be at the Ice Arena next Thursday ... And while we're on the subject ... young lady came up to request a record last time I was there. The record was "I Can't Stand Up For Falling Down" by Elvis Costello – I'm sorry I didn't catch your name, but if you're listening, could you get in touch with me here at Tudor, any time. Something was left on the dais which I think belongs to you and maybe has sentimental value, so ... the young lady who requested Elvis Costello, "I Can't Stand Up For Falling Down", at the Arena disco last Thursday night, if you're listening, please just give us a bell any time ... OK, as promised, here's the new one from 4 Non Blondes ...'

The idea had come into her head fully formed, shiny and complete, and she hadn't hesitated. Probably it wasn't much of an idea. But for the moment it was all she had.

FIVE

1

These were the times Chill liked.

Maybe it was a sort of nostalgia trip: coming home from work with the streetlamps blinking on and the frost sparkling on the pavements and hurrying into the warm house with its homey smells and coats hanging up in the hall and the sound of the TV... Yes, it had childhood and schooldays written all over it. Only in winter, funnily enough: you didn't get that sentimental feeling coming home from work in the summer.

Nostalgia trip, sure. Sentimental, sure. Chill didn't see anything wrong with that. He was firmly of the opinion that if there was no room for sentiment any more in this funny old world of ours, then you might as well chuck the whole thing. He'd done some tough things in his life, mixed with some pretty risky people – after all, it took all sorts – but he was just a big softy at heart and he didn't care who knew it. Anyone who'd seen him fussing over his Christmas tree would know that. Like a dog with two tails, he'd been. Now Trend, he tended to sneer at that sort of thing. And poor old Sean, he liked having a Christmas tree, you could tell, but he didn't want to admit it in case it wasn't hard. People had funny ideas about what was hard and what wasn't.

That reminded him: the Christmas tree was still propped up in the back garden. Still had most of its needles. Chill kept meaning to saw it up and put it out for the dustmen, but he hadn't got the heart to do it somehow. It was bad enough stripping off the decorations. Yes, he was a softy all right.

He kept these thoughts to himself, even when another wave of nostalgia washed over him as he parked the van outside the house and looked at its friendly glowing windows. Dear old Sean was with him, having helped out on the stall again today like the trouper he was, but dear old Sean wasn't exactly over-endowed in the brain cell department and you would have had your work cut out if you'd tried to convey to him what it was about this time of day that you liked, why it was that you had that sweet warm feeling, the feeling of home and security and another good day being put quietly to bed.

Never mind. Chill enjoyed the feeling, without having to express it out loud. Chill could talk the hind legs off a donkey – gift of the gab, got it off his old dad probably, bless him – but he never felt the need to talk the way so many people seemed to. He wasn't knocking these sad cases who had to ring up the Samaritans and spill it all out to trick-cyclists and what have you, no way: like he always said, it took all sorts. He was just different. Chill was comfortable with the things that he found in his mind. He found them interesting and amusing. He liked company all right, but he wasn't lost without it like poor old Sean who would probably have to ring up the speaking clock just to hear a voice if he was left on his own for five minutes. Chill was self-contained. He could listen to his mind like you'd listen to a good reliable engine ticking over.

The pounding was audible even before Chill had got his key in the front door, and when he opened up the noise was like a wall. Trend, natch.

'Christ on a bike! I wish he'd get himself some headphones.' Chill locked the front door behind him, touched his hand to the radiator in the hall. Hot, but could be hotter. He had his doubts about the boiler pump: have to take a look this weekend.

'Nah, it's not the same.' Sean shucked off his coat but, as always, hung on to the hat. It was a little black woollen effort that he wore on the back of his little cropped head like a halo. Some pop outfit wore them like that. Chill didn't have the heart to tell Sean it just made him look like a dodgy petty-crim Paddy. 'It's not the same with headphones, right, doesn't matter how loud you turn it up. It's just like in your head. It's not all round you.'

It was the serious way Sean said these things that tickled Chill. He laughed, while the booming and caterwauling continued from Trend's bedroom upstairs. 'Enough to loosen your fillings, that is,' Chill said, going through to the kitchen and filling the kettle. 'What is it, anyway? No, don't tell me. One of these groups I've never heard of.' Chill liked a spot of music himself, but he was a bit of a straight arrow where that was concerned, just your standard U2 and Bowie and maybe Guns n' Roses when he was in the mood. Trend, now, that was a different kettle of fish. It had to be new, obscure, difficult to get hold of, and preferably a right racket before it got the Trend seal of approval. Trend was the sort who hung around record shops. Not buying anything, not checking out the goods. Just hanging around posing. Which made

Trend a bit of a sad case really as he was coming up to twenty-two and to the truly trendy kids, the ones who were in the know, that was equivalent to getting your bus pass and your walking-frame. Not that Chill would dream of saying any of that to Trend himself. It wouldn't be kind.

'Shit, there's nothing in.' Sean had his head in the fridge. 'What happened to that pizza? I bet Trend ate it. I bet he did, as well. 'Cking hell, man, what we going to eat?'

'Have to be bread and butter, my old son,' said Chill. 'Unless you've got any money, have you? I haven't. Skint, me.'

He watched with amusement as Sean, anxious lines creasing his baby brow, hunted through the pockets of his jeans. Not easy, when you wore them as tight as Sean did. Tight bleached jeans and DMs, remnant of his flirtation with the British Movement or some such bozo brigade. Chill had quickly disabused him of those half-arsed notions, though they'd never gone very deep with Sean anyway: it was the music and the gear that had attracted him, apparently. Dear oh dear. What a case. It had hardly seemed worth pointing out to the poor muppet that forced repatriation was fairly high on that lot's list of priorities, which would mean Sean's mum and dad and his ninety-nine brothers and sisters being loaded on to the potato boat and sent back to County Ballyhoo pronto.

Sean and that family of his. It was a shame. He was always bragging about them. Practically the Krays, to hear him talk. If anyone messed with him – Sean's phrase, typically, was more basic – they would have his brothers to deal with: they looked out for each other, his family: they were like that. Sean's brothers! That was a laugh.

They were hopeless nomarks who ripped off the odd bit of fencing from building sites. As for Sean's family looking out for each other, maybe they did, but they sure as hell didn't look out for Sean. They never came near him. He was too much of a sad case even for them.

And now here was Sean hunting through his ballcrusher jeans for money because he really thought they were going to have to eat bread and butter tonight. Talk about a big kid. He had bits of string and boiled sweets in there. It would be marbles next.

'Here.' Chill opened his wallet: put the poor sap out of his misery. 'Go and get us all a chinky. Beef chow mein and a pancake roll for me.'

'Aaah, cheers!' All agog. He was like a kid actor in an Aussie soap sometimes, this boy. 'Is it OK if I have the curry?'

'Usually is, old son.' Dear oh dear. Sean actually liked the curries they served up in chinkies. Vinegary slop. 'Ask Trend what he wants. No, hang about, you make a cuppa, I'll ask him.'

'Right.'

Sean busied himself with the teabags, which was quite a complicated operation for him and required a fair bit of concentration, but Chill saw him cast a glance through to the passage, where the door to the cellar was. Talk about making it obvious. Like a kid peeking up at the top of his mum and dad's wardrobe for the Christmas presents.

'We'll do that in a minute, mate,' Chill said. Sean blushed.

Couldn't blame him, of course. Chill gave the door very much the same sort of look as he walked past it to the stairs, and was tempted to give a little rap on it, just to let her know they were home at last. Long day today! Business was slow at the market on Fridays, and he had to admit his mind had been elsewhere a lot of the time. Thinking of home and what he had there and how he couldn't wait to get back to it. And occasionally experiencing a sunburst of exultation at what a cracking idea this had been and how brilliantly it had turned out.

The hardest part had been convincing the others that they could do it. All they seemed to see at first was the risk. As far as Chill was concerned the risk was part of the fun, but then not everybody had his nerve. His chutzpah. He loved that word! He had chutzpah to spare. But not everybody was like him and he accepted that. The others had needed reassurance that the risk wouldn't exceed the fun and that reassurance he had given them. If they chose carefully, chose someone who wouldn't be missed, the risk was practically nil.

Of course, that was what you might call a basic premise of the enterprise. Take someone who wouldn't be missed. They were easy to spot: Chill was a bit of a connoisseur of sad cases, loners, losers, the people who for one reason or another just couldn't cut it. People who could disappear and no one would know or care.

The possibility of just making someone disappear had long been in Chill's mind along with various other interesting theories, but he thought it was the business of the dog that had made him decide to give it a go. When the dog had run away – and how it had got very far with the state it was in Chill didn't know, but there, you could never tell with animals – he had been disappointed, of course; but really it had just confirmed something that had been growing on him for a long time. Pets *were* disappointing. They didn't live long, and there was only so much you could do with them.

But a pet person, now: that was a different story.

Chill decided against giving her a knock: he'd go and see her soon. He climbed the stairs. They were narrow and very steep, and the stairwell seemed to rise to a tremendous height. It had been a bugger to decorate, and he still hadn't got around to changing the old flyblown glass lamp that hung from the top on rusty chains. It had come with the house. The poor old stick he had bought it from had had to go into a home and had left a lot of her antwacky fittings. Character, though, the place had bags of character. If he ever decided to sell he would make on it. Young professionals would snap it up, if they weren't put off by the Asian family next door – you could never tell with that sort.

His very own pet person! He got a buzz every time he thought of it. The idea was such a crack.

You could do anything you wanted with her. That was the thing. It was about control. Chill had discovered early on that he had a talent for controlling people and there was no denying that it was a hell of a laugh, that power. Show him a person who reckoned they didn't enjoy controlling others and he would show you a little fibber. But no matter how much of a clever customer you were at getting people to do what you wanted there was always a limit, and Chill wanted to go beyond limits. He had a spirit of adventure. He'd always thought it must have been a real crack to have been one of those explorers in the old Sir Walter Ralegh days. Sailing into the unknown. But everywhere had been discovered now.

If you wanted to find new places, you had to find them inside yourself.

Chill knocked on Trend's bedroom door, a jaunty

bom-biddley-om-bom knock, and swanned right in. Maybe inadvisable, because he had done this once and caught the little devil twanging the wire and what an embarrassment *that* had been. The trendy one had looked just about ready to sink into his high-tops. But what the hell: Chill was a teensy bit pissed off with Trend today, because Trend had promised to help out on the stall and then cried off at the last moment with some feeble excuse of needing to go down to the college. He was doing some part-time course that they gave free to doleys who were too sad to do anything else: leisure studies or some such. It didn't exactly make great inroads into Trend's time, certainly not enough to prevent him helping out on the stall now and then. It wasn't as if Chill asked for much. It was his house, and he didn't expect any contribution to the bills. Both Trend and Sean were signing on, and the official line was that they were renting their rooms from him: hence he got a nice hundred and twenty quid a week from the housing benefit paid direct to him, and that was very nice thank you, and he didn't want anything more. They could just treat the place as their own: they were mates, after all. But that was the point – mates didn't mind doing you favours. And just look at him in here, slumped down on the floor with his head against the bed. Wall-to-wall racket and smell of joss sticks. Chill felt like a dad with a sulky teenage son sometimes.

'All right, my old china? Speaking of which, you up for a Chinese tonight? Name your poison. Dog chow mein, prawn bollocks, whatever you want.'

He had to shout over the music, which underlined his feeling of being a teensy bit pissed off with Trend, a.k.a. Derek, and what a surprise that he didn't care to be known by *that* name. But the feeling didn't amount to much, didn't ripple the smooth surface of Chill's nature. It certainly didn't even come within hailing distance of anger. Chill didn't know anger as an emotion. It was alien to him.

'Eh?' said Trend, with his chin on his chest.

'Chinese.' Chill bellowed it, made a slanting-eyes gesture. Bit tasteless, but he had to get through somehow. 'You want one?'

'Oh yeah, cheers.'

'What do you want? State your preference!'

'Eh?'

Dear oh dear. You could have a better conversation with the wall. Or Sean, which was pretty much the same thing.

'I said what do you fancy? Beef chow mein?'

'Yeah, whatever.'

This was sulky even by Trend's standards. Probably best to leave him here to stew. Trouble was, that wasn't Chill's style. He just couldn't pass by on the other side, never could, it was just the way he was made.

'Good day at the college?' Chill leaned against the doorframe, glanced over the posters pinned above Trend's storm-tossed bed. Pop persons, and not very photogenic ones. None of your Madonnas or Kate Bushes, anyway. Geezers mostly.

'S'all right.'

There was a lull in the scrapyard din. Trend slithered across the floor to the boombox to change the cassette over, using the absolute minimum of muscular effort to do it.

'What time'd you get back?'

'Dunno. Fourish.' Trend gave that heavy sniff that Chill had noticed in a lot of dudes of his sort. It was meant to give the impression that you were, hey, no stranger to hard drugs. All kidology. Trend's narcotic experience went no further than a puff on a joint: Chill knew that because it was he who got the stuff, being partial to a spot of blow himself. He pictured Trend and his posey pals ligging around the Virgin store, all doing that sniff and all, probably, fooling each other with it; and he chuckled inside. Seeing into people always gave him a little buzz.

'Everything OK down there? While we were out?'

Trend peered up at him through a hedge of reddish fringe. 'Down where?'

'Down where, he says. The guest room, my old fruit. Where d'you think?'

Chill noticed that little frown. He called lots of people 'my old fruit': it was just a phrase of his, picked it up from his old dad. But Trend didn't like it. Funny.

'Dunno. Suppose so.'

'Thought you might have checked up, you know.'

Trend shrugged, shook his head, and treated them to another deafening selection of amplified barnyard noises.

'Ah well. I'll look in on her in a minute. Who are these when they're at home?'

'Those Nightmare Persons. They're from Seattle. Playing the Marquee next week.'

'Yeah? You know what, you should be a DJ, you should. You'd be good at that.'

Trend muttered, 'All wankers.'

'Well, they speak very highly of you. No, I know what you mean, they're usually daft old crumblies in toupees who've been hanging on to the job for years. But that's what *I* mean, see. They need someone who's really cool, you know, who really knows what's happening. I'm not kidding, you'd be a natural. They don't come much cooler than you.'

Trend made an awkward laughing sound, shaking his head. His face was crimson. It was a funny thing: sometimes it was as if Trend suspected Chill was taking the piss out of him. But there, what could you do?

'Beef chow mein then.' Chill tipped him a wink and left him.

Well, that was OK. Chill knew for a fact that Trend hadn't been able to resist taking a peek at the pet while they were out, but he knew for another fact that Trend hadn't done anything more than that. Chill was an easygoing sort of guy, but he'd made it clear from the start that there was to be no interfering with her – not without his prior knowledge and consent. She was his pet after all: fair was fair. No worries on that score, anyway. Poor old Sean, whatever sort of commotion was going on in those shrinkwrap jeans of his, was too scared of Chill to step over the line; and as for Trend . . .

Well, all sorts of interesting things were going on there, and Chill would have to have a good think about them some time. There was a reason why Trend had gone even more mean, moody and magnificent since the arrival of the new pet, but it wasn't a simple one, that was for sure.

Chill was an enthusiastic undergraduate of the university of life, and he had made a special study of stupidity: after all, there was plenty of material about. And one thing he had learned was that it varied in quality. Sean's stupidity, for example, was pure. It went all the way through him like the letters in a stick of rock. But there was such a thing as complex stupidity and Trend had it. That was what made him such an interesting sad case; but it also made him a touch unpredictable *vis-à-vis* the new addition to the household.

The new addition! Chill felt buoyant as he renegotiated the steep stairs, taking them at a daring clip simply because it was more fun than being careful.

He thought what he was doing with the girl was a daring thing to do also, but not bad. It was a big undertaking and it had its problems and difficulties accordingly: you couldn't make an omelette et cetera. Some people might have said it was irresponsible, maybe, but that all depended on how you went about it. You had to make things nice for the pet but you had to be firm as well: you had to let her know that this was her home now, but that like any home it had to be treated with respect. Chill remembered a teacher at school giving him a ticking off for balancing on two legs of his chair. The old coot had been right, too. Chill always remembered that: it had made quite an impression on him. He had been a bit of a tearaway in his time – still was, in a way – but he knew about respect.

Sean had made the tea: lovely job. 'Make that two beef chow meins, Sean,' Chill said, swigging. 'Ah. Sheer nectar, Jeeves.' He was not exaggerating his appreciation of the tea. Chill could feel the minute amount of caffeine it contained circling pleasantly in his veins, just as he could feel the stronger surge when he drank beer, the sudden elevator-swoop when he smoked some good dope, the warmth of bed when it was cold outside and the pleasure of scratching an itch and the good cleanness of stepping out of the bath. Nothing was dull or stale to him. As he often said, he was like a big kid really.

'Two beef chow meins, pancake roll, curry and rice.' Sean chanted it to himself. It was a lot for him to remember. Chill risked taxing the little pilferer's brain a bit more and said, 'Sweet and sour pork with special fried rice as well, my old china. China! There's a little pun there if you can spot it. Oh, Chill has made a funn-ee, let's sing hip-hip-hooray . . .'

Sean stood in his most missing-link, peel-me-a-banana posture, mouth hanging open. Dear oh dear. Terrible back problems the lad was going to have when he was older, if he didn't straighten up. Mind you, he had the nick written all over him – Chill gave it two years – and he would have to smarten himself up there willy-nilly.

'Who's that for?'

'Who do you think?' Chill had a particular bright, uncertain smile which indicated that his mood was dangerous, and though he wasn't feeling dangerous – quite blissful, really – he put the smile on now, just for the crack. Just to see Sean's face. 'Who do you think it's for, Sean? Do you need three guesses?'

Sean took a step backwards, 'Sorry,' he said.

'I should think so and all. Dear oh dear. I suppose we're all going to pig out on Chinese takeaways while she has bread and butter, are we? Is that what you're saying?'

He kept the smile going – wobbly, too broad, on the edge – for a few more moments, because it was just so irresistible to see Sean bricking it. It was so easy to spook old Sean, and he spooked so satisfyingly – eyes rolling, lip trembling, the whole Laurel and Hardy bit. That was Sean for you. If anyone walked into a room where he was on his own, he invariably jumped out of his skin. Probably it was because he had packed such a lot of petty crime into his short life: somebody was always after him.

'Sorry,' Sean said again, 'I didn't think . . .'

Well, he would start blubbering any minute, so Chill turned the dangerous smile off and let it go. Bit naughty, teasing the poor soul like that. He slapped Sean's shoulder. 'Nah, mate. Only winding you up. You're a good 'un, you know that?'

One thing you could say for Sean, he didn't bear a grudge. Like a small child, he could go from tears to laughter in the space of a second. Instantly he was reassured. You could find this sweet or pathetic depending on who you were. Chill, he found it sweet.

'Sweet and sour pork, special fried rice.'

'You got it.' Chill slapped his shoulder again, quashing the impulse to flick Sean's little pink ear right where the gold stud was. He was in such a devilish mood today, he hardly knew what he was going to do next.

Sean lit out for the chinky. That was an advantage of living in Grenville Street: it was real takeaway land round here. Kebabs, curry, West Indian, pizza, you name it. You could get halal burgers if you wanted. Grenville Street suited Chill just fine. Five happy years he'd spent here. A legacy from his old dad had helped him put the deposit down and get on the property bandwagon, and though the mortgage had been a bit of a struggle at first he didn't regret the move. Chill was a firm believer in the property-owning democracy. Owning your own place gave you a bit of pride. And then there was the freedom of it too. If it was your own place, you could do exactly what you wanted in it. The Englishman's home was his castle: maybe that was a corny idea, but Chill wasn't about to knock it because of that. There was too much knocking going on these days in his opinion.

Dear old dad! Chill felt a little glow, part sadness, part pride. His dad would be pleased to see him so nicely settled. His dad had known tough times, and he never forgot them even when he was well established as a butcher and could afford a decent motor and the holidays in Spain and all the rest of it. It hadn't come easy, especially when there was that bloodsucking bitch, Chill's mother, to contend with, at least until she skipped off with that geezer she'd met in Southend and what a relief *that* had been. Best thing that ever happened to him, because she was one awkward woman and it didn't matter how hard you clipped her she never saw sense. Well rid, Chill thought.

And then cancer came and took the old boy just when he was enjoying life. It all seemed so quick. One moment he was trading sauce with the old dears over the bacon-slicer and the next he was lying in a hospital bed looking as if a steamroller had run over him.

It wasn't fair, that was for sure. *Life* wasn't fair. But then Chill supposed everybody learned that sooner or later. It was just that the knowledge affected different people in different ways. You could let it get you down if you wanted to. Or you could use it as a springboard.

That was what Chill had done. Taken a flying leap. Moved on up.

Sean was gone, Trend was still upstairs doing his not very convincing impression of a little ray of sunshine, and so Chill was alone with his thoughts.

He roamed around his house while he turned them over. Anyone who had seen Ian Christopher Elderkin roaming around like this would have been reminded of a dance. A dance, indeed, very much like the first primal dances of mankind in its self-assertion, its glorying in his own existence. Humming to himself, clicking his fingers, doing neat little side-steps and quick turns, Chill went from room to room, looking at this and that, seeing that everything was in its usual place, picking up an object here and there to do conjuring tricks with. Chill's house was nobody's idea of designer living. He had two lodgers who had no respect for property, and his own ideas of what a home should contain were pretty much inherited from his old dad. If you were going to be picky and snobby you could say that the three-piece suite in the front room smelled like a tramp's coat, that the stone-effect fireplace was tacky, that the table-football game standing in the dining room beneath a film poster of Whitney Houston and Kevin Costner was a long way from *Homes and Gardens*. But Chill didn't care: Chill liked it all. And he liked to shimmy around it, feeling his body loose and sure as it moved amongst familiar things, with a *zap* here as he turned on the TV with the remote and an *alley-oop* there as he tossed a pair of boots into the closet and on, around, up and down, move your body to the sound . . .

They were deft and easy, these movements of Chill's: he was a limber man, never clumsy. But the domestic dance of Ian Christopher Elderkin was not a comfortable dance, all the same. If he was absent-minded, it was not in a relaxed way. His mind was working, smoothly and economically; and at a speed that most people would have found distressing. If he had had a tail, it would have been lashing.

When Chill at last came to a stop, his stillness was as remarkable as his restlessness had been a moment ago. The place where he stopped was the door under the stairs. He stood in front of it with his hands on his hips, simply looking at the door. His eyes dwelt on the dingily painted panelling as if he were studying a picture in a gallery. Occasionally a smile formed on his lips as he stood there, but he wasn't exactly thinking about his pet or what he was going to do with her. It was the idea of her that was behind the smile. His pleasure was something like the rarefied intellectual pleasure of mathematics.

But Chill knew that pleasure was more intense if you rationed it, and soon he came away from the door and addressed himself to some practicalities. First, plates to warm in the oven. Next he hunted through a stock of medicines in one of the kitchen cupboards. Quite incidentally he noticed various things that would come in useful for the great adventure – plasters, sleeping tablets, painkillers – but what he was after was a jar of multivitamins that Trend had bought when he was on a brief health kick.

'Ta-dah!' Found them. These should do her good. She hadn't been looking too clever when he'd looked in on her this morning, which was perhaps only to be expected. She was eating after a fashion, and she seemed to have given up hurting herself by flinging around and banging on the wall and all that malarkey, and she was paying a bit more attention to hygiene – she had consented to Sean's washing her hair over a bowl yesterday, and had given herself a lethargic sort of wash with a sponge. But obviously she wouldn't be in very good condition, not under these circumstances: she wouldn't be tiptop until she had learned to be part of the household.

Which was Chill's ultimate aim. It wouldn't be an easy job of training, and he might well have to be cruel to be kind. But then that was all part and parcel of having an exotic pet. No one would have exotic pets if they were easy to get hold of and easy to look after. Might as well have a moggy.

Also it was a challenge. It was all very well to make someone do what you wanted by sheer physical force:

you could have some fun that way, but it was pretty crass. But to work on someone so hard and so skilfully that there was no resistance left in them – to bring them to the point where they didn't *want* to do anything but what you wanted – well, now, that was something like power.

And nobody had ever got the better of Chill yet.

'*Free*zing. 'Cking hell, man, *free*zing.'

Sean was back, crashing into the house with all the finesse of Frankenstein's monster and lurching into the kitchen ditto. Never mind that it had been freezing every night for two months: Sean was still in a state of plaintive astonishment about it. It would be the same thing when he got up tomorrow morning – "Cking hell, man, it's freezing!' Hibernian amazement at non-overnight appearance of heatwave in middle of severe winter. That Sean. What a case.

Chill investigated the contents of the foil trays while Sean carried on with the brass monkey exclamations. They did a very nice sweet and sour at the Hong Kong Garden. It smelled a treat. If that didn't perk her up he didn't know what would.

'Freezing, man, 'cking freezing . . . Lessee the weather forecast . . .'

Sean clicked on the grease-smeared black and white portable they kept on a kitchen shelf. The little tune he hummed didn't fool Chill. It wasn't the weather forecast but the local news he was after. So obvious! Understandable, though, Chill supposed. Trend was the same. No matter how hard Chill tried to reassure them, they still had this suspicion that the disappearance of the girl was going to be splashed all over the news, even now, when more than a week had passed. It won't happen, he'd told them. She was a nomark. Nobody noticed when nomarks dropped out of sight. Nobody would notice if *they* dropped out of sight, for example – but that was a comparison he was too kind to make.

The local news was the usual. Hospital closure. Appeal for a bone marrow transplant for some poor kiddie. Pile-up on the A1. It was shocking, really. Chill tended to steer clear of the news: it made him depressed.

'Any change, Sean?'

'Oh . . . yeah . . . sorry . . .'

Chill stopped him in the middle of some more Houdini manoeuvres. Those jeans of his. He was going to get taken for a rent one of these days and what a shock *that* would be. 'Keep it, mate. No worries. Let's dish this up, I'm starving. No – not that one. Leave that in the oven. I'll take it down myself after we've eaten.'

'Oh. Right.' Sean was still trying to be cool about the whole thing, but it was no good. Whenever the pet was mentioned he went all self-conscious and awkward.

'And don't worry about the bucket and all that. I'll change it tonight. You've been working too hard, you have. You want to put your feet up. Take the weight off your slingbacks.'

The old chestnut got the usual gurgle of amusement from Sean. But he gave Chill a look too, daringly, a look with a question in it.

Chill didn't bother to answer the question. He just laughed.

2

Darkness.

A slice of light, leaving imprinted on her eyes the image of the figure at the top of the steps: then darkness.

Then, the voice.

'How you doing?'

Her own breathing. Darkness: only sounds, textures, smells. Textures of blanket, pillow, cold metal of cuffs, familiar to her now as the ridges in the skin of her own hands. Smells, with a new intensity and significance in her changed world. Departed smells of her own waste, removed but persistent: departed smell, fainter, of Chinese food. Newly arrived smell, of him: denim, some sort of aftershave, not cheap stuff.

Smiler. Smell of smiler. She didn't need the after-image of the compact blockish figure with the neat fair head. She knew his smell. Like she knew the boy with the hat's, faint sweat and roll-up tobacco, and the weasel one's, patchouli and leather.

Darkness, and the presence of the smiler, hovering on the steps.

Sound: clink of chain as she shifted to a sitting position on the bed.

'Put the light on.'

Sound: her own voice. Not too wobbly. Good.

'Don't need it.'

Sensation: nausea, instantaneous nausea at that familiar chirpiness in his voice.

'Put the light on.'

'Just thought we'd have a talk. Don't need the light to talk, do we?'

After-image fading now. Let it go, and let go too, for God's sake let go, the perception that he was carrying something in his right hand.

'Put the light on. Let me see you. What are you fucking afraid of?' Cracking a little there, her voice.

'Ooh. Now then. No call for that sort of language.'

Sounds: trainer-shod feet squeaking a little, descending the steps. Slowly.

'Did you enjoy the Chinese?'

'No.'

'No? You ate it all. Can't have been that bad.'

Taste: the ghost of the food on her tongue, in her gullet. Shame, because she had enjoyed it. In spite of everything, the traitor body had said yes to the plate of Chinese food. They did feed her, but not frequently, not much. It made the traitor body grateful for anything that came along. And faced with the good Chinese food, the traitor body went crazy.

Clever.

'I thought it'd be a nice treat for you. We're not the world's greatest cooks, I'm afraid.'

Change in the quality of the footsteps: slight disturbance in the air of the cellar, fluctuation in the smells: he had reached the bottom of the steps and paused there. She was learning a blind person's stern skills.

'So, how you doing, Alison?'

Al-i-son. The syllables tripped off his tongue, too lightly. Three little morsels.

'How do you think I'm doing?'

Sound: the thermostat of the electric heater clicking. He heard it too – something in his stillness.

'Warm enough, are you? It feels OK in here. Warmer than up top, to be honest. This awful weather. Never lets up, does it?'

'I wouldn't know.'

'Dear oh dear, you're a right cheerful charlie tonight, aren't you?'

Disturbance of air again: he was moving about the room, sure-footed in the dark.

Sounds – no, not sounds, at least not external ones. Sounds in her head of her mind working. Working at sudden speed from proposition to proposition.

Something like a shift in attitude to her. It meant something or nothing, more probably something. Hope in it? Think. They had kept her here, but they had done nothing to her, nothing at least compared to what they might do to her if they chose. They might yet not choose. If she approached it in the right way, they might cut their losses. All they had done was detain her here against her will.

Negotiations. Plea-bargaining.

'It's getting boring, this, isn't it?'

Her own voice, level, conversational even. Good.

'You say what, Ali?'

A-li. His tongue precise against his teeth. No, forget that.

'It must be boring for you and . . . the others. Keeping me here. Having to feed me and . . .' Nearly stumbled, nearly fell, recovered. 'And clean up after me and everything. I mean what's it all about?' Put it into her voice, put it into her voice that this was not the time of the pleading and screaming and thrashing, this was different. This was Ali and Chill, talking. 'You're not telling me it's easy, having me here.'

'Oh, Ali, it's a pleasure, believe me. Pleasure beyond measure.'

'I'll believe you. Thousands wouldn't.'

His own cheeky-chappie tone. Worth a try.

'You're no trouble, Ali. You were a bit at first, I must admit. A bit obstreperous. Is that the right word?'

His voice was a still source now, not moving. Somewhere over the other side of the room, near the heater.

Yes: she felt a faint diminishing of its heat. His arm, moving across it.

'Yep – pretty good little heater this. Lovely job. You do understand, I can't leave it on all the time, not without any ventilation in here. Dangerous. Can't be too careful.'

'That's what I mean. It's...' Oh God, stumbling, falling.

'What do you mean, Ali?'

Fingers clenching the rough blanket, her own deep-drawn breath loud as a hurricane as she tried to recover herself. 'Well, I mean it's... it's a pain, isn't it? What's the point? I'm a burden, a drag. Come on. Don't tell me you don't think that sometimes.'

'Oh, Ali.' Weary but kind, and a pause, as of someone trying to think of a simple way of explaining something complicated. 'Look. I'll accept that you're not very comfortable here just now. A bit restricted. But it'll get better. Once you're settled in a bit, it'll get better. It's always difficult, settling into a new place. Believe me, I'd like nothing better than to have you out of those handcuffs, poddling around the place doing your own thing. But I can't trust you to do that just yet. Now can I?'

'Can't you?'

'Well, hardly, poppet. I mean, you've just been trying to get me to let you go, haven't you? That's what that was all about, wasn't it? All that stuff about being a burden and what have you. It was a way – subtle, I'll give you that – of persuading me to let you go. You want to escape, Ali. I was beginning to hope you might have got that particular bee out of your bonnet, but apparently not. Oh well. You see what I'm saying? If I let you out of the cuffs, say, you'll go for that door like a bullet from a gun. So what can I do? It's up to you, really. I can try and make things as nice as possible, but really it's up to you whether you settle or not.'

'Just let me go. Just let me go now. Look, if you let me go now there's no harm done. I won't tell anyone, I won't tell the police, I know, I know you can't be expected to believe that but truly I mean it I won't tell, I mean who'd believe me anyway the whole thing's so weird they'd just think I was mad and then you, I don't know, maybe you did it for a dare or something, well if you did you've done it, you've proved it and now you can let me go and that'll be the end of it I swear—'

'Ali, Ali, slow down. You're getting all out of breath, you'll be – what's that thing? – hyperventilating. And are you crying? You are, aren't you? Dear oh dear. You've gone and got yourself all upset over nothing. And I wanted tonight to be nice for you.'

'Nice how can it be nice you sadistic bastard look what you're doing to me they'll get you for this they'll get you and they'll throw away the fucking key . . .'

Sounds, duplicated and reduplicated: her screamed words, echoing round the cellar. Sensation: sandpaper in her throat.

Then no sounds. From him, silence and dreadful stillness.

Darkness.

Smell: her own fear, with something sharper overlaying it, sharp and blood-coppery. Despair, perhaps.

At last, quietly: 'Finished?'

She flung herself down, tossed her head on the pillow. Grew still. Turned her wet face to him.

'I'm not going to have a shouting match with you, Alison. All I wanted was to talk. People don't talk enough nowadays. That's where misunderstandings start.'

A movement. Maybe a step closer. Her own eyelashes, blinking, felt like insects on her cheeks.

'I wish you'd just think for a minute, sweetheart. You've got to look at this thing from both sides. All right, it's a bit of a shock, but that's change for you. There's good and bad in everything. I mean, take the Chinese. I don't suppose you could afford Chinese takeaways on your income support, could you? Now be honest. I know what your old life was like, Ali. I know all about you. You told me yourself. Poky little flat in the YMCA with a lot of dippy teenagers playing loud music till all hours – well, must admit we've got a bit of that here with old Trendy-boots thumping away up there, but there's no harm in him. You signing on every fortnight, getting kicked in the teeth when you apply for a job because you're too young or too old or too qualified or too unqualified or they'll only pay you twopence an hour and lay you off in three weeks' time because they've got some poor sod off the Youth Training Scheme to do it for nothing. It's nasty out there, Ali. It's nasty for anybody, let alone when you're nineteen and got no job and no family who give a monkey's. The old dear up in Geordieland, she doesn't give a monkey's about you, does she? You told me so yourself. Cold, hard world, Alison. Nasty. Dangerous. See in the paper this week where they found some poor old geezer dead of exposure in the cemetery. Sleeping rough, you know. Found him there all stiff like a leg of lamb. That's not London, mind – that's right here in our very own fair city where the Yankee Doodles come and take pictures of the cathedral and think what a cute place it is, shucks, we got nothing like this at home. See? Nasty. Why would you want to be out there? Think about it.

You're safe here. You're safe and you're warm and you're fed and you've got no responsibilities. I know what the DSS are like, if you don't get a job they shove you on some nomark scheme digging holes and filling them in again and if you won't do it they stop your benefits, and *then* where are you? Out on the street, that's where. You haven't got such a bad deal here, Alison. OK, I know it'd be nice if you could have a hot bath and watch the TV and all, but like I say, that's up to you.'

Another step closer: the aftershave was strong now, his voice clearer. She could hear the minute clicks and shushings of the saliva in his mouth as he spoke.

'Now I know what would make it nicer. To have your own bits and pieces around you, your own clothes and whatnot. That's fair enough. And I tell you what, I'm going to get them for you. Flat 14, Lyle House. It's on your library card. I've got the keys—'

'I know you've got my keys.' Her own voice: it surprised her. Flat and croaking, but not quite resigned, not yet: that was something. 'You've got everything of mine.'

'Only borrowed. That's all. I'm borrowing your keys, and I'll use them to get in your flat and bring you all your clothes and bits and pieces. Everybody likes to have their own things about them. Like the poor old girl who sold me this house – she had to go into a home, and you know what those places are like, they wouldn't let her have all her own things just how she liked them, isn't that terrible?'

'You're a bastard.'

'Coh, no one told me dad. Look, I said I'm going to get your stuff for you, you'll have everything you need. I mean, what more can you want, eh?'

'Freedom.'

'*Free-du-hum* . . .' he sang it out in a mock falsetto. 'Anything else?'

Something was rumbling on the edge of her consciousness. The terror, the blast-wave of terror: it was coming for her and it was bigger than it had ever been because he was not going to let her go. Not for a minute, not for a single second had he even entertained the idea of letting her go.

'Anything else, Ali?' He was closer now. She could smell his breath and his body heat. 'Anything else?'

Just time, before the terror hit her. 'To see you hung up by your tongue.'

'Oh, charming. And I love you too.'

It couldn't be, because there was no light source in the room, but she could have sworn she saw a glint where his face was. A little needle glint, as if he were throwing out sparks. The glint of the smiler enjoying himself.

And then suddenly he wasn't there: waft of him going away.

Back to the stairs? The terror was boiling towards her like a moving cloud, but there was a chance it might miss her. If—

Sounds. Sucking clunk of a plug being pulled from a socket: she registered the lessening of heat. He was over there. He had unplugged the heater.

Another clunk, different in timbre: something plugged in. Fumbling sounds. And then together the click and the light, making her screw up her eyes in pain.

Now she saw him. Saw now that he had found his way around with a key-ring torch, but it wasn't that which was making the bright light.

'Bit of light on the subject . . . Now, where can I stand this?'

He stood it on the bar, then stepped back jauntily to admire the effect.

The terror came towards her like a world spinning out of control.

'It's cute this, isn't it? Can't remember where I picked it up from. Thought it'd make a nicer light for us, anyway.'

It was a child's bedside lamp. The shade was in the shape of Mickey Mouse's head. Big round ears and bright cartoony colours. Mickey was smiling right at her.

'No.'

'No? Don't like it? Well, no accounting for taste. I'm a sucker for this sort of thing myself. Just a big kid really.'

The flies of his jeans were open, as they must have been all the time. He had been stroking himself in the darkness. Now he turned to face her, grotesquely exposed: glanced coyly down at himself.

'Dear oh dear. Look at *me*.'

'No.'

'I know, you're shy. I'm feeling a bit shy myself. But if we don't conquer it, how are we ever going to get to know each other?'

One more moment of coy stillness, before the sudden swift closing of the distance between them. Sounds, his laughter, scraunch of the bedsprings. Smells, hot, unthinkable. The blast-wave of terror hit her just as he did.

SIX

1

Old Mrs Dhanecha was very well aware that she frequently irritated her son and daughter-in-law, but that didn't bother her. She knew she had right on her side. In fact, as far as she could remember she had never been wrong yet.

There was, for instance, the room they had prepared for her. It was the middle room on the ground floor – dining room, officially, though the family preferred to eat in the big kitchen. They had put a folding bed in it and a little chest of drawers and they expected her to think of it as a bedroom.

'You expect me to sleep here, with the window there straight on the back garden where any man could come along and peep in?'

'Amma, no one can get in the back garden. Anyway, there are curtains, close the curtains.' Ram, shuffling his feet. He always shuffled his feet when he knew he was in the wrong. He had done it when he was a little boy and he did it now.

'First you say no one can get in the back garden and then you say there are curtains if someone does. I want to sleep upstairs. What's wrong with the back bedroom? I'll sleep there.'

'But it's a tiny room, Amma. And you can only get to it through Prakash and Arun's room.'

'I don't mind a tiny room. I like a tiny room. How much room does an old woman need? And what does it matter if I have to go through Prakash and Arun's room? I can keep an eye on them. They need watching. You're too soft with them anyhow.'

Ram shuffled his feet some more, and gave in. He knew she was right. Later, when the bed and the chest of drawers had been moved and they thought she was sleeping, she heard some sort of high words going on between Ram and Trupti, but they were speaking in English and she couldn't follow it very well when they spoke fast like that. But it didn't matter. She hadn't lived seventy years in the world and raised five children and come all the way from the Punjab to be told to sleep downstairs under a window where any man could come peeping in at her.

She knew, also, that there had been a fuss about her coming in the first place. Trupti didn't say so to her face, because she wasn't *that* badly brought up, but it was plain to old Mrs Dhanecha that her daughter-in-law didn't see why she should come all this way to stay with them, just because there was another baby on the way. They had managed quite well when Amee was born and Prakash and Arun . . . oh, yes, she knew what Trupti was thinking.

Well, it was different. The air fare had been beyond them at the time and besides, Ram had been working regular shifts at the clothing factory then. You could be sure he would be home at set times in the evening. Now he was a taxi driver he was out at all hours – all night sometimes. They might think there was nothing wrong with a pregnant woman being left alone and unprotected, but old Mrs Dhanecha had been brought up differently. Trupti might protest that she could manage, but Trupti was a headstrong girl and prone to all sorts of stupid fancies. She needed someone there until the child was born and who better than old Mrs Dhanecha? Never mind these health visitors and what have you. They didn't know everything. Old Mrs Dhanecha wouldn't have gone as far as to say she knew everything, but she knew when she was right.

'What can happen?' Ram would say sometimes – when, for example, he walked down to the corner shop and old Mrs Dhanecha told him to be careful. 'I'm going down to Mirza's to get some onions. What can happen, Amma?'

What could happen? He was a foolish boy, for all the scratchy beard and the big backside sticking out behind. She didn't know this country all that well, but one thing Mrs Dhanecha knew was that anything could happen. It didn't matter where you were or who you were: *anything* could happen, and if you weren't careful it probably would. She wasn't being a fussy old woman when she told Ram to be careful, or when she shouted at the children, slapping out with hard accurate hands, if they came home late from school (and that irritated Trupti too – but then she was too soft on them anyway). She wasn't being a fussy old woman when she lay awake at night listening out for Ram's return from the late shift. They had glass screens and bars behind the drivers' seats in all the taxis now, but how had that come about? Because taxi drivers had been stabbed in the past, and one had died from it. She didn't see it as being fussy: she saw it as facing the facts of life.

She knew she was right, just as she knew she was right about that cellar under the house.

Of course, there were a lot of things she didn't understand about life here. That was only to be expected. Ram had come when he was very young, and Trupti had actually been born here – which explained a lot, Mrs Dhanecha thought. They were used to it. They watched all sorts of things on the television that Mrs Dhanecha thought the most unbearable stupidities. They were gadget-mad. They bought things off the shelf all wrapped up so you could hardly see them and then wondered why they didn't suit when they got them home. As for the children, sometimes Mrs Dhanecha was quite baffled by them. Good pure simple Queen's English she could cope with after a fashion: old English people, for example, she found she could communicate with quite well. But the children seemed to speak some other language entirely. They brought it home from school, she supposed, along with those strange enthusiasms for pointless little games and heavy crippling shoes and fizzy drinks that had who knew what mixed in with them.

'But it's brill, Grandmaji! It's wicked! You listen!' Prakash would say, plucking off the headphones of his Walkman and pressing them to her ear. Racket, the most terrible racket! And what was it doing to his hearing, having that noise drumming in his ears all the time?

'They're boys, Amma. Boys only,' Ram said. 'They like pop music. All the boys their age do.'

'It will send them mad! It will send them mad, bang-bang-banging in their ears all the time!'

But Ram only sighed and said there was no harm in it. Not that he was very much better: he was always playing tapes of rubbishy Bombay film music in his cab.

Freezing Point

And Mrs Dhanecha strongly suspected that he had more than once been tempted to a glass of beer when he was at the taxi office. There were all sorts of backsliders and wasters there: she had heard about them.

Slackness: that was the most worrying thing she found here. When she'd first visited her son and daughter-in-law, not long after they were married, she'd thought Trupti, for all her faults, was at least a reasonable housekeeper. How that had changed! Back then she had made many of her own clothes: now it was all off-the-peg stuff. Back then she made chapattis every night and was bottling her own pickles: now there were meals from packets and tins, and she was sure she had heard the boys talking about hamburgers. As for Trupti's dress, Mrs Dhanecha had never thought it overwhelmingly modest, but now she seemed to have abandoned all standards: she didn't even wear the dupatta when they went into town.

'I suppose before long you'll be walking around in a skirt with the wind blowing up your behind, na, and every man in town ogling you. Put more salt in that. If it's a heating food it makes you sweat, and then you lose the salt from your body and you have to replace it, don't you know anything?'

Trupti didn't say anything, but she gave her mother-in-law that look when she thought she couldn't see. That look that said she was an interfering old woman who was stuck with stupid old ways. Well, she could give her that look all she liked. It wouldn't stop old Mrs Dhanecha speaking her mind. After all, it was for their own good. Look at that bed they slept in – like a great big soft sponge. They would get back pains: they would be half crippled by the time they were fifty.

Slackness: no standards. Mrs Dhanecha felt strongly

about this (there weren't many things she didn't feel strongly about). Once you let your standards slip there was no end to it. There was all manner of badness in the world and it was all too easy to let it in. One thing led to another. That was why she made what her son and daughter-in-law considered a fuss over what they considered to be small matters. And if they ended up getting irritated, so much the worse for them. They ought to listen to her. They would, in the end. In her experience, if people didn't listen the first time they would listen the hundredth. That was how it had been with her late husband.

'It's just like stains,' old Mrs Dhanecha muttered to herself, as she put away the cups in the cupboard where they ought to be. Trupti always hung them on hooks, a stupid place. 'It's just like stains. You have to keep working at them.'

And so with the cellar.

Ram had actually pleaded with her to leave it alone. A grown man, with three children, nearly four, and such a backside, pleading with his mother as if she were some sort of tyrant!

'Please, Amma. Please, just forget about the cellar. It's upsetting Trupti.'

'Upsetting? What's upsetting? When you're eaten alive by rats, that will be upsetting.'

'I've told you. There are no rats. There never have been any rats.'

'How do you know? You think they're going to come up and introduce themselves to you? Ask for a ride in your taxi? You don't know rats. And a baby on the way, nara. What would your father say?'

Ram sighed and shuffled his feet. 'There are no rats,

Amma. And please don't keep going down into the cellar. It's dark and probably damp and you might fall—'

'Dark and damp, just the way rats like it! If I fall, it's because I've tripped over a rat, you'll see!'

Old Mrs Dhanecha had never liked that cellar. When she had first seen the house she had thought it was cold, dark, and full of shadows, but that was only to be expected: cousin Jagu's house in Bradford struck her just the same, and he was supposed to have done very well for himself. But the cellar, now: the cellar was a different matter. She couldn't be comfortable living in a house with such a thing underneath it, and she told them so, often. Trupti had muttered in English that she didn't have to live there, they did: thinking old Mrs Dhanecha wouldn't pick it up. She heard all right. It didn't make any difference to her. She hadn't lived seventy years and raised five children to be put off by muttering and looking. She was concerned for her grandchildren's welfare even if no one else was.

So one of the first things she did when she arrived to help her daughter-in-law through her pregnancy was to open the door under the stairs and creep down the stone steps to inspect the cellar with a torch. Still no electricity down there, though she had told Ram a hundred times that it would be better.

'There's no point, Amma. We don't use the place. We just keep the door closed and don't bother with it.'

'That doesn't make it go away. You need light. Rats don't like light.'

'There are no rats.' Mournfully.

'You wouldn't know a rat if it came up and bit you on your big behind. And what about the children? What if they open the door and fall down the steps in the dark and break their necks, what then?'

'The children don't go near the cellar. They've been told not to and they don't. They're old enough to know better.'

'And the new one? You think he'll know? When he's crawling and toddling, you think he'll know not to open that door and fall down the steps and break his neck and get eaten by rats?'

'Amma, please. You're upsetting Trupti again.'

But though Ram sighed and Trupti looked and muttered, they couldn't stop her keeping an eye on it. They couldn't stop her taking the torch down there for a daily inspection. They couldn't stop her laying the rat poison she had bought at Mirza's Mini-Mart.

Sometimes Ram would rib her about this – when he had had those secret glasses of beer, she suspected. 'Is your rat poison still there, Amma? Haven't they eaten it yet? Perhaps they don't like the taste of it. Perhaps they prefer a different brand.' She hated it when he tried to be funny. Even the sighing was preferable.

Well, it didn't matter. Old Mrs Dhanecha knew she was right about the rats, even though the poison was untouched, and even though she scanned the bare cement floor of the cellar in vain for droppings or shredded paper. She knew she was right about the rats, because she could hear them in the walls.

One wall, at any rate. Once she had pinpointed which wall it was that the tiny noises proceeded from, she spent a good deal of time crouching on the cellar floor with her ear pressed up against the unplastered brickwork. And in the same way she became aware that that wall was warmer than the others.

'Son,' she said, coming in upon Ram going over a pile

of bills on the kitchen table, 'the cellar. Does it join on to somewhere else?'

'Oh, no. Amma—'

'Never mind Amma. I want to know. You bend too close over those papers, you need glasses. Well, does it join on? What about next door? Do they have a cellar the same?'

'I suppose so. The houses are semi-detached, I suppose they'd have been built the same, but—'

'Is it one wall between? Or two walls with a gap?'

'I don't know. It wouldn't be a cavity wall, I don't think . . .'

'Well, there are rats. I can hear them. And they must have them next door too. Maybe that's where they breed. You should go and ask them. They should put poison down too.'

'Go and ask . . .? Oh, Amma, this is crazy. In the first place, there are no rats. And I'm certainly not going to go bothering them next door about it. No, really, Amma, that's too much.'

Ram was, for once, firm. And his mother, for once, did not press. She understood that you had to be careful with neighbours here: she had heard some grim stories. Ram insisted that he got on perfectly well with the people next door. It was Ian's house, and Ian was a very nice fellow, he said, who had never shown them anything but friendliness. As for the other two, there seemed to Ram to be no harm in them, even the one with the boots and cropped hair. But they could be a little wild, with parties and so forth, and Ram thought it was best if they all kept themselves to themselves.

Old Mrs Dhanecha's feelings, typically, were much stronger. She did not like the neighbours at Number 43 one bit. She had studied them closely – from the kitchen window you could see them going in and out of the back door – and she had drawn some very definite conclusions.

'Boots,' she muttered to herself, peeping through the net curtain, 'what do you want such boots for? Boots are for kicking. I know *you*.'

And, again: 'You think you're in a film, stroking your hair and pouting like that? Well, I wouldn't buy a ticket to see you. I know *you*.'

And then: 'Oh, you've seen me, have you, blue-eyes? Well, I won't wave back to you. How did you know I was peeping here, unless you can see round corners? Always so pleased with yourself, smiling, smiling. I know *you*.'

But she didn't, somehow: somehow old Mrs Dhanecha didn't know what to make of the one her son called Ian, the one who owned Number 43, the one who parked his blue van so carefully to allow room for Ram's taxi. All she knew was that she didn't like him.

'Smiling, smiling,' she muttered as she washed the boys' school shirts at the kitchen sink. 'I'll bet that's where the rats breed. I'll bet there are rats running around in their cellar, yaar, they like the company.' You only had to look at their dustbin, as she was doing now. Nothing wrapped up in bags: food containers thrown in anyhow, and overflowing. She could see foil cartons with dried-on Chinese food. If that wasn't an invitation to vermin she didn't know what was.

'Oh, Mamaji, what are you doing?' said Trupti coming in. 'You're hand-washing? But we have a perfectly good machine!'

'Good for bits and pieces. You want these white shirts clean, you have to hand-wash.'

Trupti frowned and dipped her hand in the sink, then

drew it out with a yelp and swore in English. 'Ai, Mamaji, how can you bear to have your hands in there?'

'Hotter than any machine, hah?' said old Mrs Dhanecha, and cackled with laughter. Her hands were like leather. Life was a lot less problematic if you were tough. Her body never gave her any trouble because she had resolved from an early age not to let it. It was wiry, scrawny, serviceable. The fearful cold of this winter, which Ram and Trupti said was exceptional even for Britain, did not affect it. She could walk into town in open sandals.

She could also sit cross-legged for fifteen minutes at a time on the cold floor of the cellar with her ear pressed against the wall, as she did later on that day. The fact that the poison was still untouched did not deter her. She was convinced the rats were there. Rats were cunning creatures. Mice might have made their presence known by now, but not rats. And the noises, though small, were still too heavy and definite to be made by mice. It had to be rats: she couldn't think of anything else.

And they were certainly active tonight: she could half hear, half feel the little restless noises through the dusty brickwork. Ram came to the top of the cellar steps once and did some pleading and sighing, but she ignored him. She was absorbed.

Old Mrs Dhanecha had a highly developed sense of when things were not right. She had seen some horrible things at the time of Partition, when her husband had nearly been killed before her eyes, and ever since then her sense of right-not right had been supernaturally keen, keen like an old wound throbbing its warning. It had throbbed that time on her last visit when Ram was late back from work, and Trupti was saying it often happened and there was nothing to worry about and all the time Ram was in casualty because a fare had turned nasty and called him a Paki (they couldn't even get that right) and ended up punching him in the jaw.

The cellar was like that. The cellar was not right. Old Mrs Dhanecha might wag her lean finger at her grandchildren and take them to task and stand over them while they polished their shoes, but that didn't mean she wanted to see rats creeping into their bedrooms. And as for the new one that was coming in a few weeks' time...

She wished her English was better. Those young men next door must have rats in their cellar, and she had half a mind to go round there and ask them.

2

'Ah well. Here we are again. Happy as can be. All good friends and jolly good company.'

Rob chanted with his most deadpan disgust, and it was in the same tone that he spoke into the microphone, holding it gingerly between finger and thumb as if it were a fish in an advanced state of putrefaction.

'One two. One two. Testing. Two. Two.'

Out on the ice a couple of girls who had arrived early gave a cheer and waved at him lubriciously. Rob grimaced.

'State of them. You know what I wanted to be when I was young?'

'You *are* young,' Sarah said.

'Nah. I wanted to be a roadie. Can you believe that? What a pillock. I actually wanted to be some fat old slob in a cut-off T-shirt setting up the mikes for talentless little pipsqueaks and then driving them up the motorway to

Dudley or wherever and doing it all over again. Yep. They always go, "Two. Two," into the mikes, you see. Don't know why. I mean, you could say anything really. Recite poetry or whatever.'

'Go on then. Have a recite.'

'Don't know any. Only the one about the old man from Gosham who took off his—'

'Smutty boys are lonely boys, Rob.'

Ah. Comforting, this casualness and normality, but difficult to maintain her part in it. Difficult at the best of times these days, but most difficult of all here – where it had all started two weeks ago.

She was back at the Ice Arena with the Tudor Radio roadshow. Rob was here to look after the equipment and do his running Eeyore number, just as before: his teenage assistant was here to do nothing very much except pursue girls with testosterone-soaked persistence, just as before. And just as before Porky the manager was strutting his domain like some gauleiter in mufti, periodically presenting his ham face at the edge of the dais to favour Sarah with some punter lore and to check that she hadn't fallen madly in love with him in the last half-hour.

Just as before.

And if everything turned out *exactly* as before . . . then Sarah was, quite simply, saved. If the girl with the red hair appeared amongst the skaters, laughing and chatting, then Sarah would begin to live again. It was that simple.

She watched Rob drooping off to bring more discs from the van, and experienced a sharp pang of envy. She wished she felt as Rob did about this occasion – practically nothing, in other words. It was just another Thursday night disco to him. She wished too that she could explain to him something of what she felt tonight – if only so that he wouldn't be surprised if she started gibbering at the mixing desk or flying around the high rink ceiling like a released balloon. And then she wished, most intensely of all, that she had not been alone in the car park that night two weeks ago: her mind drew a swift vignette in which Rob had not driven the roadshow van away first but had hung around to, what, help her with her car, say, because it wouldn't start, and only then had the red-haired girl and the three men come out to the car park and Sarah and Rob had seen what happened together, and DS Routh and all the sceptical constabulary condescension he represented just couldn't turn a blind eye . . .

Sarah began lining up her playlist. All this wishing: it was bull. After all, the red-haired girl might be perfectly OK and still not turn up tonight: who went to the Arena disco every fortnight without fail? A few fans, maybe; but really it was an occasional thing. Ice recreation, as Porky might put it, had yet to realize its permanent potential in the leisure spectrum. And the girl might well come, but that didn't mean Sarah would spot her in the crowd.

I would. I'd spot her anywhere. I know it. The stubborn child spoke up within her, the child that she suspected Murray sometimes saw now when he looked at her in that perplexed way, fondness entangled with impatience. *If she were here, I'd spot her.*

All right, so she'd spot her. And maybe the three guys too – the blond boyish one certainly. But preparing herself for it was asking for trouble. Instead she must stick to practicalities. She had come here with a programme in mind.

First, as soon as the disco was under way, make an appeal similar to the one she had been repeating on her

Tudor show every day. (Her producer was getting twitchy about this. Direct audience links were a feature of Motormouth Mark's afternoon show, which specialized in reconciliations on the air and such. Sarah Winter should be a more remote radio presence. But then her producer was in a general state of twitchiness at the moment anyhow. His wife was rumoured to be having an affair with a fifteen-year-old boy.) Then, if there was no response to that, broaden it to include anyone who knew the girl or thought they might know her, or the three men in the van. And then if there was still no luck, she would round off the evening by interrogating everyone who worked at the rink, from Porky downwards, about what had happened a fortnight ago. DS Routh might have already done that, but DS Routh was a policeman. And the sad fact was that when a policeman asked you questions, you clammed up. Ain't nobody here but us chickens.

Only Murray knew about this business, and Murray would not say it, so Sarah said it to herself: people would very probably think she was mad.

OK. That was certainly no fun. But the conception others had of her didn't matter so much just now. Her conception of herself did and she could not turn her back on what she had seen.

Sarah cued a dance remix that would pound away for a good five minutes, scanned the few early arrivals huddling in the stands or teetering on to the ice, and then went down the dais steps to the service doors. A security man was there, all belt and gut.

'Just going to nip out for a cigarette,' she said in answer to his look.

'You'll kill yourself with them.'

Sour pomposity. Yet he must have been all of sixty:

somehow you only expected the carcinogens lecture from acid young professionals. The pods had got everybody nowadays.

The thaw of the past two days had been a lie. The air was vicious again now, and out in the car park the refreezing of the slush had made a moonscape. After the first month of good-citizen caution on the frozen roads, drivers had mostly decided just to rev and hope: but surely tonight people would hesitate before venturing out.

Though maybe if you had one of those chunky vans . . .

'Marijuana causes sterility in men, apparently,' said Rob, locking up the Tudor van.

Sarah looked at him, then at her cigarette. 'Eh?'

'Just reminded me. You know how they go on about tobacco. Well, I was reading where marijuana inhibits production of sperm. Long-term effects, apparently. I thought: Wait a minute. All the dopeheads I know have got about fifteen kids each. You know. All called Cloud and Zappa and running around with full nappies.' Already high-shouldered, Rob had to make an extra effort to shrug. 'You tell me.'

Sarah laughed, and noticed the sound of it in the thin wide air. All her laughter was like that these days. A ration of laughter, the way people laughed when they were ill and wrapped up in blankets and you tried to amuse them.

It would be good to laugh freely again.

'Right.' She threw down her half-smoked cigarette. Yellow wands of headlights were passing across the visitors' car park: the punters were braving it after all. 'Let's start the ball rolling, then.'

'Better,' Rob said, checking the van one last time. 'I thought for one awful moment you were going to say,

"Let's get this show on the road." '

Just as before. The swirl of light: the curious noise, half din, half murmur, of the skates grinding on the ice and the skaters laughing and shouting: the mufflered parents waving and waving from the stands: the skating coach on his tight-buttocked prowl for jailbait: the clomping parade of newcomers issuing from the dressing rooms and gripping fiercely at each other's arms: the smell of burgers: the cool, shrill vastness.

Just as before.

'Hi and a big welcome to Thursday night at the Arena from me, Sarah Winter, and the Tudor Radio roadshow bringing you the best in music all the way through to eleven. To those of you who've been here before, nice to see you again... and if this is your first visit, well, what kept you? Just a reminder that the cafeteria is open and is serving burgers, fries, shakes, you name it they've got it; also that the gallery bar is open tonight till eleven, with a full selection of wines, spirits, lagers and real ales. Just one problem, they're all out of ice. No, bad joke. Here's something to tickle your double-axels... it's Blur with "Girls & Boys"...'

Leave it a while yet: the place was still filling up. Rob handed her a Coke. Warm: just as before.

Swirl of lights. White flashes out on the ice: someone using a camera, record of a great night out. Everyone was having a good time. The possibility of ghastly things happening seemed wildly remote, to be entertained only by paranoid killjoys.

And yet listen to the screams. The screams of those thirteen-year-old girls holding on to each other as they propelled themselves away from the crash-barrier, taking the plunge, exhilarated at their own momentum.

Wide-mouthed, full-throated screams. A thin line. A thin line . . .

'That's Blur there . . . Listen out for their new single on my show on Tudor tomorrow, eleven till two, plug plug . . . Remember to keep those requests coming in . . . And just while we're on that subject . . .' don't swallow, don't swallow on mike, it sounds like a whale gulping, 'a young lady came up the desk here to request a track last time . . . that's a fortnight ago . . . young lady with auburn hair, about eighteen . . . the request was "I Can't Stand Up For Falling Down" by Elvis Costello – yes, good choice that . . . Well, that young lady left something behind on the dais which I think may be of sentimental value, and we've hung on to it, so . . . If she's here tonight, do pop over here and see us . . . that's the young lady who requested "I Can't Stand Up For Falling Down" by Elvis Costello, this time last fortnight . . . and speaking of that track, here it comes . . .'

Didn't know what she'd said: whether she'd said what she meant to, or talked Martian. Shaking again. The warm Coke tasted like spit.

'Excuse me. Here. Excuse me.'

The girl leaning on the edge of the dais was no more than fourteen, and her hair was long down her back, and it was an unmistakeably pale shade of ginger. And it was an index of Sarah's state of mind that even as she perceived all this she was prepared to be convinced that this was the girl she sought.

'Excuse me. That was me. What you just said. Last week. I left summing here.'

Prepared to be convinced . . . but not *that* prepared.

'Last fortnight.'

'Yeah, whatever.'

The girl with red hair had been, possibly, Geordie in speech: certainly not local, as this girl was. The girl with red hair had also been genuine.

'Oh, right, so you were the one who left the purse?'

'Yeah, that's it.'

'Or was it a scarf?'

'Scarf, I mean.'

The giggle was uncertain, and faded away altogether under Sarah's stare.

'Shit,' the girl said. Collapse of ginger party. She exited with a flick of hair and a waft of shoplifted Charlie Red, though her expression seemed to say it was still worth a try.

Faces, faces. Faces in a crowd: you thought of them as anonymous, featureless. Interchangeable. But when you scanned them for one particular face, studied them, gave them attention, you realized how numerous the variations were on that one simple theme. Nobody really looked like anybody. Everyone was a one-off.

Faces, faces, moving, turning, uplifted, cast down, in shadow, in light. Faces observed and unaware of it were cryptic, crafty, full of secrets. This was surely why it was that babies gazed into the faces of strangers with such transparent awe. They hadn't learned to make blanks of them.

She's not here, Sarah.

Sarah eased down the low frequencies with one hand, with the other flipping the next disc out of its case.

I know it. I know she's not here.

But what she hadn't known till now was how badly she had wanted the girl to be here: what an enormous weight of expectation she had placed on this evening. Sheer professional necessity was preventing the weight from descending on her just yet, but it would, it would.

'Excuse me.'

Ginger back for another try? She snapped out of a trance of gloom.

'Excuse me . . .'

Not ginger. A mixed quartet of teenagers, the well-scrubbed sort. Good diet and a desk in the bedroom.

'Could you play a request for us, please?'

'Chris Rea.'

'No, not Chris *Rea* . . .' Doppler and wow of adolescent disgust. 'Sonic Youth . . .'

'Play both if you like,' Sarah said. 'What names?'

Lindsay and Sue and Steve and Dean . . . who, it turned out, was the one with the camera. He was clicking away like a demented paparazzo even now.

'God, Dean, give it a rest . . .'

'He's been like this all night . . .'

'Yeah, he got a good one of you falling on your arse!'

'Well, what about you? You couldn't stand up at all . . .'

No ill-humour in it: laughing mouths, strong teeth and healthy gums. The same good humour even when Dean, who was obviously a photography pain, shepherded them in front of the Tudor logo at the front of the dais and lined up another shot.

'Move your head a bit, Sue, it says Tud Radio . . .'

'Dean, how come *you're* never in these photos?'

'He'd crack the lens . . .'

Innocence and friendliness. Sarah was surprised at the heartache she felt.

'Is it all right . . .?' Dean, camera suspended, leaning tentatively up towards her. 'You know, taking a photo . . .?'

'God, yes.' Innocence indeed: they actually thought

Tudor Radio was a big deal. 'Trust me to take one? You can all be in it then.'

Big response to that. Sarah found a Chris Rea track, made the dedication, then stepped down from the dais. Friendly teenage hands supported her graceless landing.

Sudden thought, piercing empathy: was this how the red-haired girl had felt last time? The kindly inclusion, the conviviality lifting and soothing her, the supporting hands?

And then, suddenly . . .

'OK, here's the shutter. Just press there . . .'

Dean, half garrulous and half shy, passed her his far from cheapo camera as if it were a new kitten. She knew him: knew, at any rate, with some certainty, what Dean was like. He was the well-behaved and well-doing sixth former, hot on the sciences and destined for a university place. He gave his parents a minimum of grief because his enthusiasms had stayed intact even when the hormones kicked in. He had been chubby at fourteen but was now only stocky, he had his hair barbered rather than styled and only when his mother reminded him, and he would go from his present pink-and-white to stubbly without acne in between. Sarah knew Dean because she had known Deans when she was a sixth-former and, alas, had tended to see them as hopeless no-nos compared with the Andys and Trevs who cracked heartbreaking grins and slid their tight buttocks on to the seats of motorcycles. The Andys and Trevs were now beerbellied losers kicking the second-hand pushchair as they crashed in from the pub, and the Deans were sophisticated goodlookers with a lifetime ahead of them.

'OK, ready . . .? Smile . . .'

She framed the four young faces, captured them, happy

to do so and aching a little again around her heart. They wanted another, different poses: another: another.

'Are you OK for film?'

'I've got loads, I've got loads.' Dean flourished boxes of fresh film, all sheepish eagerness. 'See?'

'Oh, put it away, Dean.'

'He even took a picture of me in the lav, can you believe that?'

'Only when you were at the washbasin.'

'That's what I mean!'

'You've got all those films from last time as well.'

'I'll get round to them . . .'

Sarah kept snapping until the track reached the fade, then handed the camera back. Fulsome thanks, exchange of looks, and then it was Dean who plucked up the courage.

'Could we . . .?' A jerk of the head, and a little mime of taking a picture.

'You want me in a photo? Sure, of course. Just give me a minute to put the next track on.'

She hopped up to the dais again, amused and wondering what they would be like if they met a real celebrity. She cued James Brown, recalling an old lady who she had once seen loitering in the lobby at Tudor and who had finally approached her with the unanswerable query, 'Excuse me, dear, are you well known for anything?'

The possibility hit her as she was stepping down from the dais again and made her heartbeat do a drum fill. For a few instants she had no pulse at all and then it was pounding like the James Brown from the speakers.

'Dean – did you take photos here last time? Did I hear that right?'

'Sorry?'

The bass was terrible, like a train in a tunnel: she should have remembered the reverb needed controlling on these old tracks. 'Last time,' she shouted, gripping Dean's sleeve. 'You were here last time? And took photos?'

'Oh yes, that's right,' he mouthed, too shy to approach his face to her ear. 'We all came last time. And Andrea as well, that's Sue's sister—'

'And you took photos? Round the rink, on the ice . . .?'

'Everywhere,' one of the girls chipped in. 'Honestly, he's mad. He's like one of those Japanese tourists.'

'Here, remember that time at Lisa's party where he barged in on—'

'Have you got them?' Sarah made herself relax her grip on Dean's sleeve, which was beginning to alarm him. 'Those photos you took last time? I mean, the film, is it—'

'It's at home.' He was too polite to look puzzled. 'Well, there's three rolls, I think. I haven't developed them yet.'

And now something descended blessedly on Sarah. It came, perhaps, from her job, from thinking on her feet, covering over awkwardnesses, never being stuck for something to say. It was a neat, glib, plausible excuse.

'Listen, do you think I could see them when they're developed? I'll tell you why, we're hoping to do a display in the lobby at Tudor to publicize the Arena nights, you know, and what I thought would be really good would be a kind of montage, like a kaleidoscope effect, showing what these nights are all about, and maybe a whole lot of snapshots like that . . .'

'Yeah! Yeah, why not? Only a lot of them are – well, they'll have us on them.'

'No, that's fine, as long as it's OK with you. Like I say,

it's sort of in the planning stage, but obviously if we did use them you'd be properly credited as the photographer, and of course we'd reimburse you . . .' Hmm. She would have to sweet-talk the producer like she'd never sweet-talked before, but what the hell? As for Dean, there was no difficulty there. He was open-mouthed; and knowing Dean and Deans as she did, she realized it wasn't at the prospect of money.

'Yeah! No problem, no problem! Here, we're going to be famous!'

More open mouths, and a few bashful cringes.

'Shit, what was I wearing that night . . .?'

'Dean, don't let them have that one . . . you know the one . . .'

'I'll develop them tonight,' Dean said.

'No, no hurry.' There was hurry, of course there was hurry, though she couldn't tell them the real reason. But it didn't matter, because Dean was seventeen. There was no can't-make-it and that's-going-to-be-tricky at seventeen. You skated all night and then went home and did something else. No problem, no problem. Sarah could have hugged him, except that it would have embarrassed the hell out of him.

'How shall I get them to you? I could drop them off at the radio station, if you like.'

'Fine.'

'Oh, and the ones I've taken tonight.'

'Um . . . of course, those too.'

'Right. I'll bring the lot. I'll drop them round after school.'

'That'd be great. But really there's no hurry.'

No, there should not be hurry, there should not be this hurry of expectation inside her, dangerous, because she had brought that same hurry of expectation here tonight, expectation that all would be resolved, that the red-haired girl would be here.

So. A warning. But Sarah doubted whether she would heed it. The red-haired girl was not here tonight, but as Sarah linked arms and smiled into Dean's camera she felt beneath her feet a sure rock of knowledge amongst the mire: the red-haired girl had been here a fortnight ago. A face in the crowd.

A face.

3

Contemplating a night on the razzle, Chill, and why not? All work and no play makes Chill a dull boy, that's his motto, and heaven knows he's been on the job non-stop just lately and no smutty remarks thank *you*. No, if he ever gets to be a dull boy he hopes someone will let him know about it pretty sharpish because if there's one thing he cannot abide it's your dull dreary ditchwater types, never got a smile, never let their hair down, never loosen up, and in fact, while we're on that subject, step forward your friend and mine Derek a.k.a. Trend, a sobriquet by the way which Chill bestowed on the little ray of sunshine himself and if there was a tiny smidgen of tongue in the cheek region when he did so, i.e. Trend as short for Silly Trendy Posey Bastard, well Chill's not the person to say anything about it, and after all the ray of sunshine himself seems to like it so where's the harm?

But that Trend, now. Really doing Chill's head in just lately, he is. Now don't get him wrong, Chill doesn't expect everybody in the world to have his cheerful disposition, not at all. We're all made different and there's your heredity and your environment and what have you, as well as what you might call your individual chemical whatsname. The message the fairies wrote about Chill's cradle was Spread A Little Happiness and that's just the way he is and he'd be the last one to judge if somebody just can't duck and dive and come up smiling the way he does. And Trend's never exactly been a party-starter, more of a party-pooper if truth be told unless he's been at Chill's blow and *then* he just turns into a giggling heap and you can't take him anywhere. But the thing is, that's Trend. Chill personally wouldn't change a hair on the dear little loser's head, well maybe cut a few because he's starting to look like an overgrown privet hedge, but anyway the argument still applies. You take a person for what they are. And when you think 'Trend' you think 'Misery-guts' just the same as when you think 'Sean' you think 'Moron'. Doesn't mean you love them any less.

But there are limits, and Trend's overstepped them as far as Chill's concerned. Just lately he is one moody, sulky, mopey pain in the nether regions and Chill's just about had a bellyful of it.

It's something to do with the pet, of course. A blind man could spot *that*. Trend has been a bit unsettled right from the moment she came. Let's face it, they all have. Talk about your felines on your overheated galvanized roofing materials. But then that's only to be expected. It's quite a big thing after all, as the actress said to the bishop and that's just about enough of *that* sort of talk, thank you. It takes a bit of getting used to, having the pet in the house, and Chill would be the first to admit it. But Trend . . . well weird is the only way to describe the trendy one's reaction to the advent of the new pet at 43 Grenville Street. And Chill's buggered if he knows what's at the bottom of it, no pun intended.

Just the other day, for example, Chill was describing something to Trend about the pet, OK a bit intimate but they're mates after all and men were supposed to be in touch with their feelings and all that nowadays, weren't they? Just describing this little episode, just giving Trend the lowdown as 'twere, man to man, when all of a sudden off goes Trend into strop mode.

'Yeah, Chill, all right, when's the fucking wedding.' No question mark. No josh in the tone either, which would be all right because Chill can take a josh as well as the next man. Thrives on it, in fact. Still, Chill pressed on, choosing to ignore Mr Megasulk's reaction because really you had to sometimes if you were going to get any sort of conversation going at all, and—

'Just leave it out, Chill, will you?'

Now this wasn't your confrontational type in-your-face mode doodah, which was just as well as Chill would have dealt with *that* very promptly. But well out of order just the same. Chill, however, being Chill and full of the milk of human whatsname, tried to make a joke of it.

'That's funny,' he said, 'that's exactly what *she* said.'

And what a glare he got, from underneath all that hair! Quite took Chill aback, it did, and he wasn't generally an abackable sort of dude as anyone would tell you. There was more.

'Just shut it.' A stormy sort of voice now: did Chill detect tears in the offing, wherever the offing was? 'Just shut it, Chill.'

'Where you going?'

'Out.' And he was too. Stomp stomp.

Would you credit it? 'Out,' and then out. It was just like in one of those soaps where the mixed-up teenager says his moody piece and then exits stage left because the scriptwriter can't think of any other way to end the scene.

He came back, of course, eventually, and was no more nor less than his usual sparkling self. And Chill didn't say anything. Not Chill. Let bygones be bygones is his motto, always has been. But he did a lot of thinking. Still is doing a lot of thinking, in fact, in between all the other things he has to do, which are not few, and it's no wonder he's ready to make a bit of a night of it which he hasn't done for ages, not since Crimbo really unless you count that night at the Arena and that was different, really. Special.

Too much to do lately, deffo. Tote that barge, lift that bale, it's lucky really that he never gets tired because then where would they be? Look at today, which being Saturday is naturally the busiest day of the week at the market, not that they were shifting that many units, more's the pity, a lot of the punters taking it into their heads just to paw the stuff and unfold it and hold it up against themselves and then toss it down again and bugger off saying, 'No I'll leave it,' and sometimes that really makes Chill wild, though he's an easy-going fellow as anyone will tell you. But you'd think after a hard day like that he'd be straight home and putting his feet up in front of a roaring TV *n'est-ce pas* but oh no. He had more to do. Namely, fetching the pet's stuff from her flat as he'd promised. Always kept his promises, Chill. He said she'd have her gear and her gear she would have.

So there was just time for a cuppa and a wash to get the punter's muck off him and then it was back in the van with old Sean, bless him, right by his side and off down to Lyle House YMCA. Now he could have done this during the week but he reckoned Saturday evening was his best bet. Knowing these places and the sort of teen muppets who lived in them there'd be a lot of toing and froing on Saturday evenings. Boyfriends and girlfriends and just plain friends coming a-calling and not much notice taken of strangers in those smelly parqueted corridors. Funny, the smell of those places. Like burnt toast. They couldn't all live on burnt toast, could they?

Tell you what, though. Seeing and smelling those corridors, with the rows of cack-brown doors and the photocopied notices saying what to do if there was a fire and the sad cases trundling in and out all hair and trainers – well, it stiffened Chill and that's quite enough of *that* thank you. Stiffened his resolve or his conviction or whatever you wanted to call it. Finally crushed any teeny-weeny doubts he might have had about taking Alison Holdenby as a houseguest.

Because look at this place. They could put potted shrubs all round the block and call it Lyle House as if it were some sort of stately home and give it a posh timber sign all in lower case letters but it was still a hole to put losers in. Look at those security doors, what a laugh. Anybody could get in, anybody would open them for you. Even before he saw the flat itself, Chill knew he had done the pet a favour taking her out of here.

Easy to find, Number 14, though there was a bit of a hiccupette as Sean, who was not exactly a byword for courage under fire, suddenly started bricking it just as Chill was about to insert the key in the door. 'Shit. What if somebody sees us, man? I'm not kidding, this is dodgy, man, I mean what if somebody sees us, what if somebody says something?' Stuff like that. There was a lot more of it. The hardest part for Chill was stopping himself laughing, because when Sean bricked it he really was a sketch.

The poor old stick acted furtive and guilty at the best of times. Put him in a situation like this and he went all to ratshit. Beads of sweat, yes, Chill had never quite seen the truth of that phrase until now, they were like actual beads running down Sean's brow, not that they had very far to run, whoops, bit unkind that but really, it was such a sight to see, and the way he danced up and down on the toes of his DMs like a kid about to wet himself. A real card, that Sean. 'I'm not kidding, man, well dodgy, I'm not kidding...'

It was on Chill's lips to say that the poor droog should have thought of that before embarking on a life of virtually uninterrupted petty crime, but he let it go. He didn't like to see dumb animals suffer, and so he just said, 'There's no one around to see, my old china, and anyway nobody's interested. We'll be in and out in two shakes, don't you worry.' And then he turned the key in the lock and they were in. Into Alison's home. *Former* home.

As for the flat itself, that stiffened Chill even more, and OK in this case you can take that literally if you like because it did give him a bit of a buzz going in there and knowing it was all hers, her place and her things and there he was in amongst them and no one to say him nay. An exciting feeling. Brought home to him just what a spectacular thing he had pulled off. Here was a whole life in this flat, flatlet really, and that life was now his. He had taken possession of it. Absorbed it.

So a bit of a shiver, a bit of a thrill as he explored Alison Holdenby's little flat but still. Still and all. It only went to show, like the smelly corridors, that he was dead right in taking her in because look at this place. Tiny, tiny and sad. Little wooden bed with a flowery quilt, bless her she's tried, really tried, but what can you do? An old rug on the floor to cover the manky carpet tiles. Two plywood shelves fixed to the wall, it's like they only bother to give you two because it's not as if you're going to have anything to put on them. Table with tubular metal legs like the ones in DSS offices and a plastic chair. Two-ring cooker and a battered old fridge in a sort of recess and next door a bathroom about two feet square, lots of little scented articles in there the way girls do and ah, sanitary towels, he was going to have to remember that sort of thing. Get them whenever he bought his razor blades maybe.

Dear oh dear. A whole life in here. Didn't amount to much. Not even one vanload.

'Let's get moving, man. Come on. Let's just take the stuff and go. This is dodgy . . .'

Yes, Sean, unable to suppress the tealeaf gleam in his eye but still in a thoroughly bricked-up state and looking like he was about to wet them at the slightest sound. And so, though Chill wouldn't have minded soaking up the atmosphere a while longer, they got moving. It didn't take long. Clothes from the wardrobe – she had some nice gear, our Alison, strictly budget stuff but she made the best of it, took a pride – posters from the wall, she'd like having them, and the books ditto. All the bathroom stuff. The little black and white TV and the cute animal ornaments and the few pots and pans . . . everything, in fact, that the tenant of the flat would take with her if she did a quick flit without paying the rent. Which meant leaving the cooker and the fridge, not that she'd be needing them as they had a perfectly good cooker and fridge at Grenville Street and as for the bed, well, that would have to stay too. Chill had to admit that it would be a bit of a crack, a bit of an extra thrill, knowing that it was her very own bed she was lying on when he paid her a visit but there, manoeuvring a bed down the smelly corridors was a different matter from taking a couple of cases and boxes and besides the bed in the cellar was specially adapted. Well, you couldn't have everything in this life and it was no good kicking against the pricks, as he'd had to tell her more than once.

So, Chill and Sean carried the carryables to the van parked in the parking area at the back of the block, no shortage of room there though surprisingly one or two of the resident losers did have what could only be described as vehicles. Sean, natch, did a lot of sweating and muttering under his breath but really there was no need. After all, tealeaves wouldn't be calmly waltzing through at seven o'clock in the evening with cases under their arms, now would they? Stood to reason. A couple of vacant faces gawped out at them from lit windows, a couple of student types passed them in the corridor with a waft of grass and a drone of heavy-type conversation, but really that was your lot. No risk worth speaking of. Nobody gave a toss, and didn't that just say something about the world today, Chill thought, didn't that prove what he'd been saying to her just the other night? Cold hard world. Better away from it. Who was it sang 'Gimme Shelter', was it the Stones or was it someone else entirely, well anyway that's what he had done and as they drove away from Lyle House Chill felt pretty good about it.

But of course the thoroughly knackering day wasn't over yet because when they got home they had to unload the stuff and Trend had made himself scarce as per usual when there was work to be done. And now you'd think she'd be pleased at having her stuff brought down to her, wouldn't you? But no. Not a bit of it. Not our Alison.

Chill could have sworn she even cried a bit, though it was difficult to tell with her doing the head-under-the-blankets, curl-up-and-die routine. Dear oh lor. You tried your best, and what thanks did you get? Zilch, that's what. To tell the truth he felt a teensy bit miffed seeing her acting up like that when he'd gone to so much trouble and it was tempting to let her know it. But hey ho, sometimes you just had to bite the bullet, no cross no crown as his old dad used to say, and so Chill just kept his cool – when had he ever lost it? – and got on with the job in hand, putting up the posters on the cellar walls, laying the rug down by the bed, putting all her bits and pieces round about the place in rather a tasteful manner though he said it himself. Then left her alone. She'd perk up sooner or later.

And now here he is back in the van and barrelling down the ring road and this really is the last chore he's got to perform before he goes on the town tonight. Because the thing is there's one or two bits and pieces of hers that she won't need, like the quilt, or that he'd prefer her not to have, like the chair because there were those metal legs and you simply never knew. She'd tried to brain poor old Sean with her food tray the other day and though that had been more comical than anything it still went to show that you couldn't be too careful. The girl certainly had spunk and really that's quite enough of that, thank *you*. Honestly.

So a quick trip over to his lockup to stow the unwanted stuff away nice and safe. Also a chance to check that everything *is* nice and safe because it is the weekend after all and these lockups have had their share of break-ins. It would actually be rather a crack, Chill thinks, to come across one of those tealeaves just as he's trying to break in. See his face – and then rearrange it. Before and after sort of thing. Funnily enough, the one who tends to worry most about the lockup being broken into is Sean and he is the most incorrigible tealeaf going, or he was until Chill took him in hand, as constabulary visits to Number 43 are not exactly high on Chill's wish list. But you can only reform a nut like Sean so far, it seems. He still goes out early some mornings to lift cases of milk from the back doorsteps of corner shops where they've been left by the delivery vans. 'Look,' he'll say, when Chill comes yawning down to breakfast. 'Look. I ripped 'em off.' And there they are, twenty-four pint cartons of milk wrapped in a Cellophane package. What on earth are they supposed to do with twenty-four pints of milk? That is the question verily, but best not to tax poor Sean's brain with it. Something might snap in there.

Not a journey Chill particularly likes, the journey to his lockup, because this part of the city is pretty grim in his opinion. Here on the outskirts it's just Legoland as far as he's concerned and he wonders what the planners were on when they ran these places up back in the sixties and seventies. They built a stonking big estate of houses all looking like stood up shoeboxes with little slits for windows like your ye olde castle efforts and they build an industrial estate that's all trees and bushes and corrugated roofs and they stick the ring road in between them with a connecting underpass that no one in their right mind would set foot in and hey presto. Nobody goes out of their houses after dark because there's nowhere to go except other houses and no one goes to the industrial estate because it's so difficult to get to and so units fall empty and the more empty units there are the more little tealeaves and firebugs you get. Has its advantages in

Chill's case, though, because he can rent a lockup here dirt cheap. Right in the middle of the industrial estate there's a quadrangle of single-storey lockups, small tradesmen for the use of, with these great ugly hangar-like places on either side.

Chill parks the van in front of the lockup and steps out with a scrunch on to the frozen tarmac. Shines his torch. No sign of tealeaf interference, anyway: too cold for them probably.

Chill gets busy. Could have asked Sean to come along and help, but old Sean's got his sanitary duties down in the cellar and besides, Chill likes to have a bit of time on his own now and then. He's only human.

Plenty of room in the lockup as it happens. Chill did good business over Christmas and hasn't bought in a lot since. There'd be even more room if it weren't for the boxes of summer casuals that are supposed to be stacked neatly at the back awaiting the return of the old treacle bun and which are in fact piled up in the most cack-handed and downright dangerous manner it's possible to imagine and three guesses whose handiwork *that* was. Poor old Sean. Tries so hard to help, Chill hasn't got the heart to bawl him out. Talk about lack of organizational powers in regard to piss-ups in brewery premises or what.

Chill soon has the Alison bits and pieces unloaded and stored and the sight of them sends him off into a little dream. He wonders, at some length, what it would be like to keep a pet in here ... But though the idea's got its potential and there are some fun aspects that he dwells on for a while, in the end he decides he made the right choice. Having the pet at home right from the start is much the nicest.

'Right. That's me finished for the day.' Chill skips,

brisk. Padlock padlocked, last check around, back in the van. We're off.

Back to Grenville Street first, of course, to leave the van. Chill has every intention of getting bevvied tonight and that means no driving. A lost licence in his line of work would be a fairly complete disaster and besides, drink-drivers are the scum of the earth as far as Chill's concerned. Don't talk to him about drink-drivers. They fairly make him wild.

So he parks the van next to old Ram's taxi and finds Sean all ready to go and Trend, surprise surprise, upstairs doing a big I-don't-feel-like-it number which he takes a bit of jollying out of. But jollied he is at last and off they go, the Three Musketeers, hitting the town on a Saturday night and where it will all end who knows?

SEVEN

1

You should have made more friends.

Ah. The imp of self-pity was back. He had a new message for her. The message was that she should have made more friends.

She didn't trust the imp, and she hesitated before considering his message. The imp pretended to help sometimes, pretended to make her feel better, but he didn't really.

There used to be a car called the Hillman Imp. Then there was the word impish which was generally used in a positive sort of way – cheeky and harmlessly naughty. Strange. Imp had a nasty sound to her. She imagined something small and spiteful with a big head and black tarry skin and little monkey hands. Self-pity was an imp.

Metaphors. She had been hot on metaphors and similes at school – all the paraphernalia of language that had made her classmates in English groan in perplexity. ('This is A level standard,' her teacher had told her, with admonishing approval. 'Honestly, Alison, you'd cakewalk it.' But oh no. Alison wanted to leave. Pig-headed Alison.) But she had never thought of them as having any existence outside the covers of books. Now, here, in her prison, she found that she lived in a world of metaphor. The physical world was severely limited – a few material objects, a few sensations, chiefly fear and pain – but her interior world had taken on a vivid variety of shapes. Self-pity was an imp. Hunger was a stony desert that opened before her. Waking from sleep was a horse, a dreadful wild horse that capered about the cellar as soon as she opened her eyes, kicking out with terrible hooves. And then there was the apple of anticipation.

She had given up the daily tugging at her chains. All it did was make raw meat out of her wrists, and after a period of not caring what happened to her body she had come to a careful avoidance of injury. This was because the smiler used it. The second time he had raped her she had managed to hurt him with her teeth and in return he had burned her with a cigarette. The pain of the burn went on and on with no water or ointment to relieve it and soon she realized that that was the point. When he finally brought the can of Burneze he made her beg and do things for him in order to get it and she did them. The smiler knew what he was doing. Pain was an effective means of control, but even more effective was the withholding of relief from pain. And so she had given up tugging at the chains. There were already enough centres of pain in her body.

But instead of the tugging at the chains, she now had the tapping. And it was the anticipation of the tapping that presented itself to her consciousness as an apple. Satisfyingly round and smooth in your hands. Lustrous and tempting. Sweetness and crispness as appealing to the imagination as to the taste buds.

The tapping, and the prospect of it, was doubly satisfying because there was power in it. Alison had found a little power over her captors and it had begun with a teaspoon. The boy with the hat, stupid though he was, would certainly have noticed if she had taken a knife or fork from the food tray and secreted it (they were plastic, but she would have found a way to do some damage with them nonetheless). But when he had brought her boiled eggs one time she had risked taking the spoon and slipping it into a little rip in the ticking of the mattress and it had worked. The boy with the hat hadn't noticed. That was her first manifestation of power. The second, which in a way was even more satisfying, was knowing when to use it.

Alison had made a picture of time, which at first had been a blank space to her. She had pieced it together from many small things. The transformation of her senses had helped her. Vision furnished virtually no clues, but the potential of her sharpened hearing was almost inexhaustible. Out of those faint traffic noises she had made herself a clear pattern of the day's passing. More: she could recognize not only the shape of the day out there in the normal sane world, but the shape of the reptiles' day. There was a particular sound, a sound that her old dull hearing would scarcely have registered, that she had come to recognize as the smiler's van starting up in the morning. Cough and throb: it was unmistakable. The smiler was a market trader, and market traders started work early.

So, knowledge: knowledge of morning, and knowledge too of late afternoon when there was a different but just as unmistakable throb and cough that was the smiler's van returning. More importantly, knowledge that between those times, the smiler was out of the house.

The boy with the hat, too, usually. Because often when the boy with the hat came down to check on her and maybe change the bucket – nothing so identifiable as breakfast – the voice of the smiler would call out to him to hurry up. And if the boy with the hat *were* around during the day for some reason, she would soon know about it, because he couldn't stop coming down to the cellar to look at her and, sometimes, after his fashion, talk to her.

More problematic was knowing what the weasel one was up to. He didn't leave with the van. Often she knew he was still in the house because she could pick out the thump-thump vibration of amplified music, but at other times there was quiet and she could only doubt and wonder. The sound of the front door should have been a help to her here, but was not: somehow it didn't carry, somehow she couldn't pick it out from the other door noises. And though the weasel one occasionally came down the cellar steps, there was no sign that when he did this he was checking on her before going out. Nothing like that. He just stood there and stared. He stared as if he hated her. He stared as if she had done something to him.

She hadn't, but would do given the chance, as she would to all three of them: but that was moon talk. Moon talk was the term her new metaphorical mind had coined for anything that referred to a future, a future different from this, a future which did not include the cellar and the fan heater and the bar and the pool table and the dartboard and the mousetrap. (Never mind the possessions of her own that the smiler had placed about the room. They were not here. After the first anguish of seeing those familiar and well-loved things, raped just as her body had been raped, Alison had deliberately shut them out. Her eye might fall on them, but she would not see them.) Moon talk could be beautiful, too beautiful: beauty had no place here. Away with moon talk.

The thump of music was all she had to go on, really, as far as the weasel one was concerned. But she thought it was a pretty fair bet. From what the smiler said about him, and from what she had seen of him, she reckoned that the weasel one was the type who would always have music blaring out if he was alone in the house. And so when the van had coughed and throbbed and the traffic settled to its mid-morning rhythm and there was no music to be heard, Alison tapped.

She tapped on the wall beside her bed. Tapped slowly, insistently, repetitively. Not loudly – you couldn't tap loudly on a thick wall with a teaspoon no matter how hard you tried. Never mind. She was relying on insistence and repetition. She knew enough about the acoustics of this place by now to know that the spectacular stuff didn't pay off. There had never been any point in screaming: that was plain from the way they let her do it. The smiler even seemed to enjoy it under certain circumstances. It was like the weasel one's music: only the bass carried. The higher frequencies just didn't penetrate.

There were certain activities that Alison thought of as fence activities. Repeating them every day helped to construct a fence against insanity. One of these was running her tongue very slowly around her teeth, registering the unique shape of each one, giving a delicate attentiveness to that little sharp edge, that awkward filling, that slightly receded gum. It took her a good while: it was a task requiring at least as much concentration and effort as, say, doing a pile of ironing. And it had reassurance in it, reassurance of identity: these were Alison Holdenby's teeth just as they had been before the catastrophe. But above all the exploration of her teeth with her tongue was a fence activity, like the rhythmic counting of the links in her chains, like the list of world capitals she was compiling in her head and placing in alphabetical order. The smiler had brought her books along with her other possessions and placed them in piles over the other side of the room, out of her reach, and he had promised her them when she was 'good' – but she didn't trust that, didn't trust either the promise or the longing that the sight of the books evoked in her, because to read in here, to read under the reptiles' power would be to defile reading, destroy it for ever. No, she would stick to her own fence activities; they were good and they worked, for she felt reasonably certain that insanity was a fair distance away yet. But the tapping, now – that was different. It was a fence activity but it also had another function. Alison allowed herself to dare to hope that something might just possibly come of the tapping. Her sensitized hearing had picked up sounds on the other side of that wall.

Tiny sounds: again, sounds that her old pre-prison ears would hardly have picked up. Difficult, too, to separate from those countless stirrings on the edge of audibility that occurred when you pressed your ear to any wall: difficult to disentangle from the aural texture that every occupied place had. And she was so cautious, so fearful of what an unfounded hope might do to her mind if she let it in, that Alison clung to doubt almost longer than she needed. A devil's advocate within her poured scorn on the tiny sounds – plumbing, he blustered, plumbing, nothing more nor less than the noises of plumbing transmitting themselves through the wall – until at last he destroyed his own case. Alison knew the noises of plumbing: she had already picked that particular thread from the infinitely fine web of sound that surrounded her. This was not plumbing. The tiny sounds, irregular, fleeting, indistinct, obscure and incommunicative as they were, still indicated one thing and one thing only: human presence on the other side of that wall.

And so she tapped, steadily and rhythmically. She elected not to speculate about the human presence on the other side of that wall, because that was moon talk. Nor did she go much beyond a deduction that there was an adjoining cellar and hence an adjoining house. It was too easy to fall into wild dreams of salvation that would by sheer contrast make the reality literally intolerable. No. Best just to tap. Every day, as soon as she was reasonably certain the reptiles were all out, get tapping. Left ear against the damp plaster, left hand gripping the teaspoon and, with an awkward backward motion that was all she could manage with her shackled wrist but which was now as natural to her as breathing, keep tapping. And listening.

Alison Holdenby, nineteen years old, thin and pale, developing a breathing complaint from stale air, with sores on her buttocks and scabs on her wrists, and with so many bruises on her body that she only feels the freshest and blackest of them: Alison Holdenby, her mind grappling, with the determined intensity of some great general's, at her survival strategies: Alison Holdenby, tapping on the wall of her prison with a teaspoon, and unable to resist the return of the imp of self-pity.

Yes: here he is again. And what is his sighing little message?

You should have made more friends.

She hates to give the imp anything, but she has to admit the truth of that.

She should have made more friends when she came down here from Tyneside. Friends noticed your absence. Friends knew where you were headed on the night you disappeared. Hell, friends came with you to wherever you were going.

But she hadn't bothered with friends. What did she need friends for? She had Martin. But even if this had not happened, she saw that time would soon have shown her the speciousness of that argument. In fact, hadn't it been proved to her even before the reptiles came on the scene? Why had she continued to shop at that corner store, even though her money would have gone so much further at the supermarket, if not because the shopkeeper always said hello to her?

Why else, indeed, would she have been so pleased when the three guys started talking to her at the Arena that night?

You needed friends. And not just as an insurance against love's young dream turning sour: you wouldn't keep friends for long if that was all you wanted them for. Even if everything had turned out all right for her and Martin, she saw now that there should have been friends too. And maybe that very lack had played a part in splitting them up, at least indirectly. She had invested too much in Martin. She had made him her world. Marooned herself naked on the island of Martin, out of sight of land. No wonder that she had begun to find the island too small, too bare, too monotonous. Wanted to get off.

Foolish. But the *if onlys* could only do so much. She might have found friends and a job and a nice place to live in this city and still ended up drifting away from

Martin. Even if she had not set him the impossible task of being everything in the world to her, the irritations would have been there. The private jokes that just became wearisome after the nth repetition. The fecklessness that meant he was in debt even when he was working and the arrogance that assumed there was something amusing and charming about this. The fits of moroseness when he would conjure a quarrel out of nothing. She could see these things clearly and steadily now, and she probably saw them only slightly less clearly and steadily at the time.

She could see the good times too, nonetheless. She remembered the two of them going to an early picture show – *Manon des Sources* no less, good grief – and afterwards buying a bottle of ginger wine and some sausage rolls and taking them back to his flat. Hot August evening. Ginger wine, at the height of summer? And sausage rolls? Sure, why not? Ginger wine and sausage rolls, and motes dancing in the light of a hot bedroom. She could see these things, very clearly.

And she felt guilty. Without knowing why, she felt guilty and bad and afraid at these good memories. Alison could feel her worst bruises, she could feel the shrinking soreness between her thighs, she could feel the bronchial harshness of her breathing, but she was not aware of the marks that her ordeal had already placed on her mind. All she knew was that thinking of good times gave her a feeling of unworthiness, a feeling that she didn't deserve them, that they were not for her: she did not know that this too was a thing that had been done to her.

Alison Holdenby, tapping, tapping, sensing with an animal's prescience that outside the sun was sinking and the afternoon waning and knowing that, in more ways than one, her time was running out.

She had to pee. She usually tried to postpone this as long as possible, so as not to have the smell in the room with her all day. Partly for the same reason, partly from bad diet and lowered physical condition, she was almost permanently constipated. Peeing hurt: touch of cystitis there too. The boy with the hat had forgotten again to leave toilet paper, so she couldn't blot herself, but then she was so sore down there it hardly mattered.

She had another strategy for dealing with what the smiler had finally done to her, and done several times over the past few days. She had blanked out that part of herself much as she had blanked out the pieces of her home that he had arranged around the cellar. Like them, that part of herself had been brought here, disposed as he wanted it, used, and violated. And probably destroyed – she certainly couldn't envisage any time when that part of herself would be normal again, just as she couldn't envisage ever touching her old teddy bear that he had placed on the bar. So, she cut herself off from it: didn't acknowledge it. Like her favourite old poster that she could see now out of the corner of her eye yet couldn't see, it simply wasn't here. Survival was about reduction. Paring yourself down. She had not seen herself in a mirror since she had been brought here, and if she had it would have been more than her gauntness and pallor that would have startled her. Her sheer physical presence would have been a shock. She thought of herself as little more than a single bright spark of disembodied will.

Alison heaved herself back on to the bed, tugging up her jeans one-handed as she did so – another action that would once have seemed impossibly awkward but which now she performed without being aware of it. But today her co-ordination must have been a little off, maybe because the cystitis had made peeing a long business and cramped her. She had set the teaspoon down on the pillow before shucking down her jeans, and now when she put out her left hand to retrieve it she was clumsy. It slid off the pillow and disappeared down the narrow crack between the bed and the wall.

For some moments all she could do was gasp in disbelief. Then a great heartbroken wail escaped her before she could stop it and went on and on. One of her strategies had been to save her energy by never crying out at anything any more but the loss of the teaspoon, pure, sudden and desolating, blew a hole in the dam.

She stopped, at last, by cramming her fist in her mouth. Her own noise had disturbed her: it was as if there were someone else in here, someone wild and frightening. In the renewal of silence she found she could think, and she permitted herself to suck her thumb for a bit while she did so.

The teaspoon wasn't lost, not necessarily. It had fallen down the side of the bed, probably to the floor, but it might just have got caught up in the blanket. That could be reached easily, even with the handcuffs.

Try that first.

She moved her hand carefully and slowly, afraid of snatching and sending the teaspoon skittering further away. The gap between the mattress and the wall was narrow, but because there was give in the mattress she was able to avoid scraping her knuckles along the plaster. Slowly, now. Feel all round the folds of the blanket. There—

She had given a little moan of relief before she realized that the cold metal she had touched was the iron frame of the bed. Still, she summoned up more control from somewhere and explored again. The spoon might have slipped further along, halfway along the length of the bed maybe...

Sure. Sure it had. Its name was Tommy Teaspoon and it wriggled around like a fucking fish.

Crying was something she had not done for a long time either. The smiler had a thing about seeing her cry and so she had ruled out crying even when she was alone. But now she cried for the teaspoon until again she had to cram her fist in her mouth because that noise too was frightening. That wild crazy person was back in the cellar with her and she didn't like it.

Then almost without conscious volition Alison was sitting up and shuffling backwards on her behind till she was sitting on the pillow right at the head of the bed. Her mind caught up with her body and saw what she was trying to do. She couldn't have done it if the bed had been right in the corner of the room, but it wasn't: there was about two feet of clearance between the head of the bed and the wall behind it.

Buttocks balanced, then, on the head of the bed, right on the iron frame. Couldn't have done it if there was a headboard likewise, but no headboard, so there. Knees crooked and feet digging for purchase on the blanket. Back tensed and straight. Hands gripping the sides of the mattress. Now, lean backwards, backwards, slowly and stiffly. Don't let the spine curve, don't let the shoulders sag because there'll be too much body weight over the end of the bed and then you'll fall, fall with your chin driven into your chest, neck broken and arms pulled out of their sockets by the cuffs, just *incline* like a board until...

The back of her head touched the wall behind her. She

waited a moment and then, keeping her trunk absolutely stiff and straight, inched her buttocks forward so that her head slid, juddering, further down the wall. She inched until the muscles of her neck seemed to be snapping with the strain and then, carefully so as not to upset her balance, shifted her left hand, bringing it over the end of the bed, the cuff attached to the iron leg clanking as it turned round.

Reached down. The length of the chain was enough, from this angle, to allow her hand to touch the floor under the bed, even to creep round like a spider and explore ... It was the rest of the body that was the problem. It was twanging and juddering with the strain, pain of the underused muscles just too much, too much, and she couldn't turn her head to give her exploring hand any visual help, and the hand just wouldn't go very far under the bed, not physically possible—

No, wait, got it, Jesus, got it got it. Got it by the sharp end. Well, not sharp, but sort of pointed, it was an old-fashioned teaspoon where the handle was a kind of leaf design, got it anyway, dear teaspoon come to me ...

She grasped the teaspoon and brought her hand up, clenching it, and then her head slipped and juddered down the wall another few inches and she could feel her balance going and her right hand gripping the edge of the mattress wasn't enough to pull her up and neither hand would reach to the wall behind her to push against it—

Move.

It was a complex logistical exercise and required lightning assessments of strengths and balances and it took two seconds. She tossed the teaspoon in her mouth and splayed and braced her legs exactly like a limbo dancer and hauled herself up through eighty degrees simply through one screaming effort of the dorsal muscles and her hands scrabbling at the edges of the mattress nails breaking made up the other ten degrees and then muscles and willpower she didn't know she had squirmed her forward on the bed until she slumped, grunting reassurance to herself and seeing red spots dancing behind the closed lids of her eyes.

When she opened them the first thing she saw was the handle of the teaspoon, jutting jauntily between her lips. She squinted at it a moment, then took it out and shook it and studied the bowl end.

'Temperature hundred and two,' she said, and then she was laughing and weeping all at the same time.

But the laughing was part of the weeping and soon it was swallowed up by it. And when the weeping too was done Alison sat up and stared at the wall beside her and then at the spoon still clasped in her hand and it was as if something fragile were torn right across.

Tapping. Tapping on the wall with a teaspoon. A ring of ghostly faces stretched in astonishment seemed to gather round her. What's she doing? *Tapping?* Tapping on the wall with a *teaspoon?*

There had to be something better.

Well, there was something. Maybe not better, but something different. It was a thought that she had been squirrelling away in the back of her mind just as she squirrelled the teaspoon away in the mattress at the end of each day. She didn't know whether the thought had any chance of success if acted upon: it might conceivably make things worse. But that wasn't the problem. The problem was, she didn't know if she could do it.

Now, she told herself, let's think about this. OK, thumb

in mouth then, just for a little while, not too long in case it makes you go away. Think. Get to the root of this problem, because maybe this business of the tapping has just been an excuse not to dig down there amongst the dirt.

She thought, and tried to make herself into a mere thinking machine as she did so, just a ticking whirring brain. No body. No aching breasts and ticklish fiery soreness between her legs. Those things were here but they were not here.

Just a brain addressing itself to a question, and not a moral or ethical or philosophical one. Just an intellectual enquiry, thus. Something had been done repeatedly to her against her will. She had not been able to resist it, though she had tried with all her might. Nothing could be the same in her life after this had been inflicted on her. Therefore, did it make any difference if she deliberately submitted to the same act from a different person? *Feel sick. Ignore it. Think.* No, not deliberately submit – pretend to submit. Give the impression of submitting, in order to achieve an ulterior end. Give the impression that this is a voluntary act, freely chosen.

But then wouldn't that make it a voluntary act? If it was not forced upon her, was it not then undertaken out of free choice?

Alison pulled her thumb from her mouth and gave herself a cuff on the cheek. The thinking machine was getting out of control. For Christ's sake, there had been no voluntary acts since the moment they had hustled her into that van. She had just caught herself on the edge of the most dangerous thinking of all. She had just stopped herself taking on her shoulders some of the responsibility for what had happened since that moment.

The truth of it was that *everything* now was forced on her. If what she was contemplating was collaboration, then the collaboration too was forced on her. She had options, but the options were not her choosing any more than the cuffs and the bucket to pee in.

The option involved the boy with the hat, and if she were going to follow it through she was going to have to stop thinking of him in those terms. Sean. That was his name. There: let the name into her head. It was defilement, but her world was defilement now and all that mattered was utility or otherwise.

Sean. She had suspected from the start that if there was any possibility of exerting some sort of human influence over her captors, any chance at all of a little leverage, then it lay with Sean. Sean was stupid. He was so stupid that sometimes he forgot that what was happening in the cellar was an unthinkable outrage and spoke to her just like a fellow human being.

For a time it had seemed one of the most unbearable aspects of the nightmare: the fact that the boy with the hat – no, Sean – would remark on the weather whilst he took away the food tray of the innocent person he had helped to kidnap, imprison and torture. 'Tell you what, it's bloody colder than ever today, I can't believe it.' Like that. Conversational.

'All right?' too. Brightly, like you would say it to someone at a party as you went through to answer the door to more guests. 'All right?' Like you would say to someone who couldn't possibly be anything other than all right.

Perhaps he even thought she was. Perhaps he was that stupid. The smiler was different. When the smiler said, 'Well, now, this looks nice and cosy,' you knew and he knew that pain and humiliation would follow. But the wires in Sean's head were crossed in quite another way. What she was going through probably didn't even occur to him.

Whether she could get him to understand it, pity it, and make it stop was another matter. The way he obediently carted away the slops or washed her down whilst the smiler stood by watching was evidence enough of Sean's slavish submission: he did what the smiler wanted, no questions asked. But more than that, she doubted whether there was any sort of conscience worth talking about underneath all that stupidity.

Nor even self-preservation. She had considered trying to work on Sean with dire whispers of what would happen to him when he was found out, but it had been swiftly borne in on her that his stupidity insulated him from such considerations. His trust in the smiler was absolute. Nothing would happen to them because the smiler said so.

The trust was matched by fear: she could see it in Sean's eyes when the smiler was around. He was scared of his mentor. And that closed off another avenue. If there were only Sean, she might well have come up with some reason that would convince him he should let her go. Nothing to do with right and wrong: just something commensurate with his stupidity. He might have let her go for a dentist's appointment, as long as she promised to come back. Or, just let her go. Why not? Just for the crack. No worries. Something like that. She suspected his mind was that flimsy.

But there was the smiler and the fear of the smiler and that meant appeals to Sean's better nature or his fear or his sheer stupidity were non-starters. No, there was only one way through to Sean. It would mean capitalizing on his tendency to see her as a human being, and as a girl. It would mean befriending him and seducing him.

Feel sick feel sick no no you don't feel sick it's nothing that part of you's been disconnected anyway disconnected not part of yourself any more so use it use it . . .

OK.

Alison took a deep breath, made a circuit of her mind, checked the fence. All intact.

OK. She had acknowledged the thought, dealt with it. Could handle it. Now, follow it up.

There was no question of a trade, of course. The same reasons applied. She could let Sean do what he wanted – and she had no doubt from the way he looked at her and the way he touched her when he washed her – but that still didn't mean he was going to put her on the first bus home when he had finished. The fear would remain.

Yes, the fear would remain: good. What might Sean not do, if she pressed that fear?

Let him do it, then threaten to tell. The smiler had exclusive rights in her – he had said as much. He wouldn't take kindly to his subordinate poaching on his preserves.

Now let me go, Sean. Let me out of here, or I'll tell Chill what you did.

Shit, shit, man, all right I'll let you go, just don't tell him . . .

Alison gently fingered her lip where it had been bitten, her other hand meanwhile resuming the mechanical tapping with the teaspoon.

Well. It was a sweet scenario all right. Perhaps just a little too sweet. It depended on the paradox of Sean's conquering that fear in the first place.

It wouldn't wash. Not on its own, anyhow. Bribe and blackmail were doubtful propositions with this particular jailer, which was maybe why the smiler had chosen him. And yet... and yet...

Jailer. That was what was causing the gleam in her mind's eye, and that was why she wouldn't let the idea drop.

Jailer.

Keys.

There was a bunch of them on Sean's belt. The smiler had a set too, though he kept them out of sight. Her cuffs were opened by a key, a little brass key: she had seen it. They released her from them occasionally, now that the smiler had stolen her things from her flat, to give her a change of clothes; but only when the three of them were present, hulking round her, ready to slap her down if she tried anything. She had never been free of the cuffs when there was only one of them in the room. When the smiler came down here to amuse himself he kept them locked and seemed to like it that way.

She was unable to fight them because of the handcuffs and she was unable to unlock the handcuffs because she couldn't fight them to get hold of the keys...

But there were always embraces.

Alison kept up the tapping. She kept her ear pressed to the wall. But when the tiny noises came she hardly took any notice of them. Her mind was otherwise engaged. It was preparing itself. Her mind was like a fighter before the big match of his career, shadow-boxing, dancing on his toes, pumping himself up. And when she heard the cough and throb of the van drawing up, that was the bell.

She stowed the teaspoon in its hiding place, sat up against the pillow, scrubbed at the tear marks on her cheeks. Fixed her eyes on the cellar steps.

Voices in the hall. The smiler's, and Sean's. Then the smiler's, raised.

'Trend!'

Pause, and then again: 'Trend!'

No answer. Only two of them in the house: all the better, if it worked. No, no, that was moon talk, dangerous. One thing at a time.

Sudden opening of the door to the cellar. She tensed.

'Evening, princess!'

Oh God not him. Not the smiler. She had worked herself up for the Sean plan, it was always Sean who checked on her when they got home, she had it all ready, it—

Wait. The smiler wasn't coming down. The door was closing again and his voice was calling down the passage.

'Phoo, bucket wants emptying, Sean. Be a treasure and go and clean up, will you? What do you fancy tonight, chips . . .?'

Alison let out a pent-up breath. Should have known. The smiler wouldn't come near her unless she was clean. He was fussy like that. Always used a condom too, though he wasn't so fussy about what he did with it afterwards—

No no don't think of that now cut it off blank it out just a brain just a thinking planning cunning brain . . .

OK. It would be the usual pattern. Sean coming down to do the dirty work. Maybe she could mention that, as a lead-in. Always the dirty work, Sean, and nothing to show for it, not fair, is it . . .? She mustn't be too obvious, though. She had hardly exchanged a word with him before now except curses.

The cellar door opened again and Sean came down the steps, springy in his DMs. He was humming under his breath and hurrying. He was like a black manservant in some old racist movie. Ise a-comin', massa. Feets, do yo' stuff. His eagerness repelled Alison. Suddenly she felt she couldn't do it.

'All right?'

After a moment she nodded. And then, huskily: 'No toilet paper.'

'Ah, shit. Always forget about that.'

He had a cold outside smell about him, masking his usual staleness. The smell filled Alison with visions of the outside world, of streets, cars, trees, people who were normal. Sky.

Enough. Moon talk.

She watched him pick up the bucket, and found herself saying, 'Could do with a lid on that.'

'Eh?'

Her lips were dry: she tried to lick them, though her tongue was no wetter. 'That bucket. Be easier for you if there was a lid on it.'

He stared at her in fascination for some moments. 'Yeah,' he said. 'Yeah, it would. Didn't think of that. I reckon they've got them on the market. Pete Marr's stall, right, he's got all this stuff, you know, like brushes and them things you clean the floor with . . .?'

'Squeegee mops.'

'Thassit.'

The thing above all was not to let the insanity of this get to her. To discuss the instruments of her torture with her jailer as casually as if she were chatting with her hairdresser was insanity all right, but insanity was the rule now, and not to recognize that was to fall apart.

'Yeah. That's an idea. I'll have to see about getting one of them. I'll have to ask Chill about that.'

'Do you always have to ask Chill about everything?'
'Eh?'
'Chill. Do you have to do everything he says?'
'Nah.' He chuckled vaguely on his way out. Doubtful whether he had even registered the remark yet. Like some stegosaurus or brontosaurus or whatever: tread on its tail and it didn't yelp till five minutes later.

The hatred that washed over her was an encumbrance, and she shook it off. She waited, pumping, shadow-boxing.

When he came back it was with a clean bucket and a tray: doorstep sandwiches, a can of Coke. She shook off another encumbrance – the recognition that this stuff was keeping her alive. She had had some bad times with that recognition, times when self-loathing had carried her anguish to new limits, for didn't she have the choice of simply not eating, and didn't it show that she was a very bad person, not taking that choice? They might have force-fed her, but she doubted that that was a very easy thing to do. No, there was a way out there, but she hadn't taken it, and that showed—

Bullshit.

What came to her aid in shaking that thought off, now as before, was a voice she couldn't give a name to, but which she felt was the voice of the person she might have been and might yet be. Confident, in control, balanced, unlikely to cock things up, making the most of her strengths and dealing with her weaknesses. It was that voice that squared up to the death wish and hit it right out of the park. *Why haven't I made that choice?* it said. *Because I want my life back and I'm going to have it.*

'Thanks.' She took the tray from him and balanced it on her knees. The sandwiches were of tinned ham, hacked any old how and slapped together, jelly seeping out. A child's sandwiches. She looked up at him and he looked back. A pink, unfinished face, no more bone than the Pillsbury doughboy. Sort of face you drew with your finger on a misted window. What was going on in there? All minds were closed books but most had a cover that gave you an idea of the contents. Not these, though.

'Do you want one of these, Sean?'

The way he looked at the proffered sandwiches was just as if she had made them. *Insanity, sure. Just don't let it get to you.*

'Cheers.' He took one and was already chomping into it as he turned away.

'Sean!'

'Eh?'

She looked into the pale blue nothingy eyes, searching.

'Thanks.'

'S'all right.'

'You have to do all the dirty work, don't you?'

'Tss-yeah.' The vague chuckle again.

With difficulty she put the tray down, one-handed, on the floor. Her rug was there, her dear old rug that she had chosen and loved and seen every day back when the world was real, but she blanked it out.

'Sean, I really need a friend.'

Suddenly there was expression on the schematic face. Schoolboy who hadn't been listening, called upon by teacher.

'Need wha'?'

A drink God, I need a drink. Reassurance in that thought, actually: she must be surviving, to be able to think it.

'You know. Just to talk and that. I get lonely. And

you're always doing my dirty work and you don't get any thanks for it.'

The words were crap. Crap on her tongue. But they were tailored for him and that was OK.

'Nah. No problem.'

'Can't you just stay a minute? Can't you sit down? I just need a friend. Need someone to be near me.'

Bad choice of words: he had cocked his head. Like most dull brains, his was supernaturally alert to innuendo. He was thinking of the times when the smiler came down here to amuse himself. He knew what went on at those times. It was plain from his look. And in the look, the fear.

Keep the smiler out of it. Make him forget the smiler.

'I just want to talk sometimes,' she said. 'I haven't got anyone to talk to. I get lonely.'

'What do you want to talk about?' Puzzled.

'Anything. You, if you like. I don't really know you.' That fresh outdoors smell was wearing off now and his own unwashed-little-boy smell was coming back. 'Like, what have you been doing today?'

'Helping on the stall.'

'What do you sell?'

'Clothes.'

She experienced a spasm of incredible pain: something to do with the realization that she had probably walked past that very stall at some time. Back in her old life. *Oh Jesus can't go on—*

'Must be cold work.'

'Freezing, man. Bloody freezing.' Suddenly there was animation. 'You know, you wear like the mittens, you know, with the fingers cut off, yeah? Tell you, they don't keep you warm. It's because they don't cover your fingers, right, and they're the bits that get cold. Not kidding you, you can't move them sometimes.'

While he burbled she had shifted up on the bed and now she patted the space she had made. Just casually. Like you would make room on a settee.

'Sit down a minute.'

Sean sat.

'Can't stay long. There's Chill—'

'Why, what's Chill doing?'

'Dunno, making the tea I think. But—'

'Well, then. Like I say, you don't have to do everything he says.' Deliberate move now: make him face it. 'Do you?'

'Nah.'

'And you *do* do all the work, so it's only fair.'

'What is?'

'You know. Being with me for a while.'

Now he was shaking his head and starting to get up. 'Nah. Nah.'

'What, don't you want to be with me?' She risked a hand on his skinny back, staying him.

'Nah. Dunno. 'S'not up to me. It's Chill—'

'Why, you're not scared of Chill, are you?'

' 'Cking hell, man, you don't know Chill!' Exaggerated head-shakings. 'You don't know what he's like, shit, man, you don't know him!'

Of course I know what he's like, you cretin. Don't you think I've learned that when he comes down here?

'He's not such a big bloke.' She kept her hand on his back.

'He doesn't need to be. He's just . . . he's hard. I mean really. And some of the nutters he knows . . . You cross Chill, man, you're in big trouble. There was this guy ripped him off once. Thought he'd got away with it. No way. Chill hunted him down, really patient, really cool. Shit. You should have seen this guy afterwards, man... That's what Chill's like. That's how he is.'

It was weird. The fear was still there in Sean's voice and face, but it was partnered by admiration. He was in awe of a psychotic. It told her much about Sean, though nothing comforting.

But she could see the keys. The key-ring was attached to one of the denim loops that held his belt. Memory of how hard those key-rings could be to open... it was always a pain when you had to put a new key on...

'But Chill's your mate.'

'Tss-yeah.' Chuffed about that: even, God help him, honoured. But an awkwardness was coming over him as his stegosaurus brain registered the fact that she was slowly caressing his back.

'Well. We can be mates, too, can't we, Sean? Come on.'

'I dunno... not unless Chill says so...'

She began nuzzling against his neck. She had once cleaned pub toilets and this could be no worse.

'Just stay a little while, Sean...'

He was trembling and sweating: paralysed. Her fingers touched his hip and then, as gently as if she were handling the petals of a flower, closed around the key-ring.

'You've always been good to me...'

Her mind raced ahead, too fast. Get the keys off, stow them under the pillow maybe and then wait till he was gone, he wouldn't notice they were missing—

Clink.

'Here!' He spun round, then jumped up as if stung. A wall seemed to collapse on to Alison's head.

'Sean—'

'Here, I know your game!' He checked the keys, then took a step backward, shaking his head. ''Cking hell, man! You must think I'm stupid!'

It was her turn to sweat and tremble. But she saw then that he was smiling. He was wagging his finger at her and grinning as if the whole thing were a great joke.

'You little bugger. You nearly had me there. You little devil.'

The wall had collapsed on top of her but Alison found she wasn't badly hurt. His stupidity was her salvation. Her attempt to seduce him so as to distract his attention and get the keys and free herself and run for it and bring the police crashing in on him with six-foot truncheons – all this had produced a reaction in him rather as if she had tried to pinch the last piece of chocolate or slip an ice-cube down his neck. So the only thing to do was play along.

'Sorry,' she said, manufacturing a grin. 'Worth a try.'

Sean shook his head, bashfully complacent, as if to say you had to get up pretty early in the morning to catch *him* out. 'Little devil,' he said. 'Have to watch you.'

'We're still friends, aren't we?'

'Tss-yeah.'

She felt something like a blow to the stomach as she realized that only he would see it this way.

'Sean – you won't tell Chill, will you?'

He shrugged and raised his eyebrows, still enjoying himself.

'Please.' She kept her voice teasing, though her heart hammered. 'Pretty please.'

'Go on then. Let you off. I'm going to my tea. See you.'

He was still chuckling as he galumphed up the steps.

Could she believe him? She thought she probably could, at least while the enjoyment of the joke was still on him. Schoolboy secrets.

But all the preparation had been for nothing and she didn't know what damage she had done to the possibilities of a next time. She had rushed it, telescoped it. Should have won him over gradually, postponed the grab for the keys.

She lay back, staring up at the grey cracked ceiling. Her Mappa Mundi. The sandwiches on the tray were curling but she didn't want them.

See? It's no good.

The imp of self-pity was back. She listened to him for a while.

Grabbing the keys, indeed. As if he's going to go into some magical Sleeping Beauty trance while you take them from him. It's no good, none of it's any good. They've got you. You can't run.

It struck her that there was probably literal truth in that. She had been in here for something over a fortnight now – she couldn't be sure of the exact number of days, because time had been beyond her at first – and all that time she had been chained to the bed. She recalled being confined to bed with a childhood illness for two weeks, and how weak and uncertain her legs had been when she had got up. If she ever got these cuffs off, she would be lurching around like a stage drunk.

There. You see. It's no good. They've got everything worked out and you're helpless . . .

But she wasn't listening to the imp any more. She was raising her legs from the bed, stretching them and tensing them, bicycling them.

And all this Jane Fonda workout business is no good either. You're wasting your time. You're...

Shuffling herself sideways on the bed as far as the chains would allow, Alison placed the soles of her feet on the wall. Then she began pushing each one alternately against the wall as if she were running on the spot. It was difficult to get a purchase because she had only tights on her feet: they denied her shoes, presumably because shoes meant effective kicking. But that was OK. It meant her leg muscles had to work harder. She could feel them straining.

It was good. It kept the imp noticeably quiet and it would surely help her towards a proper sleep rather than the feverish driftings in and out of oblivion that were all she could manage now. But this was no fence activity. It had an aim.

At last she stopped and rested, feeling cool sweat all over her body. She drank the Coke and then, after a fractional hesitation in which the smell of Sean's neck and the feel of his scrawny hip returned to her like a bad dream, she ate the sandwiches. This too had an aim.

Doesn't matter how strong you are you'll never beat them...

The imp was still around and to silence him she took the teaspoon out of its niche in the mattress and looked at it. Memory of a little triumph – retrieving the teaspoon when it had seemed lost. She relived it and as she did so she grasped at a detail.

Sharp end.

She studied the handle of the teaspoon afresh. Yes, a sort of stylized leaf shape with a little engraved pattern along the edge. To call it sharp was an exaggeration, of course. It wasn't even as sharp as a blunt pencil or a wax crayon or even a palette knife.

But it did come to a point, and points could be sharpened.

Embraces alone were not enough.

She transferred the spoon to her left hand, the tapping position, and began rubbing the pointed handle against the wall.

After ten minutes she had a little shower of plaster dust and a mark on the wall.

You see. You see . . .

'Up yours,' Alison said.

She shifted her position once more, transferring the spoon to her right hand. She reached down over the right side of the bed until the handle of the spoon touched the floor.

Soft: her rug.

Remember how you used to sit on that rug and read in the autumn afternoons with the sun low and the distant noise of kids coming out of school and it was so peaceful . . .

'Up yours again,' she grunted. She flicked back the edge of the rug. Began rubbing the pointed end of the spoon against the cement floor. It grated satisfyingly. Memory of her grandma attacking a mark on the skirting board, rubbing away with superhuman patience. 'You can work at a stain,' she would say. Rubbing, rubbing.

Would the reptiles hear this? Surely not. The sound wouldn't carry, not like the tapping. And the rug would cover the mark.

OK. Tappings for when they were out, rubbing for when they were in. Not to mention the leg exercises, and then of course there was the counting of the chain-links and all those stupid capitals to be put in alphabetical order... My goodness, life was just so *busy*...

Alison Holdenby, grinding a teaspoon against the floor of her prison as if her life depended on it and aware somewhere within her fenced, divided, and tormented mind that it very probably did.

2

Friday morning, the day after the Arena disco, saw Sarah setting out for work in a state of pure excited anticipation that she had not known since she was a child.

Perhaps it shouldn't have been pure. Part of being an adult was the recognition that nothing ever was: you couldn't leap into cleanness without leaving something behind on the bank. In this case, what was left behind was Murray.

He had come to the Arena at the end of the evening to meet her and go home with her: a piece of typical thoughtfulness, knowing that the occasion was fraught with meaning for her. Being Murray likewise, he hadn't intruded questions on her, and she hadn't volunteered anything, not yet. The possibilities opened up by the fact of those photographs were too exciting, she had to save her good news up for a triumphant presentation later. So, home to her place, where she had been hungry for him. And then, relaxing on his shoulder in the small hours, she had told.

Murray was a phlegmatic man and he had been tired. The distinct lack of enthusiasm in his murmured responses was no more than partially significant. What settled it was his silence when they composed themselves for sleep. Sarah knew about bed-silences. There was the silence that meant he was nodding off to sleep. There was the silence that meant he was in a state of dreamy contemplation and might suddenly come up with some tangential remark that would set them both off laughing. And there was the silence that meant he was wide awake and thinking.

That was the silence that had radiated from his side of the bed last night. And the thoughts were not happy thoughts. She had felt them like a cold draught.

He didn't let them out in the morning. That wasn't Murray's style either. The kiss and the goodbye were fond and they were quite normal with each other and it was plain as the day that not only did he not share her excitement about the photographs but he was actively disturbed by it.

Before this thing had happened to her, she would have said, if asked what her feelings for Murray were, that she loved him. And her feelings hadn't changed. But other things had. It was a measure of how much, that she drove off to work in that state of pure excitement. No nagging worry that the person she loved might be becoming deeply alienated by her. The smell of rot setting in didn't reach her because she was breathing different air.

David, her producer seemed to notice something different about her today. The summons to his office that came when she arrived at Tudor was probably, she thought, a summons to a dressing-down, or something as near to it as David's mildness could manage. Sarah Winter the radio personality, just like Sarah Winter the human being, had not been herself lately: those repeated appeals to the girl at the Arena were not scheduled and they were off-putting for listeners; she knew that. But she came into the office so breezy that David did not so much drop it as fail to pick it up at all. Instead he asked her how the

Arena show had gone down and, riding her luck, she plugged it for all it was worth and more. A lobby display: it was crying out for a lobby display, and as a matter of fact she knew where she could get hold of some photographs . . .

The idea was sufficiently economical to appeal to the controller's parsimony, and David thought there was a chance. The dark circles under his eyes indicated that the rumour of his marital troubles might be well founded, but he seemed in brightened mood when she left him, as if her ebullience had rubbed off.

A chance, a chance. It was no more than that and she knew it, but knowing couldn't stop her palms turning damp with anxious hope every time she thought of the photos. All through the morning she was mentally revising the chance, lengthening or shortening the odds as her hope rose and fell. More than a hundred people at the Arena that night. Yes, but, young Dean was a camera nut: he had been clicking away like a maniac last night and apparently he had been doing the same a fortnight ago. Any number of faces must have appeared in the background of his shots. Besides, what about that famous photograph of a German crowd yelling their approval at the declaration of the First World War? There amongst the boaters and the walrus moustaches was the unmistakable face of the young Hitler. What were the chances of that?

She debated and debated, and tension made her feel as if she were a marionette on strings. But she did a good show, smooth and streamlined. The thing that was with her didn't get in the way, not this time. She was on the rails now, even if she were riding a mystery train.

At two o'clock she handed over to Motormouth Mark.

In the office she went through some scheduling memos with Rachel and had a convoluted phone dialogue with the press officer for a blockbuster author who had a country place ten miles away and who might or might not do a down-the-line for Tudor next week. The blockbuster author made much of her image as a down-to-earth lass who had done everything bar digging ditches with her bare hands before her rise to fame and who was, accordingly, unspoilt and approachable. The blockbuster author wanted a fee as well as the free publicity. Sarah did her best to explain that Tudor did not pay fees for d-t-l chats even to people who needed the money. The press officer said at last that she would have to get back to the blockbuster author, not seeming overwhelmed with delight at the prospect, and Sarah went out for some lunch.

She spun it out, having two more vodkas than she would normally have considered sensible, but still it was only half-past three when she rode the glass lift to the mezzanine and Tudor. Dean had said after school, and school let out at four. The vodkas had cut a few of the strings, but still the prospect of waiting, maybe for another hour, was like hard pain.

She found Dean waiting for her in the lobby.

'Free period,' he explained. 'You get plenty of those now. It's supposed to be for private study in the sixth-form block, but . . .'

His face shone with the bashful pleasure of his delinquency. Stiff in his school uniform, he held out a large brown envelope.

'One or two didn't come out very well, I think it was where the disco lights flared on the lens. There's fifty-five altogether, from last fortnight and last night. I've put the negatives in there as well. Is this where . . .?'

'This is it. See, we've only got this rather boring display of DJs' faces at the moment. Anyway, come through, come through . . .'

The impulse to tear open the envelope there and then must be conquered, and conquer it she did, taking Dean through to the office, making him tea, giving him a tour of the studio. He cast a keen but slightly disappointed eye over the technology: compared with TV, radio was chewing gum and string. And at last she sat down and opened the envelope and thumbed through the photographs.

Not looking at them: not really. Her true task was one she could only face alone. For now she had to put on a show, and she made it good. 'These are brilliant,' she said, running her eye unseeingly over the sheaf of colour prints. Which were last night's, which from a fortnight ago? Never mind. 'Really, these are exactly what I had in mind. Great stuff.' She owed it to Dean to keep it going, though her impatience was burning her up. 'Listen, how long can I keep them? I want to show them to my producer. Obviously these are your own prints, and if we used the pictures we could have them done from the negatives—'

'Keep them as long as you like. I've put my address on the back of the envelope there.'

'You sure? This is really good of you. I can't thank you enough . . .'

'It's OK.'

He was shy here, of course, shy in a way he had not been at the Arena with friends around him and a party atmosphere. But was there something else in his constraint? Was she, in other words, acting a little bit strangely over this simple matter? Calm down, don't gush, the photos will keep, she told herself.

And then Dean rescued her from deep-breathing silence. 'Can I ask you, do you know Mark Malone?'

'Sure, that's him on air now.' She shook a mock fist. 'Highest listening figures at the station, damn him.'

'Only my sister... she's fourteen. She's got this thing about him.'

'Aha.' Like most of the female pubescent population of the city.

'Yeah.' Dean couldn't grimace enough. 'She's mad about him, you know. And when I said I was coming down here today she said could I get his autograph, I mean I know it's daft and a cheek and everything but she made me promise to at least ask...'

'What's your sister's name?'

'Janine.' A world of sibling disgust was expressed in the way he said it.

This was something Sarah could do for him, at any rate. Slipping into Mark's studio during the four o'clock news, she got Tudor's resident heart-throb to inscribe 'To Janine, all the best, Mark Malone' on a six-by-eight glossy of himself. As might have been expected from a man who was good-looking, charming and hilariously funny, Mark was as gay as a picnic basket, but never mind: his audience would find out such hard facts of life for themselves soon enough.

'Oh, that's brilliant!' Dean's eyes lit up: Sarah saw that she was handing him a weapon that would win him a whole campaign of domestic battles. The object itself, of course, was a different matter, especially as he would have to carry it home, and she found him an envelope to hide it in. The balance had shifted again, and when she asked him to jot down his phone number so that she could get in touch with him at home Dean was all pleased red-faced awkwardness. She recalled the sexual mythology that had surrounded thirty-year-olds when she was his age. They were a byword for sophisticated bonking. The thought made her briefly sad. The turnaround was complete: now, at thirty, she looked on eighteen-year-olds as the ones who were enviably at it.

When Dean at last left, promising to give her regards to Lindsay and Sue and Steve, Sarah sat down at her desk and stared for some moments at the large brown envelope. Further postponement seemed impossible, yet the cloud of well-meaning hair that was Rachel was hovering at her elbow, and Sarah didn't know what her own reaction might be if the envelope contained only disappointment. She fought with herself, and then got up so abruptly that Rachel jumped backwards.

'I'm off home, Rachel. Bit of a headache. See you Monday.'

Rachel hesitated. 'Um . . . tomorrow . . .?'

Sarah was meant to be doing some recording for the arts omnibus tomorrow. Of course she was. She knew it at once, but it said much that she had needed reminding.

'Tomorrow, I mean. Dear. Don't know what day I'm on,' laughing it off.

She was home in seven minutes. The cats, prepared for a long stakeout of the fridge, looked as astonished as their coolness would allow when she thrust chunks of chicken at them. She turned on the gas fire in the living room, knelt close before it to drive out the bone-cold that resulted from even a few minutes outdoors this winter, and shook the photographs out of the envelope.

Good colour prints. Clear definition, no red eye, no decapitation. Dean had the equipment but it wasn't just that: some people could take pictures, and he could.

Lindsay and Sue and Steve. Lindsay and Sue and Steve. Damn, so many. Which were last night's, and which . . .? Cracked it: the youngsters had been dressed differently on the two occasions. She separated last night's, absently noting how awful, genuinely awful, she looked in the one featuring herself, and put them aside. Penny, obedient to the mysterious feline impulse, came along and sat on them. The rest of the photographs Sarah stacked in a pile, neatly, as neatly as if it mattered a great deal, and then studied them one by one.

A few minutes later, tears were running down Sarah's cheeks.

EIGHT

1

It just showed, Sarah thought, what an influence cop shows had on your perception of reality that she had been fully expecting Detective Sergeant Routh to say, 'This had better be good.' None of the other details of this situation fitted the popular image. Croft Wood police station looked more like a suite of admen's offices than the sweaty run-down nicks you saw on TV: no struggling crims had been dragged through cursing on their way to the cells: the room in which she waited entirely lacked plastic chairs and styrofoam cups with cigarettes stubbed out in them. And of course Routh himself had none of the glamour, or the inverted glamour that was sleaze, that a CID officer was supposed to have. And yet when he finally arrived, Sarah fully expected him to say 'This had better be good,' and was almost crestfallen when he did not.

But he was annoyed: that was plain. The way he said, 'Miss Winter, what can I do for you?' yanking back a chair with his foot as he did so, made it clear that Detective Sergeant Routh was extremely pissed off at her and, cliché or no cliché, it really *had* better be good.

'Thank you for seeing me,' she said. He grunted. He hadn't wanted to see her, and she knew it. She had had to run the gauntlet of a desk sergeant and a WPC and then finally DC Martindale, who was as robotically offensive in the flesh as his telephone manner suggested, before her insistence that she wanted to see Routh and Routh only had paid off; and even then she had only swung it by bandying the name of Tudor Radio in a manner she knew was ill advised. The three-quarters of an hour she had spent cooling her heels in this blank room of hessian and Formica might have been unavoidable, but she doubted it.

'It's about the girl I saw being abducted,' she said, and ignored his wince. 'I've got a photograph of her.'

She took the photograph from her handbag and laid it on the shiny surface of the table. When Routh placed a finger on it and drew it towards him she had to fight an absurd impulse to snatch it back. Brought up on the likes of *Rosemary's Baby*, she could not help picturing a conspiracy scenario – Routh destroying the photograph and then denying it ever existed, whilst at home a sinister figure slipped through a window and spirited away the negatives . . .

'How'd you get this?'

She told. She did not look at him, but kept her eyes on the photograph, as if it were the most wonderful thing in the world. Which it was, in fact, to her right now.

The photograph was of Dean's friend Sue. She was close to the crash-barrier at the Arena, caught in a pose that the camera made look impressively like speed skating but which was probably an out-of-control zoom with a pratfall at the end of it. Sue was laughing. She was the only skater in the frame except for a blurred shoulder in the left foreground. On the crash-barrier the letters ND HOMES were visible, part of an advertising hoarding. Above the crash-barrier the frame had caught three spectators. On the right a woman in spectacles, partially hidden by the figure of Sue, with a small boy beside her, his face blurred as he turned his head. On the left, the girl with red hair.

None other. Unmistakable.

She was leaning her forearms on the top of the crash-barrier: one hand was visible. Her head was half-turned to her left, presenting a three-quarter view of her face, but she didn't seem from the direction of her eyes to be looking at Sue. Instead her gaze appeared to be fixed on something further away, out of the frame: perhaps not in the Arena at all.

Dean's camera had accurately caught the rich dark auburn shade of her hair. Large eyes, refined nose, slightly indrawn uncommunicative mouth. The black coat she had been wearing. It was all there.

There was no exaggerating the effect the photograph had had on Sarah. When she had come across it – almost the last in the pile – the force of her emotion had not been far off from religious revelation. What could be done with it, where it would lead, were considerations that would have their turn: for the moment, kneeling in front of the gas fire and shedding noisy tears before the disdainful eyes of her cats, Sarah had simply given thanks, right from her soul. At last, here was something she could use, something to convince the sceptical police that the red-haired girl was a creature of flesh and blood and she had been at the Arena a fortnight ago just as Sarah had said.

Afterwards had come the careful conning of the other photographs, but they yielded nothing more, not even when she used a magnifying glass to scrutinize the many miniature faces that appeared in the background of Dean's shots. There was even one print that featured that very same stretch of crash-barrier, slightly deeper: the words MAITLAND HOMES were visible. But no red-haired girl leaning there gazing out. Either she had changed position at that point, or . . .

Well, Sarah felt she knew. The first shot had been taken earlier on in the evening, when the red-haired girl had been a shy spectator. The second had been taken later – when she was on the ice. Unbearably frustrating as the notion was, Sarah was certain that when Dean had taken that second photo, the red-haired girl had been out on the ice with the three young men. And Dean's eager lens, God damn it, had missed them.

It was a pity. It was a crying pity. But that was as nothing beside this stroke of luck, the first she had had. And once she had got herself under control and washed her streaked face and made herself look presentably normal, Sarah had headed out to Croft Wood like an arrow to the target. There was the prospect of triumph, of course, and she was not proof against that; but triumph wasn't urgent. Finding the girl was.

'I thought you said she had red hair.'

Routh had been staring at the photograph as if it were some optical illusion gimmick that wouldn't work and now he said this. She wanted to rage at him, but raging indicated powerlessness and she wasn't powerless. Not any more.

'Not the girl skating. This one. Here.'

Again he peered. She could see that his hair grew from a double crown. He styled it as if it didn't, hence the hedgerow.

'Hmm. You're sure?'

'I'm positive.'

'I mean it's not all that clear, is it?' He met her burning gaze, coughed. 'OK, if you're sure, fair enough. Is this the only one? She doesn't show up in any of the other pictures?'

'No.'

'The men she was with?'

'No. It was just luck that—'

'Mmm. The thing is, I don't see—'

'*Look*. I saw something happen to that girl, something suspicious. Now I know you don't believe me. OK. That's a photograph of the girl. Trace her, find out. If she's perfectly all right and nothing did happen to her that night, then fine, you can tell me to shut up and get off your back and I will. With great pleasure.'

'It's not very clear,' he said again, chin on hand.

'Isn't it? Wouldn't you know that girl if you saw her in the street? What about those security videos they take in building societies? They convict armed robbers on the strength of those and sometimes they're just fuzz.'

'That's different.'

'Why?'

'Because there you're talking about the commission of a crime and in this case, as I've told you, there just isn't . . .' He sighed, waved that away. 'So, what do you expect me to do with this?'

'Use it. Use it to find that girl.' As he continued to look dull-eyed scepticism at her she went on irritably, 'Damn it, you've got a photo, and if you've got a photo you can make posters—'

'Wait wait wait wait. You're talking about printed posters as formally issued by the county constabulary, I take it? Whoa. When did you last see a campaign like that? I'll tell you when. It was two years ago when that wee lad was murdered on the Redmile estate. That was the biggest investigation this force has undertaken this decade. We needed information desperately. That's where your poster campaigns come in.'

'You never did get anybody for that, did you? Bastard's still out there.'

The look he gave her was more than unfriendly. But he was wrong-footed. 'As you say, the bastard's still out there,' he said, shifting in his chair, toying with the photograph. 'Listen, Miss Winter, I don't give a monkey's what you think of this force or of the police in general. For someone who's got no faith in us you seem to spend a lot of time hanging round our arses, but let's leave that aside. I'm telling you straight out that you won't get a poster campaign out of this, no way. If you walk down that corridor and turn first left you come to my governor's office. My governor's name is Detective Inspector Dolby, and if I was to go to him with such a request he would be extremely surprised. In fact he would think I'd gone out of my tiny mind. He would probably ask in his dry way whether I'd neglected to give him the details of this particular investigation and I would have to reply to him that there *is* no such investigation. What you reported, Miss Winter, has been duly noted and filed but it is not being investigated because there is nothing there. And I have to say that even if it was up to me rather than my governor, I would not . . .'

He stopped then: he was looking down at the photograph rather than at her, but he seemed to feel the quality of her silence.

'I can't promise you anything,' he said.

'No.'

'You've no right to expect it. And we're up to our ears in work just now and this thing will not have top priority, far from it. But if I can keep this photo for a while...?'

She nodded. In spite of herself, she sweated a little at the thought of letting it out of her sight.

'Then there's two things I can do with it. One, I can pass it over to Missing Persons and see if it matches up with anyone on their files. Two, I can try and creep round someone in Records to do the same. If this girl's had any convictions then we'd have a file shot of her, depending on her age, that is. Slim chance, but you never know. And that really will be your lot. If nothing comes of it I'll send the photo back to you and then you'll just have to accept what I've said all along and if you try any of those stunts like calling us pretending to be Tudor Radio I shall be... well, disappointed, that's all.'

'So you believe I saw this girl, then.'

'I never said I didn't.'

She didn't press her advantage: just kept mum and let him remember their last meeting, when he had rattled the skeleton of the one-eyed man at her. That he remembered very well was clear from the tetchiness in his voice as he picked up the photograph. 'You'll trust me with this, then? You don't want a receipt for it?'

'I've got the negative.' Enough of making points. 'Look, what if she does show up on these files?'

'If she's got form, then we'll have a name and a last address. In which case I can send someone to check on her and I *hope* you'll finally be satisfied. If she's under Missing Persons, then we're into a different ball game. We'd probably need to have your statement again as a confirmed sighting.' On his feet, he paused and seemed to view the photograph with a new surprise. 'I'll say this. I wish some of our DCs were as thorough following things up. You've really given this everything, haven't you?'

Not yet, Sarah thought, getting up.

2

The waters had broken and a great weight had been lifted from old Mrs Dhanecha's mind, because it had begun to seem as if Trupti would be carrying that child around for ever and getting more and more droopy and sorry for herself. Now there was only the labour and that was easy, as old Mrs Dhanecha informed her daughter-in-law while Ram helped her out to his taxi, easy as shelling peas, especially when she had been through it three times before. Not that old Mrs Dhanecha had the greatest faith in Trupti's strength of mind. Even the breaking of the waters, an event to be greeted with joy and relief by any sensible woman, had set Trupti wailing because of her slippers. She had been in the toilet when it happened, and her slippers had got wet. What a lot of fuss, my slippers this and my slippers that. They were far too fancy anyway in old Mrs Dhanecha's opinion.

Of course she would have wished to have gone with Trupti to the hospital to offer her support during the labour. Ram would be there, but Ram was worse than useless in such a situation. He turned all to jelly, or more like a jelly than usual, when it came to women's business. Even put on that bewildered look as if the whole thing was nothing to do with him. Ha! He hadn't turned to jelly nine months ago when it all started, that was for sure.

But, Trupti would have to manage without her mother-in-law at the bedside, because it had happened at six o'clock in the evening and there were the other three children to be looked after. Old Mrs Dhanecha consoled herself for her disappointment with the triumphant realization that she had been right. There was Trupti saying there had been no need for her mother-in-law to come over, and now what did we find? Who was there to look after the children when the labour started? Grandmaji, of course. And what would have happened, she wanted to know, if Grandmaji hadn't been there? They would have left the children alone in the house to fend for themselves and set light to things and end up burned to a cinder or wander out of the house and get flattened underneath a bus, was that it? Old Mrs Dhanecha also mentioned these things to her daughter-in-law as she waddled out to the taxi, but the girl didn't listen.

'I'll phone you, Amma,' Ram said, sweating and squeezing his fat behind into the driver's seat. A blessing, at least, that he'd been at home when it happened, though she hoped he'd remember it was his wife in the car and not a fare, because it seemed to be a point of honour with taxi drivers to drive like madmen. 'I'll phone you as soon as anything happens.'

'Make sure you do! Trupti, remember, if it's a boy you promised to name him Shiva!'

'I didn't promise, Mamaji . . .'

'Or Ashraf, after my grandfather.' Still answering back when she was practically giving birth! Old Mrs Dhanecha hoped the girl wouldn't make a show of herself in front of the doctors. 'Don't worry about the children. I'll see to them. Lucky I'm here. Lucky I came . . .!'

The taxi bucketed away, nearly clipping the wing mirror of the van parked next door. Drive like that and he'd be delivering the baby himself, Mrs Dhanecha thought, her hands on the iron spikes of the front gate. To her own surprise and outrage she found she had shed a tear, and recovered herself by rounding on the children who were gathered in a solemn large-eyed row on the doorstep.

'In, in!' She clapped her hands, shooing. 'You want to freeze out here and catch pneumonia? You want your baby brother to come home and find nothing but dead bodies?'

'I want a baby sister,' said Amee.

'Sister, brother, neither of them will want to know you with that dirty face. In, in.'

Ram and Trupti were far too lax about the children's washing, and now that she had them to herself old Mrs Dhanecha made up for it. What they failed to understand was that ordinary washing wouldn't do for children. They needed scrubbing, and scrub them she did, standing them by the sink and working the flannel vigorously with her own hand.

'Ow, Grandmaji, it stings!'

'Pah, nothing. Your nana put out a fire with his bare hands when we were first married. His hands were just like meat in a butcher's shop afterwards. Do you think he complained? Now put on your shalwar and then I'll plait your hair. Your mother at the hospital bleeding and sweating to give you a baby brother, sister then, and you stand there in jeans like a tramp off the street, nara.'

'Oh, Grandmaji, I want to watch *Home and Away*.'

'You sit in front of that stupid box all the time, your brains will rot away and all come running out of your ears. Such rubbish they put on. All killing and blood and guts, God knows what ideas it puts in people's heads.'

Concerned as she was for her daughter-in-law, anxious

as she was for the ring of the telephone, old Mrs Dhanecha could not deny that it was good to have charge of the house for once, and show the children what a really well-run household was like. None of that junk food, for one thing. She cooked a channa dhal with cauliflower, highly seasoned, and proper chapattis, and made the children sit down at the table to eat, away from that infernal television.

'Can I have more water, Grandmaji?'

'You've drunk two glasses already. You'll be up and down all night.'

'But it's so hot, Grandmaji!'

'You call this hot? At home your nana would have fresh green chillies by his plate. There'd be tears running down his face at the strength of them.'

But they stopped their complaining when she made jellabies afterwards. These were the real thing, not like that overpriced muck they sold at Mirza's. The three sticky faces around the table weren't talking for once, but they said as plainly as any words that Grandmaji wasn't so bad after all.

Old Mrs Dhanecha didn't eat much herself. Just as with heat and sleep, she found she could get by with very little food nowadays; and besides, she was worried. Not worried with a sense of things being not right – that was a different feeling entirely. It was the not knowing that troubled her. She hated being in the dark about anything.

'How long will it be before the baby comes, Grandmaji?'

'Who knows? When I had your uncle Dilip it was all over in a few minutes. When I had your father he kept me waiting all day and half the night. He hasn't changed much. He's always late now. Ha! I could—'

Mrs Dhanecha broke off at the ringing of the telephone. Arun was up and running but she beat him to it.

Ram. He started babbling away in English until he remembered himself.

'Trupti's quite comfortable, Amma. The nurse says it will be a while yet.'

'Nurse, nurse, where are all the doctors?'

'Ssh, Amma. There are doctors too. She's resting quietly.'

'What about the baby? Is it the right way round? Your auntie Poeya, she came out feet first. You never heard such screaming. Is—'

'Please, Amma. Everything's all right. The doctor said there'll be no problems. Now I've rung work and they're giving me the time off. I'm going to stay here till the baby's born. Can you put the children to bed about half-past eight and—'

'You think I can't put children to bed, nara, when I brought up five of my own? You think I'm going to put them away in drawers with the laundry, or something?'

'No, Amma. Look, I've got to go. I'll ring you as soon as there's any news.'

'Tell Trupti to breathe in threes—'

Too late: there went the pips.

For some moments old Mrs Dhanecha was occupied with indignation. As if she needed telling what to do! Then the indignation gave way to relief. It was going to be all right. The fool had not driven Trupti into a snowdrift, and it was not going to be a breech birth. Breech births were no joke, though he wouldn't understand that. Men didn't understand anything. Ha! They were hopping about if they so much as cut their finger. Imagine if men had to go through the pain of childbirth. You'd never

FREEZING POINT

hear the end of it. They'd make films about it.

She washed up the pots briskly, singing to herself, letting the children watch television. It was an indulgence but now that her mind was more at ease she was contemplating a little indulgence of her own. Drying her hands on a towel, old Mrs Dhanecha stood in the hall looking at the cellar door.

Well, why not? If she left the door open she would be able to hear the telephone. She hadn't checked her rat poison today, what with one thing and another.

Old Mrs Dhanecha fetched her torch and tested the beam. Fading already. The batteries came from Mirza's, of course. Such rubbish they sold there. Carefully gathering up the skirts of her sari – she had no intention of falling down and hurting herself with the children in her care, if only because it would give Ram the opportunity to do that sighing and say I told you so – she went down the steps of the cellar.

The poison was untouched. Mrs Dhanecha studied it and then shone her torch round the bare walls.

'I know you're around,' she said. 'I've heard you.'

Rats, rats in the dark.

Crouching down and applying her ear to the wall, old Mrs Dhanecha listened for a few minutes. She could hear something, but it was very faint and low, nothing compared to what she had heard just lately.

And as she listened it dawned on her that this was not the random scurrying of rats at all. The sound was rhythmic and level in volume, and it always came from the same place behind the wall. Old Mrs Dhanecha was not a woman to change her mind or admit she was wrong, but she was capable of a shift of gear. Maybe it wasn't rats after all making that noise, but she was certainly right in thinking there was some living creature at the other side of the cellar wall, and she was equally certain that the sounds were not made by any of the men who lived next door, for she had heard louder noises during her daytime cellar checks when they were out.

If she went round with some rat poison they would know she had heard noises, and they might do something about whatever was hiding – or kept hidden – under their house. Maybe they would invite her in out of the cold and she would see for herself – but no, people in England did not invite their neighbours into their houses. Besides, she did not trust this man Ian, nor his friends. Old Mrs Dhanecha's curiosity was aroused and, with the children and the new baby in the house, and Ram so often away late with his taxi, she preferred to know exactly what she was living next door to. There wasn't much she could do, but she would try.

Old Mrs Dhanecha made her way back up the cellar steps, muttering under her breath. The children were still gathered round the TV set in the sitting room, enraptured. Another of those soap operas. What did people want to watch them for? They were just ordinary life. You could see that every day for free.

In the kitchen she climbed on a stool ('Get down, Mamaji, you'll fall,' pah) and took the fresh package of rat poison from the top cupboard. She had got it from Mirza's the other day, just in case. Mirza had made some stupid joke, but she hadn't time to listen to his rubbish.

Should she do this? Ram wouldn't like it. Ram had warned her.

But Ram wasn't here.

'Arun. Arun, I want you.' She had to tap the boy's head to get his attention. 'You and that television, na. An axe-murderer could come in and chop you up in little pieces and you wouldn't know a thing about it.' She began tugging on his arm.

'Oh, Grandmaji, I'm watching—'

'This will only take a minute. Come, come.'

She couldn't rely on her English, not to talk to people she didn't know. Especially young people. But Arun spoke it like a native. It was his Punjabi that was terrible.

'Ask them *what*, Grandmaji?'

'Rats, rats, ask them if they've got rats. Down in the cellar. This is poison to kill the rats, say they're welcome to have it, we've got plenty. Come, come, it's only adverts now. Amee, listen out for the phone in case Abba calls.'

Arun, a good boy if a little stubborn like his father, went along with her, Mrs Dhanecha leaving the front door on the latch, down the icy path to the front gate and then round to next door's gate and up the similarly frozen path – dirty and unswept, she noticed – to the front door of Number 43.

'Knock again, Arun. They must be in. That van's here. Knock again.'

A light came on in the hall. A silhouette paused behind the frosted glass of the door, then it opened.

'Yeah?'

Ah! The one with all the hair and the face he thought was pretty. The one who wouldn't meet your eyes. Old Mrs Dhanecha studied him a moment, but she was more interested in peering past him into the hall.

'Excuse me, we're from next door, Grandma says . . .' Arun went straight into his speech, hooking one hand behind him and holding out the box of rat poison in the other. The pretty boy frowned at them through his hair. And old Mrs Dhanecha craned her neck and peered. The door was only half open, but she could see a slice of dingily painted wall and a radiator.

And, hanging on the radiator, what was surely a pair of women's tights.

Mrs Dhanecha tried to see more, but the pretty boy, glancing behind him, suddenly moved across to block her view. Their eyes met for a moment.

'Hallo, hallo, anything I can do?'

It was him: the one who owned the house, the one Ram called Ian. He was there all of a sudden, smiling, smiling. The pretty boy melted away.

Arun looked up at her, while the one Ram called Ian smiled from one to the other. Mrs Dhanecha had been right: he did not ask them inside. She gave the boy a nudge, and he went through his speech all over again.

The Ian one didn't stop smiling. He seemed to be speaking seriously, and he took the box of rat poison in his hand, and Mrs Dhanecha understood that he was saying thank you; but he didn't stop smiling. At least with his mouth. He was like something out of one of those stupid television adverts, she thought. Blond hair and a cheeky boy's face and a white-toothed smile that didn't reach his eyes.

Now he was asking something of Arun. Something about his mother and the baby: Mrs Dhanecha caught that. Arun, shuffling, replied. Mrs Dhanecha searched the Ian one's face, but she couldn't see past the smile. And he had positioned himself so that she couldn't see into the hall either.

'Cheers then.' She knew that: Ram sometimes said it, instead of saying goodbye in proper English. The door was closing.

'Cheers, cheers.' Arun hopped up and down, task over

and eager to be home. Old Mrs Dhanecha hesitated. The hall light was still on, and she had half a mind to press her face against the frosted glass and peer in. But of course, she wouldn't see anything.

'Well?' She took hold of Arun's hand to stop him skipping away. 'What did they say?'

'Ian said he didn't think they had rats, they'd never seen any.'

'Did he indeed. What else?'

'He said thank you for telling him, he'd put the poison down in case.'

Old Mrs Dhanecha made no comment.

'And he asked about Amma and I said she'd gone to the hospital to have the new baby and he said that was good news and all the best to Amma and Abba. Grandmaji, can I watch TV now?'

'No more. Bed.'

'Oh, Grandmaji . . .!'

'All right. Fifteen minutes only.'

Back inside Number 41 old Mrs Dhanecha locked the front door and then went through to the kitchen to make hot milk. The sight of the cellar door made her hesitate. After a moment she opened it and looked down into the musty darkness.

'Well,' she muttered, 'whatever you are on the other side, I'm on to you now.' But that Ian had taken the poison too readily, with no surprise, no questions. It was as if he was laughing at them. What was there to laugh at? As for the pretty boy, he had looked at them as if they were ghosts.

'Don't trust them, na, don't trust them,' crooned Mrs Dhanecha, and closed the cellar door.

Ram said they were all right, of course, but then Ram

was easily taken in. He was always admiring Trupti's jet-black hair but old Mrs Dhanecha, investigating the bathroom cabinet, had seen the little bottle she used to cover up the grey streaks.

A pair of tights, what was that all about? Mrs Dhanecha had never seen a woman going in there, and Mrs Dhanecha didn't miss much.

She heated milk in a saucepan and filled three mugs. Soon there would be the smell of baby's milk in the house, all being well. She wondered if she should get Arun to ring the hospital and find out what was going on. But no, it was their bedtime, and Ram would phone when there was news. If she didn't hear by ten she'd ring herself: she'd heard they had Punjabi speakers on the hospital switchboard.

'Here. Drink up and then bed.'

'Oh, Grandmaji, can't we stay up? Can't we stay up till we hear about the new baby?'

'Babies don't come if you wait for them. Drink, drink.'

They wailed that they weren't tired, but she wasn't having it and shooed them up to bed. Of course, *she* wasn't tired, but then she never was. As soon as they were quiet she set to work on the ironing. The children would be well turned out for school when she was in charge.

The smell of laundry again brought to mind those tights hanging on the radiator. Drying, she supposed. No use hanging out washing in this weather.

Mrs Dhanecha cocked an ear for sounds from next door. Often she heard the beat of pop music, and sometimes a vague banging around. Tonight, nothing. They were in, though, she knew that. There was something strange going on at Number 43, and Mrs Dhanecha would be keeping a very close eye on that house from now on.

3

'Shit, Chill, have they gone? Shit. What was that all about? Shit, man. I don't believe this.'

'Language, Derek.'

'What are you doing?'

'What am I doing? Pouring myself a glass of foaming fourpenny, that's what. Why, what should I be doing?'

Trend stared. Chill was in his most impenetrable mood. Pouring superlager into a pint glass, he held the dark liquor up to the bare bulb in the living room and smacked his lips. Then he began waltzing round the room, holding the foaming glass at arm's length in front of him. He didn't spill a drop. 'Tell you what. Ta-da, pom pom. When Sean gets back, let's tell him that rat poison's cocoa and see if he drinks it.'

Trend shook his head. 'Shit.'

'Oh dear oh dear, very monosyllabic. What you want is one of these, my old fruit. Go on. Down the little red lanes with it.'

Trend took the can of superlager but did not open it. He watched Chill waltzing.

'You,' Chill said, ruffling Trend's hair as he danced by, 'have got something on your mind, my son. Come on. Out with it. Tell your uncle Chill.'

Trend smoothed down his hair and then cracked the can and drank morosely.

'You know what.'

Chill stopped waltzing and struck a theatrical pose. 'Olé! You know what, I think I'm wasted on that stall. I reckon

I should be on stage. Andrew Lloyd Webber stuff, all singing, all dancing. I've always fancied that. No? Or how about me as one of those Chippendale-type geezers? Just develop my pecs a bit, slap the baby oil on, it's a doddle.' He popped open the top two buttons of his denim shirt and slid it off one shoulder, winking. 'What do you think?'

Trend muttered, 'Shit,' again and slumped down on the sofa, shielding his eyes.

'OK, OK. I get the message. You're all in a tizzy on account of Granny Gristle poking her nose round here and really, my old china, I cannot for the life of me think why?'

'It was the cellar, for Christ's sake.'

'Ah, ah, ah. About the *rats* in the cellar, matey. The rats what we haven't got. That's all. Granny Gristle thinks they've got rats in their cellar, she thinks we've got rats in our cellar, she's got bats in the belfry, I said oh yes thank you we'll have to watch out for that much obliged et cetera, et cetera, end of stor-*ee*.' Chill did not hitch his shirt back. The fair skin of his shoulder shone under the bare bulb. 'Well, isn't it? Be honest.'

'What if she comes back? What if she wants to see—'

'Oh yeah, what, comes round here with a warrant from Grannies HQ demanding to inspect our cellar? Get real, man. Loosen up. She's just a nosy old woman who's probably half cracked anyway.'

'She saw those tights,' said Trend, his eyes not quite on Chill. 'She saw those tights hanging on the radiator. I know she did.'

'Ooh shock horror. Granny Gristle spots tights drying on radiator, hold the front page.' Chill began dancing again, a slow snakey roaming about the room, with Trend as the centre of the figure. 'What if she did? We're three bachelors gay, are we not, *mon ami*? Footloose and fancy-free and surely entitled to have, ahem, lady guests in our own domicile? Any road up, the tights might be ours. Builders wear them, didn't you know that? Builders wear tights under their trews in the winter, outdoors all day, keeps their assets warm. Good idea, I reckon. Might start doing that myself on the stall. Cheers, down the hatch.' Without interrupting his slinky progress Chill tilted the pint glass and drained it in one go. 'Ah. Lovely. Toss it off, that's my motto, always has been.' He held the bottom of the empty glass to his eye and studied Trend through it. 'I spy, with my little eye . . . oh dear oh dear, you're still not happy about it, are you? Look I'll wear the blinking tights in the street if it'll make you feel better. Yeah! Yeah, I'll put them on! You watch me!'

Chill was out of the room and back like a firecracker. He had the tights. He flicked them at Trend's face and then waved them like a flag.

'Just forget it, Chill.'

'No. No indeed, my son. Ooh, bit of ladder there, never mind. Here goes.' He kicked off his engineer boots and then peeled down his jeans. He had short strong thighs and calves, dusted with fair hair. Trend started laughing, the cross laugh of a child that will soon be crying. 'You laugh, my son.' Chill toe-kicked his jeans away, stripper-style. 'I've got the legs for it, me. Legs right up to my arse. That's the trouble with us men, you see. Cover our bodies up all the time, don't make the most of them.' Chill's eyes danced, palest clearest blue, sparking. He suddenly whipped off his shirt and struck a muscle pose in his boxers. 'Look at that. Not an ounce of fat. You too could have a body like this. Play your cards right and you could have this one. Whoops! What am I saying. Beer's gone straight to my head.'

Trend was laughing and frowning at the same time. He looked like a man in pain.

'Here we go. Christ, how do they manage?' Struggling with the tights, hopping on one foot, Chill overbalanced, lurched across the room and crashed on to the sofa next to Trend. 'Ah, of course. They sit down first. Fancy me forgetting that.' He slid the tights up his legs and then stood to pull them up round his buttocks. 'Coh. Really quite sensual, that, you know. *Dead* smooth on your skin. You feel that. Go on, you feel.'

He cocked his hip at Trend. The muscles of his back stood out.

'Get off.' Trend twitched. His laughter had stopped, and he started it up again like a cracked engine. 'You're a crazy fucker, you are.'

Chill looked down at himself. 'Not quite *me*, you reckon? Nah. I know what you mean. I'm more your basic natural outdoors type.' He removed the tights and then stood, a few inches from Trend, carefully unrolling them. 'Never been shy, me. Not in my nature. Well!' He looked down at his crotch and addressed it with mock indignation. 'I don't know what *you're* getting excited about. Honestly. You're uncontrollable, you really are. Ah well, somebody's in for a treat later on.' He flashed a sideways grin at Trend. 'But she'll just have to wait.'

Trend flinched as if the grin were a slap. But Chill was already strutting away, retrieving his clothes. 'Better cover myself up else I'll catch my death. And what old Seany-poo would think if he strolled in and saw me like this I don't know. He's been gone a long time, hasn't he? Surely he hasn't forgotten the way back from the video shop. No, don't answer that.'

The painful laughter broke out, briefly, like a dry cough. Dressing, Chill looked brightly down at Trend's lowered head. 'Well, cheered up a bit now? That's the way. Because there's really nothing to worry about, Trend my old mate. You'll worry yourself into an early grave, you will.'

The front door banged, and a cold draught brought in Sean, ears red and nose shinily leaking.

' 'Cking hell, man. *Free*zing. 'Cking *freez*ing.'

'Need to wrap up warm in this weather, mate. Need plenty of clothes on,' said Chill, with a wink at Trend. 'Well, what'd you get, what'd you get?'

'*Predator 2*, man. It's ace, man. 'Cking brilliant. Seen it twice. It hasn't got Schwarzenegger this time, but it's ace, I'm telling you.'

'Oh, Sean. Thought you'd get something you hadn't seen.'

'Nah. It's ace, this. Watch it loads of times.'

'Go on then.' Chill cracked a can and sat down. 'Slip it in. Slip it in the slot, my old mate.'

Trend got up. 'Going for a slash.'

''Cking hell, man, you'll miss the start, it's ace, the start—'

'Pause it.'

Trend pulled the door of the living room shut behind him, listened a moment, then went softly down the passage. Outside the cellar door he listened again. He sniffed and drew his sleeve across his nose.

The door squeaked a little as he opened it and he hesitated again. But there was no sound either from the living room or below. Closing the door behind him, he descended.

She was lying on her left side, facing away from him.

Her hair, fanned out on the pillow, was lank and greasy. He found that disgusting.

He had approached within two feet of the bed before she stirred and lifted her head and looked round at him. He knew that sometimes she feigned sleep but this time it seemed to be real. There was a red crease-mark on her cheek and the corners of her eyelids were sticky. That disgusted him too.

'Hello?'

Didn't know where she was for a minute. He stood looking down at her while her gummy eyes searched the room and at last focused on his face.

'I . . .' She licked her dry lips. Her eyes fixed themselves on his as if they were two normal people, and as if he could do something for her. 'I'm thirsty. Can I have some water or something?'

The dark cloud that hung permanently over Trend's spirit seemed to break and tear and spit lightning. He drew back his foot and lifting it high, swinging it round like a footballer taking a volley, he kicked her.

She didn't scream even as he continued kicking her, even as she writhed and scrambled and tried to press herself to the wall out of range of his boot, but he hardly noticed this fact because of the raging noise in his head. For the same reason he didn't hear Chill coming down the steps, didn't know he was there at all until he felt himself pulled roughly back and then Chill's face was close to his.

'What you doing?' Trend was covered in sweat but there was no sweat on Chill: just a bright, questioning alertness. 'What you doing, Trend?'

Trend managed to meet his eyes, for a few seconds. He sniffed, and used Chill's own word.

FREEZING POINT

'Playing.'

Chill's finger came up. It was wagging, and he was smiling.

'Ask me first, Trend mate.' The sound of the girl's sobs filtered through and Trend watched the wagging finger. 'You ask me first. OK?'

The fustiness of the room mingled with the smell of beer on Chill's breath and the scent of his body. Trend's eyes flicked to the huddled figure of the girl, making a noise now like a mewling cat.

'OK.'

The black cloud rumbled and Trend turned away and shambled towards the steps. He had reached the top step and might have been just out of earshot when Chill turned to the girl and said solicitously, 'Sorry about that, sweetheart. I must apologize for my friend. He's feeling a little queer today.'

NINE

1

Zilch. Zero. Doodley-squat. Nothing.

Nothing. That was what Detective Sergeant Routh's researches with the photograph brought to light. Nothing in the files. Nothing from Missing Persons.

The only grain of consolation to be had from the whole enterprise was that Routh actually sounded disappointed himself, as if he had gone from wanting to be rid of Sarah to wanting to believe her. So there was that. It was something. But not much to set against nothing.

Routh came to her house himself to give her the news, and to return the photograph to her, late on Tuesday afternoon: she had not been long home. Murray was there with her. The two men gave each other that guarded assessing look that two men always did in the presence of any woman under seventy, but Routh seemed glad that she was not alone.

'That's it then,' Sarah said. 'There's nothing more you can do.'

Routh seemed glad too that she had said it for him. But being Routh he could not leave it at that.

'Well, we've followed it up as far as it will go. Left no

stone unturned, as it were, and we haven't found anything nasty under any of them. So it's good news.' There was perplexity on his face. He knew it was good news, he knew it was not good news for Sarah, and he didn't know quite where to take his stand.

'Thanks for getting back to me so quickly,' Sarah said. She could tell that he had done some pretty strenuous string-pulling, partly for his own benefit – he wanted this business over with – but partly for her too. She wanted to express her thanks more fully, but it was hard to enthuse over an unwanted gift, hard to dredge anything up from such emptiness.

'Thank *you* – for all your help over this.' That wasn't right either, and he knew it. 'This' didn't even exist as far as he was concerned, and here he was thanking her for helping him with it. There was at least wry understanding in the bleak look they exchanged.

Bleak, and bleary. Routh's eyes and nose were red, and it only now occurred to her that they had not been so last time.

'I thought your cold had got better,' she said.

'It did, I think. I've got myself another one. I've got this feeling that until this winter's gone I won't be free of a cold and I'm just going to have to ride with it. Do you know what I mean?'

'Yes,' said Sarah. 'I know what you mean. Well, I'll see you out. Sorry for all the trouble.'

'No trouble. That's the way it is in this line of work. Digging and digging down to the root and then finding there's no root after all. So don't think it's anything exceptional, Miss Winter, just say to yourself OK fine, and put it behind you.'

'Uh-huh.'

He couldn't forbear giving them both a searching look as he left, as if he were wondering how she would cope this time. Last time, smashed phone boxes and a nervous breakdown, this time . . .?

Perhaps unfair to attribute such prurient curiosity to him. At least, without acknowledging that there was sympathy there too, sympathy in the way he shook her hand and told her again to put it behind her, sympathy that would have sent her screaming up the walls if her mind had not already jolted and moved on like a train over the points.

'Good of him to come,' Murray said when Routh was gone. He picked up Charlie, but the cat knew the attempted caresses were only a distraction and struggled huffily. Murray put him down. 'Is it too early for a drink?'

'It's never too early for a drink,' Sarah said. She went through to the kitchen and reached for the vodka. Ah. There ought to be a word, she thought, for that peculiar upward swoop your hand did when you picked up an empty bottle expecting it to be full. After about three seconds she gave up trying to remember exactly when she had polished it off. There was wine in the fridge.

'Thanks.' Murray sat in the armchair, but forward, with his elbows on his knees, a posture that meant all was not well. The photograph lay on the coffee table. Sarah picked it up and looked at it, drinking her wine in swift gulps.

'Well, like he said, Sarah, they followed it up as far as it would go. You can't fault them on that.'

'No.' No, she found no fault.

'Well, at least now you know for sure.'

This remark passed lightly over Sarah's mind. In the new interior world she inhabited it had no meaning.

'I know you've . . .' He was feeling his way. 'I know it's

been hard for you. All this. I know why you had to keep on with it. I guess it must seem weird now that it's over. But at least you can tell yourself that you—'

'How well would this photograph reproduce, do you think?'

'What?'

She refilled her glass, her eyes on a face framed with auburn hair, looking out across ice. 'This photograph. Or the background part of it, anyway. Say you blew it up from a negative and then, I don't know, photocopied it.'

'Why are you asking me this?'

'Well, you know. Who better? Mid Anglia Pursuit Publishing, they deal in all that sort of thing, don't they?'

Murray set down his glass. He looked like a man who had made a spectacular plunge and found the water only three feet deep. 'What are you talking about?'

'Posters. Having posters printed, with this photograph on them.'

His lips were thin. 'Why?'

'Because . . .' She shrugged and laughed shakily and knew she was throwing herself on his mercy. 'Because I can't think of anything else.'

Murray snatched up his glass, drained it in a savage jerk, was on his feet all in one movement. 'Well, I can,' he said, pacing nowhere. 'I can think of something else. But if it hasn't occurred to you then I'm not sure whether it's even worth mentioning.'

'What is it?' For a moment she was as helplessly hopeful as if she didn't know deep down what was coming.

'All right then. Drop it. That's the other thing you can do. Drop it, and get on with your life.'

'I can't get on with my life. That's just it. The only way to go forward is to—'

Freezing Point

'What, have posters printed?'

'*Yes*. If you'd just let me explain . . . I know the police couldn't match the photograph but all that means is that girl's got no criminal record and that she hasn't been reported as a missing person. That doesn't cover everything. And I know – I *feel* something's happened to her. I *know* there was something wrong that night and I've got to find it out and this photograph is the only thing I've got to go on. If I recognize her face then other people must too.'

'These posters.' His face was taut, holding something in, just. 'I presume you mean you're going to have them printed at your own expense?'

'Can't see any other way.'

'And then – what, plaster them all over the city?'

She shrugged.

'I see . . . You know flyposting's an offence,' he said, and he laughed because the words were ludicrous and the laugh was bitter because the situation should have been ludicrous and wasn't. 'Posters. "Do you know this girl?" sort of thing?'

'That sort of thing.'

'They'll go apeshit at Tudor, you know that, don't you? Dragging their name into this. I mean, I presume that's the idea. An appeal from Tudor Radio. You just can't do that, Sarah.'

'No. I know.' She hadn't thought of it. She thought of it now, and then her mind moved smoothly over the points again. 'Well, I won't then. The appeal can be from me personally. Nothing to do with Tudor. I'll just put my phone number on the posters.'

'Oh, boy. That puts the lid on it, that does. You will be setting yourself up for every crank and pervert in the city.'

'It's no different from having your number listed in the phone book.'

'Having your number listed in the phone book is not an indication that you're going off your rocker and – oh, *shit*, I didn't mean that the way it sounded. It's just . . .' He stared at her, frowning, and something about her blankness seemed to make a decision for him. 'No. No, I *do* mean that the way it sounds. You will be acting as if you are off your rocker. Now I know you are not, and you know you are not. So why act like it? That really is storing up trouble for yourself, isn't it? I mean, we aren't talking about sticking an advert for your lost dog in the newsagent's window. This is heavy stuff.' He left a pause. 'Too heavy.'

She reached for the wine bottle, and flashed him a look when he made a gesture as if to stop her. 'Murray, I don't expect you to understand, not fully. No one can really get inside another person's mind and think what they're thinking and feel what they're feeling, and I always felt you recognized that and it was one of the things I liked about you. But I at least expected you to support me in this—'

'Oh, support, support, I thought this was supposed to be a relationship, not the bloody social services!'

Immediately, plainly, he deplored that lapse. But he was so fired up that he could not find the path back from it. 'Look, it's – it's because I want to support you that I *don't* want to support this . . . this obsession. Not just because it's dangerous and destructive but because it *isn't you*. That's what you've got to see, it isn't you.'

'Don't tell me what's me and what isn't me, Murray. Nobody has a right to do that. Not even you.'

She was taking a stand. He could have handled that.

But the stand she was taking was right alongside her obsession, arm in arm with it, inseparable. And she saw in his eyes that he couldn't, wouldn't handle that.

Still, he searched for a way back, searched for ground he could walk on.

'If you must go ahead with this poster business,' he said, grinding the words out, 'then please, don't put your own phone number on them. Just – just put a PO box number or something.'

Swiftly she considered, rejected. 'No. It's cumbersome. Someone might pick up a phone but might not bother to write. I want information, any information, and I want it quick and that's the best way.'

'All right. All right. So you put up these posters with a picture of this girl and your phone number. Think. If something bad has happened to this girl, aren't you putting yourself at risk from—'

'Oh right, so now you do believe something's happened to her? You believe it after all, do you? This is new.'

'Look, not necessarily—'

'You can believe that something's happened to her. You can accept that, and still say drop it, don't get involved, don't put yourself at risk. That is one shitty selfish attitude, Murray.'

If he had been a more selfish man that accusation would have hurt less. As it was, she had touched him with a live wire. And after the burn came numbness. He moved over to the door like a sleepwalker and when he at last spoke it was in a dull, suspended tone.

'I want to help you with this, Sarah. But I can't. The help you need I can't give.'

'Obviously.' It was meant as a simple statement of fact but it came out tangy, dismissive, a last word, and it was enough to send Murray out of the room, out of the house, a muttered 'I'll see you,' said only as people said it when 'Goodbye' was too warm.

2

She was in to work so early the next morning that Rachel, floating into the office high on whale songs and camomile tea and seeing Sarah at the filing cabinet, gave a tiny scream like a butterfly in extremity.

'Hey, what's up, are you OK?'

'Fine, thanks, Rachel, fine. Listen, you remember when we did that interview with the woman from the Missing Persons Helpline? Must be a year ago now. I'm trying to find the file.'

'I remember. Sweet lady. Rosy cheeks. Reminded me of one of those cooks, you know, in an apron. It's not under M?'

'Can't see it.'

Rachel approached the filing cabinet dubiously, as if it were a complex machine liable to overheating. 'Oh . . . have you looked under C?'

Sarah raised an eyebrow.

'C for charities. The Missing Persons Helpline's a charity. Was there something from them this morning?'

'No, no. Just thought we might do a follow-up. Topical. TV's very big on it at the moment. Ah, here it is.'

'Isn't that terrible?'

'What's terrible?'

'That it has to be a charity. Coffee?'

'Please. Oh, and could you find out the number of the printers who do our posters and inserts, stuff like that?'

The woman she had interviewed from the Missing Persons Helpline was not available. Sarah talked instead to a charming young man called Terry. As well as his Irish lilt Sarah could hear the sound of him bending over backwards in an effort to help. But failing. The Missing Persons Helpline was there to collect, record, analyse and publicize information about people reported missing by friends and relations. With their limited resources, Sarah knew, they did this admirably, but their resources could not be allocated to a snapshot of a nameless stranger – except possibly in one regard. Terry couldn't promise anything, but if she'd care to let them have a copy of the photograph he could try to do a match-up with their file pictures. It would be a hell of a job and like he said he couldn't promise anything . . .

Sarah had a lever – free radio publicity for the Helpline in return – and she didn't think it would be ignoble to use it under the circumstances. With such good nature, however, it was hardly needed. She made a note to have another print developed from the negative.

'Here's the number of the printers,' said Rachel. 'They're called Roberts Webb. Sounds like Charlotte's Web, doesn't it? Did you ever read that book when you were a child? I cried and cried. I've never brushed down a cobweb since. Having a party?'

'Hm?'

'The printers. Invitations?'

'Oh . . . no, nothing like that.' There was nothing to be gained by telling Rachel about it. She would only find it upsetting. Rachel got upset when the leaves fell off the trees.

Roberts Webb were very ready with the quotes, and a little too ready with the questions. Sarah made the mistake of mentioning Tudor Radio. Ah, one of their regular clients, would this be added to their account . . .?

It was too risky. As Murray had said, her bosses would not take kindly to her using the station's name to pursue some quixotic scheme of her own. She flannelled Roberts Webb for a while and said she'd get back to them.

Murray. For all her determined briskness, the thought of him kept pouncing on her. She wondered whether to give him a ring at work, and then wondered what the point would be. Murray had as much stubbornness as any other man, which was plenty. Besides, he had walked out on her: he had refused to put himself on the line at a critical time. Some part of herself murmured that such a failure was not irreparable, that there might even have been a comparable failure on her side, and that under normal circumstances . . .

But the voice was faint: the circumstances were not normal, and they drowned it out.

The Yellow Pages was full of printers. For some reason she picked on one that looked the oldest and least flashy – 'Geo. Finney & Sons, Printers. Est. 1926.' Somehow that 'Geo' reassured her. You could trust a 'Geo'. She phoned, imagining an old brass two-piece telephone on the other end, and made an appointment with them for lunchtime.

Geo. Finney & Sons plied their trade from an old backstreet that had undergone urban renewal, meaning that most of the houses had been demolished to be replaced with a car park and a public toilet that had cottage written all over it. The printers' neighbours were an evangelical chapel and a shop called The Druid's Breath that sold fantasy games and bong pipes and where, it was plain, you could score a hit just by lifting an eyebrow. But Geo. and his sons had only modernized as far as the fifties. It was pure Ealing in there. There were ashtrays in reception and a hat stand and a pimply youth straight out of *Billy Liar*. Specimen posters advertised the city panto. Sarah began to wonder whether they charged in guineas.

But there was one old-fashioned aspect to the business that was very welcome: a belief that the customer was always right. Like an old shopman who would sell you three nails and wrap them, the crewcut codger in the sleeveless pullover who dealt with her only wanted to oblige. He had no interest in the poster beyond the technical: what it said and what it was for was up to her. Nor did the notion of reproducing a face from the background of a snapshot faze him, though it was quite a challenge.

'It won't be clear. It'll lose definition the more you blow it up. Then again, the eye will correct that if it's seen from a distance. Given the quality, I'd suggest equal dimensions for your lettering block and your picture.'

There was one problem. The price he quoted her for colour reproduction was beyond her means. If she were to have enough posters to make any impact – she reckoned a hundred – they would have to be black and white. Even that would cost her a packet. She briefly toyed with the idea of just ordering one and photocopying it. But that would surely be an infringement of copyright or something; and besides, an image as indefinite as the photo of the red-haired girl would come out of a photocopier as little more than a splodge. She knew that from the hustings leaflets with their murky mugshots that came round with the NUJ elections.

It would have to be professionally printed and it would have to be black and white and her credit card would have to stretch like chewing gum; that was all there was to it. The pity was that the shade of the girl's hair, her most striking and recognizable feature, would go for nothing. She would have to revise the text she had been planning in her head all morning to include it.

The wording was simple, and no doubt both Sergeant Routh and Murray would call it wildly inaccurate and provocative. 'MISSING. Relatives are anxious to trace this girl, last seen at the Arena Ice Rink, Thursday, 10 January. Auburn hair, pale complexion, medium height. Any information please telephone 0173 349261 in strictest confidence.'

Weird, no doubt, when you thought about it. How come these anxious relatives didn't mention the girl's name? Well, it didn't matter. There were plenty of weird people about. The person who would find it most weird of all, of course, would be the girl herself, if she saw one of the posters. She might well come at Sarah spitting fury and demanding to know why the hell her face was plastered all over the city. Well, that didn't matter either. Because if the girl was in a position to do that then everything was OK. If the girl was in a position to do that then the stopped world would begin to turn again.

'So that's white ground A5, block roman sanserif, "missing" in bold... We'll do our best with the photo, but it'll be fuzzy, I'm afraid. Not even newspaper quality.'

'But you'll be able to tell who it is?'

'There'll be a likeness...' For the first time there was a hint of curiosity. 'Been naughty, has she?'

'Oh... I don't think so.' She experienced a moment of intense wonder at what this nameless girl might be like, where she lived and what were her dreams and what were her nightmares... 'When will they be ready?'

3

silly.

silly, thinking she could take control of the situation, silly

Oh God the pain, like brightness, pain like unendurable brightness

fight it fight it *breathe* use breathing slow

slow

slow

slow breaths taking the pain away floating the pain away floating it away like a boat on a stream slow

no good no good none of the strategies worked now not with this the pain was too much she couldn't cope with it she had lost it lost control lost control

never had it. Never

Face that. Yes, face it.

Pain dimming a little, ready to flare and blind her again any moment but face it, face it now. Been a fool. Again. *Encore une fois* Alison Holdenby they tell me you're leaving at the end of this term your English teacher's as puzzled as I am by

come back. Going away, come back, face it, fool, no control, and now

oh God

please the pain it's too much the pain

try rage try *rage* rage at him the smiler did this to her bent her finger back until God knows God knows what he's done to it bent it back when he was *playing* rage rage at him rage so big no room for the pain

better

better. A little better.

Face it. Face it or go under.

Should have known. Big plans, oh so big plans. The seduction of Sean, oh yes, Sean was going to be putty in her hands and in her hands too sooner or later was going to be the key to the cuffs, the master strategy. Announcing round of applause please ladies and gentlemen the seduction of Sean in which Miss Alison Holdenby that daring young escapologist will work on the stupid boy with the hat and thereby effect her release from captivity never before attempted hurrah hurrah . . .

When? Yesterday or day before?

damn damn damn she had had a grip of time she had mastered it but now it was slipping away from her again melting and blending

it was because of the pain the pain took over but *not now* fight it

rage

OK. OK . . . Day before yesterday, then. Must have been. Cellar door opening. The three of them coming down.

A cake. They had a cake because it was Sean's birthday and they brought it down to show her and she should have been used to it by now, the bar and the Mickey Mouse lamp and the litter tray and all the crazy horror but that cake, oh God

cake with pink icing and candles and then Sean blew out the candles and the smiler

the smiler with a gesture big glad-handed gesture
said
she's all yours mate happy birthday and they watched the smiler and the weasel one watched while Sean
and
they laughed
or the smiler did laughed and laughed the weasel one just stared

it was over quickly over very quickly and the smiler made a comment fastest gun in the west and more laughing and Sean blushing and

oh God can't have these thoughts memories knowledge in my head any more can't take them any more going to explode my head is going to

Why so bad? The big plan after all the big plan had involved it, she had been nerving herself, building up to suffering it, putting up with having Sean

near her

and that had been the plan so why so bad then

because because, oh so bad, probably could never have gone through with it but at least in control, in the plan, alone and in control and not watched by

them

and an aim behind it, suffer it to get keys, let him do it then sharpened spoon in the eye and grab keys different entirely different from the holding down and the cake and the laughing and Sean's beery giggling breath

Well. Pre-empted. The plan like a child's dream now, child's dream of magic, flying, omnipotence.

no

balls to that poor-me no-hope *resignation* no no no there just

might be another chance to

don't know something like she had planned there would be another time when she would be alone with him he was still the dogsbody feeding and cleaning when she could

work on him somehow pick the moment, lull, invite, and then the sharpened spoon and the grab for

let him touch me you're mad you're crazy have him do that again no way I can never not even to be free after that I can never

oh God the pain finger calling up reinforcements now body bruises and burns and between her
rage
fight
The spoon. Poor Mister Spoon. Grinding grinding till the muscles of her right arm felt like barbed wire inside her skin but still Mister Spoon wasn't sharp, not sharp at all, Mister Spoon was a wimpy sort of guy, he didn't want to be a killing machine, not Mister Spoon, his mother raised him to be a kitchen utensil and he was happy that way
going mad going mad were mad people happy did madness make things better because welcome if so come on in madness come on and make me smile
No. No, no, that was the pain, that wasn't her. And the pain would stop. *This* particular pain would stop because the smiler was working it that way, the smiler wanted her to do something and that was why he was withholding those strong painkillers, those beautiful pills that she craved so.
He said so. Said it right out. 'I want you to do something for me, Ali.' No – some joking first. About Sean and his
his
performance
and then the laughter, more laughter, laughing his head off before wiping his eyes and then: 'I want you to do something for me, Ali.'
And then when she had told him where to go – and it was long, seemed long, since she had wasted energy on such defiance but the outrage, the outrage at this pretence as if she had any choice, she couldn't help it—
then—

crack

and dreadful new perspectives of pain opened up while he studied her as if she were a plant with blackfly

or

anything but a girl a human being open-mouthed and writhing and said it again: 'I want you to do something for me, Ali.'

And then: 'I'll leave you to think about it.'

And left her. Not to think about it but to think about the pain, see all round it, know its shape and size and its unearthly brilliance, its power, power against her only, interested in no one else, only for Alison this pain and conscientious, peeling and stripping Alison to her essence, an implacable teacher.

No control. No control at all.

Should be doing something should be tapping or sharpening, sharpening or tapping, one or the other, I'm backsliding, losing time losing momentum

losing nothing losing NOTHING all futile all absurd no control

only the pain now. Just the two of them, the pain and her, and the pain was bigger. The pain diminished her, made nothing of her.

And then, suddenly, sleep.

No good, though. Sleep took the pain into itself and did things with it. Nightmare things, making unconsciousness the dark side of the staring moon of agony. She came retching upward to waking and to the sight of the smiler standing over her.

'Blimey, Ali. You're sweating like a pig, girl.'

Eyes blurry, still imprinted with the stills of nightmare, she tried to make visual sense of him. Fixed him at last, sturdy figure and blond head, emblem of torment.

'Sorry. I forgot – now how does it go? Horses sweat, gentlemen perspire, ladies feel the heat. You look as if you're feeling the heat, Ali. Must admit I am a bit myself, if you know what I mean, looking at you there, I mean you're not at your best as I'm sure you'd be the first to admit, but you're still a little cracker. Look like a million dollars in a paper sack, you would.'

Her mouth was too dry to conjure any spit worth launching at him, even if—

Suddenly Alison was dazzled and yearning. He had brought his hand out from behind his back and was holding up a small brown glass bottle.

'Remember I said I wanted you to do something for me?'

She didn't know if she nodded or spoke. Her own gestures were taking place on the other side of the world. There was nothing here but that bottle of pills. But he seemed satisfied.

'OK. Second question. Are you ready to do it? Or should I wait a bit longer? I mean, you can tell me to – what were your words? – go and fuck myself again if you like. It's up to you. But if I go and fuck myself, not speaking literally of course, then I take these with me.' He gave the bottle a shake. It rattled, thrilling music. 'What do you reckon?'

She longed to speak and was paralysed, between pain and joy.

'Gave you a couple of these one time before, I think. Pretty good, aren't they? I mean these aren't your average over-the-counter painkillers, you know. I get them special from a mate of mine. He says he gets them on prescription for his back but, well, ahem, let's just say I wouldn't be totally flabbergasted if they'd fallen off the back of a pharmacist. He's like that, my mate. Salt of the whatsname, but a bit of a fly boy. But there, it's easy to judge, isn't it? We're all flesh and blood when it comes down to it.'

Tongue like dry pumice slow across her lips. 'Please . . .'

'I didn't break it, you know, though I dare say it might feel like it. The old finger. I do know what I'm doing in that department. No need to break bones if you know the right moves. But it'll hurt, I know that, hurt like buggery and carry on hurting—'

And suddenly it wasn't the pain but the merry mercilessness in his eyes that unlocked her throat and said for her: 'I'll do it. What – whatever you want me to do.'

He winked at her. 'Nice one. You know it makes sense. It won't take a second.' He placed the bottle of pills on the floor, saw her eyes stretch towards it. 'You'll get them, don't you fret. *After* you've done this little thing for me.' He pulled a card from the back pocket of his jeans, held it in front of her face. It was curved a little from the shape of his buttocks. She looked at it, wondering if this was one of his curious jokes. It was a picture postcard showing Nottingham Castle. He turned it to show her the other side. Blank.

'Picked it up last week when I went up to Nottingham to do a bit of buying from the wholesalers. Winter gear, you know, chunky knits, padded jackets. All that's selling at the moment, your actual fashion gear's a dead loss.' He took a ballpoint pen from his breast pocket and uncapped it. 'You're not going to believe how simple this thing is. But I know you, I know how stubborn you can be, and this was the only way really.'

She stared at him. There was a glitter about his face: he was seeing her pain and lingering.

'I'll tell you what to write,' he said, his voice kindly. 'And you write it. On that postcard. There. What could be easier? Start with... well, start with "Dear Mum". Sit up, gel. Come on. Write it on your knee. Bit awkward, I know, but you're pretty supple, aren't you? I should know that.'

He placed the pen in her unresisting right hand. The damage to the left had been a careful choice. Still she stared at him. The understanding was there, but somehow bewilderment, a dull lump battered by pain, would not let it past.

'Dear oh dear, you're a bit slow today, treacle. Come on, "Dear Mum", don't tell me you don't know how to spell that, little bookworm like you. I think it's about time your old mum heard from you, don't you? Now I know the two of you don't exactly get on like a house on fire. You told me all about that the night we met. "Old cow wouldn't care if I fell off a cliff," I believe were the words. Shocking, really. Mind you, my old mum was a bit of a cow herself. I was just lucky my dad was a prince, bless him. Trouble is, you haven't even got that consolation, have you? I remember you telling me.'

Alison burned: the memory was a mortifying flame, eating her alive. *God forgive me. God forgive me that I told.*

'But still and all, you know what they say, blood's thicker than water. And just in case your old mum up in Geordieland should take it in her head to wonder what's become of you lately, this little postcard should set her mind at rest. Nothing fancy. Just to say you've moved on to Nottingham and you've got work there and doing very nicely and how's yourself...'

The postcard had slipped from her fingers and fallen on to the blanket. He watched it.

'You are going to write this card, aren't you, Ali?'

Her silence betrayed nothing of the clamour in her head. Clamour wild and desperate but ultimately empty. In her distant, dim, stupendously unconcerned mother she had never dared to place anything that was recognizable as hope. But hope there must have been, in some far outpost of her imagination, because nothing but a hope being crushed could have caused this wild clamour.

Wild, and empty. The pain was not going to let her refuse to write the card. No way. The pain was a crazed tooled-up junkie and it wanted those pills and it was going to have them. It would kill a hope bigger than this to get them. Oh, yes.

'Now you see why I had to do it?' he said, all innocent reason. 'I mean, this isn't a thing I could *make* you do. Not directly. It's got to be your handwriting, obviously. So you've got to choose to write the card. Voluntary sort of thing, which I've said from the start is the best way to go on after all. Isn't it?'

He gazed down at her, down into the well of her self, and his smile was reflective now, full of unfathomable enjoyment.

'You going to write it, Ali?' He picked up the bottle of pills, did a little Latin American shimmy as he shook them. 'Yeehah, yeehah, *caramba*. You want the peels, *amigo*, you have to write the postcaaard . . .'

And finally it was the sight of him going into his crazed fun mode that made her pick up the postcard with her tortured left hand and hold it as steady as she could against her knee and write 'Dear Mum'.

'Ah, you little treasure. Good stuff. Right, what's next . . .?'

Alison Holdenby's courage and resourcefulness had

reason enough to lie down and die. Consciously she wasn't aware of them at all. But even as she wrote, something was urgently throwing ideas at her through the fog of pain and despair.

Such as: signal to your mum through the postcard. Obviously he was going to read it, but there might be a way ... Change handwriting? No, he had all her things, plenty of specimens of her handwriting among them, he could compare, probably would knowing him. Grotesque misspellings? Doubtful if her mum would notice anything: worth a try if it was Sean, but the smiler was no fool, the smiler had brains ... Address, then, address—

'Oh, by the way, don't think of writing some false address on it, princess,' he said. 'I've got your donor card and that's got your next of kin's name and address on it, so I'll know. Sorry, probably you're thinking nothing of the kind, bit insulting of me that. But just in case. Ready? "As you can see I've moved on to Nottingham. Got myself work here, catering. Cash in hand. So I'm doing OK. I'm staying with friends at the moment, I'll let you know when I'm settled properly. Hope you're well, love Alison." Got that down? Good girl. Would you put kiss kiss, I wonder? No, maybe not. I don't see the Holdenbys as a kissy-kissy lot somehow. And from what you've told me about your mum I don't reckon she's the sort who's going to hold her breath waiting for you to send her a permanent address. Not a single letter from her amongst all your stuff, and I notice there's no phone number on the donor card. I mean, I could be wrong, but I reckon I've got a fair picture of the old dear. Raleigh House, now. Sounds to me like one of those godawful council blocks. They always give them fancy names, there's probably one called Drake and one called Hawkins et cetera.

Washing on the balconies and dogshit on the stairs.'

It was penetration and she felt he enjoyed it even more than the other kind.

'And there sits Ma Holdenby in front of the TV, occasionally twitching the nets to nose at the neighbours. Not a great letter writer, Ma Holdenby. Got this idea that it's posh or something, and anyway, that daughter of hers chose to clear off and leave her, so let her get on with it. Well, there we are. Like I say, there's no love lost between you and your mum, Ali, that's quite obvious, so I don't suppose telling her this little fib can bother you that much, can it? Let me see.'

He held out his hand for the postcard, and Alison was subject to a last mutinous impulse to tear it right across – not because it would do any good, not because it would stop him making her write another one eventually, not because she hoped her mother would ever ride to the rescue – but just to turn the tables, ever so slightly. See his face, as he enjoyed feasting on hers.

But the pain in her left hand, intensified by gripping the card, screamed and babbled, a detainee cracking and telling all. She gave him the postcard and he read it over carefully while she gazed at the bottle of pills as on the stirred body of a lover.

'Lovely job,' he said at last. 'Writing's a wee bit shaky, but I suppose that's only to be expected.'

He was sick enough to take the pills away again now: she knew that. The knowledge passed between them in a glance, and he twinkled at her. But then it was as if the knowledge gave him pleasure enough, and he unscrewed the cap and dropped two pills into his palm.

'Should only take one of these at a time really, but never mind.' There was a plastic cup of water by the bed

– plastic tray and paper plate with biscuits too, her very own tea service – and he passed it to her with the pills. Alison swallowed them down and lay back, waiting for them to begin their glorious work, wondering if he was finished with her. It was too much to say that she didn't care as long as this pain eased, but she was definitely strengthened. Not just by the painkillers but by something he had said that only now sank in: he hadn't broken her finger. It had certainly felt that way but, as he had said, he knew what he was doing: pain was his purpose rather than disablement. There was a prospect, then, of healing, of the pain receding of its own accord in time. If she were free of pain she would be clear-headed, and if she were clear-headed she could plan . . .

'Alison.' Tapping the postcard against his white teeth, he studied her. Penetrating. 'Don't go getting any ideas. I'm saying this for your benefit, pet. I admire your spunk, I really do. You've got this bee in your bonnet about not liking it here and you're sticking with it. But like I say, it's about choice. You can choose to be a good girl and then you can have those cuffs off and move about the house free as you please. Or you can be stubborn and pin all your hopes on getting away. But the thing is, if you're ever in a position to do a runner, we'll come after you. Or send someone to get you. This is all there is, Alison: this is your life now, and you'd better get used to it. Your old mum doesn't give a toss, and even if she does in a couple of days her tiny mind will be set at rest because Ali's written her from Nottingham and everything's hunky-dory. That old boyfriend of yours doesn't give a toss – found that last letter amongst your stuff, by the way, very nasty, surprised you kept that one. Your landlords don't give a toss – when they finally get shirty about the rent, they'll just find you've vacated the premises and done a midnight flit. Nobody gives a toss, Ali. See? See what I'm getting at? A complete loser like you, sweetheart – isn't this your natural place, really? Wasn't this just waiting for you? It's right for you, Alison, it's what you deserve, and I honestly think as soon as you begin to see that you'll feel better about things and you just won't *want* to go.' He picked up a biscuit, nibbled a piece, then put it back on the plate. 'Yuck. Soft. Well, any road up,' fresh and brisk, 'better be off. You'd keep me chatting here all night, you would. Got to be up early in the morning. Off to Nottingham again, you know.'

'Give my regards to the Sheriff.'

Didn't know why she said it. Maybe the painkillers kicking in and giving her a high. Maybe because spitting in his face was a dreary old trick now and what she really needed was to wrong-foot him, take him by surprise as she never could, take control if only for a couple of seconds. Maybe it was just the flippancy of the doomed.

The laughter began after a long frozen moment in which she seemed to see into him: an X-ray instant that revealed dark twisting places, alien guts of blackness. And then the laughter, loud and hearty, and he snapped his fingers and pointed and gasped, 'Nice one. Nice one, Ali,' and as he left her she knew how little her life meant to him and how easily he would toss it away in just such an instant, quick, easy.

TEN

1

Ian Christopher Elderkin, a.k.a. I. C. Elderkin Unisex Fashions, a.k.a. Chill, a.k.a. the smiler, set out in the cold dark morning for Nottingham.

His mind, that smooth, strange, seamless mind that had served him so well over thirty years, was fixed on various details: immediate ones like looking out for schoolchildren crossing the road on this treacherous morning of freezing fog, less immediate ones like the purpose of this journey, which was to send the postcard to Alison Holdenby's mother from a Nottingham postbox so that it would bear a Nottingham postmark. Detail: it was so important, and he was fortunate that that smooth unfathomable mind of his had always had such a firm grasp of it.

It was certainly a dismal morning, but Ian Christopher Elderkin registered none of the displeasure that all over the city was making less equable people groan and shiver and bicker with each other as they rattled cans of de-icer or struggled into burdensome overcoats. He saw the bare trees, iron-black and seemingly past all possibility of leaves, that lined the old city streets, but he was not depressed by them: he saw the dirty frozen snow that crusted driveways and kerbs, everlasting as rock and impervious to spade and shovel, but the sight imparted nothing to his mood. He had the capacity of keeping his mind and his emotional perceptions quite separate. It was sad about the old girl creeping along there about a tenth of a mile an hour and liable to crunch like a bundle of twigs if she fell: he conceded the sadness even as his thoughts bristled and bounced like a jaunty dog.

Which is not to say that Ian Christopher Elderkin was not engaged with the world he saw through the windscreen of his van. He was very much engaged with it in so far as it interested him. It was a good forty miles' drive to Nottingham and he had no company, but he did not fear being bored, because there would always be something to catch his interest.

There, for example: that family emerging from one of those narrow pathways, beloved of muggers, which threaded the Bluebell estate, a sixties catastrophe with a name that must have seemed a bad joke even then. She, twenty-five going on fifty, with one of those raw-boned thin-lipped underclass faces that seem incomplete without a clenched fag: he, unshaven and resentful in a worn carcoat that had turned the colour of the smoke in the bookies'. Behind them, ignored, two frowzy children, fruit of his ratty loins, despised by him in spite of or perhaps because they were the only thing he had to show for a lifetime of non-achievement. And each of the children being pulled along by a lurching half-grown dog, Alsatian-gargoyle crossbreed. The children couldn't control those dogs: all it needed was a cat or a speeding pushbike and they would be off the lead, pelting into the road, squashed under a car, with a pile-up to follow. Yet the parents didn't care. Their stupidity was simply too deep for them to care. In some ways their stupidity freed them, but they were also prisoners of it.

The interest Ian Christopher Elderkin felt in these things was close and attentive, but it was certainly not sympathy; and it did not resemble empathy except perhaps in the aesthetic sense, as one may experience empathy with a work of art. Studying people and getting the measure of them, especially with regard to their stupidities, gave him a satisfaction that was not quite sensual and not quite intellectual, though it contained elements of both – a fair enough definition of the aesthetic response, perhaps; but one thing was certain. No matter how far he penetrated into other people's lives and minds, he never moved outside himself. He could learn a great deal about a person by looking at their shoes, but he had no impulse to step into them. No out-of-body experiences for Ian Christopher Elderkin. He was in there for keeps and he liked it that way.

By nine he was out of the city and on the A road. There was less to interest him out here in the country, because there was hardly a person to be seen – just flat fields ribbed like corduroy and an unending glare of sunless sky. But he could open up the van's powerful engine, an adequately compensating pleasure. Part of the reason for his coolness of temperament was this balance.

He intended to do a little buying in Nottingham, but the chief reason for his journey was the postcard. It was a detail and might even be an unnecessary one, but he saw no reason to take chances. The girl might not have been telling the whole truth about her mother's lack of interest in her – unlikely, he felt, because she really wasn't the fibbing sort, she was all openness, which was one of the things that had drawn him to her; but it was just possible. It was his firm opinion that it was better to be safe than sorry.

At least, for now. He was still enjoying having his very own pet person and wanted nothing to imperil that enjoyment. He was not at all bored with her, not yet: which was not to say that he couldn't envisage a time when he would get bored with her. He could see that happening all right, one of these days. But the strange vivid mind of Ian Christopher Elderkin didn't trouble itself with picturing that day or what might lie at the end of it. It was sure to be interesting, and that was all that mattered.

2

Of all the cold places the city has to offer this cruel winter, the railway station must be one of the very coldest.

Why? Something about railway stations. They are Victorian inventions after all, creations of a tougher age when women died in childbirth and thieves dangled to the cry of a thousand throats. And the city's railway station still sprawls over seven long platforms with Victorian expansiveness, even though the old Gothic frontage has been demolished.

Besides, railway stations force people to be outdoors, a rarity in an indoor age. There's no escaping it: if you're going to use the railway you have to stand on the open platform at some time. The bizarre unfairness of this is visible on the faces of the people waiting on platform two for the Inter-City from York to King's Cross: pinched and reddened, stamping, hunching themselves into their coats, they seem to be irritably questioning their own sanity, or the sanity of the transport system. How do they come to be standing in the middle of an expanse of shelterless bare concrete with nothing but a view of coal-tips behind peeling hoardings, and with the bitterest weather imaginable concentrating its entire ghastliness on their shivering selves? There must be something wrong somewhere.

The curious xylophone noise that precedes an announcement over the PA sounds: the train is approaching platform two – is visible, indeed, rounding the long slow bend past the marshalling yard. Sudden and urgent attentiveness on the part of the huddlers and stampers, pressing forward, as if the train were a taxi and you have to hail it.

Fusty train smell as the doors open, yielding brisk journeyers, on their way somewhere, workaday. Nobody to meet anybody: that was all put away with the Christmas decorations. Busy solitude is the rule once again. Clip-clop of heels, consulting of watches. The doors close on the new travellers, the train moves on and leaves an empty platform.

All except for one figure which, having disembarked, seems in no hurry to get away from the piercing railway station cold. Setting her one battered suitcase down on the platform, she squats on it and rolls up a cigarette.

About twenty-one, this girl: sturdy in build; about five foot four. She has very fair, almost translucent skin and brown eyes – the only clue to her original hair colour, which hasn't seen the light in many moons. At present it is boot-polish black with undertones of red and cut short, too short really for the little cluster of tight braids that decorates the crown. On her hands she wears cut-off mittens, revealing fingernails bitten to the quick: on her feet, monkey boots: on her body, a grey knitted pullover that reaches to her knees, and black leggings. There is a small rucksack over her shoulder.

If there is an element of show in the way she squats on the case — there is a seat three feet away — a touch of On-the-Road, free-spirit, don't-hassle-me pretension, then it must be so ingrained as to be unconscious, for there is not a soul around to see her. Perhaps the girl realizes this, because after a few puffs on the rollup she stands, hefts her case and makes for the station exit.

Taxis waiting in the street outside, but they are not for her. Opposite the station is a huge brick monument called the Great Northern Hotel, but that is not for her either, though she gives it a narrow-eyed, world-weary onceover. In the beer garden of the Great Northern stands a tall beech tree, and it has been strung throughout its branches with coloured light bulbs, already switched on in the murky afternoon. Just a way of drawing the traveller's attention to the place, perhaps; but it has a curiously uplifting and festive effect when seen from a distance, almost as if the city were enjoying a permanent Christmas. The girl, however, has only one word for it. Grotesque. It is a word she uses a great deal.

She applies it, for example, to her landlord, or rather to the man who was her landlord until yesterday, when he threw her out. The reasons he gave for this included drugs, persistent non-payment of rent, and the hole that she kicked in the door of her room. She considers these reasons pretty grotesque. The door was a poxy door anyway. Poxy is another word she uses a lot.

The girl leaves the Great Northern behind and crosses the footbridge over the ring road. The footbridge leads directly into the city's largest and shiniest shopping mall: the city is, perhaps understandably, determined that no one shall miss it. Having lived here for a while before, the girl is not impressed by the shopping mall. She thinks it is grotesque, also poxy.

If not as grotesque and poxy as her ex-landlord. Were it not an article of her faith that she never lets anything get to her, she would describe herself as well pissed off with her ex-landlord. He wasn't even a proper landlord anyway. It was an illegal sublet. She should have reported him. Would have, in fact, if he hadn't found her stash. That made it more difficult.

The girl passes the gleaming doors of Tudor Radio and descends to the lower level by the escalator. Conveying by her dogged lope that she is only using this place for access, she makes her way to a side exit and emerges from the mall into the streets of the city centre. A down-and-out is panhandling in the doorway of an empty shop and she makes a point of tossing him a handful of coppers.

If her poxy landlord had his way, she reflects, loping, she might well be in the same position as that down-and-out now. There's nowhere for her to go back in poxy Doncaster: the mates she had there have turned shitty on her and only let her crash for the one night. But no worries. The girl with the suitcase and the rucksack and the look of streetwise disdain isn't just trolling around for the sake of it. The girl with the boots and the porcupine-quill braids and the junkie inwardness about her small mouth has a destination in mind.

The girl called Zoe has somewhere to go.

3

'Meet you for lunch?'

Murray sounded wary rather than urgent on the phone, but the declaration of intent was plain enough. He worked way out in one of the new town business parks, and meeting for lunch was no casual thing. She met wariness with cool friendliness, and he was waiting for her in the lobby at Tudor when she came off air.

'Changing the national character, this weather,' he said as they walked to the nearest maniac-free pub. 'We're getting like Swedes or Finns or something. See how stern everybody looks? All working away like beavers and then getting morosely sloshed.'

They talked of neutral matters over a ploughman's and over the noise of four indistinguishable men in middle-management suiting who were competing for the most intimate knowledge of Portugal. Murray stuck to mineral water: Sarah had downed two vodkas almost before she was aware of it. When she saw him giving her glass a significant look she interpreted it charitably as a reference to the fact that she would have to drive home later.

True, of course, and a bummer. It wasn't enough to say that she fancied another. She could have put her lips to the optic and just suckled.

At last, Murray stopped juggling and let everything fall. 'Sarah, I'm sorry I haven't . . . you know, haven't . . .'

'I haven't either. Phoned or anything.'

'No. Must be a record for us . . . Actually I meant to say sorry in another way. For being sarcy and stroppy and stomping out and everything.'

She accepted this — was glad, indeed, to see him and to hear him, glad and warmed and ready to be reconciled

– but she was alert too. Alert to the fact that he was apologizing only for style, not substance. She waited.

'About those posters... I mean if you're still set on that there's a firm who does insert printing for our place who—'

'I've already done it.'

'What?'

She upended her glass for the last inspiriting drops. 'Come on. I'll show you.'

The Embassy had been the city's largest cinema until an out-of-town multiscreen had killed it stone dead. Plans to turn it into a concert hall surfaced, like the Loch Ness Monster, periodically and dubiously. In the meantime the huge building remained, smack in the centre of the city. Probably only dynamite could get rid of it. But its huge expanse of wall offered an opportunity to everyone who wanted to stick up a poster, from the ubiquitous Socialist Workers' Party to local garage bands using dad's photocopier.

There was a lot of defacing, of course; but there was so much to deface that the most determined vandal couldn't cover it all, and Sarah found the poster she had put up last night still clean and intact. Murray had said nothing as she led him here and after he had read it he said nothing still for some moments.

'I wonder if I should have had them made larger,' she said, 'but I wanted them to fit on notice boards and such.'

He faced her. 'When?'

'They were ready yesterday. Finney's were really quick.'

'How many?'

'A hundred. But I've only put up about twenty-five so far. I did this last night. I put some on empty shop windows, some along the embankment—'

'You did this at night? How late at night?'

She shrugged. 'Late. I mean, you have to. Like the old joke says, bill stickers will be prosecuted, poor old Bill.'

'That . . . that is bloody dangerous, Sarah. This whole *thing* is bloody dangerous, but creeping around the city centre late at night . . .'

'Oh, not really. It's like you said, we're all Swedes now. Any mugger who'd hang around in dark alleys in this weather must be mad . . .'

Her breath, vaporizing, was flavoured with vodka, and oh how she wanted another. She studied Murray's face, sidelong. Great passionkiller, too, this weather. Bleak white light on indoor complexions and red noses, not just him of course, she must look the same. And yet the Scandinavians were famous for unfettered libido. Funny . . .

'You're going to make yourself ill,' he said.

'Then I'll go to the doctor.'

'I think you should anyway.'

Suddenly she felt wildly angry, but it was all inside. She only said, 'Do you indeed.'

'Yes. Sarah, for God's sake, you're stressed out, you've got to at least admit that. You're on a high wire all the time – you know you are. Maybe a doctor could help you, just give you something to bring you down a bit.'

'I'm perfectly all right. In fact I feel better than I have since . . . for a long time. I'm doing something positive. Aren't I?'

His eyes dwelled on her for a moment. He pointed at the poster. 'You put your phone number.'

'I told you, it's the only way.'

He sighed. It was not a nice sigh, and he realized it at

once. 'I don't know . . . maybe it will work. Where else are you going to put them?'

'All over the college, I thought. Places where young people go, that Rock Café place, the football ground, the swimming pool. The underpasses round the ring road—'

'Christ, no. All right, I don't mean it like that, but at least – at least let me come with you next time. I mean, if you're really set on it . . .'

Ah. He had spoiled it. That *if* said it all. The flyposting had been no fun in the dark echoing streets, and she would gladly have accepted his help – *if* it had been freely given. But she wasn't going to accept conditions.

'You mean you're going to trail along behind me as if I was some harmless crackpot tracing ley lines or bloody corn circles, oh let her get on with it, poor dear, just see she doesn't come to any harm. That's it, isn't it? No, no, Murray, forget it. You might see somebody you know and it would be terribly embarrassing for you.'

This was unreasonable. But sometimes it took the flailings of unreason to knock the mask off truth. Sarah knew she was thinking and acting with amphetamine intensity and that no one could be expected to understand, entirely, what was going on in her mind. But that didn't mean she had to fall over herself with gratitude at being offered measly half-measures. The path she had set herself to tread was a path of absolutes. It was all or nothing in her world now.

Still she gave him another chance. She said, 'Only come with me if you want to, Murray. I mean really want to.'

All or nothing.

'What I want is to see you back to normal. Relaxed. Happy. For your sake, not mine. And with this going on . . .'

Nothing.

'Look, Murray, I'd better be getting back, I've got some pre-recording to do.' He seemed a long way away from her: too far for any wranglings to be worthwhile, too far for anything but the most basic gestures. 'I'll see you.'

It was her turn to walk away.

Unreasonable, sure; and there was pain waiting for her, she knew. The part of herself that loved him still had an appointment with agony, but the appointment was postponed. Everything was postponed. That was the way it was. There was a war on.

4

The hammering at the front door was so loud and long that even Trend, flat out on his bedroom floor with aural thunderheads clashing around him, picked up on it at last. He stretched out a toe to the volume on his music system, listening out for Sean going down the stairs.

The knocking went on.

'Trend!'

Sean's head, peeping in.

'Wha'?'

'There's somebody at the door.'

'Well, answer it then.'

'Shit, I don't know, man . . . Who do you reckon it is?'

'Eh?'

' 'Cking hell, turn it down, man. Listen. Who knocks like that?'

They stared at each other a moment, then ran to the front bedroom, Chill's.

'Can't see anything,' Sean said, lifting a corner of the grey net curtain. 'No meat wagon.'

The hammering went on.

'Better answer it,' Trend said.

'Jesus, I don't know about this, man. Maybe we'd better wait till Chill gets back.'

'Yeah, but that won't be till tonight. He reckoned he was going to open the stall when he got back from Nottingham.'

'I got a bad feeling about this, man. Really bad feeling.'

'I don't know . . . maybe it's that old granny next door.'

'Eh?'

'That old – oh look, all right, I'll answer it.' Trend was as grandly magnanimous as if he were taking Sean's place on the scaffold.

The knocking had stopped when he got downstairs. Instead a pair of eyes were watching him through the letterbox.

He stopped dead.

'Trend!'

'Who's that?'

'Zoe. Open the poxy door, will you?'

Trend hesitated for two eyeblinks. Then he hurried forward and flung open the door as if he were welcoming a saviour.

'About time. Were you in bed or what?'

'Nah, got the stereo on. Where'd you spring from? I thought you were living in Doncaster.' Trend stepped aside to let Zoe in, eyeing the suitcase.

'Moved on. Hiya, Sean! What's the matter, expecting the filth or something?'

Sean, peeping over the banisters, giggled and then came at a galumphing booted run down the stairs. 'Yeah. Nah. What you doing here?'

'Oh brilliant. What a welcome. Put the flags out everybody, Zoe's here.'

There was something about Zoe's tone that was always a little off-centre. Her joking contained the smothered belligerence of the drunk. Perhaps it was simply her voice, which had a peculiarly grating pitch, the youth-culture gutturals overlaying a recognizably middle-class accent.

'Never knew you were coming,' Sean said.

'Didn't know myself. Got thrown out of my poxy digs yesterday. So I thought bollocks to Doncaster. Poxy place. Come back down here, look up some old mates. Where's Chill?'

'Out.' Sean had just noticed the suitcase. 'Where you staying, then?'

'Buckingham Palace, where do you think? Jesus. What time will Chill be back?'

'Five, half five. Give us that here.' Trend took the suitcase.

'Cheers. Got any drink in?'

Sean's jaw hung. 'What, you reckoning on staying here?'

'Dunno. Got nowhere else. That's why I came down. It's up to Chill really. Isn't it? I don't reckon he's going to turn me out on the street. I thought when the landlord chucked me out, sod you I thought, I know someone who'll let me crash at his place.'

Sean kept trying to catch Trend's eye. But Trend wouldn't be caught. Zoe looked from one to the other, frowning.

'What?' she said. 'What, is it me? Are you up on something and I'm straight? God, I hate that. That does my head in when that happens.'

'Nah,' Trend said. 'You want a beer? Come on. Here, you got anything?'

'Only blow. I was speeding the night before last, that's

when I kicked my poxy door in and that's how come the landlord got stroppy.'

'Yeah?' The mention of criminal damage perked Sean up for a moment, and he lost his look of a guilt-stricken dog. 'What did he do?'

'Told you, chucked me out.' In the living room Zoe plonked herself on the sofa and hoisted her feet up on to it. Trend handed her a can of lager. 'Cheers. No, it was the stuff as well, he was getting really scratchy about that. God. It's not as if I was dealing. He's just totally grotesque basically. So what have you guys been doing with yourselves? Must be what, over a year since I saw you.'

Still Trend would not catch Sean's eye, though Sean was pantomiming alarmed signals anyone could have seen from a mile off.

'Oh, you know,' Trend said, cracking a can, 'bit of this, bit of that. Listen, don't worry about getting a place to stay, I mean like you say it's up to Chill but I'm sure you can crash here. Can't see why not.'

Zoe stared at Sean, who was roaming about the room like a punch-drunk fighter. 'You sure you're not on anything, Sean?'

'Nah, mate.' Sean gave a nervous giggle, shook his head, sweated, roamed again. 'Nah.'

'Got any tapes?' Zoe said after staring at him some moments longer.

'Yeah.' Trend was prompt. 'Sean, go and fetch my woofer. And that Those Nightmare Persons tape.'

Sean was unused to this confidence in Trend. But he went, and was back in seconds, almost dropping the tape player in his haste.

'Jesus, Sean, watch it,' Trend said, taking it into his arms like a sick child. 'What's the matter with you?'

'So what's Chill doing with himself nowadays?' Zoe had a way of thrusting forward her neck when she was interested, and she did it now. 'Still got the stall?'

'Yeah,' Trend said, dismissive. 'Here, Zoe, you say you got some blow on you?'

'Yeah. My blow.'

'Ah, come on. Just one.'

Zoe groaned. 'All right then. But I'm going to have to find someone soon, I've only got an eighth and I've lost all my contacts here. Can you still score down the Gladstone Arms?'

'Oh, don't worry, Chill gets it sometimes, he must know somebody.' Trend watched greedily as Zoe extracted a small ball of silver foil from a pocket somewhere beneath the vast jumper and unwrapped it.

'Got any skins, I'm nearly out.'

'Yeah, sure, got all the gear.' Trend darted to the sideboard, produced a ceremonial tray set out with rolling machine, Rizlas, matches, a square of cardboard and a bottle top.

'So, Chill's doing all right then?' There was a sickly whiff of cannabis resin as Zoe burned off a corner of the brown lump and crumbled it into the bottle top. 'Seeing anybody?'

'Oh . . . you know Chill,' Trend said.

'Yeah. I do know Chill.' Zoe lifted her chin and her top lip came back to reveal tobacco-stained incisors. The action was almost exactly like that of a snarling dog. 'So what's that supposed to mean?'

Sean was roaming faster now. He was all over the room like a trapped bluebottle.

'Nothing,' Trend said, uncertain for the first time. 'Just . . . you know. Chill's not the sort who goes in for the long-term relationship sort of thing.'

Zoe gave a snort. 'Long-term relationships are totally grotesque if you ask me,' she said, covering the teeth again. She tore off a strip of the cardboard and made a roach. Trend's shoulders relaxed. 'I was seeing this guy for a while in Doncaster, but he just couldn't get his head together. Smack, you know. Been doing it since he was seventeen. I couldn't hack it in the end. Put that tape on, then.'

'Oh, right.'

'These indie?'

'Yeah.' Trend watched intently as she distributed the crumbs of resin expertly along the length of the joint, licked the paper and closed the machine.

'You still got an indie club here?'

'Yeah. I don't go much. It's crap.'

'You should see the scene in Doncaster. I mean the people there are really grotesque.' Zoe unclipped the machine, tapped out the joint and lit it. 'Here, Sean. You want some of this? Might mellow you out a bit. You look like you need it.'

If it failed to mellow Sean out, the joint at least induced him to sit down; but he still twitched like a live cable as he sat, and he would not give up the effort to catch Trend's eye. It was a dead loss. Trend had the giggles on his third puff, and when Zoe rolled another – she needed two to feel anything at all – he was completely gone. As for Zoe, when the dope kicked in its effect on her was to turn her truculence into morose introspection. Clearly her navel was a spectacle of interest beyond the possibility of exhaustion.

Time became slippery: it whizzed along, stretched forever, and still fitted into half an hour. When the tape was over Sean switched the TV on and gazed at it shaking his head and murmuring in wonder at what he saw while Trend cracked up, howling and clutching his sides. Then the munchies hit. Zoe headed for the kitchen, Trend and Sean shambling after her.

'What you got in? I'm starving. I'm starving...'

'Everything,' chuckled Trend, his arm round Sean's neck. 'We've got everything in. Everything in the world.'

'Oh, wow, haven't you got anything without meat in it? You meat-eaters, man, you do my head in. Look at all these lumps of rotting flesh, I mean it's really grotesque.'

'There's some cheese,' Sean said, and the way he said it made Trend howl again.

'Is it vegetarian cheese?'

'Don't know, I haven't asked it,' Trend said, and fell about, yelping.

Zoe gnawed the hunk of cheese anyhow, clutching it in her fist and prowling about the kitchen. And then, pointing: 'What's that?'

That was a large bag of cat litter.

'Nothing,' said Sean.

'You got a cat?'

'No,' said Trend, 'not a cat,' and then he really started laughing.

'What's the joke?' Zoe's mood swung through a hundred and eighty degrees and she unveiled the teeth. It was hard to tell with Zoe where narcotic paranoia ended and her straight personality began: probably one was an expression of the other. 'What's the big joke? Is it me? Are you laughing at me?' She began hitting out at Trend, paddling at him with open hands, and the sight of that set Sean off. One moment he was gibbering, the next he was in stitches.

Zoe was smiling too, but only at the sensation of her hands windmilling and pummelling, exhilaration at the violent momentum. 'Yeah? Yeah? Come on. Tell me the joke. Come on, tell me.'

'I can't,' Trend said weakly, falling backwards on to a kitchen chair and putting up his hands in surrender. 'I can't, honest. It's Chill's.'

'What's Chill's?'

'Nah, nah, nah,' gasped Sean, protesting through his laughter tears, helpless.

'The surprise,' Trend said, and the hair and the dope and the ingrained sullenness could not disguise something quite new in his face, a glinting perception of – at last – control. 'Wait till Chill gets back. He's got a surprise for you.'

5

When Sarah drove home late that afternoon she became aware of something that was neither a sensation nor an emotion but which seemed to fill the car like an elusive odour. And when she placed it at last she could find no more acceptable term for it than: aloneness.

Not solitude: the word had a quiet contemplative sound, and that was far removed from what was going on in her mind. And not loneliness either. Loneliness implied a lack: it was something that required to be and could be remedied by human presence. And she saw now that even if Murray had come through for her, this aloneness would not have been altered in the least. The most whole-hearted support would only have been like kisses on the other side of a wall of glass.

The driving was hazardous, and she was glad she hadn't

given in to the drinking urge at lunchtime. What made this winter so primeval was the way its elements were undifferentiated: the fog was a continuation into the air of the treacherousness coating the road surface. They were living in a freezing broth. Just before the turning to her own street she saw a couple hopelessly trying to push-start a car, their feet slithering under them. Headlights passed them indifferently. At the beginning of the winter any number of willing hands would have joined them, but the siege mentality had moved on to a different stage. People could only stand being all in it together for so long. Sooner or later they started fighting over the rat cutlets.

Sarah had forced herself into a state of inexpectation about going home. She had got the posters only yesterday, had had time to put up just a few last night. She had left the answering machine on, but it was a city of over two hundred thousand people and what were a few posters against that . . .? So when she got in to find the answering machine blinking and beeping she managed to wait all of three seconds before pressing the play button and crouching down before it like a supplicant.

Two messages.

One: her mother. 'It's all right, it's only me. Just wondering how you were, love, that's all . . .' A lot of people of her mother's generation and background automatically prefaced telephone calls with 'It's all right'. Legacy of the time when the telephone was the unavoidable instrument of bad news, maybe. Sarah hadn't been to see her lately, but her mother's rich husky tones managed to conceal the reproach as she mentioned it. Even found an excuse for her: the weather. It was twenty-odd miles to the market town where her mother pursued her jovial Chaucerian life now, and what with the roads... Sarah stamped ineffectually on guilt, mentally made that promise that was her sole vow and oath nowadays: *when this is over...*

Second message. Charlie and Penny both joined her on the floor, a twin outboard motor of purrs.

A lot of phonebox noise, and then the voice.

'Hallo, darling... listen, I don't know who she is on that poster, but I'm sure I fucked her from behind once. Tell you, she loved it. Do the same for you if you like...'

He went on until his invention ran out, which wasn't long. The cats studied her with almond eyes, composed, removed from it all. Sarah put out a slightly unsteady hand, scratched Charlie's head.

'Do you suppose I could have that drink now?'

She had it, but she did something first. She removed the microcassette from the machine and threw it in the bin, or rather fitted it into the top layer of overflowing rubbish. Then she found a spare in a drawer and slotted it into the machine.

Crank calls. Well, Murray warned me. OK. Goes with the territory. I can handle that.

But if she was going to throw away every microcassette that contained one she'd better get in quite a supply...

That thought made her pour a double instead of a single. And after she had fed the cats and done something that was like a child's version of tidying up she sat before the TV with another double in her hand and tried not to think about the lubricious voice murmuring its fantasies on to an answering machine.

Penny, granting a rare privilege, jumped on her lap. Sarah stroked the delicate head and noticed three unfamiliar books on the coffee table. What the hell...? Then she remembered: Michael Malinowski's book review feature, coming up soon. Too soon. She hadn't even opened them and knew she wouldn't. Because there was something else on the coffee table: the sheaf of posters.

'Don't get too comfy, Pen,' Sarah said. 'I've got to go out again soon.'

6

Well, the day had been a bit of a dead loss and Chill would be glad to get home.

Not as far as the trip to Nottingham was concerned, of course. He'd not only posted the card to Ma Holdenby, object of the exercise, but done a very nice little deal with the Khunti brothers, unfortunate name that but cracking blokes and very nice quality gear, and they must have had a collective rush of blood to the head or something because you wouldn't believe the price he'd knocked them down to.

Which was all very well if you could actually shift the gear but when he'd got back around lunchtime and opened up the stall he'd found that the punters just weren't buying, in fact the punters just weren't around to buy and who could blame them on a day like this? Talk about corporal punishment of deceased equine mammal. Of course it was midweek and some stallholders didn't bother to open up at all then, hardly worth the petrol money, and it had crossed Chill's mind to do the same, but there, he supposed he was a workaholic and always would be, got it from his old dad no doubt. At least there was old Lou on the next stall to talk to but with the best will in the world there was only so much you could take of the old walking emphysema rabbiting on about her daughter's operation and all in all Chill was pretty glad when the time came to load the van all over again and file the day away in a drawer that was definitely *not* marked Great Days in Ian Christopher Elderkin's Life.

He cheered up a bit on the way home, thinking of what he would do when he got there and so forth, and by the time he pulled up outside Number 43 he was all sweetness and light and goodness knows what else, his normal self in other words. Now one thing Chill could say for certain, he never lied to himself, and so there was no denying that he was knocked back by what he found when he got in. Well and truly knocked back. Flummoxed if you will. And it was so long since Chill had been flummoxed that it was like being flummoxed for the first time almost. Loss of flummox virginity sort of thing.

Not so much at the fact of Zoe being there – though she was undoubtedly a blast from the past that Chill had not expected to see in this neck of the Midlands again and maybe *that* was a teensy bit misguided of him because if ever there was a bad penny then Zoe was the counterfeit piece of coinage and no contenders. But still and all. His flabber was not gasted quite so much by the sight of Zoe's pricelessly lowlife mush gawping at him from his own front room as by Trend. Specifically, Trend's attitude. Which skewed as it was by the ingestion of a certain amount of cannabis resin was still unmistakably defiant, cocky, saucy, and downright taunting.

Of Chill. That was what took the actual biscuit. The trendy one, who despite his numerous qualities was really the most hopeless nomark that ever slouched the earth without picking his feet up, was enjoying this. For reasons of his own which Chill didn't choose or indeed need to enquire into, Trend was stirring it.

'Zoe needs a place to stay. I told her she could crash here. S'all right, isn't it, Chill?'

Thus Trend, while Chill picked his jaw up off the floor. Thus Trend, lounging and zonked but not too zonked to give Chill a look like he'd just picked one wing off a fly and was wondering when to pull off the other one.

Sean, meanwhile, was doing his don't-whip-me-bwana number, as far as he was able with the fumes of the old wacky baccy curdling what brains there were in that little round head of his. Plainly Sean had been in a right four-by-eight about the whole situation right from the start but poor old Sean was a bit of a weak vessel and there was only so much you could expect from him. Sean in a state. Trend smug (and jeez, smugness did *not* suit that boy one little bit). And Zoe dragging her arse out of the chair at the sight of Chill and leaping up like he was Christ coming down on a cloud. There was only one thing to be in this situation.

Cool.

'Hiya, Chill my man, long time no see!'

Here came Zoe, weaving her way towards him past whatever imaginary obstacles her junk-addled brain perceived in the room.

'Zoe! How you doing? If I'd known you were coming I'd have baked a cake, baked a cake . . .'

Straight into his arms to give him one of those sloppy junkie hugs. Chill waltzed her around a bit, laughing. Also taking notice: Zoe was in no hurry to let go of him. This was something he would have to think about. It was surprising and also not surprising, no false modesty or anything, just that Zoe and himself had had a bit of a fling way back when. And he had had a strong feeling at the time, and had a strong feeling now as she looked into his face with her weird smashed eyes, that Zoe considered herself and Chill to have what you might call a special relationship. Not exactly a Zoe 4 Chill romance together-forever sort of thing, Zoe being very anti anything that was enjoyed by people who did not spend their lives either out of their heads or ripping off gear from Debenhams, but still a Thing nonetheless.

And guess what, he had a feeling Trend knew it too. The eyes watching the pair of them through that forest of hair were beady. Definitely beady.

'So, how did you end up here? Thought you were up north in ee-ba-gum land, gel. Thought you'd be wearing a flat cap and hobnail boots by now.'

So he got the story, told in Zoe's own unique style of paranoid fantasy, with a lot of outraged breast-beating about the fact that her landlord had been doing something *illegal* in subletting this bughutch she'd been kicked out of. In the Zoe worldview the law was a piece of shit, to be treated accordingly, but oh how she yelped when it failed to protect *her* arse. All fired up to write to the papers about it, she was. Disgusted of No Fixed Abode. What a case.

But the sad ramblings did have a point at any rate, and the point was Zoe was without a place to lay her tie-dyed head and, having no doubt pissed off the whole lowlife population of Doncaster to the point where they wouldn't even give her squatroom, where had her thoughts flown but to her old flame Chill, only the easily nicked price of a train ride away and possessor of a four-bedroom house and well known for his generosity to waifs and strays and sad cases in general?

And Trend, the little devil, had welcomed her in and

as good as promised her the gaff was hers for as long as she liked.

Well. Here was a facer for Chill and no mistake. He stalled a bit by whipping her up a quick omelette and chattering away nineteen to the dozen about old times and flattering the poor mare till she was grinning like the easiest nightclub Tracey, the old brainbox meanwhile ticking over like nobody's business, but he had a feeling that this wasn't the whole of it by any means and that Trend, who was looking smugger by the minute, still had another trick up his sleeve. And then, when Zoe had stowed away the meal after about ten million assurances that the eggs had been laid only by chickens who wanted to and the bread had been humanely harvested by a Central American collective, and when Chill had cracked the last remaining can of lager as a refresher to his wits and prepared himself for taking control of the situation – then, Trend did it. He pulled the other wing off the fly.

'Oh yeah, I was telling Zoe,' he said casually, as if butter wouldn't melt in his mouth or anything else for that matter, 'you've got a little surprise for her, Chill.'

'Yeah, what is this surprise, for crying out loud?' Zoe said. Not stroppily, really: she just talked like that. 'Come on, what's it all about? Show us.' Hanging on to his sleeve and giving him that weird rubbernecked stare of hers. Talk about spotlight on Chill.

But then, Chill had never been averse to the spotlight: put him in it, and he'd dance. And even in this situation, which was definitely hairy, there was something in Chill which just rose to the occasion. For one thing, he didn't like having his decisions made for him: he'd rather take the responsibility himself, no matter what the consequences. Free will sort of thing. And besides, there was bravado. Bravado was his middle name. Give him a challenge and he'd take it up, simple as that.

Of course he could have just given Zoe some bullshit, popped her a couple of tenners, and shooed her out of the house, end of story: he didn't think Trend would push it any further now that he was actually here. But then there would have been a crucial loss of face, and losing face in front of a nomark like Trend just wasn't on Chill's agenda.

And would he have done that in any case, without Trend's little intervention? Chill thought not. It was the bravado thing again: seeing how far you could go because that was what life was all about. Take whatever comes your way, that was his motto, and in this case it was Zoe wanting a place to stay. And a place she would have. Now it was written all over her that she was practically itching for the two of them to pick up where they had left off, and that was fine by Chill because in spite of being a dysfunctional junkie lowlife with the personality of an attack dog, Zoe was one hell of a goer when it got down to brass tacks and he wouldn't be at all averse to slipping her a length now and then if his strength was up to it. But it wasn't just that. It was the challenge.

Also, it would be a hell of a crack to see her face...

'Surprise, what surprise?' Chill said, milking it a bit because he wanted to see *Trend*'s face and Trend needn't think he'd forget this little trick. As it happened it had turned out fine and dandy, but the intention behind it had been something quite different and let Trend beware, just let Trend beware. 'I don't remember any surprise... Oh! *That* surprise. Aha.'

Chill looked from Zoe to Trend, from Trend to Sean. Dear oh lor. Hardly a brain cell between them. Well, there was a breathless hush in the close tonight and no mistake. Hanging on his every word, they were. And Chill had a bouncing, high-stepping realization: he was on top again.

'The surprise,' Chill said, all enigmatic, and tapped his nose and winked at Zoe. Then he flung open the living-room door and did an exaggerated after-you bow. 'Come and see it.'

ELEVEN

1

It went in stages. First she thought it was a dream and then she thought it was a nightmare and then she thought it was inevitable and then she thought it was an opportunity. Somewhere about the second stage her mind very nearly went over the edge of the chasm of babbling insanity, but now she was back on firm ground. Just.

First the dream. An event so incredible, so unexpected, so closely resembling the dreams of rescue that had haunted her sleep in the first days of her imprisonment before she had suppressed them by some mighty effort of unconscious will because they were just too beautiful to be borne ... And still scarcely to be believed even now. The world contained only three people besides herself: creation had been undone, and there were only the smiler, the weasel one and the boy with the hat; this was the cosmology of Alison Holdenby. The arrival of another person was as stunning and dislocating as an alien visitation. For the first moments there was only awe at the inconceivable.

Awe, as she lifted her head from the pillow at the sound of the cellar door and saw – no, *beheld*, only the word *beheld* could convey it – a newcomer descending the steps. Smiler, weasel, hat, they were there too, but they were shadows beside the blinding light of the newcomer.

Yes: Alison understood, then, what people meant when they talked about a religious experience. Paralysed by wonder, she thought: *I am saved.*

For the same reason Alison didn't think it incumbent upon her to do or say anything even if she had been able. The newcomer – the girl – didn't look like a police officer or anything like that, but it didn't seem to matter. She was here. She was not one of them. It was all over.

Hard to say at what precise point the dream turned into nightmare. The sacred wonder persisted, she was sure, even when the girl approached the bed with unsteady steps and then stopped and just . . . *stared* at Alison, stared with her neck thrust forward, stared from a face that seemed to have something missing – not so much expression as meaningful expression, expression you could grasp and understand. But then, redemption was certain to be mysterious. And Alison was sure the glorious hope did not even leave her when the girl turned her head to the smiler and he grinned at her in return. He was, after all, psychotic. Nothing less was to be expected of him.

And then the vision spoke to her.

'You into bondage, or what?'

The police were fond of gallows humour, it was a consequence of their job, like when that copper went to arrest Nilsen and just said, 'I've come about your drains', and as for the clothes and the hair and the studs all along her ear, well, she was surely working undercover, had to be, the outfit was almost exaggerated in its sleaziness . . .

Thus Alison Holdenby tried to hold on to the vision,

Freezing Point

tried to call back the ecstatic light that was fading from her, even as the girl sauntered up and down the length of the bed, studying her.

'Is this a joke, or what?'

From the smiler, a shrug and a theatrical spreading of the hands, like a conjuror displaying a baffling trick.

'What do you think?' he said.

The girl shook her head. 'You're shitting me.'

'Feel those cuffs.' Even more the conjuror. 'Go on, feel them. Are they real or not?'

The girl felt. And while she felt, her face was a few inches from Alison's: but she didn't look into Alison's eyes at all.

Didn't see her.

And perhaps that was when the dream turned into nightmare.

'Shit, man.' The girl straightened up, shaking her head some more. The weasel one and the boy with the hat were merely standing by like pageboys at a wedding: it was to the smiler that the girl addressed herself. 'I don't believe it. I mean, what's she done?'

'Nothing,' the smiler said. 'She's just ours. She's our pet.'

The girl took that one in. Her eyes searched his face.

'How long's she been down here?'

'Oh, I don't know, a few weeks. It's all right. Nobody knows about it. Nobody's looking for her. We were dead careful.' As she continued to stare at him he paused and drew a deep breath and cupped his fingers, as if trying to put something very complex and subtle into simple terms. 'We . . .' And then he looked delighted as it came to him, a flash of inspiration, the *mot juste*. 'We did it for a laugh.'

No dream now. All nightmare. Because the way the girl was shaking her head and pacing from wall to wall of the cellar and muttering and glancing at the bed and shaking her head again meant only one thing. There was disbelief there all right, but it was—

It was *admiring* disbelief.

'You really are a nutcase, you know that?' the girl said, stopping a few inches from the smiler and gazing raptly up into his face. 'I've always said it, Chill mate, but now I know it. You are a complete and utter nutcase.'

'Now, now, don't give me all the credit,' the smiler said, mock-bashful. 'It was a team effort, you know. Team effort.'

The boy with the hat looked sheepish. The weasel one just looked.

'Where'd she come from?' the girl said. 'What about the filth?'

'She came from nowhere,' the smiler said calmly. 'And the police don't know a thing about it. Why should they? It's just our little secret.'

'The police are coming.'

Alison spoke. It was a nightmare and in nightmares your throat locked tight and you had to move heaven and earth to speak, but she managed it at last. The girl goggled at her: just as if a dog had talked.

'The police are coming all right,' Alison said, and she focused on the girl, tried to fix those blank eyes with her own, tried to speak right through to the girl's soul. 'They'll come. You don't think people can just get away with this sort of thing, do you?' She pushed herself into a sitting position, ignoring the screaming pain that had returned to her hand. 'They'll come sooner or later. That's why you've got to let me go. What they've done –

you're not part of it. Can't you see? Look, I don't know who you are but—'

'Sorry,' the smiler cut in, 'my fault that, should have introduced. Zoe, this is Alison. Alison, meet Zoe.'

'This has got to be a wind-up,' Zoe was murmuring. She had a half-smile: literally a half-smile. One side of her mouth was turned up.

'They've done this to me and—' Alison's voice was halting, a cut-up of speech, so long since she had needed coherence like this, so long since there had been any frame of reference outside the insane world of the cellar and the reptiles. 'Look, can't you see, this is real, they've done this to me and they can't get away with it and you've – you've got to be the one, can't you see . . .' Searching, searching for a spark or response in the girl's – *reptile?* – vacant eyes.

'She rambles a bit,' the smiler said breezily, 'but she's all right really. She's got her own stuff here, and she eats what we eat and so on. It's a bit of an odd setup, I suppose, but she's all right, our Alison.'

The toilet bucket stood by the bed. The girl, Zoe, poked it with the toe of her boot. What was that expression on her face?

Fascination?

'Don't – don't be afraid of them,' Alison said, stretching forward to the limits of her chains, trying to get Zoe to look her in the eye. 'You've done nothing, you're not part of it, you – you've got to let me go, tell them, make them . . .'

Already she knew. Knew that only appeals to Zoe's self-interest were any use: that it was no good looking for normal human feelings in a girl who freely associated with these three. That was the nightmare: that the person who should have been her saviour was just like them.

Just like them? Could it really be that this Zoe was turned out of exactly the same warped mould? Surely not. She must at least have self-preservation inside that pasty skin.

'Listen. Zoe, listen to me. They kidnapped me. See? Kept me here and . . .' She swallowed painfully. 'What they've done, it's . . . you don't just get away with it, the police, the police will be searching, they'll do house-to-house, this is heavy stuff, Zoe, it's really heavy stuff what these bastards have done and – and don't you see, you're in it too unless you let me go, tell them . . .'

Exhaustion deprived her of her voice, but there was a small victory. Zoe looked her in the face. Just for a few moments: then turned on the smiler.

'Jesus, Chill, what is all this about the filth? Huh? If you've got me down here just to get me in schtuck as well, I'll frigging kill you, I mean it. If you've got the pigs on to you for this, then I'm out of here, I'm out of here right now—'

'Hold your horses, Zoe, just hold your horses a minute.' The smiler put his hand on her arm, caressed up and down. 'Listen, do you think I'm stupid?'

'I'm not kidding around, Chill—'

'Do you think I'm stupid? Just answer me that.'

Shake of the head. Sulky look, and something else. It could almost have been a smoulder, up into the smiler's eyes.

'All right then. Just think a minute. We've had her for weeks. Nobody saw us take her. Nobody gives a monkey's about her because she's a bit of a loner, our Alison. There aren't any police doing house-to-house or even doing *anything* because no one knows. Sean here kept his beady eye on the local papers and the TV because to be honest he was bricking it a bit at first and thought there might be a bit of comeback but was there, Sean? Was there? You tell her.'

'Nah, mate.' Sean, the good lieutenant. 'Nothing.'

'See?' The smiler was still caressing, up and down. 'It's all right. Do you think I'd be down here chatting away if the bizzies were on to us? Don't you think I'd be frantic? Going bananas?' He spread his arms wide. 'I ask you, Zoe, do I look worried?'

'Don't listen. Don't – don't – listen to – him.' This was a new kind of sobbing that was racking Alison's body now, and she thought she had been through every variety of grief. It was quite dry and it was silent: it came in irregular spasms and it punched holes in her speech. It was agony distilled and purified. 'He's a lunatic, he'll say – anything, you've got to – help me for God's – sake—' She lurched up, almost throwing herself off the bed, trying to *reach* this girl. 'Zoe ... please ...'

Zoe looked sulky again. It was plain that she didn't like being asked to do anything. She jerked her head in Alison's direction. 'Is she always chained up like that?'

'Only because she's uncontrollable otherwise,' the smiler said. 'Honestly as far as I'm concerned she could walk around the house just as she pleases, there's nothing I'd like better. Just be one of us. But she's got these stubborn ideas in her head, and so we have to restrain her. No choice really.'

Zoe shrugged: gave Alison a sidelong glance. 'Look,' she said reluctantly, 'it's not up to me. *I* can't do anything.'

'Call the police, then!' Screaming now. 'Get out, get out now and call the police—'

'No way. Stuff you, sunshine. What do you think I am? No way. You don't catch me grassing anybody up. No way, man.' At last there was animation in that doughy face, but it was not of the right kind. Zoe was backing away from the bed as if Alison were the devil bargaining for her soul. 'I'm no grass. Hey, where you coming from, man, asking *me* to be a grass?'

Alison made no sound. The wailing she heard was in her head. It came from a despair that had something hysterical about it, laughter from the abyss. For she knew where Zoe, at any rate, was coming from. A place where there was nothing worse than being a grass. A place where you could cheat and steal, rape and kill, and none of it carried any moral charge compared with the sin of grassing up. A topsy-turvy world where nothing was wrong except telling on wrong-doing, like a great playground where the toys were knives and needles. *Wonderland*, she thought wildly, *I'm Alison in Wonderland*, and then she closed her eyes as the sobs thumped into her again.

'We know you're not a grass, Zoe,' the smiler was saying soothingly: the girl was quite upset at the idea. 'Look, it *proves* that we trust you, bringing you down here in the first place, doesn't it?'

'No one calls me a grass,' she muttered.

'And there's no need for all this talk about police anyway. She's safe, isn't she? Warm and fed with her own clothes and everything? I mean, let's get this in proportion. There's some poor sods out there living rough on the streets.'

'Too right,' Zoe said with a sniff. 'Saw one as I was coming through town today. Gave him a quid.'

'They don't – get *raped*.' The words tore Alison's throat.

'Eh?' Zoe cocked her head. 'What's she talking about?'

The smiler tapped his temple.

'Raped – me.'

Zoe looked from Alison to the smiler, her tongue running along the cusps of her teeth.

'Depends who you want to believe,' the smiler said, shrugging. 'Like I said, she gets ideas in her head. Nothing much I can do about that.'

'You can – look if you – want.' Alison began to struggle with the button of her jeans. 'See – the bruises.'

'She does things to herself,' the smiler said, keeping his eyes fixed on Zoe's. 'She's a bit funny that way. But like I say, it depends who you want to believe. Put it this way, you know me pretty well, don't you? But you don't know *her*. You don't know what she's capable of. But it's up to you, Zoe. If you really think you've got to go and tell the police about this, then I can't stop you.'

'Jesus, man, now you're doing it, calling me a grass, I can't believe this, it's doing my head in . . .' Zoe was moaning and pressing her fists to her temples like a child in a tantrum. New nightmare perspective: Zoe saw herself as the one to be pitied in this situation. Alison knew her. Even in the cellar where the damp walls reeked of screams, it was Poor Zoe.

'Nobody's calling you a grass, Zoe,' said the smiler. 'Nah, nah,' from the other two, at his look.

'I never asked for any of this, man, it's just not fair,' she whined. 'I just come here looking for a gaff, and I get all this crap, I mean what have I done . . .?' Suddenly she darted a venomous look at the smiler. '*Have* you been filling your boots with her?'

The smiler made a cross-my-heart gesture.

'What do you *think* he's been doing?' Alison yelled it out, and Sean jumped, pale.

'Get off my back,' Zoe muttered.

'You're in it with them! Don't you see, you stupid cow, if you don't do anything you're an accomplice, the police—'

'Get off my back, I said!' Suddenly Zoe was by the bed, up close, so that Alison could see the saliva glistening on her teeth. 'Stop giving me this fascist crap about the police, all right?'

'She's got a nasty tongue on her, I'm afraid,' the smiler sighed.

'Too right she has. Who are you calling a stupid cow? Eh?'

Spots of saliva landed on Alison's face. Zoe noticed them, with interest.

'You don't have to put up with that, Zoe,' the smiler said. His words were like neat smooth stones and he was smiling as he said it again. 'You don't have to put up with that.'

Something dawned on Zoe's face, a sick light. 'Too right,' she said again, and Alison was ready for the slap a couple of seconds before it stung her face.

'That's for calling me a grass,' Zoe said.

Alison did not see them go. Her eyes were closed by then and all she could hear was that wailing inside her head. But she knew all she needed to know, anyhow.

When she opened her eyes again she did not think about Zoe for some minutes. She spent the time instead taking an inventory of her body's ills. The burning in her cheek where the girl had slapped her was only a minor addition to the list, well below the terrible throbbing that was her left hand and the constant gravelly dragging of her breathing. She noted something new as well, new but familiar: a faint grinding in her belly that meant her period was due. She would have to ask Sean for sanitary towels next time he cleaned her up. If he knew what they were.

In that little flexing of contempt for him she recognized something: sanity. Astonishingly, it was still with her. And it was about then she must have entered the third stage: dream, nightmare, and now inevitability.

Of course. Of *course*. What did she expect? The reptiles brought the girl down here. Escorted her. If Alison hadn't been so high on wild hope, she would have seen from the first moment that they were showing off their acquisition to their guest as you would show off an aquarium. Come and see this...

And entirely without fear of her reaction – at least, on the smiler's part, and he was the one that mattered. That said it all. The smiler was a psychotic, but naïve he wasn't. He saw through people: God help her, he had seen through Alison. He was like a damned X-ray machine. And he had the measure of this Zoe creature all right: he must have known, with utter certainty, that there was no risk in showing her the little secret at the bottom of the cellar steps.

Inevitable: to be here at all, Zoe must be one of them, with the same hole where her conscience should have been. Conscience, heart, feelings – whatever it was that prevented the majority of people from abducting innocent strangers and torturing them, Zoe lacked it too. Such people, Alison supposed, found each other.

Just another reptile in the house. The disappointment should have been too crushing to bear, and for a time she felt it so. The fourth stage came when she forced herself to think about Zoe, to recall the details of the dream that had turned to nightmare. That was when she stopped seeing the situation in black and white. That was when she saw opportunity.

Because things *were* different now. There was a new factor in the ghastly equation: a shift in the balance. This Zoe might have about as much fellow feeling as a sewer rat, but she had feelings all right. Alison had seen them. They were directed towards the smiler.

There was no room or time for disbelief at this. Obviously in the reptilian world what he had done and was still doing was no occasion for outrage, and she would just have to accept that. But what was also plain was that Zoe felt she had some claim on him. She wanted his attention – everybody's attention, but especially his. Alison could see it in her. The smiler wasn't the only soul reader.

Zoe in the house – for she had spoken as if she were staying here. Zoe in the house. It must make a difference.

What sort of a difference she began to learn the next day.

2

The night had been long, a trudge across a desert of pain, but the morning brought beauty in the shape of a pill.

Sean brought it, along with a cup of milk and a cold bacon sandwich. For a moment she thought this was on his own initiative, which suggested changes more profound than she had dared to hope. But then he said, 'Chill told me to give you this,' and she knew otherwise.

'Sean . . .' Since the episode of his birthday the rapport

she had been trying to build with him didn't come easily to her; she felt literally nauseous when he was near her. But he was still her only window on the world. 'That girl . . . that Zoe. Is she staying here?'

'Yeah.' Sean was distracted, in a hurry. Also, she felt, a little unnerved.

'What's she like?'

'Eh?'

'Do you like her?'

'Yeah.'

'I mean, you're not going out with her or anything?'

'What, me?' Sean's eyes widened. 'Nah, man, not me. Listen, I got to get going.' His boots pounded back up the steps. Soon she heard the cough of the van: Sean and smiler off to work. A faint pulse of music indicated that the weasel one was still here.

Zoe too? Or had she gone out?

The question lapped gently and uninsistently at her mind whilst the pill worked on her like a tender nurse. She thought briefly of the spoon but the diminishing of pain – the only pleasure she knew now – made her languid. She slept, and when she woke Zoe was in the cellar.

The girl was going through her things, the books and clothes and little ornaments that the smiler had brought from her flat and placed about the room. She had hold of Alison's old teddy-bear, and when she saw Alison looking at her she tossed it up to the ceiling and caught it.

'Whee,' she said.

Her face was cracked by a sort of serious smile, and she moved as if she were walking on the moon. Alison was no expert on drugs, but the girl was definitely on something.

'What you got there?' Zoe high-stepped over to the bed

and investigated the remains of the bacon sandwich. 'Oh, that's foul. Oh Jesus, that's foul.' She hurled it across the room. 'You're a meat-eater. Should be shot, man.' She made a gun with her fingers, pointed it at Alison's face. 'Pee-ow. You ever try acid?'

Ah. Alison shook her head.

'Nah. Course not. Not enough *meat* in it for you . . . Where'd you get all this stuff? You rip it off?'

'No . . . It's mine.'

'Lousy materialist.' Still wearing the too-steady smile, Zoe squatted down beside the bed. 'Show you something. Show you something dead smart. Had it done in Doncaster, this guy . . .' Zoe came to a mental precipice, fell off. When she got back up she seemed surprised to find herself squatting in the same position. 'Show you something, right? You ready?'

Alison nodded.

'I said, are you *ready*?'

'Yes.'

'Because this is important, right, this isn't just any old thing because this, yeah, is beautiful, you see what I'm saying?'

'Yes.'

'Oh wow . . .' Zoe became absorbed in contemplation of her own hands for a few minutes, then abruptly pulled back her sleeve all the way to the shoulder. 'There. See that?'

There was a small tattoo of a butterfly on her upper arm. The pallor of her skin made it look like a bruise.

'Yeah? You see it?' Zoe's dilated gaze zigzagged over Alison's face. 'You ever see anything like that?'

Still groggy from sleep, Alison groped for the right answer. The girl was out of her head, and unpredictable.

'It's . . . really nice.'

'It's a *butterfly*.' Mouth stretched wide, Zoe dragged the syllables out: ber-ter-flyeee. Then the smile switched itself off and she scooted away, scowling. 'Don't show it to *her*. She'd probably *eat* it. I'll bet she *eats* butterflies, yeah, death junkie.'

Cross-legged, Zoe cradled the teddy-bear, studying its mangy fur and crooning something in a falsetto so high it was almost beyond hearing. Alison studied her in turn, wondering. What parts of the girl's personality – or version of personality – did the drug expose and make vulnerable? What could she use in this situation? Where were the handles?

Zoe's head jerked up. 'So how long you known Chill?'

Known him. Dear God.

'I don't know him at all really.'

She had plucked the answer out of the air, but it seemed to please Zoe. The girl started giggling, rocking herself backwards and forwards.

'Me and Chill,' she said, suddenly solemn, 'we go back a long way. Tell you what, he's got a great little body.' Pouting her lips lubriciously, Zoe made grasping motions in the air.

Say it? Yes.

'I know,' Alison said. 'I know he has.'

Zoe's eyes slid round, shifting pebbles. 'You,' she said, crawling crabwise towards the bed, 'you don't know anything. Me and Chill, right . . . me and Chill . . . Listen, you don't know *anything*, man.'

'I'm not a man,' Alison said.

While Zoe tried to work that one out, Alison digested the newest and maddest realization. It was so mad that it should have finished her off, smashed her mind and sent it spinning off into space. And yet, paradoxically, it was her firmest hope yet of taking control, the first real handle she had been offered. It was the realization that Zoe was jealous of her.

There. Chew on that, Ali, and see if you can swallow it. This girl is jealous of you. If you can take that knowledge in without your brain going nova, then nothing will ever faze you again. After this is over, there'll be no such thing as weird. Been there, seen it, done it.

After this is over . . .

'You're full of crap, you know that?' Zoe began a swaying circuit of the cellar, touching the walls. Sneering: not smiling now. 'Full of meat, full of crap.'

'Doesn't Chill eat meat?' Maybe unwise to antagonize her: the girl was stoned enough to set fire to the place or something.

'That's not all he eats,' Zoe said, showing her teeth, cocking her hip. 'You don't know *nothing* about him, *girl*.'

'Ask Trend.' It was an inspiration, but inspiration born out of observation. Sean the loyal lieutenant had been allowed to

don't think about it

but with Trend it was different. He hadn't been near her, not in that way. Something else was going on there, something with hatred and resentment in it, and she was beginning to perceive what. 'Ask Trend what Chill does down here. I'll bet he'll tell you.'

Zoe lurched over to her. She was all eyes, all teeth. She paused, and pointed a finger so that it almost touched Alison's nose.

'I could kill you, couldn't I? Easy. Easy-peasy.'

'Yes. You could. I don't know whether Chill would be too pleased, though.'

'Easy-peasy,' Zoe said again. But her expression altered and she backed away from the bed, stumbling. Alison let out a pent-up breath.

'Or,' Zoe said, beginning to dance, a slow swaying that reminded Alison of a caged animal, 'I could let you go.'

'You haven't got the keys,' Alison said after a stunned moment.

'I could get them,' Zoe said, wearing a beatific smile now as she swayed and shuffled and tossed her plaits. 'Or I could, like, *saw* through those chains. Or . . . I could just use *magic* and you'd be free.' Suddenly she gave Alison a sidelong look that was almost plaintive in its childishness. 'Do you believe I can do magic?'

'I don't know. Maybe.'

'I can, you know. It's earth magic and you wouldn't know anything about it. La-la-la-la-la-la-la . . .'

Whatever song she was hearing in her head was lost in translation. Alison watched her weaving about the cellar, repelled and fascinated, wondering what the chances were, wondering what she could say that would—

'But if I let you go,' Zoe said, 'I don't think Chill would be too pleased about that either. Would he? Woody WOODPECKER. Woody WOODPECKERRR . . .'

Zoe began twirling in slow circles, shouting, and she was still twirling and shouting when the cellar door opened and the smiler, still in his coat and gloves and flushed from the outer air, came down the steps.

Quickly: more quickly, at any rate, than was usual with him. It was almost as if he had lost his cool for a moment.

'What are you doing down here?'

Yes: he could smile all he liked, but there was definitely a loss of cool there. He had been taken by surprise and he didn't like it. Alison took that knowledge and hugged it.

'Chill!' Zoe had sashayed over and grabbed him in a dancing hug before the question sank in. 'Why-ee?' she said in a baby voice, pulling away.

'Wondered where you'd got to, that's all.'

'Oh, *yeah*? You just don't want me down here, only you're allowed down here and you don't want anybody else coming down here with your precious Alison I wonder why I wonder why you don't . . .' Her voice rose to a manic fast-forward speed and she started beating at the smiler's chest with her fists. 'How come that's what I want to know how come how come how come . . .'

He had no difficulty in fending her off, but the cool had definitely slipped. She was screeching. He gave Alison a dark glance as he gripped Zoe's wrists.

'Chill, Chill, hold me, please, hold me . . .' All at once Zoe was whimpering. She was trying to creep into his coat like a frightened puppy. 'There's all . . . things, there's all things coming . . . Ugh! Look at them, look at them . . . don't let them get me, Chill . . .'

'All right, gel, all right. Bad trip, that's all.' He held her, but he wasn't holding her. Alison, X-ray machine number two, saw that all right. She intercepted another lowering glance from him, and wondered if he would make her suffer later. But that was complicated now, too. 'Come on,' he said, steering Zoe up the steps. 'Come and lie down.'

'You lie down with me-eee . . .'

'All right. If you like. Coh, dear oh dear, where'd you get the stuff anyway?'

They were gone and Alison was alone again.

Alone, and with many demands on her attention. She was hungry: she was thirsty; the grinding of her imminent period had returned, and the much grimmer hand pain, though distant as yet, was making its slouching way towards her. And there were whispers of reproach for things omitted: the spoon lay untouched in the mattress, and she hadn't exercised her legs today.

These things mattered, but they seemed to matter less just now beside the hazy shade of opportunity called up by the unpredictable presence of Zoe. Among her strategies she had found a new one, though it was also the oldest in the world.

Divide and rule.

3

The new baby was a boy, as old Mrs Dhanecha had known it would be. In her triumph about this she passed over the fact that they hadn't named him Shiva as she'd wanted. Kishen was a good enough name, she supposed, and in the family, though her cousin Kishen had been a good-for-nothing. Anyhow, sometimes you had to pretend to give in, just to keep them sweet. Ram and Trupti were only big children themselves, as far as old Mrs Dhanecha was concerned.

And once again, what a blessing that she'd insisted on coming, because Trupti clearly wasn't up to running the household alone when she came back from the hospital. It wasn't just the bodily fatigue; the least upset and she was crying into a tea towel, which was no good to anybody.

'It's the baby who should cry, not you,' old Mrs Dhanecha informed her daughter-in-law, wringing out nappies and giving them a slap against the side of the sink. 'You've got a healthy son, what is there to cry about?'

'I don't know, I don't know,' Trupti sobbed. 'Didn't

you ever feel like this after yours were born?'

'Pah, I remember when Ram was born I was up and about the kitchen the very next morning,' old Mrs Dhanecha said, slapping nappies. 'When he grew up and I saw what he was like, that's when I cried. Ha!'

She made the joke with some idea of cheering Trupti up – not that it seemed to work, because her head went straight into the tea towel – and also because old Mrs Dhanecha was more worried than she cared to admit. Trupti really didn't seem to be bearing up under the strain, and Ram wasn't much help. He was working a lot of overtime to meet the extra expense, and all he did when he got home was fall asleep in the armchair. Then there was Amee, who was grumpy because she hadn't got a baby sister, and Prakash sulking because he wasn't the baby of the family any more. The only one who seemed normal was Arun, who was his usual lively self: old Mrs Dhanecha always said he was the one who took after her.

'You're just tired, that's all,' old Mrs Dhanecha said, a little grudgingly, because tiredness was not something she generally made allowances for. 'And then there's this weather. That's enough to make anyone cry. Doesn't the sun ever shine in this country?' She thwacked another nappy.

'Oh, Mamaji, do you have to keep making that noise? It goes right through my head.'

'If you had a mangle I wouldn't need to. What does Ram spend his money on, that he can't afford to buy you a mangle?'

'The dryer, Mamaji. Put them in the dryer.'

'Pah, they come out all prickly. Put them on Kishen, before you know it he'll have a rash, you'll have to take him down to that surgery with all those fanatics coughing and spluttering in the waiting room, then he'll catch something off them and you'll be burying him before his first haircut.'

Trupti wailed again.

Old Mrs Dhanecha paused in her thwacking and looked at her daughter-in-law in perplexity. Sometimes she had to remind herself that this generation just wasn't as tough as her own. Little things upset them. But what could she do? Tenderness didn't come naturally to her.

'Ai, you're a good girl, Trupti,' she said awkwardly. 'Don't cry. Look what a fine son you've got, nara, beautiful eyes like his grandfather's. And you've got milk too, your fourth and you've got so much milk, what about that?'

'Too much bloody milk,' Trupti muttered in English. 'I feel like a bloody cow.'

Old Mrs Dhanecha thought she understood that, but chose to ignore it. 'And such a healthy baby too,' she went on. 'After all, he might have—' She was about to say that he might have been born with his head where his behind should be or something like that; but she remembered that such straight talking always seemed to upset the girl. 'He might have come out looking like Ram, ha!'

But that joke didn't go down too well either. And then Kishen started crying and it really set Trupti off.

'There he goes again! I can't stand it sometimes! Crying, he's always crying!'

Not the only one, old Mrs Dhanecha thought grimly. 'It shows his lungs are working,' she said.

'I'm sure the others didn't cry that much. Maybe there's something wrong with him.'

'He's hungry, hungry only.'

Old Mrs Dhanecha was right, of course. And when the baby was fed and changed he settled down as good as could be and even Trupti began to look a little more cheerful.

'It doesn't last long, that's what you have to remember,' old Mrs Dhanecha said, dishing up the children's tea. 'Before you know it he'll be running around like Prakash and you'll wish he was a baby again. Is Ram working late again tonight?'

'He's always working late. I think he'd rather work than be with me,' Trupti said, with a renewed flash of mournfulness; but old Mrs Dhanecha had appropriated the tea towel, and the moment passed. The children came stampeding for their teas, earning a rap each with the wooden spoon from their grandmother. 'Make less noise,' she said. 'You'll wake the baby.'

After tea the children returned to the TV and old Mrs Dhanecha shooed Trupti after them. She could have the washing-up and ironing done while Trupti was still sighing; and besides, the girl really did look worn out. Old Mrs Dhanecha also hoped for an opportunity, while they were hooked up to that idiot box, to visit the cellar and check on the noises through the wall. What with one thing and another, that had rather gone by the board just lately.

Her curiosity hadn't diminished, however. In fact it had grown, because it wasn't just scratching noises that had been coming from next door the last few days.

Oh, no. Just as alarming, but much louder.

The monotonous thump of what they called music she was used to, but just lately it had been vibrating through the walls at all hours of the day and night. To her it had a violent and disturbing sound, like the strokes of a hammer or the pounding of an overtaxed heart. But the music wasn't the worst of it. They had been quarrelling next door, quarrelling at the tops of their voices, and voices didn't normally carry through the walls at Grenville Street. One voice carried in particular: the girl's.

Old Mrs Dhanecha had seen the girl, through the kitchen window. She was not impressed.

'And where did you come from?' she had muttered to herself, the first time she had spotted the girl cramming rubbish into the bin. 'I haven't seen you before. What has the world done to you, that you wear a face like that? And such hair, did you plug yourself into the electric socket, na? I suppose you're carrying on with one of those shifty fellows. Well, good luck to you. You'll need it.'

Was this the girl whose tights she had seen hanging on the radiator next door? She supposed it must be: though it was odd that she hadn't seen her around before, because old Mrs Dhanecha didn't miss much. Well, she would reserve judgement.

She didn't have to reserve it long. The men's voices didn't carry so well, but the girl had a voice like a hyena: she was forever screaming and shouting. And once or twice there had been the sound of things smashing too.

Were the men fighting over her? Didn't say much for their taste if so, she thought. And she couldn't imagine the pretty one being interested at all.

'Prettier than she is, ha,' Mrs Dhanecha said to herself now, drying the dishes. She remembered the pakoras she had made earlier, and put two each in the children's lunchboxes for tomorrow. They would miss her when she went back home: it would be back to crisps and all that rubbish.

The kitchen was tidy: also quiet. Old Mrs Dhanecha

hesitated and then pressed her ear to the party wall.

Ah, there was music, though not as loud as usual; and voices too. She could pick out the girl's, though the others were just a mutter. She strained to catch words, but couldn't make anything out of them. Not that she needed to: she knew that tone all right. What a temper! There were worse things, after all, than crying into a tea towel.

Old Mrs Dhanecha left them to it and went softly through to the hall. The flicker of the television from the front room showed that all was well: nothing short of a power cut would budge them. She peeped into the dining room where Kishen's cot had been placed. Fast asleep. Good.

She took more precautions than usual because Ram had become very unreasonable about this business of the cellar since Trupti had come home from the hospital. 'Amma, you're upsetting Trupti with all this talk of mysterious noises.' 'Amma, please don't go down to the cellar any more. Can't you see how Trupti's feeling?' Blah blah blah. If he was ever in the house for five minutes at a time he'd know that *everything* upset her. Talk about the price of bananas and she had her head in the tea towel. Besides, now that Kishen was here her vigilance against the unknown creatures next door was even more important. But she might as well humour the foolish boy and keep her visits a secret. Children never knew half the things you did for them anyhow.

She found the rat poison untouched, but was not greatly surprised. She'd almost put the idea of rats behind her completely now.

Old Mrs Dhanecha settled herself by the cellar wall to listen, but she had only been there a few moments when she gave a start and looked round her in puzzlement.

Either whatever was behind the wall was very big, or—

But no: the noises her keen ears had picked up were coming from somewhere else entirely. A second crash and a high-pitched squeal confirmed her suspicion, and she scuttled back up the steps and down the hall to the kitchen.

Prakash was there: he had been helping himself to milk but he now stood frozen with the carton in his hand, listening wide-eyed to the screams and thumps coming from the other side of the party wall.

'Grandmaji,' he said, 'are they fighting next door? What are they doing?'

'Hush, hush,' old Mrs Dhanecha said, holding up one finger and pressing her ear to the wall. The girl was yelling and screeching, far worse than before: she caught the English word *bastard* several times, worse words too, words you couldn't help knowing in these times. A heavy crash seemed to strike the wall right next to her ear, and then the baby was crying.

'What's going on?' Trupti, looking distraught. 'What are they doing? They've woken him now. Just when we'd got him off. Now he'll never be quiet . . .'

Kishen bawled: the other children came running through: Trupti reached for the tea towel: next door there was another resounding crash. Old Mrs Dhanecha gathered the baby up and brought him through to the kitchen, shushing him on her shoulder, and wishing for the first time that Ram was here. Something ought to be done . . .

'What's happening, Grandmaji?' Amee danced around on her toes. 'What's all the noise? Why's Amma got a tea towel on her head?'

'Ssshh!'

There was a moment's silence, even Kishen pausing to

draw breath. The scream from next door that shattered the silence made even old Mrs Dhanecha's heart miss a beat.

That decided it.

'Here, take him,' she said, putting the baby into Trupti's arms. 'Arun, run and bolt the door.'

'What is it—'

'Go, go!'

Panting a little, old Mrs Dhanecha hurried into the front room and picked up the phone. She would just have to trust her English: the message was simple enough.

'Police, police, police,' she cried as soon as the 999 call was answered. 'Forty-three, Grenville Street, come quick, quick.' Ignoring the tinny voice enquiring in her ear she recalled the word they were always using on the idiot box and which seemed the only one that conveyed what was happening. 'It's murder, they are doing murder...'

4

She had definitely gone downhill, old Zoe.

Last time around she had just been your average junkie lowlife with a bonnetful of bees and a fistful of resentments and a tendency to fly off the handle if you committed some unforgivable sin such as looking away from her for two minutes: but a goer nonetheless and capable of being a good laugh when she let her henna down. And it was on that understanding that Chill had taken her in this time – plus, of course, there was the challenge that Trend had laid down and which Chill had taken up willingly. Let Zoe in on it? Sure. Why not? Let's push it as far as it will go. Double dare. Spirit of adventure sort of thing. No problem.

Except there was problem because Zoe just wasn't the girl she used to be. Or rather, she *was* the girl she used to be, ten times over. Zoe to the nth degree sort of thing. Concentrated essence of Zoe. A bind, in other words.

Chill blamed the junk himself. Not that he was taking any sort of moral line on the stuff, far from it. Personally he wasn't keen on anything stronger than blow but if other people wanted to indulge then that was up to them. People should be free to do what they wanted, that was Chill's creed in a nutshell. He was a libertarian if you liked. No, what he was talking about was the plain facts of what the stuff did to you when you took it in the quantities that Zoe had over the years.

Paranoia: that was the heart of the matter. Of course, tell that to a junkhead and he'd deny it strenuously. He'd assure you that he was not paranoid in any way, shape or form, and then start climbing the walls and wanting to know why you had joined the international conspiracy against him. But there you were: ipso fatso as the saying went. Junkies ended up paranoid. And if the junk was circulating in the veins of someone who was a paranoid case to start with, then you ended up with . . . Well, you ended up with Zoe, in a word.

It was a bit of a shock, all the same, to see how far gone the poor mare was, and Chill wasn't a shockable dude by and large. There he would be, in the kitchen with Sean rustling up some dinner and chatting about this and that, and suddenly this manic muppet would come crashing in demanding to know what they were saying. And never mind that the subject of the conversation was how cheap the Singh brothers were selling their plaid shirts four stalls along, oh no. In Zoe's whatdoyoucallit idiosyncratic worldview that was only a blind.

'You're talking about me, aren't you? What were you saying? *Tell* me. *Tell* me what you were saying.' Stuff like that. It was funny within limits, but only within limits. Really, the girl had a problem.

The trouble was, Zoe didn't really have any interests outside of drugs and shoplifting. Not that Chill expected her to sit there doing petit point of an evening, but it came to something when she switched the TV off when he'd been watching it for all of five minutes and stuck her behind in front of it waving her hands and calling for attention.

'It's boring,' she said when he protested. 'Don't be so boring. It's only so you can ignore me. It *is*. That's what you're doing. You're ignoring me, Chill. Stop frigging ignoring me, man, it's doing my head in.'

Dear oh dear. That was all you needed when you came home from a hard day's graft. It would have been easier if the others could have shared the burden a bit, but small chance of that. Sean and Zoe didn't have much to say to each other once they'd swapped tealeaf anecdotes, and as for Trend, the girl didn't have much time for him, probably because she liked to corner the market in monosyllabic self-pity and didn't want any competition. But then, it wasn't their attention Zoe wanted, alas and alack. From the moment she had arrived Zoe had been doing a big Romeo and Juliet number on Chill and there was nothing he could do about it.

Not that Zoe would have thought of it in those terms, being very anti all that romantic bourgeois possessionist bullshit and more than willing to bend your ear on the subject if you had a few days to spare. But whether she would admit it or not, it was plain that Zoe had come here hoping for the start, or the restart, of a beautiful friendship. Now obviously she hadn't gone without in the meantime and Chill was a mite puzzled as to why it should be such a big deal for her (there was his general irresistibility, of course, but he was too modest to take that into account). Maybe she was getting a touch insecure about herself, because though the old boobs were holding up well her clock was certainly showing the strain of dedicated substance abuse and nobody, to put it bluntly, was going to put her on the cover of *Vogue* without the addition of a paper bag. Whatever it was, Zoe had a big thing about him and he could hardly take a shower without her banging on the door and wanting to know how long he'd be and what was the matter with him and why was he trying to avoid her. Et cetera, et cetera.

Except of course it wasn't really the shower or the TV or any of those things that sent her into jealousy meltdown. No, no. What it was all about – and maybe this shouldn't have surprised him but it did, Chill had to admit to a certain amount of gobsmackedness at it – was the pet in the cellar. Just when you had life sussed, he thought, it came up and pinched you on the bum and the pinch in this case was the realization that Zoe was not at all happy about Alison.

Now if she had been not happy in the sense of disgusted or outraged at the very idea of having a pet person then he really would have been in trouble. But that had never been on the cards because Chill knew his losers and he would never have let Zoe past the cellar door if he'd suspected her of those sort of straight-arrow feelings. No, good old Zoe didn't have any problem with the idea. What she couldn't handle was another girl on the scene. Boy, did she hate Alison's guts.

It was a tricky situation. As far as Chill was concerned, you took your pleasures where you found them. Having Zoe share his bed at nights was fine by him: Zoe staying at Number 43, fine also, if a bit wearing. He didn't see why it should change anything. After all, Zoe was a long-time habitué of squatland where casual and indiscriminate shagging was the rule rather than the exception. But as soon as he went near the cellar door, Zoe went into her demented Rottweiler routine.

'What do you want to see her for? What makes her so interesting? Dumb cow tied to a frigging bed. You must really hate me if you prefer her company. What are you going to do down there, play frigging I-spy?'

Well, of course the games he had in mind were considerably more exciting than that. He had missed playing them this past week with Zoe around, and he felt that it was important, too, that Alison should know things hadn't changed around here. It was still his goal to beat her, to win her submission, so she needn't go getting any ideas. But impressing these things on her was easier said than done with Zoe forever at his heels. What was more, he suspected Zoe was still sneaking down there when he was out, even though he had warned her off when he had caught her that first time. The dozy mare wasn't quite cracked enough to try and let Alison go, he thought, but he still didn't like the idea.

He'd tried reasoning with Zoe on the subject. Starting from the premise that he and Zoe were not exactly a genuine item only sent her into one of her screaming fits, so he concentrated on denial. Sure, there was a girl tied up in the cellar, but he never actually did anything with her. It was just a dare, a laugh. He wasn't interested in her that way... Well, if Zoe was dumb enough to swallow it, it was no skin off his nose. Trouble was, saying it once was no good. Zoe needed to hear it about fifty times a day, and by number forty-nine it was tempting to tell her the truth. Just to see her face. It might actually shut her up for once and what a blessing *that* would be because Zoe's wobblies were pretty hard on the old ears.

'You liar! How do I know what you've been doing while I'm out? You could be doing anything, you could be doing *anything*, you could be doing *anything* . . .' Bit of a hallmark of Zoe's tantrum style, that, the stuck-record feature. 'You don't give a toss about me anyway, nobody does! I could be lying dead for all you care! You'd just laugh! You're laughing at me *now*, you're laughing at me *now*, I know you are—'

'I'm not laughing at you, Zoe.' Hands up. She did look a tidge ludicrous clenching her fists and stamping her feet and making with the old teeth like that, but he knew better than to let it show. 'Honest, Zoe. Cross my heart.'

'You are, you are, you're always laughing at me, you're always talking about me behind my back, I bet you talk about me to *her*, you *do*, you *do*, you *do* . . .'

And then Zoe would cop hold of whatever breakable object lay to hand and give it the old heave-ho. Dear oh lor. Talk about your bovine livestock in a retail pottery establishment.

It was lucky that Chill had the patience of a saint, because there were times when he felt a strong urge to swing for her. But when he finally did snap it wasn't with anything as clumsy as fists that he registered his displeasure.

It was a simple thing. He had come home to a late tea and he was sitting at the kitchen table happy as a sandboy digging in to his steak and kidney pie when Zoe started in on him with her vegetarian food police routine.

'How can you eat those slabs of meat? That's just so grotesque. Don't you know an animal was killed so you could eat that muck?'

'This one died of old age, by the taste of it,' Chill said. Trying to lighten the mood, gloss things over, even now. No one could say he wasn't a trier.

'I can't believe it. I can't believe you're eating that.'

'Horses for courses, gel,' he said, munching, 'and speaking of horses—' But that little joke went by the board because just then she grabbed a fork and started flicking the food off his plate and all over the table. 'Muck,' she was going, with a little flick between each word, 'muck – muck – you – can't – eat – that . . .'

'Lay off, will you, Zoe, I was enjoying that!' The thing was, he was still prepared to find it a joke. Zoe being zany sort of thing.

But Zoe wasn't being zany. She was away.

'You and your meat, you're totally grotesque sometimes, I mean anybody would think you don't care how it disgusts me but then you probably don't care, do you?' She flicked a soggy piece of pie-crust and it landed on his shirt and stuck there. 'You don't give a toss about me. You'd rather have meat. You'd rather have your bit on the side in the cellar than me, wouldn't you? I notice *she* eats meat. Perhaps that's why you like her.'

'You're a headcase, Zoe. You really are.' He gave up on his tea. If that gravy stain didn't come out of this shirt . . .

'I must be a headcase to let anybody treat me like this. I'll bet that's what you call me when you talk to her, isn't it? You call me a headcase, I'll bet you do, I'll bet when you're down there you say, "Zoe's a headcase," and crack up laughing, you *do*, you *do*—'

'Give it a rest, Zoe.' He got up.

'Where are you going? Why are you always avoiding me? You're going down there, aren't you? You're going to see *her*, aren't you?' She had hold of his arm and her fingers were like birds' claws. 'What's so special about her? All she does is lie there, she's retarded or something, what's the point? What's she got that I haven't? Eh? What's the big deal? Is it because she's a meat-eater as well? Poxy meat-eaters sticking together, is that it, yeah? You sit down there and talk about what poxy *meat* you've eaten lately?'

And that was when Chill snapped.

'No,' he said deliberately. 'But she's certainly sampled my meat and two veg a few times, I can tell you that.'

And it really was worth it after all, to see her face. It was quite a crack, in fact, and he had to laugh. But after the first few thunderstruck moments the wobbly kicked in, and it wasn't quite so funny any more. This time her screams were so loud that Sean and Trend, who were pretty used to it by now, came running from the living room.

'It's true, isn't it? She said ask you – she said you'd know . . .' Zoe was screaming into Trend's face, and the poor bloke was looking fit to fly. 'I knew it, I knew it! I hate you all!'

Inclusive. But it was Chill she had a bone to pick with, no doubt about that, and it was Chill she flew at with the old fists going like windmills. It was a dodgy moment because she was so fired up she very nearly connected with his jaw and if that had happened he wouldn't have been able to answer for himself. But luckily there was the three of them there and dragging her off him wasn't so difficult. Calming her down was another matter.

Whatever she'd been taking today it was no sedative. Round and round the kitchen she went, screeching and spitting and hurling everything that came within reach, either at the wall or at Chill's head, with the three of them struggling after her and grabbing at her and falling over chairs like a regular Marx brothers outfit, and poor old Sean nearly came a very nasty cropper when she got hold of the bread-bin and swung it at him. It just seemed to go on and on. It must have gone on and on, in fact, because the next thing Chill knew there was a loud knocking on the front door and he didn't need Sean's pettycrim sixth sense to know that that was the old bill come to enquire what all the noise was about.

Aplomb. That was what this situation required and that was what Chill came up with. He disposed of his troops in three seconds flat. Sean, down to the cellar to clamp a precautionary hand over Alison's gob; Trend, upstairs to fetch his boombox down and put it on in the living room, loud. As for Zoe, Chill just took hold of her chin and looking into her eyes said the two simple words, 'The filth'.

Even Zoe's dope-fugged brain could work out that once the old bill had set eyes on her, half-stoned and blithering, they'd be round the place looking for the stuff, and they'd find more than they bargained for if they got below stairs. Zoe pulled herself together – or as together as she could – and retreated up the stairs pronto.

Chill opened the door on the third knock, a can of beer in his hand.

'Evening, sir. This is Number 43, isn't it? We've had a complaint about the noise from your place. All right if we come in?'

They were the usual dogsbody PCs, all gangly legs and

nasal accents. No fools, though. Eyes darting all over the place.

'Sure, yeah, come in.' Chill stood aside. The officers followed their ears into the living room, where Trend was really doing a very good impression of an average young tearaway lounging on the sofa with a can of Special Brew. No more nor less.

'Turn it down, Trend, will you?' Chill said, and then to the coppers, 'Sorry, I suppose we've been making a bit of racket, yeah?'

'You tell me, sir.' They were sniffing around, but thankfully there was for once no smell of dope in the room.

'Well, yeah, I know we have. Got a bit out of hand. It's my fault. I shouldn't drink on an empty stomach.'

'And you are Mr—?'

'Elderkin, Ian.'

'Are you the householder, Mr Elderkin?'

'Yep. This is Derek, mate of mine. Like I say, it's my fault. We got into this stupid argument. Derek's a vegetarian and I'm not and we started arguing about it and next minute we were shouting the odds.'

'Hm. Shouldn't drink if it makes you like that, sir.'

Chill produced a hangdog grin. 'That's what he told me.'

'Been having a bit of a session, have we?' PC Number 1 said to Trend, as if he were slightly deaf.

'Yeah.' Trend glowered up at him in his best sulky-drawers fashion. 'Not against the law, is it?'

'Only if you disturb other people.'

Trend grunted and swigged.

'Anybody else in the house, sir?'

'Just the two of us.' And Chill added, seeing Trend swallow convulsively and feeling a swoop of daring glee,

'Would you like to have a look?'

But PC Number 2 had had enough and was putting away his notebook. 'Well like I say, sir, there's been a complaint from your neighbours, so keep it down unless you want to see us again. Just show a bit of consideration, eh?'

'And I should lay off that stuff if I were you,' PC Number 1 said, addressing Trend in his inimitably patronizing way. 'Worse than meths, it is.'

Chill showed them out. Ten feet down the hall passage was the cellar door. He saw a tiny crack of light showing: Sean, the drongo, hadn't quite pulled it to behind him. It was hard not to laugh out of sheer exhilaration.

But he kept up a suitably chastened and embarrassed expression until the plods had gone down the path to their cruiser, and only then did he shut the front door and let his laughter free.

5

PC Fletcher and PC MacMahon paused a moment by their patrol car, looking up at Number 43 Grenville Street.

'Nice houses, these, aren't they?' PC Fletcher said.

'You could make them nice, with a bit of work. Obviously those two aren't too interested. See the state of that room?'

'Young and foolish. Bloody hell, it's cold.' They got in. 'Isn't that heater working?'

'Sort of.'

PC MacMahon radioed in whilst his companion blew on his fingers and cursed the cold. Then: 'Hello.'

A face had appeared by the passenger window. An

ancient Asian woman with piercing black eyes and a tiny wizened face was knocking on the glass.

'I think this is our neighbour,' Fletcher muttered, winding down the window. 'Can I help you, madam?'

'You get them?' The old woman pressed her face into the car. 'You stop them killing?'

'You would be Mrs Dhanecha from next door, yes?'

'Yes yes.' The old woman's breath was steaming, but she didn't seem aware of the cold. 'What you do? You stop them?'

'We've dealt with the matter, yes, madam, and thank you for making the call. They were having a bit of a party and we told them to keep the noise down. They shouldn't give you any more trouble, but if they do—'

'Party, no party. Shouting, killing!' The old woman was practically in the car with them. 'Killing, I heard!'

'Madam, I assure you there's nobody dead in there. It was a drunken row and we've ticked them off about it. Now as I say, if they do make any more noise, you let us know about it. Now I should go inside, you'll catch your death. Good night now.'

'Christ,' Fletcher said when the old woman, reluctantly and with many backward glances, left them and went indoors. 'Imagine living next door to that old witch.'

'I know the sort,' MacMahon said, starting the car. 'Always got their ear pressed to the wall. Bloody Pakis are the worst.'

TWELVE

1

They had called it, in all apparent seriousness, Hampton Court. With a name like that it was bound to end up as a dive, Routh thought.

They had run it up as the focal point for one of the city's least lovable housing estates, back in the seventies when truckloads of cockneys had been ferried up the A1 with promises of a better quality of life. Probably the place had looked very nice in the original drawing, with little stick men strolling along the covered walkways and sitting on the park benches. The direct correlation between flat roofs and endemic crime had yet to be established then, he supposed.

'Here we are again,' DI Dolby said as they parked in Hampton Court's vast empty car park. 'The old stamping ground.' Quite a fulsome communication from DI Dolby, who carried dryness to extremes.

'What can you do with this place?' Routh asked. Rhetorically, he supposed, though not entirely so. The question really did bug him. The post office was grilled and barred as if to withstand a missile. Next door a butcher was setting out a window display. The meat was all grey. The newsagent's had nothing in it: it was just floor space, a pile of *Suns*, and two cans of Coke. The one shop unit that did not look run into the ground was, weirdly enough, a Nepalese restaurant. It had a high reputation and people who were interested in that sort of thing came from miles around. Worth the journey, as the guide books would say. Tourists in their own country.

The Lord Burghley – well, the name said it all. The centrepiece of Hampton Court, the pub reminded Routh of caravan holidays when he was a kid. The site always had a club that looked like this. Round orange tables, swirly carpet, yards of blank windows with curtains that didn't fit. Most pubs were unappetizing places at quarter to nine in the morning, but this was the pits. It did a good trade, though, he knew that. Half the ripped-off gear in the city changed hands here.

A WPC was stationed at the door, a second uniform showed them the rear door where the raiders had got in. It was steel, but what the hell. They'd had time to work on it. The nearest houses were half a mile away across a frozen prairie of playing field.

'No dog?' Dolby said.

'Well, yes. Alsatian,' the PC said. 'She shuts it out on the flat roof effort at the front. Says only her husband can control it and she's scared of it. Poor thing's half dead with cold.'

'It must have barked,' Routh said, uselessly. Of course it barked. Round here, there was a Sheba or a Sabre in every garden and they barked all the time. Probably had them put down at the vet's if they didn't.

'Where's the husband, then?' Dolby said.

'Away, she says. Since Wednesday. Apparently they've

been having marital difficulties and he's gone away for a bit to, er, think things over.'

'Right. What'd they get?'

'Takings from the safe upstairs, the float out of the till, boxes of cigarettes from the stockroom. Oh, and the change and the cigarettes from the machine as well.'

Dolby grimaced at Routh. 'Everything but the Durex. Local yokels?'

'Certainly knew the score. Probably drinking in here the night before,' Routh said.

'Mm. All right, let's have a look at her.'

The landlady of the Lord Burghley was more steely than the traditional brassy, but then she surely wasn't looking at her best. A thin-lipped, small-eyed woman of fifty, she was nursing a small brandy and a large bump on her head. She had refused to go in the ambulance, saying she wanted to see the police, and a doctor from the Hampton Court medical centre had patched her up for now. It showed guts, because she had been badly knocked about. Likewise the upstairs flat where they had got her. Routh nosed around, picking up the odour of stupidity. Professionals would have turned things over, but not like this. The gondolas and shire horses had been smashed because the meatheads had found themselves in a playpen, and played. Maybe, after all, she'd been lucky. The bump would go down.

The bedroom was in less of a state: not so many moveables. The bed gave Routh a pang. It was king-sized, with brass posts and a lacy valance. A desperately romantic bed. Someone had been trying hard.

'Can you give us a description?' Dolby said. 'Just an idea for now. We'll take your statement when you're up to it.'

'Men. Youngish, but not that young, at least one of them might have been forty, he was fat and he had this voice...'

The landlady came no further than the threshold of the bedroom. Routh suspected she would strip and gut the place afterwards. It was here they had tied her up to the brass-railed bed with her husband's ties – he could see the ligature marks on her wrists – and here she had spent the whole night and early morning, calling out when she recovered consciousness but unheard. The police had been called when the cleaner turned up for work and found the back door bashed in.

'One had a balaclava. Another had one of those stockings over his head. The fat one just had a scarf pulled up over his nose. He had dark hair, quite long...'

'Familiar?'

She shrugged. 'They weren't regulars, if that's what you mean. There was a group playing pool in the bar last night I didn't know, but you get all sorts in here. It might have been them, I suppose.'

Routh made a note and intercepted a look from Dolby. He knew what that look meant. It meant that later he was going to have the delightful task of interviewing the Lord Burghley's regular clientele. Better put on some fake tattoos.

'I presume this is what they hit you with,' Dolby said, stooping. He picked up a decorative wrought-iron candlestick by the candle end.

'Must have been. We keep it on the bedside table. I used to think it was pretty...' She pulled her lips tight. 'They were wearing gloves, anyway.'

She had seen her cop shows. 'Have it dusted in case,' Dolby said to Routh, stepping round the bed. 'No alarm on the premises, Mrs Coleman?'

'Don't bother with it any more. Not round here. Everybody's alarm's always going off. Vandals, kids. You get so sick of the sound of it you turn it off.'

She gave Dolby a straight hard look, and Routh saw the little crime-prevention lecture die on his governor's lips.

'That's why John wants us to pack the place in, it's so bloody rough round here. You get some nice customers, good friends to you, you know, but mostly they're just scumbags, they really are. But we put so much into the place . . .'

'Where exactly is Mr Coleman?' Routh said.

'Yarmouth. His sister's got a little boarding-house there, he goes to.' All at once she wasn't there, wasn't seeing them. Her husband hadn't been here when this happened, and both she and Routh were wondering whether reconciliation was now out of the question. The trio of tealeaves had screwed this place more than they knew.

'It's got to be some little turds who've been watching the place. Home territory for them. Probably about half a mile from us right now,' Routh said as they went downstairs.

'Yes, it's a thicko job. Nasty though. Get Martindale down here, he can go over the place with the prints boys. And tell him to take Mrs Coleman's statement only when she's been checked over at the hospital, I reckon she's going into delayed shock. Ah, Mandy, is it?'

The cleaner had her rubber gloves on but she hadn't dared touch anything, she explained. Should she—

'If you could sit with Mrs Coleman till her husband arrives, that'd be a great help. DC Martindale will take your statement later . . . Probably need another PC down here to deal with the nosy parkers,' Dolby said, turning fastidiously away from some flat faces pressed against the bar windows. 'It's the locals who'll give us this one, as long as we can sort out the real info from the grudge stuff.'

'My next door neighbour poisoned our cat and owed me twenty quid, therefore he did it? Mm. You can usually tell.'

'Hope so, you're going to be talking to them. No, Martindale can do some of it. You take the flats above the shops for now. And the bar staff who were here last night, fetch them in. I'll get on to the press officer and see if we can make tonight's *Telegraph*.'

They went outside. Such life as the bleak quadrangle of Hampton Court possessed was going on as normal. An overcoated weirdo made a furtive exit from the Bengali off-licence with his morning bottle of cider. A couple of half-feral dogs nosed among the frozen chip-papers. The doors of the medical centre were blocked by a log jam of pushchairs. A postman was making his first delivery. No seven o'clock mail here: too many early posties had been coshed for their bags in the winter dark. The icicles hanging from the dismal concrete awnings would have looked pretty anywhere else: here they looked like daggers.

Routh gazed up at the balconies above the shops. Two storeys of flats.

'Somebody must have seen or heard something,' Dolby said, reading his expression. 'Hopefully somebody saw the vehicle.'

'Uh-huh. And everybody'll keep shtum because they're frightened of a comeback.'

'Well, you'll just have to be persuasive, then. See you.'

Routh grunted and picked a gingerly path along the frozen walkway to the off-licence. By the look of these places he was going to be subjected to some pretty fusty smells and he would need the fumes of strong peppermints. In the shop he asked a few questions on the off-chance but the shopkeeper had nothing. He closed at seven every night and went home. Live above the shop? He looked at Routh as if he were mad.

Outside again, Routh was about to make for the stairs at the rear when something caught his eye.

It was a poster pinned to a notice board that stood in the centre of the square. The notice board had been well designed to survive Hampton Court: it was set in an arch of steel that had been riveted into the concrete. There were notices forlornly advertising meetings of the residents' association and community coffee mornings, but he was not interested in those.

As soon as he saw the poster he realized how much this thing had been on his mind, because he recognized that photograph at once, though he hadn't had it for long. *MISSING*.

Dear God, she hadn't let it go after all. And that, unless he was very much mistaken, was her own phone number she had put on the damned poster.

Paul Routh had been feeling sad for much of the morning, but the saddest thing of all was seeing that someone had drawn a pair of glasses and a moustache on the face of that unknown girl.

2

'Sorry to disturb you, Miss Winter—'

'You've got news, what's happened?'

'No, no, nothing like that. I just . . . Mind if I come in?'

Routh's first thought when Sarah Winter opened the door was that she looked terrible: pale, drawn, tired, her usually neat dark hair a mess. And his second thought was that she looked terrible, in a different way. The eager enquiry – *news* – lit up her face with a light that he could only describe as feverish.

And then the light went out as abruptly as if something really had switched off inside her. She stood aside to let him in and said indifferently, 'I thought the county constabulary had me down as a waste of time.'

'I'm here on my time, not theirs.'

She didn't respond to that. He followed her through to the sitting room. Another mess, and he doubted that that stuff in the glass was mineral water.

'I saw your poster,' he said. He was old fashioned and would not sit until invited, so he stood. 'At least, I presume it's yours.'

'This one?' She held up a copy from a pile on the table.

'There's more?'

'I've put up about fifty. Still got some more to do.' She sank down on the sofa, pushing a cat aside, and reached for the glass.

'Is this off your own bat? I mean, the radio station . . .?'

'They don't know anything about it. So, have you come to nick me for flyposting?' She saw his look and let it go. 'Sorry. Where did you see it?'

'Hampton Court. Investigating a break-in at the pub there.'

'Was it intact? The poster?'

'Er, it had been defaced a bit.'

She nodded. 'A lot of them have. I might have to have some more printed.'

'How much is this costing you?'

'Is that a police question, or are you asking?'

'I'm asking. Look, it doesn't matter, I can guess.'

'It's up to me what I do with my money.'

'Yes, of course.' He felt at a disadvantage. He always did when he was with her, but this was something more. It was like sitting by and watching while someone dug a deep hole in the wrong place. 'Where else have you put these posters, then?'

He marvelled while she told him. She had been all over the city doing this . . .

'Well.' Her look was shrewd: she might be a wreck, but she was still sharp. 'Looks as if you might be changing your mind about the flyposting after all.'

He stirred. 'I am going to warn you about it. Not as a copper, just as . . . It's dodgy, that's all. Shopowners can turn very nasty about it even if it's an empty premises. Plus . . . I presume you're doing it at night. Alone?'

She nodded, looking into her glass.

'The gentleman who was here last time, isn't he—'

'No.' She drank quickly.

Ah. Well, Routh could understand it if the guy couldn't handle it . . . but then again he couldn't understand it. If he threw in his hand over a thing like this, then . . .

'Any response?'

'No,' she said. 'Just a few heavy breathers. And an old woman who thought it was her granddaughter. I went to see her. She was bats. Her granddaughter was thirty-three years old and lived in Canada.'

'Uh-huh. Well, there's a lot of nutters around. They see a phone number written up, they ring it.'

He saw a flicker of gratitude that he wasn't going to tick her off or say I told you so. But the simple fact was, he was stymied. If she hadn't considered her own safety before she certainly wasn't going to now. She was going ahead with it, just as she had said she would. What could he do?

Why not treat her as if this were a normal rational thing to do? As if she were a fellow copper on a case?

'Well, you seem to have covered the city pretty well. You following up any other, er, lines of enquiry?'

'I've sent a print of the photo to the Missing Persons Helpline. They're going to try and match it with their files, but obviously it's not easy and it's not priority.'

'No. Good idea, though.' Maybe that was humouring her a little too obviously. But he was humouring her? Hell, he didn't know.

'Why did you come?' she said, startling him.

'Because I saw your poster,' he said, playing for time.

'And you wanted to ask me what the hell I was playing at.'

'I wanted to know if you'd had any luck. And . . . to see how you are.'

'As in, have I flipped?' She sipped, though the glass was empty. 'Well, I haven't gone back to the shrink, if that's what you want to know.'

'Oh, to be honest I don't believe in all that trick-cyclist stuff anyway.'

For the first time there was half a smile. 'Does that mean you think I'm sane?'

'Yes, I think you're sane.' The tone was casual, but he found the words were significant for him once they were out. 'By the way – when did you go to Hampton Court?'

'Couple of nights ago.'

'Oh. No, just wondered, if you were there last night you might have seen something of these raiders.'

'And if I had,' she said, unable to disguise a certain sour triumph, 'would you have believed my testimony?'

He had to give her that one. She saw him wince, and she smiled, a whole smile this time. It occurred to him that she was not doing a lot of smiling lately. The unfairness of it left a taste. He was a believer in bothering, in giving a toss, and so plainly was she: but here was that belief being undermined. There were little crims on probation for ABH having a lot better time than she was.

He felt for his notebook. 'Here,' he said, 'this is my own number at Croft Wood, that'll get you through to me without the switchboard palaver. And this is my home number.'

She looked, literally, baffled as he handed her the sheet of paper. 'What for?'

'To ring me. If you need to. If you need any help that I can provide.'

He wondered if he should say more, emphasize that this didn't mean the official line had changed, that he couldn't promise anything . . . But she simply nodded and he saw that she understood. More, she looked relieved: even as if she might burst into tears.

He felt curiously relieved too. He had at least picked up a spade.

'Well,' he said, 'I'd better be off. Got a glamorous night ahead of me.'

'Somewhere nice?'

'Back to the Lord Burghley,' he said, and his gloomy tone was only a little exaggerated. 'We reckon the blaggers must have been sussing the place out over a pint, so it's a question of getting to know the regular clientele. If you don't hear from me again you'll know I've been eaten by a pit bull.'

The laugh was reluctant, forced maybe, but there was a gesture in her summoning it up at all. Back in his car, waiting for the windscreen to clear, he felt the weight of things unsaid. She must have thought it strange: he'd given her short shrift before.

He felt the same now – but he was looking a little more closely into what he did feel. The fact was, he had never really seen her as the cracking-up type, even when he'd learned about that episode she'd suffered five years ago. But the alternative to the neurotic-woman scenario just didn't add up either. Nothing had come to light about this girl and that very strongly suggested that there was nothing *to* come to light.

But she believed it. She was going to one hell of a lot of trouble – and he'd played down the risks because he suspected she'd had a bellyful of being patronized – and there was no doubting that she believed heart and soul that something had happened to that girl.

Of course, people believed that the Second Coming was scheduled for Wednesday week. They put up posters about that too. But as he examined his feelings – cliché to say gut feeling, he supposed, but then Routh saw nothing wrong with clichés – he knew that they didn't include that sort of dismissiveness. He wouldn't be here now if they did.

Either she was cracking up, or . . .

He didn't follow the thought to its logical conclusion:

he was late, there was an investigation under way, the Lord Burghley raiders were his quarry. He just wondered, as he started the car and drove away, whether that was an excuse.

THIRTEEN

1

'Sean.'

'Eh?'

'They were fighting again last night, weren't they?'

'Nah.'

'I could hear them.'

' 'Cking hell, man, this stinks.'

'I'm sorry. If I hadn't got these cuffs on I could get up and use the toilet properly.'

'Nah, don't start that.'

'You going to work in a minute?'

'Yeah.'

'I'm getting bedsores. It's really painful. Couldn't you get me some cream or ointment or something?'

'Dunno. I—'

'Please.'

'Look, I'll see, all right? 'Cking hell, got enough 'cking problems.'

'What were they fighting about? Was it me?'

'. . . Look, I got to go. I'll see you.'

She was satisfied.

2

The inventory took longer now. She began it soon after Sean and the smiler left for work, and she reckoned she spent a good half an hour reviewing the ills of her body. There had been some promotions and demotions, and a few new recruits including the bedsores and a cut lip where Zoe had punched her yesterday. The pain in her hand had lost much of its authority, but some old-timers like the chafing of the cuffs on her wrists had surprisingly gone up in the world. As for the grinding in her belly, that had dropped out of sight altogether since she had come on yesterday: there was discomfort instead, because it was heavy. The smiler – (*not smiling quite so much*) – had brought her a pack of sanitary towels down last night, shortly before the shouting had started, but changing them was an exhausting struggle with the cuffs and she knew she was going to need a new towel soon.

She postponed it, and devoted what she calculated as the next hour to the sharpening of the spoon handle. There were changes here too. The point of the handle was a long way from a stiletto, but it made a dimple when she pressed it lightly against the tip of her forefinger, and there had been a subtle alteration in the sound of it when she ground it against the floor. Sometimes she had a feeling as if it were going to snap. But alarming though this was, there was not the cosmic terror in it there would formerly have been. The war was being fought on other fronts.

At last she resigned herself to the dreary task of changing her towel. She disposed of the used one in the bucket and lay for a moment panting and considering whether just to leave her jeans round her ankles: it was warm enough. But then she applied the two benchmark questions which she used to decide everything nowadays. One: would the real Alison Holdenby, who had once existed and would exist again, have done it? Two: was there any advantage to be gained from it?

She gathered herself a moment, and then pulled her jeans up and buttoned them. She lay still, recovering her breath and listening.

The sounds of Zoe and the weasel one were hard to disentangle. A blast of music could mean the presence in the house of either or both of them. But she had worked out that slamming doors and pointless clumsy noises came from one source only, and soon she heard them. The crazy girl was up there somewhere, and it was odds on that crazy girl would presently be down here. Zoe couldn't help herself. The smiler didn't like Zoe coming down here, that Alison knew, but still Zoe came: to stare, to tease. Occasionally, as far as she dared, to hurt.

Alison was well aware that in Zoe she had chosen a weapon that might easily blow up in her own face. Zoe hated her; and though she sought to turn that hate to her own account, Alison's control over events was severely limited and she knew it. What she was trying to do was crazy, possibly; but Zoe was crazy and her captors were crazy and what had happened to her was crazy and crazy situations called for crazy measures. *Well, now, here's this little old atom. Let's split it and see what happens. Who knows, we might be able to crawl out of the wreckage.*

And here came the atom now. The cellar door was opening and –

Alison flinched. Zoe, if it was her, had clicked off the overhead light as she closed the door behind her, and in the utter darkness that immediately enclosed Alison there was all the pristine fear of her first days in the cellar, when terrors had been doubled by black mystery. Of late the reptiles had just left the light on all the time, and Alison's mind had forgotten or repressed the dread of that darkness and what agonizing enigmas it might be teeming with . . .

'Zoe! Zoe, is that you? What's the game – what are you doing . . .?'

She knew it was Zoe: she recognized the sounds and smells of her. Resentful pigeon-toed shuffle, shallow junkie breathing, grassy woolly joss-stick odour – all coming slowly towards the bed.

'Zoe . . .?'

The face of a devil, lit from underneath by a torch, thrust itself before Alison's and the scream was ripped out of her before she knew it.

'Oh *yes*! Oh wow . . .'

The voice of Zoe came out from behind the devil's face and dissolved into dopey laughter. The beam of the torch swung around and Zoe used it to guide herself back to the light switch, staggering and cracking up all the way. When the light came on Alison saw that the devil's face was a cardboard mask of Spiderman.

'You crease me up.' Zoe pushed the mask up on to her head: it was fastened with an elastic band. 'You crease me up, you do. Oh wow. Oh Jesus.' She lurched around, hissing and squealing.

'Funny,' Alison said, her heart thundering in her ears. 'Really bloody clever.'

Her tone, and a glimpse of her expression, were enough to trigger one of Zoe's spectacular reversals of mood. She sauntered back to the bed and snatched the mask off, flourishing it in Alison's face.

'I cut it out off the back of a cornflakes packet. I thought it would be a laugh but obviously not.' She sucked in her cheeks sulkily, shifting her weight from one foot to the other, looking down at Alison now this way, now that. 'You know what? You're really boring, you are. You are dead frigging boring. I mean what are you into anyway?' She slummocked over to the pile of Alison's books, tossed them around. 'What's this? *The Great Gatsby*. Oh wow. Grotesque. *Fatherland*, what do you call this?'

'It's a thriller.'

'Fascist.' Zoe threw the book in the air so that the pages fluttered, let it fall. 'What music you into?'

Alison's mind, stumped for a moment, reached painfully back into the lost world. 'I like The Beautiful South.'

Zoe snorted. 'Oh, Jesus. Boring. Boring, boring, boring—'

'I don't get much chance to be anything else down here, do I?' Bizarre, even now, to find herself talking about this as if it were normal: as if she were talking about being stuck in a council flat with a screaming baby rather than chained to a bed in a cellar with her life in the balance. Was reptile-speak her first language now? Would she ever be able to talk to real people again?

But forget that. Press ahead.

'What do you mean?' snapped Zoe, very paranoid.

'Just what I say. How can I be anything but boring, for Christ's sake? I can't do anything. Not yet anyway.'

She aimed for, and hit off pretty well, Zoe's own niggly inward tone. And it was in the same tone that she carried on, ignoring Zoe's stare, 'I just wish Chill would hurry up and let me out of these bloody chains so I can walk around the house a bit. That's all I want. Not much to ask.'

It was too much to say that Zoe sneered – her face was like that anyway. She just cranked it up a notch, and the result was not pretty. Satisfying, though: satisfying to see that lurking uncertainty.

'You,' Zoe said, swaggering and slack-jawed, oh yes she was rattled, 'you're not going anywhere, man. You think Chill's going to let you out of here, you're off your head, sunshine, I mean, whoo—'

'Of course he's not going to let me go,' Alison said, making it sound snappy, impatient, 'not in that way. But he's going to let me live in the house if I want to. That's the whole point. He wants me to be part of the group like you, he always did. But I wouldn't, not at first. Well, I've still got my doubts. I mean, I *think* I can trust him now and I think he's ready to trust me, and then we can take it from there. He promised me it'd be soon—'

'No way, man, no way, you are full of crap, I mean you are seriously . . . you are seriously out of it, man . . .' Zoe roamed, bug-eyed. 'Jesus, you are not telling me that if he lets you out of this cellar you're not going to be straight out of the door and legging it, I mean—'

'Well, of course, that's what I thought at first,' Alison said, 'but seeing as they're only going to come after me there's no point. I mean, he's told me that. I'm not stupid. I know what Chill's all about and I think I can handle it now. I mean, like you say, he's a bit of a nutter . . . but Christ, I've been thinking, he really must *want* me here, you know? It's frightening in a way but then again it makes you think . . .'

She was already trembling as Zoe turned and bolted up the steps because she didn't know, she just didn't know what sort of fire she was playing with here and how much she might get burned. And when Zoe came stomping back down the steps more wild and bug-eyed than ever she was convinced for a moment that fire was exactly what she was going to get because the girl was carrying a rusty tin and—

oh my God that's surely paraffin or something and she is going to torch me right on this bed—

then she saw what was written on the side of the tin. And saw that in her other hand Zoe was carrying a paintbrush.

She stayed silent while Zoe poked at the lid of the tin with the handle of the paintbrush and sweated and swore and at last grabbed the plastic knife from Alison's food tray and levered the lid off with that, breaking the knife in the process and hurling it across the room. She stayed silent while Zoe dipped the brush in the gooey brown gloss.

front door must be painted with that brown front door big deal no use

and began daubing the walls of the cellar, grunting as she went along, fast, manic, like some crude parody of the artist inspired.

FASCIST. MEAT IS MURDER. LYING FASCIST BITCH LIVES HERE. LYING BITCH. The letters were huge. There was a slogan for each wall, and after the last one, right next to Alison's head, Zoe scrawled an arrow to underline the point. Then, panting and chortling, she added a few swastikas.

And Alison stayed silent. She waited till Zoe came to the end of her abbreviated attention span. It didn't take long. Soon Zoe tossed the paintbrush down on the floor and stood in her cockiest hipshot pose, admiring her handiwork. And even then Alison didn't say it until she had engaged the girl's eyes with her own.

'Well.' She spoke slowly. 'Chill's going to kill you. He wanted it to be nice for me here. Fetched all my stuff and everything.' She let out a long low whistle. 'You've had it now. Blimey, Zoe, I don't know how you're going to get out of this one. I mean, maybe I could try and say Trend did it or something, you know, perhaps it'd be better coming from me—'

What happened next was surprising only in retrospect. And though it felt horrible, it indicated success too. Zoe upended the tin of paint and shook it all over Alison, with special attention to her face.

'Now you look like *crap*,' Zoe screeched, throwing the empty tin at the wall. 'You look like what you are and that is crap, man, let's see how he likes you *now* let's see how he likes you *now* . . .'

She was still chanting it as she pounded up the steps and even after the cellar door banged behind her Alison could hear her wailing and storming about the house.

There wasn't much she could do about the paint beyond wiping her eyes clean and spitting out what had got into her mouth. Besides, she very much wanted the smiler to see it when he got home. It was only paint; he had smeared worse things on her in his time – and that was just it. She was *his*, to do these things with if he chose. The messages daubed on the walls and on her unresisting body said something quite different. They said he was losing control.

FREEZING POINT

3

It had been a funny old day. For one thing it had started snowing mid-morning and though *that* should have been no surprise in this perishing winter it was a bit of a facer in a way because you got used to the weather being nothing but bare skies and cold air and everywhere frozen solid and suddenly this feathery stuff came drifting down and it was... well, peculiar. Here it was practically March and it was as if the winter were starting all over again. Christmas and all the lot. Gave Chill a bit of a lump in the throat, in fact, seeing the snow come down like that, all sort of swirling. *The Lion, The Witch and The Wardrobe* stuff. Nostalgic. He really was a sucker sometimes.

And for another thing, there was Sean. All morning the poor old stick had been more of a chocolate teapot than usual as far as usefulness went, and in the end there was nothing for it but to ask him straight out what the matter was and, well, *quelle surprise* when he did because it turned out that Sean had found another brain cell from somewhere and put the two together and come up with a conclusion that all was not well at Number 43.

Of course, Sean was a natural-born worry-gut. Nothing was wrong that Chill couldn't handle but Sean, being a bit low on stock in the nous department, he had to be reassured about it and that was Chill's not exactly enviable task for most of the afternoon. It was Zoe, of course. Zoe and the little contretemps her presence in the house tended to provoke and the resulting teeniest bit of a bad atmospherelet: these were the things that were preying on what passed for Sean's mind and Chill supposed that was fair enough. To someone of Sean's bricking tendencies the situation probably did look a tidge hairy. But what he had to impress on Sean, with one-syllable words and pictures and speech bubbles, was that this was *Zoe* they were talking about. Zoe, the nomark of nomarks. Loser of the year. Undisputed heavyweight champion sad case. All of Zoe's wobblies put together didn't amount to a hill of beans because not only could Chill twist her round his little finger but Zoe simply wasn't a person you had anything to fear from. Zoe, alas poor cow, was never going to do anything more important than OD in a doorway and give the whole town a high when they cremated her. Just the way it was. Chill would never have let her through the door otherwise.

And really what it came down to was whether Sean trusted Chill's judgement. Because if he didn't, they were in deep schtuck, weren't they? It was hardly worth reminding Sean – was it? – that they were all in this together, and that if Sean tried to walk away from it he would find himself with no legs to walk with. And honestly, Chill wanted to know, had he ever let Sean down? Of course not. So it wasn't too much to hope that Sean wouldn't let him down either. He didn't need to say 'or else'. It was an unspoken telepathic communication doodah. And then Chill slapped him on the shoulder and Sean gave him his little retarded Bambi look and they said no more about it. It was that sort of chat. Friendly.

Funny old business, though. Funny to think of Sean getting upset over a spot of argy-bargy on the domestic front when you considered his background because the O'Blimey clan weren't exactly the Waltons. Even when they had one of their innumerable weddings they ended up pushing each other through plate-glass windows and cutting the best man with a Stanley knife and bagatelles like that. It just went to show, he supposed, that it was all a matter of temperament. You could be sublimely, ineffably thick like Sean and still be a worrier. Now Chill, he could meet triumph and disaster and look those two whatsnames in the thingummy, but he knew that that wasn't anything to do with anything, e.g., the fact that he had had a prince of a dad whereas Sean had been brought up by a smalltime thug with a face like a bag of chisels. As far as Chill was concerned God mixed the ingredients before you were born, and the rest was just cooking. Character is Destiny, that was his motto. I Yam What I Yam. Popeye sort of thing.

And what Chill was, was cool. And he had to remind himself of that fact when he got home that evening, with things turning out as they did.

The snow had stopped falling by then. It had settled, and all along Grenville Street it was sparkling under the streetlights and one or two kidwinks were out playing in it. All bundled up they were in duffels and bobble hats and they looked like they would just bounce like rubber balls. It quite brought a tear to Chill's eye, especially when it was plain from that bite in the air that the lovely stuff would all be frozen solid again by tomorrow morning and it would be back to grazed knees and people chipping away at their front paths with shovels. Hey ho. That was the mood he carried indoors with him: just sort of resigned and a bit melancholy in a nice way.

And cool. No doubt of it.

He should have known of course that something was up simply from the fact that Zoe stayed aloft in the bedroom instead of flinging herself in his arms like Cheeta greeting Tarzan and hanging round his neck and wanting a second-by-second rundown of every single thing he'd done that day and threatening to top herself if she didn't get it. Et cetera, et cetera. But he just supposed that she was shooting up or coming down or some such substance-related activity and that she would join them once she had finished shooing the pixies off the duvet and it was not, actually, to be truthful, wholly unpleasant being able to walk in the house and make a cuppa and take the weight off your slingbacks without getting a faceful of Zoe straight off. It proved his point about the pet exactly. With the pet you were in control. It was the ideal relationship—

But apropos of the pet, that was where the funny old day began to turn into a funny old evening and no mistake.

Off Sean went to do his little chores down below – never complained about those, bless him – and there was Chill nosing in the fridge wondering whether to go a bit crazy and actually cook something tonight and Trend just come in from college with his file and his notebooks and pens just like a real college boy, it was sweet to see really – and suddenly, trouble. Chill should have known really. The moment you lay back in the bath the phone was sure to ring.

'Chill!' Sean slammed into the kitchen with his eyes on stalks. 'You got to come and see! 'Cking hell, man, the mess down there, it's like unbelievable . . .'

Chill's first thought was that the pet had found some way of making her quietus with a bare whatsname and that the mess Sean was referring to was of the gory sort, and as the intellectually challenged one was more incoherent than usual and could only stand there catching flies there was nothing for it but to leg it straight down there and see for himself. And though what he saw in the cellar wasn't as dramatic as all that it was still...

Well, it made Chill see red. Fair dos, the mess could be cleaned up and he'd been a bit of a devil himself down here when the fancy took him and it wasn't the end of the world and all that, but still. Enough was enough and this was not on. This was well out of order. If Zoe couldn't handle the idea of his pet then fine, just keep away from her.

His pet. That was what made him see not only red but scarlet and crimson and every other shade you could think of. He was a tolerant sort of guy but what people had to understand was that you didn't encroach, not with Chill. He had fences up and they served him well. A quick shafting for old times' sake did not give Zoe the right to carry on like this. This whole malarkey was a finger in the face and nobody gave Chill the finger, period.

'Sean,' he said, 'there's some turps under the sink. Try and clean her up, I know it'll be a job but do your best. The blanket's had it, just chuck it.' He met Alison's eyes: they were peculiar, almost expressionless; she was just lying there as if she didn't care. 'Sorry about this, sweetheart.'

He started up the cellar steps. Trend was standing at the top, gawping. Peculiar look on *his* face, too.

'Come on, old fruit, you can lend a hand.' He paused. 'Did you know anything about this?'

'Get out of it, man, I've only just got in from college!'

'Yeah. Course. Sorry, mate.'

Of course, it was Zoe's work. Had her fingerprints all over it. The thought made Chill see red again.

And yet he was still cool as he started up the stairs to the bedroom. Red and cool. Like a strawberry maybe.

He even managed a little chuckle to himself at that. And he didn't hurry. He just walked upstairs to the bedroom (*his* bedroom, actually) as if he were simply going up to change.

There she was. This year's Miss Snakebite relaxing at home. She was lying on the bed the wrong way round, with her DMs on the pillow. It was *très* Zoe, that. Even alone she was posing.

She turned her head when he came in and peered up at him through her multicoloured fringe. He could tell from her eyes she was coming down from something. Like little fuel gauges, those eyes, and the needle was nearly on empty.

'Hiya, Chill,' she said in her best little me voice. 'How you doing?'

Now this really got his goat as well. The way she thought she could wriggle out of it by pretending not to know better. This zany Zoe act. How can you get mad at such a crazy mixed-up butterfly sort of thing.

Cool, and red.

'I've had such a bad time,' she said, watching him.

He didn't answer that. Just went over to the wardrobe and began taking out her clothes and piling them on the bed.

'What are you doing?' She sat up. 'Chill?'

'Making a few changes, my sweet,' he said.

'Eh? What's up? That's my gear. What are you doing with my gear?'

'Moving it.' He glanced round at her. She didn't know which face to put on: Tiny Tears or Baader-Meinhof. What a case.

'Where?'

'To a place you seem to be very fond of, gel.' He added

her ratty brush and comb to the pile. 'That was quite a little stunt you pulled down there today.'

'Don't know what you're talking about.'

Now you could ask anyone about Chill's patience and they would tell you it was practically unlimited. But that same anyone would also tell you that he did not like being made a fool of and when Zoe spoke to him like that, as if he was one of her deadbeat coterie who all talked in that dumb defensive riddling way, then...

Cool. Cool and red.

'I'm talking about your little alterations down below, treacle,' he said, keeping it chirpy. 'I'm glad you've let me know how you feel at last, any road. You should have said. Could have done this earlier.'

'What is this? Chill? What—'

'If you're so jealous of Alison, my old beauty,' he said, turning to face her, 'then you can swap places with her.'

And now the needle was definitely on empty. Zoe was wide awake, Zoe was with us, and Zoe was leaping off the bed. Never seen her move so fast.

'You're out of your mind – you're out of your frigging mind if you think you're going to put *me* down there—'

'Like you said, Zoe, I'm a nutter,' he said, gathering up her clothes, 'a complete nutter.'

'No *way*! You can't make me go down there! You're full of crap, man, you're just...'

Zoe speechless, now there was a first for you. 'Oh, I think I can,' he said, tipping her a wink. 'I can do anything I want to.'

'No way. No way.' Zoe's teeth were on show and her eyes were darting everywhere. Talk about a cornered rat. 'You're cracked, man. You've totally flipped. I'm out of here.'

'Well, there is that, as an alternative. But not the way you think. Not just dossing down somewhere for the night and creeping back in the morning. You go out of here, sweetheart, you don't come back.'

She was dumbfounded. Gobsmacked. Flabbergasted. And maybe after all he shouldn't have pushed it but it was so good, seeing her like that.

'It's no skin off my nose,' he said, very casual, 'because to be honest you won't be missed. Certainly not by me. Sorry, Zoe. I call a spade a spade, always have. Sad, but there it is. Bit of an absence of magic in the old interpersonal relationship department.'

Whoa. Now *there* was a hell of a look. Curdle milk, it would.

'You liar. That's all bull, man. You don't want me to go.' She was hissing, literally hissing. Saliva everywhere, charming. 'You can say what you like, Chill. You're stuck with me because if you throw me out of here I'll go straight to the police.'

'Oh, come off it. You, a grass? You, having a chat with the filth? I'll believe it when I see it.'

'I'll tell them, Chill. I mean it. You chuck me, I'll tell them everything.'

'You can give it a go if you like. I suppose it might give them a giggle before they lock you in some nuthouse full of junkies on cold turkey.'

All right, honest injun, he was just a teeny bit concerned now because life was after all full of surprises and it was possible, it was just possible that Zoe might . . .

'I'll tell. I'll tell. I'll tell.' Zoe going into parrot mode there, but it was undeniably effective because she wasn't chewing the scenery this time, she was looking straight at him as if—

As if she meant business.

'Well, that wouldn't be very sensible of you, would it, Zoe? Because you'd just be telling on yourself. You're in this up to your neck, gel. You're in it just as much as I am.'

'Crap.' That was a very nasty smile she had on there, a knowing smile. 'You must think I'm stupid. You did it, you and your poxy mates. I've got no worries, Chill. I don't give a toss any more and when you go down I'll cheer because you are one using son of a bitch.' The smile had faded. It was something else now, something vicious and quiet. 'If I grass you up they'll give me a medal.'

'Try it,' he said.

The thing was, all this business about swapping places with Alison was just a ruse. He hadn't meant it, though of course Zoe mustn't know that. It was just a way of teaching her a lesson, a way of making her see sense. See how lucky she was, if you liked. And when he said 'Try it' that too was just a way of testing her out. Calling her bluff.

And once again it was the eyes. Windows of the soul, yes indeed. It was the look in Zoe's eyes that told him she wasn't bluffing, at least three seconds before she bolted for the door. He should have used those three seconds but he couldn't because he was stunned. Completely poleaxed by the realization that Zoe was going to the police.

He caught up with her on the landing. Her hair was the nearest handhold and she yelped like a kicked dog when he yanked her back by it. Another mistake, as it happened, because it left her arms free and if any further evidence were needed that she meant business here it was in the way she hit out at him, no tantrum this time, her fists were really swinging and if she could just connect and get free of him then there was no doubt of what she was going to do.

And so he yanked her round by the hair so he could get a good look at her clock and then wound up his fist and gave her such a right-hander as she never saw. This, he felt, was no more than was necessary under the circumstances but the best laid plans of mice and men and all that, and what happened next was just one of those things. Zoe went flying backwards and unfortunately there was nothing behind her but a steep flight of fourteen stairs. She must have been out cold even before she started falling because she went tumbling and thundering, over and over, like some enormous rag doll, hell of a noise it made, and as if he hadn't had enough bad luck for one day when she reached the bottom it was her head that struck first, back of her skull right against the wall, a sort of sideways bounce and then slide, and on the subject of noise the sound *that* made wasn't one he'd forget in a hurry. Nor Sean and Trend, he supposed, because there they were in the hall below wondering no doubt what all the commotion was about and now seeing with their own eyes and there was no doubt about it, by the look on their faces he was going to have his work cut out getting them through this little crisis and he was going to have to be . . . well, one thing above all.

Cool.

4

Trend was the first one to touch her. Surprising, that: he wasn't entirely without bottle after all. Put his fingers on her neck, the way he'd seen it done on TV probably. Sean, meanwhile, was not exactly bearing up under pressure. Talk about giving birth to a litter of infant felines.

"Cking hell, man, I don't believe this, I mean this is unbelievable, this isn't happening, man, this is not for real..." He kept walking up and down the hall, backwards and forwards, head down and muttering. What this was meant to achieve Chill didn't know. Maybe it was some Hibernian ritual. Maybe it was what his ancestors did when they saw Cromwell coming.

'I can't feel any pulse,' Trend said. Really getting into his Dr Kildare role, he was.

'Oh Jesus oh God I don't believe it I don't believe this is happening...'

Dear oh lor. As if this Mother Macree stuff wasn't bad enough, the pet down in the cellar was shouting her head off, wanting to know what was going on. Trust them to leave the door open. It was time Chill got a grip of this situation.

'Sean,' he said, 'close that bloody door, she's doing my head in. And stop that wittering, for God's sake, it's not doing anybody any good.' And when Sean still wouldn't come out of his tizzy Chill grabbed him by the front of his shirt and held his forefinger up before Sean's button nose. 'You hear what I'm saying, Sean? You hearing me?'

'Yeah. Yeah. I hear you, Chill.'

'Jolly D. Now then.' He turned to the crumpled heap at the foot of the stairs. Well, what else could you call it? It certainly wasn't Zoe any more. He did his own Dr Kildare stuff, even getting a mirror from the loo and holding it in front of her mouth, but it was plain to him all along that poor old Zoe was as dead as the hand jive.

You only had to look at the mess in her hair to know that. On the wall, too. Yuck.

Well, well, RIP, Zoe whatever-her-last-name-was. He supposed it had always been a toss-up between the drugs and that temper of hers.

'Ambulance!' said Sean suddenly. Brainwave sort of thing.

'Bless you,' Chill said, getting up and wiping his hands. He looked at Sean standing there in eureka posture. Dear oh dear. It was going to be quite a test of his skill, getting them through this.

'What do you call, 999, yeah?'

'Sean. Sean, mate. Listen a minute. How can I put this? There's no point in calling an ambulance because Zoe is dead.'

Sean's jaw hung. You could hear the cogs slowly turning.

'She is no more,' Chill said. 'She has ceased to be. She is an ex-Zoe.'

All right, maybe the humour was a bit black, but he was trying to rally the troops and boy, did these troops need rallying.

'Oh Jesus.' The penny had dropped and Sean was back to walking up and down. 'Oh wow. Oh Jesus.'

'Shouldn't we phone the ambulance anyway?'

That was Trend, and really it was a little disappointing because up to now he hadn't handled this at all badly and it was a shame, a real shame that he had to go and let himself down like this. But Chill didn't lose his rag. He just took it calmly and slowly.

'The thing is, mate,' he said, taking hold of Trend's sleeve, 'if we report this we're opening up a whole can of worms. Now you know as well as I do that what happened to Zoe was an accident – ' he held Trend's eyes steadily – 'but you know what the old bill are like. They're not going to see it that way. Now are they? Be honest. Foul play I think is the old bill term. Now if it was just me . . .' He smiled, shrugged, took a look at Sean to make sure he was following this. 'But it's not just me. That's the whole point. Because what are we? The Three Musketeers! All for one and one for all and all that. Do you follow me? Any filth come sniffing round here and we're all in deep shit. And I do mean deep and I do mean *all* of us.' He kept the smile going while he let that one sink in. 'Now it's a crying shame about Zoe and I don't mind telling you I'm completely gutted by this whole thing. But life, you know, it goes on. I'm not so gutted that I don't care what happens to me any more and neither are you, I'm sure. Right? And no matter what we do it's not going to bring Zoe back to life. A *fait accompli*, that's what you call it. So now we have to move on. I mean, I don't know about you, but I want to enjoy the rest of my life. Don't you – Sean?'

'Yeah.' Obedient to the last.

'Trend?'

'. . . Yeah.' Not quite meeting his eyes, but it was good enough.

'Right then.' Chill put a hand on each of their shoulders. 'So let's take a look at what we've got here. There's poor old Zoe suffered a tragic accident which for various reasons we can't let anybody know about. Agreed? So. What do we know about Zoe?'

'Not a lot,' Sean said, hanging on his every word now, just waiting to be told what to do. Dear oh lor. And they wondered where Hitler got his recruits from.

'Precisely. That's the sort of person old Zoe is, was

rather. She's got no folks that I know of, no folks that she keeps in touch with anyway. She's got no fixed abode. The last place she was signing on at was Doncaster. I mean basically she moves on from squat to squat, footloose and fancy-free, Zoe doesn't live here any more sort of thing, yeah? I think that's a fair picture of Zoe's lifestyle, am I right?' Trend's eyes kept wandering to that heap at the bottom of the stairs. Chill gave his shoulder a squeeze. 'Isn't that right, Trend? So. Zoe's – what's the word? – confrères, aren't the sort to notice if she drops out of sight, now are they? Zoe's not your forwarding-address sort of girl. I hate to say it, but really nobody's going to know or care that Zoe's snuffed it. Shame and all that, but that's the sort of girl she was. Now are you with me so far?'

From Sean, a breathless 'Yeah!' Just like one of Deputy Dawg's sidekicks, he was. But Trend was a mite distracted. He couldn't keep his eyes off that heap. Corpse, if you wanted to put it in Agatha Christie terms. Maybe it was because there was a bit of a whiff coming from that vicinity, a whiff like a baby that needed its nappy changing. That happened with violent death, apparently. Like the old hanged convicts dripping from their trouser legs. Interesting in a macabre sort of way.

'Trend?' Chill said. 'You with me?'

'No . . . I mean, yes, I see what you're saying, but . . . Christ, she's *here*, Chill, what are we going to do, we can't just leave her lying there, we've got to—'

'We've got to what?'

Trend hung his head. 'Get rid of her, I suppose.'

Chill smiled. It was always nice when they got there themselves and you didn't have to say it for them.

'What, like . . .' Sean mashed his lip between yellow

teeth. 'Like, chop her up or something?'

Chop her up. Hark at him. Dear oh dear. He'd been reading too many true crime magazines, this one. 'Sean,' Chill said patiently, 'this is Zoe we're talking about. Our mate. She's . . . she's died tragically, and it's up to us to give her a proper burial.' He was speaking slowly for the benefit of the terrible two, but in the meantime his brain was leaping and sprinting ahead: in fact, it had reached this conclusion five minutes ago.

'How are we going to do that?' said Sean.

'Yeah, Chill, we can't do that, it's like . . . touching her and everything, it's . . . oh God, I don't know, this isn't for real, it's a nightmare, I'm going to wake up in a minute, please God . . .'

Hmm. Quite a sensitive soul, our Trend, apparently, underneath all that hair. Maybe it was time to hang tough.

'Listen, my old china,' Chill said, 'I'm not going to repeat this, so listen up. She is dead and we are going to get done for it and we are going to get done for a few other things besides if we do not get rid of her pronto. Got it? Now if you like we can just leave her there until she gets a bit high and the environmental health geezers come calling, yeah? And then they bring the bizzies in and the bizzies take a look at what we've got in the cellar while they're about it and maybe then we can all be in the Scrubs together nice and cosy. If that appeals to you as an alternative scenario then do say, my old fruit, you just come out and say it and we'll take it from there.'

He had moved close to Trend as he spoke: he could feel his own breath rebounding from Trend's face. When he had to work on Trend, physical proximity always seemed to clinch it. Funny that.

Success, anyway. Maybe Trend had looked at the prospect of thirty years inside and realized he wouldn't be able to buy any new records or T-shirts for the duration.

'Where?' Trend muttered.

'Well now, it'll have to be somewhere safe,' Chill said, chipper again, on the up, ready for action. 'Somewhere she won't be found. We don't want anybody messing about with her grave. Poor old girl deserves a bit of peace.'

'Garden!' Sean cried. Full of bright ideas today, he was. Practically see the little light bulbs above his head.

'Possible,' Chill said. 'Thing is, we're a bit overlooked out the back there. Windows on all sides. I mean, even in the wee small hours you don't know whether or not somebody might be clocking you up through their curtains. That's urban living for you. And here's another thing, right. At the moment there's absolutely nothing to link us with Zoe. Last anybody knew of her she got chucked out of digs in Doncaster, and if she told any of her scummy mates she was heading down here they were probably too stoned to listen. So basically there's nothing to link her with 43 Grenville Street. But you put her in the back garden, that's a hell of a link, do you see what I'm saying?'

It was quite exciting this, in a way. Quite a buzz in it. Sherlock Holmes sort of stuff. The old henchmen were a bit slow on the uptake, but they were getting there. If they could pull this one off, then it would be congratulations all round, in fact he'd take his hat off to the pair of them and the drinks would be on him.

'Dump her in the river, maybe,' Trend said. There, he was getting into the spirit of the thing now.

'River, possibility,' Chill said. 'Trouble is with our river, it's not much of a river. People tend to find things in it. Good thought, though, mate.'

'Out in the country somewhere, then.' He was on a roll now, was Trend. 'Just take her out somewhere in the country and . . . and bury her.'

Precisely the point Chill had got to, five minutes ago: in fact he had moved on to a consideration of just how easy, or hard, it was going to be digging a hole in this freezing weather. Hard, he suspected: literally. But now that he had got the muppets out of their blue funk and into a relatively positive frame of mind he didn't want to knock them back again.

So, 'Brilliant!' he said. 'Let's start clearing up.'

5

The scene is not unlike a Christmas card. The snow on the ground, though rapidly freezing, is still fresh enough to give that soft, suggestive, enchanted look, and it coats the boughs and twigs of the trees like delicate icing. The sky is clear and starlit, casting indigo shadows across the old rutted farm track that leads through the trees into an inviting blackness right at the heart of the composition. All it needs is a fox in the foreground, alone in his rural kingdom, pausing with lifted head as if to reckon the hours till dawn.

Probably, indeed, this secluded copse is the haunt of foxes – badgers too: but they have made themselves scarce tonight. The composition, and the three o'clock peace, is disturbed by the arrival of a van, which crawls down the old farm track towards the bull's-eye of darkness. Stops, at last, with a wink of red brake lights.

The three people who get out are well wrapped up

against the cold, though one of them shivers and mutters about it until he is hushed by his companions. From the rear of the van they take out spades and shovels, and the clinking of these in the wide starry silence seems huge, ear-shattering. There is something else in the back of the van, but after a moment's whispered discussion they leave it there and lock the doors. And then they move off into the trees, plainly led by one of their number who is less wrapped up and whose fair hair can be seen glinting palely amongst the lower twigs.

The crunching and scrunching of their shoes on the half-frozen snow presently stops, and is replaced by thick, slow, chunky, laborious sounds, sounds that go on for a long time, long enough for frost to draw its strange maps on the windows of the van and for the tracks made by the tyres to set into crystal. When the three figures return through the trees, carrying the spades and shovels, their breathing is harsh and loud and one of them slumps against the side of the van, protesting. But the pale-haired leader says or does something to revive him, and then opens the van doors again, and together they take out the other thing that is there. Which is much less noisy than the clanging spades. Just a muffled sliding sound as they drag it out, and a faint rustle and crackle from the black polythene in which it is wrapped.

They bear it off through the trees, one at each end, one holding the sagging middle. The heavy laborious noises continue, and when they cease the stars have altogether faded, though the darkness is unbroken and dawn seems a long way off. It is not so very far though: despite the snow and ice, winter is receding inexorably; things will change just when it seems they will never change.

Two of the figures are slow and subdued in their movements when they return through the trees to the van; but the pale-haired one is brisk, a splash of animation in the iron-bound scene. He even lets out something that resembles a laugh, and which is as strange and clamorous in the stillness as the earth-waking clatter of the spades and shovels being put back in the van. All except one, which the leader, apparently tireless, uses to churn up the snow where they have walked. And he is not finished yet; because when at last they climb into the van, and reverse carefully along the farm track to where it meets the tarmac road, he gets out again and painstakingly does the same thing to the tracks made by the tyres, walking backwards and churning up his own footprints as he goes.

Finally, satisfied, he hops up into the van. The engine coughs, the tyres find an elusive purchase on the frozen road, and the disturber of the peace pulls away from the scene, its drone diminishing until it is altogether lost in the grander perspectives of silence.

6

Ram was working the early shift, which was surprisingly busy, mostly with fares to the railway station. He often had a little grumble about this and he was doing it this morning: something about milkmen and newsagents and how everyone sympathized with them having to get up early but no one seemed to care that taxi drivers had to do it too. Old Mrs Dhanecha, who had been up an hour before him anyway and was making his breakfast, didn't listen too closely. She'd heard it all before and besides she had something on her mind.

'And with the baby as well,' Ram moaned, his head in

his hands. 'Crying for his feed every two minutes. I don't think I've had any sleep at all.'

'Pah, I heard you snoring. Anyway it's not you who has to feed him, though God knows you've got the bust for it. Here, eat.'

'When did I snore?'

'I don't know, the middle of the night. I was awake. I didn't get much sleep myself, not that I need it.'

In fact old Mrs Dhanecha had been awake most of the night. It was a noise from next door that had woken her – she proudly acknowledged herself the world's lightest sleeper – and made her go downstairs and peep out of the front room window. And after that, her mind had been so busy with speculation that sleep had been impossible.

'Amma, I can't eat all this.'

'Eat it and be quiet. You go out to work with nothing in your stomach, you'll start feeling weak by ten, then you lose your concentration and before you know it you've driven your taxi into the side of a bus and they have to drag you out in pieces—'

'Amma, please. Besides, you're always telling me I'm too fat. You can't have it both ways.'

Old Mrs Dhanecha had an answer for that, but she decided to suppress it. She sat down at the kitchen table and watched her son through several mouthfuls and then said, with something less than her usual confidence, 'Son, last night I saw something strange.'

Ram raised his eyebrows. 'Not the rats again.'

'Rats, who said anything about rats? This was outside.'

'What on earth were you doing outside in the middle of the night?'

'I saw it through the front window, stupid boy. I heard

a noise and I went down and... It was those fellows next door. They were putting something into that van of theirs.'

'What sort of something?'

'I don't know. I couldn't see. Something big, wrapped up in plastic. Don't sigh at me, boy. Your father used to sigh like that and it never did him any good. I saw it and it wasn't right.'

'Why not? Ian's a market trader, he's got a stall in town. That's what the van's for, moving his stock.'

'At three o'clock in the morning?'

'I don't know. Maybe. Market traders have to start early. Like taxi drivers.'

'Pah, that's typical of you. You don't want to know.'

'No, Amma, I don't want to know because it's none of my business. If Ian wants to load up his van early that's up to him.'

'Early is one thing. Sneaking out in the middle of the night when everybody's asleep is another. Anyway, they came back. At half-past five they came back. I heard them.'

Ram pushed away his plate. He had an odd look on his face. Like he was constipated, old Mrs Dhanecha thought.

'What?' she demanded. 'You don't believe me? You think I've gone mad?'

'Amma, I'm asking you, please leave it.'

'I saw them—'

'I'm not saying you didn't. Just for once, believe me, it's best if you leave it. Maybe this stuff they were putting in the van... if they didn't want people to see it, then maybe...' Ram blew on his fingers.

'You mean stolen? You mean they've been thieving?'

'Sshh, Amma. I'm not saying either way because I don't know. But these market traders, sometimes . . . you know. They've got a bit of a reputation.'

'Thieves! Thieves right next door, nara, and you say leave it!'

'Yes, leave it. It's best not to get involved in these things. You can't be too careful. I mean it, Amma.'

Old Mrs Dhanecha sat back and scowled at him. 'If everyone was so careful, the thieves would run the country.'

'You haven't seen my tax return,' Ram mourned.

'So we do nothing while they load up their van with stolen goods? What about the police?'

'*If* that's what it is. We don't know that, Amma. And as for the police . . . you know what happened last time.'

Old Mrs Dhanecha scowled some more. She hated it when Ram wagged his finger like that, but she was stuck for a reply. The memory of that incident rankled, because she had made a fool of herself. At least, in other people's eyes: Ram had done a lot of smug sighing when he had found out about it. Old Mrs Dhanecha still felt she had been right to call the police, simply because she always was right; but she had to admit that the response of the police had been discouraging, and she didn't like the thought of being involved with them again. She had seen that look in the eyes of certain shop assistants, and it was a signal to check your change. No, she wouldn't turn to the police.

'And besides,' Ram said, putting on his lofty man-of-the-house voice, pah, 'I don't want Trupti getting upset again. You know she's not been feeling well. Something like this will only set her back. So please, Amma, just leave it, na? Now I'm going to work.'

FREEZING POINT

Old Mrs Dhanecha, unusually for her, sat on at the kitchen table, thinking. She was a little annoyed that she hadn't thought of Ram's explanation herself. Thieving! Stolen goods! Well, she could certainly believe it of that crew next door. In fact, she could believe much worse of them. And where did the girl fit in? Was she part of it? She hadn't been there last night.

Leave it, Ram said. What he really meant was, he was frightened of them. She could understand that: she was a little frightened of them herself. But that didn't mean she was going to leave it.

7

'It was just a bit of a barney, Ali. We've been having quite a few as you may know, and this was really the last straw.'

The smiler had brought down a kitchen chair. He was sitting on it a few feet from the bed, legs crossed, smoking a cigarette. He looked tired, but at peace with the world.

'I'm really sorry about all this,' he said, waving a hand at the daubed walls. 'Soon as I get a minute I'm going to redecorate. Cover it all up. I mean, she was always a bit of a scamp, our Zoe, but this was beyond a joke and I told her so. And that's how it all started. That's when the sparks really started to fly and I thought, that's it. I've had enough. Sorry about all that racket. Proper shouting match it was.'

'What was that other noise?'

'Hm? Oh, I threw Zoe's suitcases down the stairs. Bit melodramatic, I suppose, but at least she got the message. So it was ta-ta Zoe and, I've got to admit, good riddance.'

Her eyes searched his face. Once this would have been

like putting her hand into maggots, but things had moved beyond that now.

'She's gone?'

'Gone with the wind. That's that vegetarian food for you.'

Her senses were different, now, from other people's. Not just the extra acuteness of her sense of smell and hearing: she was tuned in to the frequencies of his madness, could detect its fluctuations like waves crackling in the air. She was picking up something now. For all his relaxed posture and casual tone, something supercharged and dangerous was flickering around him, and she feared it. The fear was simply a condition without regard to circumstances: on any rational level she had already run the gauntlet of fear and there were no new terrors under the sun. But looking at him like this, hearing him, receiving his pulsing signals of wild hilarity, she was afraid. And he knew it, and it was joy to him.

'How could she have gone?' She spoke quietly, lying flat: she was weak. Her period was having an exhausting effect on her, and her aches and pains were many. She knew her strength was not what it had been, possibly her will too: that much was his victory. 'I don't believe it.'

'Well – ' he chuckled – 'things have been a lot quieter today, haven't they? Surely that proves it.'

'She was obsessed with you. She wouldn't have gone. She would have . . .'

'What?' He leaned forward, and his gaze was like a light bulb in her face. 'What, Ali?'

'She would have stitched you up.'

'Oh, no. Not our Zoe. She's one of us. No matter how badly we fell out, she would never . . . Blimey, Ali, whatever put that idea in your head?' His eyes narrowed as he dragged at the last of his cigarette. 'Anybody would think you'd been hoping for it. Planning it, even. No, but of course, that'd be daft.'

'You can't be sure.' Her chest was labouring: she could feel an inexplicable panic rising in her.

'Beg pardon, sweetheart?'

'You can't be sure, you can't. If you threw Zoe out... if she's out there somewhere... you can't be sure she won't turn you in.'

'Oh, I'm sure, Ali. I'm dead sure. I wouldn't be sitting here with you now if I wasn't. Now would I?'

He was saying something more, but she wasn't hearing him. All within her head was deafening chaos, landslide, collapse. When her consciousness came crawling out of the smoking ruins of hope it was to hear him say, as he rose up out of the chair, '... so, now everything's back to normal, sweetheart. We can get to know each other all over again.'

FOURTEEN

1

'Time off? Why on earth would I want to take time off?'

David, Sarah's producer, sported a beard that was reminiscent of some small inoffensive animal in its blond silkiness, and he put up a nervous hand to stroke it very much as if it were a creature not to be startled.

'Well, the same reason anyone would take time off. To rest up. To refresh yourself. Maybe sort things out in your life that work doesn't leave time for. We're all human. But there's a tendency to forget that in broadcasting. It's not just the listeners who mistake the persona for the real person.'

From anyone else she would have felt this was patronizing. But David's concern was too genuine to be resented. Her indignation was defensive, and all the more strident because of it.

'If I've been doing lousy shows,' she said, 'then tell me. And I want detail. Is it the material, is it presentation, is it tone—'

'If you'd been doing lousy shows I would tell you all about it, believe me. If only because I know how much you'd hate the idea of letting yourself down professionally.

But you're not doing lousy shows, you're doing your normal shows and you're straining. I can tell.'

'If it comes over on air then it matters. If not, it doesn't.'

'It hasn't come over on air, not yet,' he said. He didn't meet her eyes as he said it, though. 'But eventually it might do. Look, when I spoke to you the other day about that animal rights feature you looked blank. It was quite obvious that you hadn't done a single moment's preparation for it.'

'But I—'

'And you went ahead the next day and did an excellent interview as if you'd studied the subject from the cradle. Exactly. I don't know what sort of catching-up schedule you put yourself through but I wouldn't fancy it myself. Sarah, all I'm trying to say is you don't *need* to be in this sort of situation. You're obviously exhausted and under a lot of strain – sorry if you mind me noticing these things, but I do. Whatever's behind it, it's none of my business. What I can do is try to help. And like I say, there's no need for you to be under the extra pressure of doing fifteen hours of live radio a week. There's nothing to stop you taking . . . well, say, three weeks off.'

'Make a bit of a hole in the programming, surely?' Oh, gags, she had a million. She wasn't even fooling herself with this flippancy.

'Well, normally it would be hard to get a stand-in at this short notice. But as it happens . . . you remember meeting Simon Austin, who's joining us from Radio Wessex? He's moved up earlier than expected and I'm sure he'd be pleased to sit in for a few weeks.'

'Sounds like you've got my replacement all lined up. Great. Do I get a reference?'

He sighed unhappily. 'I'm no good at this. Personnel management they call it. Sarah—'

'No, no, look, I'm sorry, David, that was out of order. I just... if you tell me to take time off, I mean really insist, then I will.'

'You will?'

'Oh yes. And I'll also never forgive you.'

It was David's habit to keep on his desk a perfectly neat row of perfectly sharpened pencils, like a set of panpipes; and now he ran his finger along them nervously, counting them.

'Ah.'

'And that doesn't mean I don't appreciate your concern. I know you're trying to help. If you could help, I would let you, believe me.'

He smiled a little. 'I can recommend some good sleeping tablets, if that's any use.' There was something behind the words which contradicted the smile: she remembered the rumours about his marriage. She smiled too.

'I've gone past that point, I think,' she said. 'But I will get back to... normal. I will, David, that's a solemn promise. But work's the one thing that's anchoring me to normality at the moment. I don't need any cure because that *is* the cure. Does that make sense?'

'Oh God yes. I think there's only so much that it can do in that way, but yes, of course I see. Well, it's your decision. If you're absolutely sure you don't want to... oh, you know, jet off to sunny climes for a fortnight, get away from this awful winter...?'

'That's just it, you see,' she said softly. 'I can't get away. Not like that. I wouldn't be getting away at all.' *Nowhere to run*. The phrase sounded tough and sexy and exciting, until you lived it out.

'No.' David gently reassured his beard again. 'No, I know what you mean... this isn't something you can talk to me about, is it.' He did not inflect it as a question.

'Not really.'

'Well... all the best with it, anyway. At least it's the weekend. I can make you have *that* much time off.'

'Oh yes,' she laughed. 'I won't argue with that.'

And the laughter was close to the edge, closer than she had come throughout the whole exchange, and she was glad when David had to take a call and she could get out of there fast.

Because this weekend was exactly what she had been dreading and the thought of it, its endless mind-teeming leisure, had been at the back of her excessive reaction to David's suggestion. It was late on Friday afternoon, and the working week was over, and tonight Sarah had an appointment with emptiness.

Murray had rung a couple of times, but she wasn't ready to face him: couldn't see, in the dark glass of the future, a time when she would be. But that was only an echo in the emptiness, not the emptiness itself. What appalled her was the simple knowledge that she had no more posters to put up. She had plastered them everywhere she could think of and short of having another batch printed and putting them up all over again she didn't know where to go next. She had kept her eyes fixed on this task, like following the yellow brick road, and now the road had run out. If the posters were Plan A there ought to be a Plan B to follow it but damned if she could think of one.

She had learned, at least, to control her impatience when she got home: she made herself take off her coat, stroke the cats, and mix a drink before playing back the day's messages on the answering machine. Tonight there weren't even any crank calls: just a message from a mail-order company with an unrepeatable offer. The emptiness echoed again.

Booze alone wouldn't even begin to fill it, she knew that. She needed to construct something for the evening; something artificial, maybe, but then much of her life seemed unreal now, a matter of acting out a succession of parts. Circumstance had cast her as the depressed and neurotic solitary and so she decided on the classic depressed and neurotic solitary's Friday night: bottle of spirits, takeaway, and an all-action video.

The first two were easy: the video proved to be a problem. She roamed the hire shop for half an hour, picking up titles, recoiling and putting them back. Normally she could watch anything short of a video nasty with complete detachment, her mind coolly holding the knowledge that the blood was tomato ketchup and there were make-up girls drinking coffee ten feet away from the exploding set. Tonight the images on the video covers swarmed at her like unbearable bees. Guns and killers. Hands in black leather gloves opening doors. Faces lurking in shadow. Dying cops clutching their guts. They were acting but they weren't acting, not really. Shiny jagged prisma on a menacing world. She couldn't take one home with her, couldn't trust herself. Her mind wasn't safe any more: she had to beware the black ice.

But she had come out to get a video and somehow she saw going home without one as a failure, another mocking echo in the emptiness. And so half desperately, half laughing at herself, she snatched up Walt Disney's *Bambi* and paid for it at the counter and took it home and switched it on while she unwrapped a balti takeaway.

Maybe *Bambi* told her more about herself than the most disturbing psycho-thriller could have, or maybe it simply told her why the movie was still around fifty years on. Whatever: it wrecked her. From vague childhood memory, she expected a cutesy fable about baby animals with a lot of painstaking golden-age animation of raindrops and snowstorms. What she saw was primal, and utterly without reassurance. Nobody vowed colourful vengeance over the dead body of Bambi's mother: no heavenly music wafted her to a better place. She just got shot, offscreen. You didn't need to see it: your mind knew what it looked like. Doves cowered in the thicket at man's approach. *Don't fly, don't fly*. One panicked and flew. *Bang*. 1942, it was made. It was pretend and it wasn't pretend. All the dark wonders and terrors of childhood were there, but the adult world offered no protection. Fire swept through the forest, driving the animals before it. The gallop of the stags was a march past of violent energy. Hunting dogs scrambled over each other to get at the doe. The ending, with the birth of new fawns, promised renewal yet it was as biblically stark as the rest. All flesh is grass. The whole thing was about mortality and there wasn't a dead body in it.

She had had the video. She had had the takeaway. Sarah completed the classic pattern by drinking, weeping for no reason, and finally falling asleep on the sofa amongst the remnants of her bleak debauch.

When she woke and blinked at the ceiling it was several moments before she knew where she was, and then there was disbelief at the light in the room. Her drunken sleep on the sofa had actually carried her right through till morning – late morning, by the feel of it. She was about to look at her watch when she realized she couldn't move her right arm. It was crooked up above her head and something was pinning it down. And her left arm, by her side, that was the same...

Her groggy brain registered a passionate purring, and she turned her head to see Penny curled up on the arm of the sofa, trapping her right hand beneath that billowing body. Down below Charlie, the original copycat, had parked himself on her left hand ditto. Fastidious as they were, they didn't seem to mind that their mistress had turned into a sleazebag.

As memory and hangover converged, however, Sarah found that she did mind. Extricating herself from her feline manacles, she stood swaying in the centre of the room for a moment debating where to start: bathing or binning? She had just decided on a shower when the telephone rang.

She picked it up on the first ring, and the voice, as is usual with such promptness, was hesitant.

'Hello...? Er – is this 349261?'

'Yes, Sarah Winter speaking.'

'Oh... right...' Callbox background; a young woman's voice, low and tentative. 'Well – it's about that poster. You know? It said to ring this number?'

'That's right.' Sarah readied herself for some lunatic outpourings.

'Only... that girl in the photo. I know her.'

Sarah sank back down on to the sofa. The hope that came at her was like a juggernaut and she was half afraid to be in its path.

'Go on.'

'Well... what's this about? Is she in trouble?'

'I don't know.' Sarah had dreamed of this for so long it should have felt unreal, but it didn't: it felt like the realest thing that had ever happened to her. 'That's what I'm trying to find out.'

'I mean, is this anything to do with the police? You're not a copper, are you?'

'No, no. Nothing like that. I work for Tudor Radio . . . but this is just a private thing. I need to trace that girl urgently, that's all.'

'Only I don't want anything to do with the police, you see. I want to help, but—'

'I promise you, this is nothing to do with the police. All I want is information.'

'Well, OK. My name's Nicola, by the way. All I can tell you, that girl on the poster's my next-door neighbour. I . . .'

Crackle and confusion. Something had happened.

'Hello?' Sarah said. 'Nicola? Are you there?'

'Yep, sorry, just had to put some more money in. Yeah, she lives next door to me. I mean I don't know her name, I only know her by sight, just to say hello to in the corridor and that because she's really quiet, you know, but it's definitely her.'

'Where?' Sarah fumbled for a pen. 'What's the address?'

'Well . . . look, like I say, I don't want to get involved. The thing is, I shouldn't be living in this flat by rights. The tenancy's in somebody else's name but he's shacking up with his girlfriend and he let me move in here. You know, you're not supposed to sublet, it's against the rules, and I don't want anybody finding out—'

'Nicola, I promise you that's completely confidential, it's your business, all I'm interested in is finding the girl on the poster and if you can just – just, please, give me an address, that's all I'll need . . .'

If her anguish didn't come across on the phone, then the sincerity of it must have, because Nicola said, 'OK then. As long as you keep me out of it. She lives at Flat 14, Lyle House. That's all I know. Like I say, she keeps herself to herself, and . . .' A pause, Sarah's eyes squeezed shut. 'Actually, I haven't seen her around lately.'

2

Sarah recognized Detective Sergeant Routh's car as she pulled up outside Lyle House. When he got out she saw he was wearing pullover and jeans: CID civvies.

'You must have driven like the wind,' she said.

'I live quite close to here, actually. College Park. You know, the tacky phoney-Barratt houses. The mortgage is a sin.'

She wished devoutly for some of his calm. 'I'm sorry about ringing you like this. Only—'

'That's why I gave you my number. Anyway, Saturday morning, this is better than traipsing round Sainsbury's.' He shrugged, and she saw that some of his calm was exactly what he was trying to give her.

'Well,' she said, 'thanks. I couldn't believe it when this girl rang . . . and immediately I thought—'

'I'm as interested as you are,' he said: then seemed to find that a bit unfortunate, and went on quickly, 'So what exactly did she tell you?'

'Just what I told you on the phone. She recognized the girl's photo because she's a neighbour, and that this is the place.' She turned to look at the block of flats, which had the slightly toytown appearance that came from a combination of low budget and highfalutin architect. 'And that she . . . hadn't seen her around lately.'

'Any chance of talking to this Nicola?'

Sarah shook her head. 'It had to be in confidence. I'm sure you understand. Anyway, she said that was all she knew.'

Routh sniffed. 'Well, let's go in and see if the mystery girl's home.'

The security door was no problem: an exiting Chinese girl, textbooks under her arm, held it open for them. The corridors were loud with visceral music. Sarah couldn't speak, couldn't even allow herself the conscious realization that this was where the girl lived: all she could do was hold herself in, keep breathing.

'Right.' Routh stood before a plain brown door with 14 in plastic numerals on it. 'Come in Number 14, your time is up.'

This flippancy wasn't like him. She could only guess that he was nervous too. When he knocked and knocked again and there was no reply it was her response that was the calmer one.

'Not in, maybe,' she said.

'Damn.' He knocked again, impatiently. 'What do you think? Ask the neighbours?'

Remembering Nicola's reluctance, Sarah shook her head firmly.

'Hm. Just what is this Nicola up to, that she's got to be so secretive?'

'Nothing that the CID would be interested in. But I've got to respect her confidence.'

He grunted. 'So near and yet so far... Damn. I'd really like to get this sorted out now, once and for all.'

She looked at him uncomprehendingly: realized that she had been viewing the address as an end in itself, and had thought of nothing more practical than camping outside this door for as long as . . .

As long as what?

'Come on,' he said. 'There must be a warden or something.'

There was a warden, ensconced in a typical jobsworth office full of mugs and paper clips: but he was a brick wall until Routh brought his credentials into the proceedings.

'Tenant of Flat 14 . . . Holdenby, Ms Alison,' he said, consulting a Xeroxed list as if it were hieroglyphics.

'You know her?' Routh said.

The warden's bald head shone defensively. 'There are forty-two tenants here and they keep changing all the time. I only know them if they give trouble. I'm just responsible for cleaning and maintenance.'

'And security, presumably,' Routh murmured.

'Wait a minute, though. I have got another internal letter for Number 14 . . . sure I have.' He hunted in an overflowing pigeonhole. 'Ah. Two in fact. Fancy that . . .' It was fortunate that his face was already florid.

'You distribute the mail yourself?' Routh said. 'Didn't I see numbered lockers in the lobby there?'

'That's where the GPO stuff goes,' the warden said loftily. 'Internal mail, from the landlords to the tenants in other words, comes to me and I slip it under their doors.'

'The landlords are . . . ?'

'Lyle House is run jointly by the YMCA and the Sadleir Housing Association. Sadleir do the direct administration.'

'You have keys to all the flats?'

'I have a pass key that I may only use on my own initiative for cases of emergency involving danger to life or property. In all other circumstances, no employee or representative of the landlords may enter a tenant's flat unless the landlords have previously given three days' written notice of their intention to do so.' The warden sounded aggrieved at this. 'What's she done, anyway?'

Ignoring him, Routh pointed at the letters. 'Is that what they could be? Notice of intention and all the rest of it?'

'Possibly. Notice of rent arrears, notice of essential maintenance work, all sorts of things. Well, unless there's anything else, I'd better go along and deliver these.'

'We'll come with you,' Routh said.

Half resentment, half self-importance, the warden preceded them back to the door of Number 14. Routh stopped him just as he was bending to slip the letters under the door.

'Mind if I do it?'

Obviously the warden minded a good deal, but he couldn't argue. Sarah watched in perplexity as Routh kneeled down and inserted the letters slowly through the crack, pausing when they were halfway there.

'How many of these have you delivered lately?' he said.

'I don't know . . . a fair few, I think.'

Routh kowtowed, his eye against the foot of the door, inching the letters forward. 'Well,' he said in a muffled voice, 'I reckon they're all still right there on the doormat.'

'Oh God,' Sarah said.

Routh straightened quickly. 'What about that pass key?'

'Well, I don't know. I appreciate that you're police and all, but the rules are very strict about this, and I really would have to get permission from the landlords first, you know, I'd have to ring the Sadleir office and—'

'Do that then. Wait, when do they close?'

'Twelve on Saturdays.'

'Quarter to... Right, ring them, and while you're about it tell them not to hurry off home yet because I might want a word.'

While the warden was telephoning they waited outside the door of Flat 14.

'What it must be like to have such power,' Sarah said.

The anxiety and tension behind the flippancy was obvious; and it was with a certain quiet solemnity that he replied, 'Only with things like this. It doesn't help you in your real life.'

After a moment's silence she asked the question that was like a placard round her neck.

'What do you think's happened to her?'

The warden was back before he could answer. He huffed and he puffed and he reluctantly conceded that Sadleir Housing had given him permission to open the door and had also said they would be glad to offer any assistance with the detective's enquiries.

'Fine, let's have a look then.'

Routh was first in, and the warden thrust himself after: but even a glimpse over their shoulders was enough to show Sarah that no one was living in this flat. She didn't know what she felt. The putting of a name to the face that had haunted her had left her curiously numb. Holdenby, Ms Alison. Alison Holdenby. In primitive times to know a person's name was to gain power over that person. She wasn't sure it wasn't the other way around.

'How much of this belongs to the landlords?' Routh said, prowling.

'The fridge and cooker are part of the fittings. And the curtains. Not the bed.' The warden placed a hand on the radiator and became indignant. 'If she's terminated her tenancy, she's supposed to turn off the heating. And ensure all personal effects have been removed. The cost of storage—'

'Well, it looks like she's been gone a while,' Routh said, picking up a shrivelled apple from the kitchen worktop. 'And taken everything she can carry with her.' He looked into the wardrobe, grunted. 'Midnight flit, by the look of it. Get a lot of that?'

'It happens. They don't appreciate these places,' the warden said sourly, scooping up the pile of mail from the threshold.

But she did live here, Sarah thought. The girl I saw that night at the Arena lived here. She tried to penetrate the atmosphere of the stripped flat, studied the Blu-Tac marks on the walls as if they were a dot-to-dot puzzle that might reveal the girl's personality. Holdenby, Ms Alison. Alison Holdenby.

They were breathing Alison Holdenby's domestic air but the girl was still a wraith.

'Well, she's not here,' Routh said, looking at Sarah for the first time. 'And not coming back, by the look of it. OK. Thanks for your help,' to the warden, who had been as unhelpful as possible. 'Let's go and see what the landlords can tell us.'

Outside something of the numbness left her, to be replaced by dizzying dread. She put her hand on Routh's arm. 'What do you think?'

'Like I say. I think she's done a runner. She's still the registered tenant but she's emptied the flat and hasn't been back.'

'Behind with the rent.'

'It's a classic. But we'll find out what Sadleir can tell us. You do want to come?'

She didn't need to answer.

'OK. We'll say you're a friend of hers.'

She looked at him. 'That's what I am,' she said.

The offices of the Sadleir Housing Association were part of a large Edwardian villa near the city centre. It was a neighbourhood of doctors' surgeries and the receptionist seemed to have caught offensiveness from her medical sisters, squawking, 'We're closed, we're closed,' until a youngish woman in a navy two-piece came through to silence her.

The woman introduced herself as Prue Cooper. She was the chief housing officer at Sadleir but, she added as if she had seen a buck coming, 'I must emphasize that we administer Lyle House jointly with the YMCA.' She had the sort of hairy face that layers of foundation only seem to emphasize and her hair, the colour of a golden retriever, was aggressively styled. While she invited them both into her office, she addressed herself solely to Routh, and not just because he was the copper. Sarah had noticed there were some women who did that.

'Well, I dare say the gentleman at Lyle House will have given you an idea of what this is about,' Routh said. 'We're trying to trace the tenant of Flat 14. According to the warden her name is Alison Holdenby. Now it's plain from when he opened the flat for us that Miss Holdenby has removed her personal effects and is no longer living there, and presumably the association weren't aware of this.'

Prue Cooper tapped at her computer keyboard as fast as her fingernails would allow.

'No,' she said, 'we most certainly were not. In fact it looks as if you've only just anticipated us, going in there. Miss Holdenby is in a month's arrears with her rent. It looks as if several letters have gone out about this and the last one would have been a final warning, which would have required that she see either me or the deputy housing officer, and if she failed to make the appointment a notice to quit would have followed.'

'For a month's arrears?' Routh said.

'Thirty-four days, to be exact. You must understand that there are certain procedures we have to follow. They tend to look worse than they are. It's the association's policy to seek any kind of alternative arrangement to eviction if it's at all possible. Arrears can be paid on an instalment plan. We're not in the business of putting people on the streets. But we have to have some kind of co-operation from the tenant in question and in this case it looks as if there's been no reply whatsoever. Let me just get the tenant's file . . .' The tubular skirt made getting up and sitting down a complex business. 'Right, here we are. No – no reply to any of our communications. The housing benefit office contacted us three weeks ago to inform us that as Ms Holdenby was no longer in receipt of income support her housing benefit had automatically been stopped. This made her personally responsible for paying the rent and we sent out a letter to that effect.' Prue Cooper talked as if she were dictating a letter, and now she started a new paragraph. 'And now Number 14 is empty. Well. I'm afraid this does happen, unfortunately. The association has a very careful policy with regard to tenants' rights and the right of privacy in particular, and inevitably it's open to abuse.'

'So what's the procedure now?' Routh said. 'Once a tenant's done a moonlight flit, what happens?'

'After the expiry of the three days' notice of our intention to gain access, we go in. Any property left behind by the tenant is placed in storage and if unclaimed after a certain period is disposed of to charities. Once the tenant is held to have broken his or her tenancy agreement the tenancy is formally recorded as expired.'

'But you'll try and track the tenant down in a case like this?'

'Obviously, yes. We have to change the locks as a matter of course but in the meantime we make every effort to contact the tenant because of the outstanding arrears. Depending on the amount and the circumstances, the responsibility for this may eventually be placed in the hands of a debt collection agency. But we make our own enquiries first. Of course in this case the DSS can't help because the tenant has apparently signed off benefits, so our first line of enquiry will be the tenant's next of kin.'

Sarah sat up.

'You have details of that?' Routh said.

'When a tenant signs the tenancy agreement we require the name, address and telephone number of his or her next of kin in case of emergency.' The housing officer inclined her sculptured head. 'Can I ask, is Ms Holdenby being sought by the police in connection with any crime?'

'Not necessarily. But I'd like to have that address if I may.'

After a working lifetime of being smoothly and condescendingly obstructive this plainly did not come easily to Ms Cooper. But she wrote the address down, half shielding it as if they were playing consequences. 'We will of course be contacting the next of kin ourselves, once we've gone through the procedures and taken a look at the flat. Sometimes there's the question of damage to the structure and fittings in these cases.'

'Everything looked pretty intact,' Sarah said. She got a varnished smile in return.

'Is there any other information you can give us about Ms Holdenby?' Routh said, his eye on the file under Ms Cooper's crimson-tipped fingers.

'I'm afraid not. It's not the policy of the association to request any personal information. All we're interested in when we take a prospective tenant on the waiting list is their housing needs, which are assessed on a points system. With Ms Holdenby that was . . . yes, here it is. Her previous address was a privately rented bedsit. Bathroom was shared and heating was inadequate – obviously that gave her the points and she was offered Flat 14, Lyle House last September. She signed the tenancy agreement on 23 September.'

'Has she ever been in arrears before?' Sarah said.

'No . . . no trouble before,' Ms Cooper said, speaking as if Routh had asked her. 'But unfortunately, there's no telling with these things. As I say, we keep no personal details beyond name, status and next of kin. And disabilities, if any, as that's relevant to housing needs. Ditto if a tenant becomes pregnant we like to know about it. Otherwise we take the tenants on trust. This applies to our own properties as well as Lyle House, which is something of a special case as it's funded by the YMCA. Lyle House is designed as a low-rent facility for young single people and so . . . well, I think that speaks for itself in terms of the problems we encounter. That being the case it would be helpful if the police could let us know if . . . well, whether this investigation is something we need to be concerned about. If for example a tenant has been dealing in drugs in one of our properties that would be a matter—'

'We'll let you know,' Routh said getting up. 'Thanks for all your help.'

Outside a few flakes of snow were in the air, suspended rather than falling. Standing under the porch of the building, Routh handed the piece of paper to Sarah. 'Mrs J. Holdenby. Relat: mother. 44 Raleigh House, Duckham Road, Newcastle-upon-Tyne.'

'She got behind with the rent,' Routh said, 'packed up her stuff, and did a bunk to somewhere else.'

'She'd never been in that sort of trouble before.'

'Always a first time.'

'Why? I mean, why would she do that? She had a reasonable place. Better than a bedsit. She'd put herself on the waiting list, so she must have wanted it. Why throw it all up?'

'Well, it looks like she signed off the dole, so she must have got work. A job somewhere else maybe. Or gone off to shack up with a boyfriend. Could be anything. There's no way of knowing.'

'Yes there is.'

Routh turned his head, but she wasn't looking at him. She was looking at the piece of notepaper with Ms Cooper's schoolteacher handwriting on it.

'No phone number,' he said.

'No,' she said. 'An address, though.'

'Yes, an address at the other end of the country.' He sighed and took out a squashed packet of cigarettes. 'You know, don't you, that this is me doing this? Not the force?'

'Yes, and I'm grateful, I'm as grateful as can be.'

'I don't mean that. I mean my hands are tied. If there was an official investigation I could forward a request to the Tyneside CID asking one of their boys to check up with this Mrs Holdenby. But as it is... I'm trying to think if I know anybody in the force up there, somebody who'd do me a favour. The nearest I can think of is in Scarborough.'

'It doesn't matter,' Sarah said. 'The address is all that matters, and I've got that.'

'What? Oh, Sarah... Look. You've done great. You had a bad feeling, you followed it up, you didn't let it drop, and now you've cracked it. You've got absolutely nothing to reproach yourself for, quite the opposite, because you've done it. You've found her.'

'Where is she then?'

He sighed. She passed him one of her own cigarettes, lit it for him.

'I can be in Newcastle in less than three hours. I wouldn't fancy driving, but you can get an Inter-City direct from here,' she said. 'After all, why shouldn't I? I haven't got anything else to do today.'

'And just what are you going to say?'

'That I'm a friend. Looking for Alison.'

Routh coughed rheumily.

'You shouldn't smoke with that cold,' she said.

'Shouldn't smoke with lungs, but I do,' he said. 'Look, I can't stop you doing this. But like I say, I can't help you with it either.'

'I don't expect you to. You've helped me a lot already.'

'I mean, I am off duty today. We've got the Lord Burghley blaggers down the nick all pointing the finger at each other and everything should be hunky-dory. But that doesn't always stop my governor getting me on the bleeper when the fancy takes him.'

'No, I appreciate that.'

'The girl did a flit from her digs. That's all.'

'It may well be. But I'm going anyway.'

She left a pause. The pause was neutral: he could fill it if he wanted to.

'Oh, what the hell,' he said. 'A day trip to Newcastle still beats Sainsbury's.'

3

It was not only the longest conversation she had had with Routh but the longest conversation she had had with anyone for a good while. This was not simply the enforced proximity of the train journey: he was the only person who was not entirely out of place in her transformed interior world. Routh did not stand on the safe ground of normality impatiently beckoning her to come back to it. Because of his job, he didn't live there himself. And it quickly became clear to her that this was from choice. What emerged from his plain recital of how he had come to decide on police work as a career was a simple perception on his part: the perception that there were two worlds. There was the world you usually inhabited and which you saw as generally safe and civilized and predictable. And alongside it was another world where nothing was certain, where human life was chaotic and imperilled and dark holes yawned. And the two worlds were not separate: some people lived in both, and anyone might cross over, voluntarily or against their will. Once that perception had been reached, his stubbornly methodical character had done the rest.

'My family don't think much of my job,' he said. 'And after all, why should they? It means that for most of my life I associate with criminals. But then, I don't think much of my family.' He said it casually, but she could see how far he had had to travel to arrive at that casualness.

Something else was cleared up on that train journey. They were in a smoking carriage, and he expressed mild surprise that she was one of the dwindling caucus of tobacco-users.

'Don't expect snotty yuppies to smoke, eh?' she said, feeling now she could say it, keeping it light. His expression was one of pure bemusement.

'Did I ever say that?'

'Not in so many words,' she said smiling. And nothing more needed to be said. That his puzzlement was genuine showed that his change in attitude to her was genuine too.

The Tyneside air was if anything softer than they were used to at home, where the harsh winter sat on the chest of the low-lying inland city like an incubus; but the same frozen detritus clogged and saddened the streets, and the movement of the traffic was a tense creeping that defeated even the taxi driver's manic brio. It was nearly an hour after they had got down from the train that they arrived outside Raleigh House, and it was only then that Routh raised a question that Sarah had suppressed.

'Suppose she's not in?'

'Wait till she is, I suppose.'

'She might be away for the weekend.' Then he sensed her anxiety, like a twanging in the air, and crossed that out. 'Well, we'll get to her somehow.'

Raleigh House did not look like the kind of place where people went away for the weekend. It was not so much a high-rise as a medium-rise, as if the builders had got discouraged halfway through. It was surrounded by a grim playground all painted in the sort of desperate primary colours that make tolerable drabness look unspeakable. Outside the block Sarah stopped, looking around her, thinking of those Blu-Tac marks on the wall of the little flat.

'What?' Routh said.

'She wouldn't have thrown that all away, just like that,' she said, half to herself. 'It doesn't make any sense.' She looked at him, and they went in.

Though it smelled like a zoo, the lift was working. When they came out on to a dingy gloss-painted landing a thought struck Routh and he said, 'Have you got that photograph of the girl with you?'

'I always carry it. Why?'

'It just occurred to me that that Nicola might have been mistaken. And that this Alison Holdenby might not be the girl you saw at all.'

She thought of it: couldn't bear to think of it. 'Come on,' she said.

The door of Number 44 was opened by six inches after a lot of knocking.

'Mrs Holdenby?'

'What do you want?'

'My name's Detective Sergeant Routh. This is DC Winter. We're just making some routine enquiries, we won't take more than a few minutes of your time.'

The door-chain rattled, and they were admitted. Entering the flat was like approaching a furnace. It seemed as if no windows had been opened here, ever.

'What's it about? Is it those joy-riders last week? I heard them but I didn't see them.'

O fat white woman whom nobody loves ... the line rose in Sarah's mind before she could suppress it. Mrs Holdenby, voluminous, short-breathed, with pink-rimmed suspicious eyes, preceded them into the living room on fat bare feet stuffed into worn slippers. With its hectically patterned curtains and cushions and carpet the room was like a migraine.

'Nothing like that,' Routh said.

'I wouldn't say if I had seen them because what's the point? They'll only get you back for it. They want putting away. But all they get nowadays is a pat on the head. You want to bring back the birch.'

She stared accusingly at Routh, then with a grudging look turned down the volume on the vast blaring TV. A caged budgerigar chirruped into the silence.

'It's nothing to do with that, Mrs Holdenby,' Routh said. 'We're just making a few enquiries about your daughter. Alison.'

'Why, what's she done?'

The question, and the tone of it, spoke unhappy volumes. A policeman mentions your daughter's name: surely your immediate response is 'What's happened to her?'

'Nothing as far as we know,' Routh said. 'We're just trying to trace her whereabouts. She left her last address rather suddenly and various people including her landlords are concerned about where she's gone.'

'Well, she's not here.' Mrs Holdenby sank into an antimacassared armchair. It was so uniquely moulded to her shape through years of use that no one else could have sat in it. 'You can look if you like. What's she been up to? You can't hold me responsible, whatever it is. I'm not her keeper.'

Sarah intercepted a glance from Routh, remembered the photograph. She passed it over.

'This is Alison, isn't it?' she said.

'Aye, that's her. What's she doing there? Has she been stealing or summat?'

'I assure you, Mrs Holdenby, we're just trying to trace her because . . . she appears to be missing,' Routh said. In that simple sentence he had made a grander gesture, Sarah felt, than in coming all the way to Newcastle with her. 'Now we found your name as next of kin, so—'

'Where'd you find my name?' There was a box of chocolates on the arm of the chair and Mrs Holdenby began feeding herself with them. Her mouth relished them even while her eyes puckered and frowned in suspicion. 'I've done nothing, where did my name come from?'

'From Alison's landlords,' Routh said. 'Now—'

'She'd no business giving my name to anybody,' Mrs Holdenby said, through husky chewing breaths. 'She needn't think I'll pay up if she gets into debt. I haven't got money to throw away.'

'It's a common requirement of employment and tenancy that you give a next of kin address, Mrs Holdenby,' Routh said.

She snorted. 'It's all forms nowadays. Have to fill out a form to do anything.'

'Mrs Holdenby,' Sarah said, 'we're very concerned about Alison. Have you seen her or heard from her or had any communication with her recently? It is important.'

'Well, I had that postcard,' Mrs Holdenby said, munching.

Sarah and Routh exchanged a glance.

'A postcard from Alison?' Routh said. 'When was this?'

'Oh, I don't know, the other week.'

'Do you still have it? Could we see it?'

Sighing and reluctant, Mrs Holdenby heaved herself out of the chair and fetched a rack of letters from the sideboard.

'I put it in here somewhere, I don't know why. It's got a castle on it, nothing pretty. She always had to be different like that. Here it is.' She gave the postcard a disdainful glance, before handing it over.

They read it together.

Dear Mum. As you can see I've moved on to Nottingham. Got myself work here, catering. Cash in hand. So I'm doing OK. I'm staying with friends at the moment, I'll let you know when I'm settled properly. Hope you're well, love Alison.

Routh pointed to the postmark, but he didn't need to. It was the first thing Sarah looked at. The postmark was dated two weeks ago. The incident in the Arena car park was nearly a month ago.

She had written this postcard after then.

Thus, nothing had happened to her that night.

Thus, she was all right.

Thus, everything was all right.

Thus, that was the end of it and Sarah should be feeling great surges of relief.

No surges. Sitting on the sofa beside Routh in an overheated flat in Newcastle, Sarah waited for them, waited for the accumulated pressure of the past month to break, burst, release.

And she found emptiness.

'This is definitely from Alison?' Routh said. 'I mean, it is her handwriting?'

'Oh, yes. That's her writing. It's typical, really. Mrs Carrington upstairs, she got a postcard from her son in Barbados. It was a beautiful picture on the front. And look at that thing.' The expression of contempt barely altered Mrs Holdenby's features. It fitted her as she fitted the chair.

'And this is all you've heard from her recently?' Routh said. 'She hasn't sent on her address or anything?'

'I wouldn't expect her to. She's not interested in me, never has been. She says she's got this job, but that won't last. People don't want to work nowadays. More likely she's after some lad like last time.'

'Last time?'

'That was why she moved down south in the first place. Following some lad. Not to get married and settle down or anything like that, oh no, not Alison. Anything in trousers.' Mrs Holdenby's puffy hand scrabbled vengefully among the chocolates. 'She's always been like that. Never any use to me. She always had her nose stuck in a book as if she were summat special. Fat lot of good that did her. Then as soon as she's old enough she clears off and leaves me just to chase some lad down south.'

'Do you know the lad's name?' Routh said.

Mrs Holdenby shrugged. 'Michael... Mark... summat like that. She never introduced him to me properly. Ashamed of him probably. Like I say, she goes her own way, always has. Her father was the same. Takes after him. Off she went. Me stuck here on my own. Get a postcard if you're lucky. That's my daughter for you.' The chocolates were all gone and Mrs Holdenby glared at Routh and Sarah as resentfully as if they had eaten them. 'Well, whatever she's done, she needn't come to me for help. What *has* she done?'

4

They had sandwiches and coffee in the station buffet, waiting for the Edinburgh–King's Cross train, talking but not talking.

'God, the heat in there,' Routh said. 'It's a wonder that budgie survives.'

'Thinks it's at home, maybe. They come from Australia, don't they?'

'Do they? I've never thought.' He got out a cigarette, then saw it was a no smoking area and irritably broke it in two.

'You're not happy about something,' he said. 'Is it because it looks like this girl's a bad 'un? Don't take any notice of that. It looks to me as if she just had to get away from that old bat before she went brain dead. Made a life for herself, and good luck to her.'

Sarah nodded.

'Look, I do know how you're feeling. From the work I do. It's a long road and when you get there you expect, I don't know, flags and trumpets and instead it's an anticlimax.' He eyed her narrowly. 'It *is* the end of the road – you know that, don't you?'

She nodded again.

'I mean,' he said, frowning more in perplexity than impatience, 'you can go and stick posters all over Nottingham now if you like, but I don't see the point. You were afraid from what you saw that something had happened to her. A couple of weeks after that she writes her mum a postcard from Nottingham saying she's moved over there and she's working and everything's fine. You can't get much more clear-cut than that. Can you?'

'No. No, you can't.'

'Sounds to me as if she's . . . well, like a lot of young people have to be now. Rootless. Bit naughty doing a runner from that flat maybe, but it's no big deal. The main thing is, you don't have to worry any more because she's *all right*. You do see that, don't you? Sarah, I'm not asking this because I want you off my back even though it might have seemed like that at first. I'm asking because I'm worried about you. I can see what you've been through and I can see that everybody's been saying let it go, let it go as if letting it go is easy and it isn't, I know. Letting it go is the hardest part.'

She took a blind sip at her coffee, forcing it down her tight throat.

'I should be glad, shouldn't I?' she said.

'Of course you should.' He seemed relieved that she had spoken at last. 'But like I say, I do know how you're feeling.'

Did he? If he did, he had the advantage over her. Sarah hardly knew what it was she was feeling. It was emptiness but it had something sharp about it too. The closest word she could think of was failure.

FIFTEEN

1

'Steve Jordan's coming in this morning,' Rachel said.

'What?' Sarah paused, her hand above the telephone keyboard. 'I thought he was set for Wednesday.'

'He's not going to be able to make it. David rescheduled for today. Just ten minutes before the news, usual thing. I'm doing the new sheet now.'

'Great. Well, at least it gets him out of the way, I suppose.'

'Oh, and there's a memo about the Arena roadshow. Apparently the Arena people might want to reschedule that too because they've got this personal appearance coming up. Some famous figure skaters. Not Torvill and Dean. Russian, I think. They've got these tremendous names.' Rachel peeped tremulously through her hair. 'Sarah . . .?'

Shards of memory, slipping like icicles through her fingers.

'Sarah, you OK?'

'Hm? Oh yes, fine. Well, that's OK. I was thinking of asking to be taken off the roadshow anyway.'

Rachel looked surprised. But after a glance at Sarah's

face she turned back to her word processor.

Sarah dialled the number right to the last digit before pressing the cut-off button. She closed her eyes, imagining how it would feel to enter that warm tasteful room again, to sit among the areca palms and unravel her tortured mind like a conjurer pulling ribbons from his sleeve.

His name is Mr Peter Foley. Her name is Miss Alison Holdenby.

Rob moseyed through clutching a hank of jack-leads like a bouquet of flowers. Seeing her on the phone, he raised a hand gloomily and backed out.

Either she hung on to this phone like a receptionist in a soap opera or she used it. Now which was it to be?

Given the way she had felt yesterday, the way she had felt this morning, the way her brain was revolving like a mouse in a wheel — given all that, was there any choice?

She put the call through. Jane, her old psychotherapist, remembered her at once —

Dear God. You never forget the real fruitcakes.

— and at once, too, she was back in that unnervingly smooth, too reassuring world, the doolally world where a soft carpet was laid out for your erratic feet and you knew the things you were saying were strange simply because they met such a bland unsurprised reaction. Jane was delighted to hear from her: it was as if five years ago they had spent some memorable holiday together. Jane suggested she come over and see her tomorrow evening, just for an informal chat. Jane didn't ask for details. Jane didn't say, 'What the hell are you coming back for, you're supposed to be cured!' Jane took it all for granted. That was what was so godawful about it.

But the mouse was spinning in the wheel so fast it was

going to do itself an injury and there wasn't, there just wasn't any choice.

Sarah went through to her studio, busied herself with her preparation, all the defence she had against failure and emptiness.

Jackie, preparing for the news in the adjoining studio, spoke through the relay.

'Sarah, have a good weekend?'

'Different,' Sarah said. 'Had a day out in Newcastle.'

'Oh.'

'Steve Jordan's coming in today. So if you hear my teeth grinding on air you'll know why.'

'God, he's creepy, isn't he? That damn jacket of his smells like a dead cow. Well, I suppose it is a dead cow.'

'I have to introduce him as Steve Jordan of Steve Jordan Entertainments now. Talk about Lord High Everything else.'

'I heard a rumour that Radio East were—'

Jackie was interrupted by Ravinder, the news editor, who darted into her studio and flung a flimsy on her desk.

'New headline,' he said. 'Go with this for now, but I'm hoping there'll be more before eleven. We're in a queue for Croft Wood police and it's coming on the IRN tele as well.'

'Shitty death,' Jackie said, reading. This colourful expletive never failed to startle coming from the impeccable Jackie, who groomed like a ballroom dancer. 'They've found the body of a young woman in a shallow grave near Huntley. No other details yet. Whoa, this'll be a biggy. Sarah, where are you going—'

'Shan't be a minute.'

It was no good, of course. Neither Routh's home

number nor his extension number at Croft Wood produced him. He was CID and a body had just turned up: what did she expect?

A good question. She was galvanized, but by nothing as recognizable as fear or foreboding or expectation: she couldn't, in any case, be sure that any of her responses were appropriate any more. All she knew was that the emptiness had changed character. She was a pure vessel of anticipation, waiting to be filled. Waiting for knowledge.

The minutes ticked through to eleven, and nothing more came through. Jackie led off with what she had.

'... The body of a young woman has been found in a shallow grave in woodland near Huntley, seven miles north of the city. A farm worker made the discovery early this morning. The area has been cordoned off and detectives from Croft Wood police station are at the scene. No further details have been released as yet.'

The red light came on and Sarah knew that if she could get through this one she could get through anything.

2

Nothing.

Nothing left.

No more Zoe. No more mind games. No more fantasies of manipulating the reptiles until they tore each other apart. Now it was back to the boy with the hat and the weasel one and the smiler, just them and her world without end for ever and ever and last night the things the smiler had done *back to normal* he said *back to normal* he said and she thought there were no screams left in her but he found some and—

Fantasies! Of course. She had done it again. Just like

her master plan of seducing Sean. A plan that rested on one crucial false assumption: that she was in control of events. That she was the only piece on the board that could make a move. So it had been with Zoe. Fantasy gaming. Dungeons and Dragons. And here she was still in the dungeon and Zoe was...

Well gone. There was no doubt of that. But how much to believe of what the smiler had told her? Could he be completely confident that Zoe wouldn't tell? One hundred per cent certain?

Of course he could the smiler is never wrong the smiler knows everything you can't fight him you can't fight the smiler he's won admit it he's won.

The imp of self-pity was back. But it had changed its tone. It used to speak in a niggling whiny tone. Now its voice was faint and hollow and resigned. As if it were—

Dying. Dying like the rest of her.

No.

The negative came from that other Alison. The Alison she should have been and might still be. And yet there was no denying that the voice was fainter too, no strength behind it, sapped.

Sapped by the pain and the sickness and the terror that only needed despair to attain completeness.

And there was nothing to keep her from that despair now. She had no more plans, no more strategies, no more hopes.

Nothing.

Nothing except the spoon.

And maybe the spoon was nothing really but they were old friends and she couldn't bear to part. And so she was still grinding, grinding the handle of the spoon against the floor. Her wrist wore a bright thong of pain but absence of pain was unknown to her now and it was just a matter of priorities. When the thong tightened beyond bearing then the priorities would change but for now the grinding could go on. And should go on. It was a sentimental thing. Nothing more.

Nothing to be gained, either, from the *if onlys* that kept brushing her like the memory of lost love. Things were as they were. She had taunted Zoe until Zoe had taken her bizarre revenge with the paint and the paint had caused the final quarrel and as a result of the quarrel Zoe was gone and the smiler was in control again. All right. What did these things mean, now?

Nothing. They meant nothing because they were coming to the end of things now, her and the spoon. There was just the grinding and the waiting. Things might happen to her, indeed they surely would, but she could make nothing happen: nothing.

Thus Alison Holdenby, chained to her bed of pain, grinding the handle of the teaspoon against the floor and sweeping her mind clean, filling it with nothing.

And then the tip of the spoon snapped off.

She had induced in herself such a state of passivity that she stared at the spoon with as much baffled astonishment as if she had caused the seas to part. And then a trapped and desolate wailing fought its way up inside her because the spoon was no longer as it had been and the spoon was her only friend . . .

But the wailing didn't come out.

Alison held the spoon up close to her face. She pressed the pad of her forefinger gently against its fractured tip.

The spoon was still her friend. In fact it had revealed a new, devilish, exciting side to its friendly old nature.

Worn thin by the grinding, about half a centimetre had

snapped off the handle end. Not straight across, but at an acute angle. The spoon now had an edge and a point. It was a little blade.

Alison had a weapon.

3

Nobody much wanted to be there, except for the regional TV crew. They had had nothing but early lambs and traffic pile-ups since Christmas and here they were with a real body – at least, there was a body somewhere beyond the cordon and behind the screens of plastic sheeting.

Routh had had a look at it, but a look was enough for him. He still wasn't too good with dead bodies, though it was as well to cover it up in the force where macabre humour was something of a way of life. A colleague of his told the tale of his first green visit to the morgue, when a waggish sergeant had removed the block supporting the cadaver's head. Because of rigor the head had sunk slowly backwards with a violent juddering motion as if the corpse were in fits of suppressed giggles. Routh's colleague told this tale often. So often that Routh suspected he had never really got over it.

Fortunately the other DS with whom he was supervising the dig had a strong stomach, and now that the forensic pathologist had come up from Cambridge they could take a back seat. A miserable and frozen detachment of uniforms were combing the surrounding area. The divisional photographer had just arrived, after a run-in with the farmer who owned this land and who had tried to stop him parking his car in the adjoining field. The Super was here as Senior Investigating Officer and, like the megastar he was, was giving some early flannel to the press. Altogether something like fifty people, armed with various degrees of authority, expertise and technology, had gathered at this bleakest of spots, to scramble about amongst frozen mud and sullied snow. It was tempting to ask yourself what it was all about, until you remembered there was a dead girl in amongst the spiky trees and she sure as hell hadn't put herself there.

Routh had already done more than his share of wondering — not his habit at all, because his mind worked best when it was fixed on practicalities. The wondering, of course, was a consequence of the weekend. Already, faced with this scene, that wild goose chase terminating in a Newcastle tower block seemed like a freakish dream, and certainly not like real police work. Indeed, he had hardly seen it as such at the time. It had been an act of capitulation to an obsession that he had begun by seeing as unreasonable and ended up seeing as reasonable enough, simply because he knew what it felt like to have a gut feeling so strong you couldn't let it go. Whether he had begun to share that gut feeling, just a little, was a difficult question. Just now, with the prospect of a heavy and tangible investigation ahead, it all seemed foolish and annoying. And yet, he couldn't help wondering. For the past month a missing girl who wasn't missing had hovered in the back of his mind, and now here was a dead girl dumped in a shallow grave. None of it fitted, of course, and from the glimpse he had had of that blue death-stretched face she could have been anybody; but it was a coincidence that his tidy mind found awkward and irritating.

The press had got all they were going to get out of the Super and were now concentrating on the farm worker's dog whose curiosity had set the whole thing going. The dog did not want to pose for pictures: like everyone else, it was cold and wanted to go home. Routh ticketed evidence bags as they came through for the forensic science van: bits and pieces, nothing that gave him a buzz. Traces showed up well in this white frozen world, but that was a mixed blessing: whoever had put her here would have spotted them too.

The Super, lordly as a sheik, made an entrance through the polythene sheeting where the pathologist and the forensic science officer were doing their work. Routh knew the drill, and felt a grim admiration. Even taking the rectal temperature of a living person seemed to him an outstandingly unpleasant thing to have to do. He was glad to note that the Super came out more hurriedly than he went in.

'Paul, how's it going? Any pickings?'

The Super was a first-name man. It gave you the creeps, as it was no doubt meant to do.

'Nothing that shouts, sir. To be honest I don't expect anything. This looks like a careful one. And unfortunately Farmer Giles brought a tractor through here just the other day, which has messed things up.'

'Ah. Well, she's been dead for more than forty-eight hours. How long she's been down there's a different matter. She's practically deep frozen, makes it harder to tell. The doc's about finished here, I'll authorize the removal of the body and then we'll see what he comes up with at the post-mortem.'

'Any sort of ID, sir?'

'Nothing. They stripped her. White female, early twenties, shoved in a couple of big bags, that's it. Tell you what did show up, though – needle marks on her arms. If she was into junk we might have her prints, they've usually got some sort of form. But it certainly wasn't junk that killed her. Her skull's bashed in.'

'Cause of death?'

'The doc's cagey but yes, I'd bet on it. 'Orrible murder, Paul, I'm afraid. Keep those poor sods at it, we're going to need every scrap we can get. As you say, this looks like a careful one, not just a couple of druggies fighting over their stash. And tell Farmer Giles to bugger off home, it's not his land while we're on it.'

'He doesn't like the media around.'

'Who does?'

The media... At Tudor Radio she would surely have got the news by now, Routh thought. It bothered him, because she bothered him. Her reaction to the successful end of her peculiar quest bothered him most of all. He knew about anti-climax, but this was different. She had been dull and withdrawn: shell-shocked almost. He had rung her yesterday to see how she was, but she had stonewalled him: he couldn't get through.

It bothered him.

The Super had the uniforms push the camera crew back: they were bringing the body out. It was covered now, but Routh knew well enough what it would look like. There would be plastic bags sealed around the hands and feet to preserve any contact traces, giving it the look of a baby in scratch mittens. There would be weird skin colorations wherever gravity had sent the lifeless blood. There would be a grin. Various people would have to look at these things closely and for a long time, which was something the killer didn't have to do.

And once the post-mortem and the inquest had officially established what they all knew – that that girl in the bag had been unlawfully killed – then it was going to be

Routh's duty, along with his colleagues, to get that killer. This was not a small matter. It was a hell of a big deal and it was not going to leave him time or space to be bothered by trivialities like Sarah Winter's mental state.

And that fact bothered him too.

4

Chill wasn't a liquid lunch type of bloke. Normally come one o'clock he would nip into the market café for a cup of tea and a wad or else send Sean to the sandwich shop over the way for a couple of crusties and a sausage roll. Just your basic comestibles to keep the old bod moving till shutting-up time. But every now and then, once in a blue moon really, he had the urge for a swift half at lunchtime and he didn't think it was much of a self-indulgence with all he had to do. There was always the possibility that left to his own devices Sean might sell everything on the stall for ten pence or burn the market to the ground, but then what was life without risk anyway?

And today it so happened that Chill fancied a beer at lunchtime and decided to take a walk down to the Mayor's Parlour, which was a basic sort of boozer as city centre pubs went and not liable to be overflowing with office workers finicking over their lasagne and backstabbing like nobody's business. Not that he had anything against that sort, he just wanted a bit of peace to play the bandit without somebody squeezing past him with a plate of salad. So he made his decision, and call it fate or destiny or whatever but the fact was to get to the Mayor's Parlour you had to pass the old closed-up cinema and that was where he saw the poster.

Well, it certainly arrested him and no pun intended.

He was so used to Alison's pretty face being his own private property that his first reaction, seeing her pasted up on the wall there amongst the gig adverts and the to-the-barricades-brothers and all the rest of it, was that it was a bit of a cheek. And his second reaction, he would be the first to admit, was a sensation that was rather like swallowing a whole ice cream and feeling it slide all the way down inside you right to your toes.

But once that was over he got a grip and he bellied up to the poster and took a good look. And swiftly concluded that the old ice cream feeling was a bit premature, because this sure as hell wasn't a police poster. Somebody else had done this — somebody who could be reached on that phone number, presumably. 'Relatives', it said, which was weird because he couldn't imagine Ma Holdenby, from what he had heard of her, being exactly on tenterhooks about poor Ali, even if he hadn't sent that postcard. Well, *somebody* had missed her at last, that was for sure.

And that was when his third reaction set in and it was a reaction that made him smile. Because for all his big talk about Alison not being missed and no one knowing or caring, there was a part of Chill that was a wee bit disappointed at just how easy it had been and that same part now felt a little shiver of excitement. After all, it had been a big undertaking and it would be a shame if *nobody* noticed. Just like if you climbed Everest or whatever. You wanted a bit of credit. Chill was a down-to-earth sort of guy but he was susceptible to glamour like everybody else: the whole idea of being able to say to yourself: *I did that!* Like hearing your own record played on the radio. You got a thrill.

Still, life was like an ashtray, there was always a but in it, and the but in this case soon occurred to him. If somebody was missing Alison, they were going to go on missing her, and sooner or later the police were going to prick up their piggy ears. Of course, this was a possibility that had been present to Chill right from the start but it wasn't something he had given a whole lot of thought to, at least not until Zoe had had her extraordinary fit of public-spiritedness. And now that the Big Z was safely out of the way he had tended to assume that things would just be back to normal on the Ali front. It just went to show you should never assume.

Well, well. So Ali had friends after all. He had already modified his initial opinion of her as a total loser, because there was no doubting the girl had guts. And now this. It was interesting. It was food for thought. It was, possibly, dangerous. He would have to see. And he could start by ringing that telephone number.

Chill had a memory like an elephant, not his only resemblance so he'd been told, and he didn't need to write the number down. He carried it in his head to the Mayor's Parlour and waited till he'd ordered his pint and downed the first golden mouthful before trolling over to the payphone and dialling it.

An answerphone, which was fine: he just wanted to see.

'Hello, this is Sarah Winter. Sorry I'm not able to take your call just now, but if you'd like to leave a message after the tone I'll get back to you.'

Well, that was one sexy voice. Somehow familiar too. Chill contemplated saying something after the beep, just for a crack, but decided against it. Devil-may-care was his middle name but he was going to have to go against his nature and be a bit cautious from now on. He could feel it in his water.

He put the phone down.

Sarah Winter. Whoever she was, Sarah Winter had an interest in young Ali. That meant Chill had an interest in Sarah Winter, but this poster was unofficial, a desperate plea for information. No one knew where Alison was, except Chill and his losers and they weren't about to volunteer any information. Still, food for thought again. He restricted himself to two pints because he wanted the old brainbox in perfect working order. And once again it was surely a case of fate or destiny or whatever because never had he needed a clear head more than he needed it that evening when, after an afternoon filled with your average amount of graft and more than your average amount of cogitation, he got home to Number 43 and switched the TV on.

Funny, really, that it should be him who switched it on because usually it was one of the others, the gruesome twosome being constitutionally incapable of spending two minutes in the house without plugging themselves into some electronic media or other. But as it happened tonight Trend was quietly snoozing on the settee when they got in, worn out from the exhausting business of underlining things with his magic marker no doubt, and Sean being a bit loose on account of all the chinky curries went stampeding straight up to the loo. And so it was Chill who plonked himself down in the front room and cued the idiot box and found himself right in the middle of the regional news.

Literally.

' 'Cking hell, man, I've got the trots something chronic, I mean it's like a tap—'

'Ssh!' Chill held up a hand to stem the returning Sean's flow of urbane wit because this was serious. Dead serious.

'... A post-mortem is being carried out and the results of the forensic pathologist's findings are expected to be released tomorrow. Police have yet to confirm that a full-scale murder inquiry is under way but Detective Superintendent Alan Rich, who is leading the investigation, has this appeal for members of the public who have any information that may be of assistance...'

Normally it would have been quite a sketch to see Sean's reaction to this, but Chill ignored the Celtic heebie-jeebies going on all over the room and turned the sound up. Maybe a bad move because it jolted Trend awake so that the first thing the hairy one saw when he opened his eyes was a full-colour all-action shot of that memorable spot in the woods swarming with police and the next thing you knew there were two of them at it. Talk about your decapitated domestic fowls.. Frantic, they were.

Yes, this was serious, and it was also a serious test of his leadership qualities – in other words, whether he could get the poor droogs through this one without their overburdened brains exploding. So he took it one step at a time. First he left them have their respective kittens, because nothing short of a machine gun would have stopped them anyway. Then he went through to the kitchen and brought back three cans of beer and told them, simply and quietly, to sit down.

'Sit down, what good's sitting down going to do?' Trend moaned. 'They've found her, Chill, the police have found Zoe!'

'Jesus. Oh Jesus, this is unbelievable, man. I mean this isn't fair, this isn't right...' Sean was doing his caged-animal number and very monotonous it was. It was time, Chill thought, to hang tough.

'I've asked you to sit down,' he said. 'And now I'm telling you. Sit down or I'll break *your* arm and then when you've listened to the crack I'll break *your* arm.' It was heavy stuff and he didn't like doing it but it did work, mainly because they knew he meant it. They sat, muttering.

'All right. Now get this down your necks and let's do a bit of thinking here.'

'Come off it, man,' Trend burst out, 'what is there to think about, it's on the TV, man, it's on the TV!'

'That's right,' Chill said, 'and exactly what did they say on the TV? You don't know because you were having the vapours. Luckily I paid attention. And all it is, they've found a naked girl's body up near Huntley.'

'What do you mean, that's all—'

'I mean that's all. Unidentified dead object. We know it's Zoe but they don't. They don't know anything about it.'

'They'll find out,' Sean said, shaking his head. 'The pigs, man, they'll find out.'

Touching, really. This faith in the supernormal powers of the constabulary. They'd certainly found out Sean's petty blags on a regular basis, but then Sean did everything but write SEAN MCGOOLIE WAS HERE in big letters at the scene of the crime.

'Well,' Chill said, 'maybe they will. Identify her, I mean. I suppose they've got their little ways. But then where's that going to get them?'

He left a pause there, mainly because his own mind was working ferociously – because things were getting hot, no doubt about it, things were definitely getting hot around here – but also because he was working his audience.

'Nowhere,' he went on. 'How are the old bill to know what happened? You've got to remember who we're talking about here. Our Zoe. A drifter. Here today gone tomorrow. Nobody gives a stuff about Zoe.'

'She was here, though,' Trend said. 'She was living here.'

'Who knows that?' Chill said. 'Us three. Who else?'

Sean piped up, 'Alison.'

Chill gave him a look, half-sorrowful, half-amused. 'Yes, Sean. I was talking about people who matter.'

Sean went red. Bless.

'There might be somebody,' Trend said, in this dogged voice that was beginning to do Chill's head in rather somewhat. 'She was getting stuff in town somewhere. She might have said something to her pusher.'

'Oh, come off it. You know that lot, no names no packdrill. And even if they did by some chance in a million try to link her with this house, what is there to show? Her stuff went on the bonfire and I personally took what was left down the dump.'

Hmm. He had gone a little bit wrong there, even raising a visit from the bizzies as a remote possibility: the pair of them had gone as white as a couple of sheets. He had to admit that dear old Number 43 was not exactly a house you'd want to be made the subject of an investigative detective-type scrutiny doodah.

Not in its present state, anyhow.

Chill fell back on his personal appeal. It was a mite cheap, but it seldom failed. 'Look,' he said, arms wide, 'have I ever led you wrong? Have I ever got you in deep schtuck and not got you out of it smiling? Huh? Have I?' It was real friends, Romans, countrymen stuff this, and it was working on Sean at any rate; he had calmed down and was giving Chill his ja-mein-Führer look, which was just fine.

Trend, though, was a different matter. Sulky acquiescence was the best he was getting out of Trend and Chill wasn't sure it was enough.

'I'll bet you any money the police won't get anywhere with this,' Chill said. 'I mean *nowhere*. But if they do, we'll be covered. OK? That is my solemn promise to you, *muchachos*, whatever happens we will be covered. OK?'

'OK.' Not quite in unison. Trend a little bit behind there.

'Now the thing to do is act completely normal, stay cool, and keep up with the news reports. That's all we can do and that's all we need to do.'

'Man, we should have buried her deeper!' cried Sean. Just as excited by the idea as if it could make a difference.

'Well, who knows,' Chill said. 'All in the lap of the gods, these things. Must admit I didn't think they'd find her *yet*, but there we are. Life's full of surprises. But they needn't be nasty and this needn't be nasty either, if we just stay cool. And like the old lefties say, in unity there is strength. Know what I mean?' He cocked an eye at Trend. 'We're all in this together and I find that a happy thought myself. I mean, I'm feeling pretty cool, but if either of you sort of wasn't around any more, then ... I don't know what I'd do.'

Yes, cool. Veritable cucumber, in fact, now that he had put the old henchmen straight. But still, things were definitely getting hot.

Setting the muppets the little task of ordering a takeaway, Chill went to the kitchen and turned on the transistor, searching for a local station. He would have preferred Radio East because you didn't get the irritating adverts, but the reception was bad so he settled for Tudor. He checked that there was no news, and then he made his way down to the cellar.

She didn't look good, the pet. Seeing the photograph on that poster brought home to him just how much she had gone downhill lately. He studied her, while she looked back at him with those big, unfathomable Alison eyes.

'Hmm,' he said at last, turning to go. 'I don't know about you.'

5

Maybe this being a DJ wasn't such a good idea, Sarah thought as she drove home late that afternoon. Maybe it actually fostered schizophrenia. Today there had been the profoundest split between her two selves. Sarah Winter of Tudor Radio had presented a smooth series of records spliced with jingles and commercials, gone through an events rundown with the loathsome Steve Jordan without once assaulting him even when he referred to a wet T-shirt competition as 'one for the ladies', handed over to Jackie for the news at hourly intervals, and generally spread her usual not-too-salty pâté over the middle of the day. The other Sarah Winter had been falling apart every time Ravinder came through with a news flimsy, cracking up every time the IRN teleprinter chattered into motion, and generally tearing herself in pieces with wild speculation. The division was so complete that she almost expected to see a doppelgänger riding home in the car beside her.

Yet nobody had noticed a thing. And maybe this really was what it felt like when your mind slipped its moorings. It wasn't the voices that had you gibbering but the fact that other people couldn't hear them. If she hadn't reached that stage yet she fully expected to. This suspense alone was enough to finish her off, she felt. Because there was no more news. Somebody had put a dead body in a wood outside the city and it was the body of a young woman but beyond that the police either didn't know or weren't saying.

And Sarah's own personal hotline did her no good. She had tried ringing Routh all day without success and she tried again as soon as she got in. No use. He had, she supposed, too much on his plate. The answering machine was bleeping, but there was no message. Just a silence and a click after the tone, which wasn't uncommon: there were a lot of people who couldn't bring themselves to speak into these things. Or maybe it was Murray, wanting to talk to her in person. It didn't matter.

She set herself the task of cooking. Even if she didn't eat, she had made the effort, that was the idea: also, hanging over the stove gave her an excuse to have booze at her elbow, it was traditional. And the booze set off some sharp self-questioning as she thought about the events of the weekend and what she had learned today. The questions weren't nice. They revolved around what she wanted. Could it be that she was actually *disappointed* on finding out that nothing more dramatic had happened to the red-haired girl than a moonlight flit to Nottingham? And that she was all a-flutter about this discovery near Huntley because maybe something had happened after all?

In other words, did she need to be proved right so badly that she wanted Alison Holdenby dead?

What sort of person did that make her?

'Mad or bad,' she said, feeding most of her meal to the

cats. Either she accepted that she was mad or she accepted that she was bad. No alternatives.

And yet there was a part of her that refused to accept either. Perhaps because there was still a part of her that believed that she had seen the beginning of something wrong in the Arena car park and it still hadn't been cleared up. It was a part of her that Paul Routh had at last come to respect, but the respect, she knew, had its limits.

She rang his home number nonetheless, when she had done the washing-up for the uneaten meal and tidied up as a sop to her conscience and then smuggled the vodka into the sitting room with her. Still no answer. She had barely replaced the receiver when the telephone rang at her, making her jump so violently that Charlie shot off her knee.

She picked up and got an earful of racket.

'Hallo? Hallo . . .?'

'Hallo, is that Sarah Winter?'

'Yes, who's this?'

More racket. It wasn't a bad line after all: something very noisy was going on at the other end.

'Shut up, will you . . . Hallo? This is Nicola. D'you remember, I rang you about that poster . . .?'

'Oh right, yes—'

'Shut up . . .! Sorry about that. I'm at this party . . .'

'Sounds like a good one.'

'Yeah, I'm going to be well away. Listen, what I was ringing to say – how'd you get on? You find her? I saw them changing the locks on her flat today.'

'Yes, she's not living there any more I'm afraid. Apparently she moved to Nottingham – you know, without giving notice. But that's as far as I've got. I haven't got her address in Nottingham or anything.'

'Oh, right, that'd be it then. Thought it was funny I hadn't seen her. Must be those guys . . .' A blast of music drowned out the rest of it.

'Sorry, what was that? Nicola?'

'Turn it *down* . . . Yeah, I was just saying, I reckon she must have moved in with these guys that Ashley saw.'

'What's that?' Sarah's knuckles were white. 'Which guys? Who's Ashley?'

'He lives upstairs at Lyle House. He's here tonight and we've been, you know. Talking. That's what I was going to say to you. He reckons he saw these guys moving suitcases and stuff out of her flat.'

'When was this?'

'Couple of weeks ago, he reckons. He's not sure. He's a bit pissed . . . Yes, you are . . .'

'Did he get a good look at these guys?'

'Wait a minute . . .' The background noise took over. Sarah tried to control her breathing. 'Hallo? No, not really. Just young guys. One had blond hair, bit like Jason Donovan he says. That's it. They were carrying these cases and stuff and putting it in a van, you know?'

'What about the van?' Sarah had to stop herself screaming it. 'Can he describe the van?'

'Wait a minute. Ash . . .'

Sarah closed her eyes. Slippery shards of memory, icicles in her fingers . . .

'Yeah, he says it was a light blue transit van. What did you say it's called, Ash . . .? Su-what? Subaru.' Nicola repeated it with sloshed earnestness. 'Subaru. That's what he says it was.'

'What about the girl? Was she with them?'

Nicola relayed it. 'No, he didn't see her. Just the guys

carting the stuff. Anyway, I reckon she must have gone off with them, you know. Maybe shacking up with one of them. Funny, isn't it? She always seemed so quiet.'

'Yes, it is funny,' Sarah said.

'Anyway, thought I'd let you know. Better go now while the loo's free. Ash, get off...!'

'OK, Nicola. Enjoy your party. And thanks again, I mean it.'

She put the phone down, and by knitting her fingers together got her hands to stop shaking at last.

It had to be. Blond hair like Jason Donovan. The van. It had to be.

Sarah paced herself. She rang Routh's home number only at five minute intervals, and allowed herself to refresh her glass only after half an hour. Meanwhile she kept the teletext on the TV paged to the local news, switching to screen whenever there was a scheduled bulletin. She got nothing from that she didn't already know, but at half-past ten she finally got Routh.

'I've been trying to ring you – sorry, stupid thing to say, I know you must have been busy.'

'You heard about the body, obviously.'

'Uh-huh. You're involved?'

'Practically everybody is. Listen, you know I'm not supposed to talk about this, but... Well, obviously it went through my mind too. When I heard. All I can say is I'm sure, I'm almost one hundred per cent sure it isn't her. But we've got to wait till she's been identified.'

'What happened to her? Sorry. I know you can't say that either.'

'Well...' She could almost hear the shrug on the phone. 'Somebody killed her, that's all that matters. And we've got to find him, with sweet f.a. to go on.'

She should perhaps have heard the warning note there, but she was too wound up. She dived in with Nicola's story, and when she was through she thought for a moment that his silence meant he was as excited by it as she was.

Then he spoke and the weariness in his tone was unmistakable.

'Well, well. Like this Nicola says, it looks like she's done a bunk with the guys in the van.'

'But she wasn't seen with them. It was just them carrying the cases and stuff.'

'Yes, well, the old gender roles aren't dead after all. Look, Sarah, I don't see the point of this. We knew the girl had left the flat and done a runner and it seems a reasonable assumption that she didn't take her stuff away in a rickshaw, so—'

'But that was the van I saw, that was the same van and the men too, they were the same men—'

'You don't know that.' Now there was an edge to the weariness. 'You don't know that at all and even if it was, so what? You saw her at the Arena with these same guys and that same van, OK, I'll accept that for the sake of argument but it still doesn't mean anything except that she's, I don't know, friends with them, involved with them, whatever. And maybe living with them in Nottingham right now.'

'Why didn't she take her bed?'

'What?'

'She left her bed behind in the flat. Why not take it with her, if there was a transit van available to move her stuff? You saw her mother, you saw the place she came from. That girl must have scraped and struggled to get her little flat kitted out. Don't you remember how chuffed you were with your own bits and pieces when you first left home? Why would she leave it behind?'

'I don't know. Maybe if she's moved in with some fella she doesn't need it. Sarah, none of this is . . .' He stopped before saying *important*, but she filled it in. 'I know you can't help wondering, but really I just haven't got time for this. Whether this Holdenby girl is living in Nottingham with some guy or without some guy or with her bed or without it or whether she's living in some bloody commune eating wild rice, it's . . .' He sucked in a breath. 'Look, you can't even be sure what this guy at the party did see or didn't see. He—'

'He was probably mistaken. I know. I've heard it before. Maybe he was just imagining it. Maybe he had a breakdown five years ago and you can't trust anything he says.'

A sliver of silence.

'That's not fair,' Routh said.

'No. Forget I said it.' Shortly.

'Sarah, I'm . . . I'm sorry, it's just I'm so knackered and I can't think straight and I don't know, I really don't know what I can do about this right now. I mean, once again it's a question of . . . of you know, this van, it's just a van, and without the registration number . . .'

'I know.' The softening in her tone was the result of her own weariness, which attacked her suddenly and completely; but it closed up a little distance, at least. 'I know.'

'Listen. This body that's been found, as soon as there's an ID on it you'll know about it. I mean you'll probably get it at Tudor as soon as it's released, but I'll let you know if not. And this business about the van—'

'Put it out of your mind?'

He was solemn. 'Yes. Do that.'

'All right. I'll let you get to bed.'

'I must admit I'm ready for it . . . There's a funny thing. I've just realized, I've still got the same bed I bought when I first left home . . .' He turned brisk again, after a still moment. 'Look, I'll try and talk to you tomorrow. You get some sleep too.'

She might, she thought as she put the phone down, and then again she might not. She had a lot to think about.

SIXTEEN

1

It came through at five to three the next day, an hour after Sarah had finished her show. She was haunting the newsroom where Ravinder had spent most of the day trying to winkle something out of the press office at Croft Wood when all at once the teleprinter supplied what she had been waiting for. She had time to glance at it before Ravinder hustled it through to Jackie.

The body in the wood was not Alison Holdenby. So far so good. It was the end of something, but not for Sarah. Not since Nicola's phone call.

She listened to Jackie on the relay.

'Police have identified the body of the woman found in a shallow grave near Huntley yesterday as that of Zoe Bayliss, a twenty-two-year-old from Maidenhead. The results of the post-mortem carried out by Dr Vejay Odedra, a pathologist at Addenbrookes Hospital, indicate that the dead woman died as a result of a fractured skull...'

Rachel was beckoning Sarah to the phone in the office.

'Sarah? Paul Routh. You've heard?'

'Just now.'

'OK. So now you know. ID'd her from her record, by the way. She had quite a few convictions. A very posh and bewildered man's just been brought up from Maidenhead. Mr Bayliss. First time he's seen her in years. "But I gave her everything", all that stuff. So. Second thing. I'm sorry I was so dismissive on the phone last night.'

'That's OK.'

'No it's not. It was rude. But I still stand by what I said: put it out of your mind. Got to go.'

Put it out of your mind. Well, she wasn't sure she wanted to any more. But there were people who were professionals at putting things out of your mind and she was booked to see one this evening. Jane and her cool compress of understanding.

She would still go, Sarah decided – mainly because if she cried off Jane would see it as more revealing than turning up. But she felt that she would be there under false pretences.

2

It came through at three o'clock. Chill had taken the little tranny to work with him, propping it up on a shelf at the back of the stall and cocking an ear whenever the news came on. And just when he was thinking he was getting in a tizzy about nothing out it came. Radio East, three o'clock bulletin, headline story. They'd identified her. And it was funny how the mind worked because all he could think for a minute was: *Bayliss. Of course, that was Zoe's surname. I did know it, but I forgot.*

And then he began to think of other things and his thinking was fast and furious.

Freezing Point

'Sean!'

Fortunately really that Sean had wandered over to chew the fat with Nige at The Kandy Man across the way. This was a thing best told to him in private. Didn't want the poor sod having hysterics all over the market.

'Sean, come on, quick sticks. We're packing up.'

'Eh? It's only just gone three.'

'Well, I'm glad to know you've learned to tell the time at last.' Chill said, snatching off Sean's hat and ruffling his hair. He loved this rough humour, bless him. 'Come on. I've had enough for today. I want to get home.'

Yes, home. Home is where the heart is. Other things too. And Chill needed to be there.

Chop chop then, gear in the van and shutters up on the stall, Sean falling over his feet in his haste. No asking why the haste: just ready and willing, that was Sean. He was a good boy. You could trust him. You learned which ones you could trust, through experience.

Chill waited until they were clear of the city centre before pulling over in a quiet spot by the old municipal park. The trees, he noticed, were looking a treat, all delicate white frost on their bare twigs just as if somebody had iced them with one of those nozzle doodahs. He noticed such things, Chill. Some people went around with their eyes closed.

'What's up?'

Sean had done a good job of not bricking it all day. Almost cool, he'd been. Chill hoped he wouldn't let himself down now.

'They've identified poor old Zoe, mate,' Chill said.

'Oh no oh Jesus man—'

'So they're going to be digging up everything they can about Zoe, excuse the pun,' Chill said, gripping Sean's arm good and tight, 'and looking for whoever killed her. OK? Got that?'

'Jesus . . . Jesus . . .'

'Yep, I know him, the one who turned up at the door with three nails and said can you put me up for the night, but he's got nothing to do with it, Sean my old son, so listen up. OK. Now. What do we do, Sean?'

'I don't know . . . I don't—'

'We stay cool,' Chill said, tightening his grip. 'We carry on just as normal. And we stick together. Thick and thin, my old china. And if the police do turn up on our doorstep at some point – I only say *if* – then we're just like the three monkeys, right? We don't know anything. It's over a year since we saw Zoe. Yes, we know Zoe, so do a lot of people, but the last time we saw her round our manor was over a year ago. We haven't seen or heard anything of her since then. This is what you call getting our stories straight, my old duck, and it is very important. Got it?'

Sean nodded dumbly.

'Good lad. Nice one.'

'What about Trend?'

'What about him?'

'He's got to say the same thing, hasn't he?'

'Oh yes, he certainly has, my son. Absolutely. That's why I want to get home pretty sharpish and tell him what I've just told you. So. Orft we jolly well go.' He keyed the ignition. 'You're OK now, are you, Sean? You're cool?'

'Yeah.' Sean swallowed, nodding. 'Yeah, I'm cool.'

He was, too, in his way. Chill was proud of him. Now if he could only be as proud of Trend . . .

The house was silent when they got in. Absolutely no sound. Not a dicky bird.

'Is Trend at college today?' Chill said, pausing in the hall, his hand on the banister.

'Tuesday? Don't think so.'

Chill called up the stairs. 'Trend! Coo-ee! Daddy's home!'

'Maybe gone down the job centre.'

'Mind that flying pig.' Chill chuckled, but he didn't feel very chucklesome. Things were getting a bit too hot for that. And when he legged it up the stairs to check on Trend's room they got about a hundred degrees hotter at a stroke.

Sean was in the kitchen making tea and he jumped a foot in the air when Chill came crashing in.

'Whoa, man, what's—'

'Gone.' There was no help for it, Chill was going to have to let his cool slip for a moment. He did it by picking up the mug-tree and swinging it like a club and smashing it down on to a stack of dirty plates.

Just that. Then he felt better.

Sean was watching him with scared eyes.

'Sorry about that, mate. But he's pissed me off good and proper this time. He's done a runner, our Trend. He's cleared all his stuff out of his room. All gone. While we were turning an honest penny, Sean my son, our old friend Trend ratted on us.' Chill held up a warning finger. 'And don't start calling on Jesus because he is not going to help us. It's up to us now, Sean.'

'What's he playing at?' Sean was flapping, but he was keeping it within limits. 'Where's he gone?'

'One of two places. Either straight down the cop shop to spill the beans, or else he's hiding out somewhere wondering what to do. You know what I think? I think he panicked. He must have heard about them identifying

Zoe, had a rush of blood to the head, got his stuff together and scarpered. The main thing was to get away from this house and away from us.'

' 'Cking hell! What a swine!' Sean looked more crestfallen than anything else. Funny really. A lifetime of petty crime and general worthlessness, and he was still shocked when someone behaved badly.

'You took the words right out of my mouth, as they say, my old son,' Chill said. Now he was gutted, no two ways about it. He had lost control for a moment and that was evidence enough of how he was feeling. But feelings weren't going to get the baby washed. It was quick thinking that was required, and Chill, no slouch when it came to putting the old grey matter into overdrive, had never thought so fast as he thought now.

'What we gonna do?' Sean was mournful but resigned. 'What we gonna do, Chill?'

'Move fast, my old mate,' Chill said with a sharp clap of his hands. 'It's Speedy Gonzales time, Sean. We get busy, we can wrap this all up tonight and be home free. Only I need you to play your part, Sean. You've got to be on the ball because this is serious stuff, you hear what I'm saying?'

'Yeah. Yeah, I got you.' Total absence of will now, old Sean. What you might call an instrument.

'Right. Number one, we've got to deal with our old mate Trend. Now you know as well as I do that he's a ditherer and that means there's a good chance we can get to him before he drops us in it, yeah?'

'But we don't know where he's gone.'

'Oh, I know my—' Nearly said *I know my losers*. 'I know my old chum Trend. He stuck so close to us he didn't exactly form a large circle of acquaintances, now did he?

There aren't that many places he can park his ghetto blaster. If he's laying low with some of his poncy mates, I'll find him. And then . . . well, I'll sort him out.'

'How?'

Chill tapped his nose and a big grin spread across his face before he could stop it. 'You trust your Uncle Chill. Once I find him, I'll sort him.'

'Don't you want me to come?'

'Nothing I'd like better, my old china, all things being equal. But this is where number two comes in, you see. You've got a little job to do here.' He jerked his thumb over his shoulder. In the direction of the cellar door.

'What?'

'The pet, Sean. Her as is. I know it seems hard and I must admit I've got a little lump in my throat myself just thinking about it, but she's got to go. Things are just getting too hot around here and this little stunt of Trend's has really put the lid on it. Do you see what I'm saying? If there is any constabulary attention coming our way we can't afford to have Allyboo down there, we really can't.'

Wow. Looked like Sean was going for a new record in gormless amazement.

'You mean we're going to let her go?'

Dear oh dear. 'Well. Ahem. Only in the sense of setting her spirit free sort of thing. Come on, Sean, get real. It's just a case of finishing what we started. It was always risky and now it's too risky and she's got to go. Waste her, remove every last trace of her little stay here, and get our kicks from stamp collecting in future, yeah? I don't know about you, but this is all getting a bit much for me.'

'You . . . you're kidding me, man.'

Chill just looked at him.

'Oh, wow, Chill . . . this is . . .'

'What is it? It's no big deal, that's for sure, not if we look smart about it.' Chill looked at him some more. 'You're not going to do a Trend on me, are you, Sean?'

'Nah, man, no way, never! It's just . . . I mean, what are we going to do with her?'

'After she's popped her clogs, you mean? Well, I think where we went wrong with Zoe was not thinking it through. I reckon we should dispose of Ali a lot further away. In fact I know just the place. So don't worry your head about that. You just concentrate on getting the job done.'

'Me? Come on, man, why me?'

'Sean. You're not listening. Like I said, we're in this together. I don't know. One minute you're telling me I can trust you and the next minute—'

'You can trust me, Chill, you can!'

'Can I really?' Chill took a step towards him.

'You can, you can, honest, I'd never let you down, I swear . . .'

Real distress on the poor muppet's face there. Chill smiled, took another step forward, and put his arm round Sean's shoulders.

'Good boy. Look, I know how you feel. I'll be sorry to see her go too, I really will, I was getting dead fond of her. But sometimes you have to be tough to survive and I'm afraid this is one of those times. And listen, it's because I trust you that I'm giving you this job, see? There's not many people I'd trust with it, I'll tell you that.' He gave Sean a squeeze. 'Now, I'm going out to find old Trendyboots and in the meantime you . . . well, you do what you have to do. All right?'

Sean looked rather like Stan Laurel about to do his

boo-hoo bit and Chill had to be careful not to laugh as that would have destroyed the mood more than somewhat. But still, the boy was holding up well.

'How . . . how do I do it?'

'I'll leave that up to you, mate. Just try not to make a mess.'

3

Well, here he was hitting the road again, hardly been home ten minutes and not a crumb of tea inside him. But there was no help for it because speed really was of the essence and he would just have to grab a bite later, all being well.

All being well not only on the Trend front but on the home front as well because he had the tiniest suspicionette that Sean might not be up to the job. Oh, he would try, there was no doubt about that – Sean was nothing if not a trier and he would give it his best shot – but there was a distinct possibility that Chill would come home to find the job only half done or even not done at all. Well, in that case he would simply have to gee Sean up. Just his encouraging presence should do the trick. Dispatching the pet himself was something he contemplated only as a very last resort. It wasn't that Chill was squeamish. He just preferred to keep his hands clean. In case.

Trend, though: that was a different matter. With Trend it was personal.

Well, hopefully tonight it would all be over, bar the hard work of course. Because besides the cleaning up and the pet's toys to be got rid of there was the question of poor old Ali herself. And that would mean, in a nutshell, driving the bod up to Nottingham and dropping it in the Trent if poss. Nottingham was where she was, ahem, living and Nottingham should be the place where she was, apparently, bumped off by person or persons unknown. Maybe it wasn't perfect but he still thought it was a pretty good idea though he said it himself. Improvisation sort of thing.

Chill was an optimist, but even he had to admit it was too much to hope that Trend might be hiding out at his first port of call, which was a set of bedsits just a short drive away from Grenville Street. This was where Trend had lived before joining the Three Musketeers and though he had been highly delighted to leave on account of a new tenant called Mucker who was built like a brick whatsname and had a habit of recreationally beating up his neighbours in the communal kitchen it was just possible, Chill thought, that Trend had tried to find a bolthole back here. One thing Chill had learned was never to underestimate the stupidity of his losers.

No go though. Of the old loser school Chill found only the hulking Mucker still in residence and inclined to take umbrage at his questions or maybe just his existence which made Chill rather glad that he had brought along a spot of protection just in case. But he shimmied out of there without having to use it, pointless confrontations with meatheads not being top of his agenda today of all days, and hit the road again.

The shopping mall was just closing and the sad cases who hung around the record shops were on the point of dispersing when Chill caught up with them. Several Trend lookalikes here and even a few who were sad enough to count themselves mates of his. Not such good mates, though, that they wouldn't dob him in if Chill leaned on them. Which he hardly needed to do, as it happened, as one look at his face seemed sufficient to make them fall over their hightops in their eagerness to tell all. Now Chill could spot a lie at forty paces and it was soon clear to him that when they said they hadn't seen him and didn't know where he was it was nothing less than gospel. But his ears pricked up when the assembled drongos started casting around for someone who might know something and the name of Rabbit came up.

Chill knew Rabbit, or knew of him. Rabbit had a prominent place in Trend's mythology on account of having once played bass guitar in some godawful band who couldn't even get a pub booking. Chill also remembered Trend droning on about some unbelievable Lebanese brown he had had at Rabbit's place, unbelievable being the operative word as Trend didn't know good dope from his elbow and would probably start rolling his eyes if you crumbled him a caramel toffee. And so when it transpired that no one had seen Rabbit around today either and that Rabbit still inhabited the same semi-legendary squat, Chill felt something click and with a cheerful cheerio to the hairies he was on his merry way back to the van.

'Ssh – be vewy quiet,' he said to himself as he belted up, 'I'm hunting wabbits.'

But that was only a little frolicsome froth on the surface of his mind because underneath, Chill's thoughts were solemn. And as he made his slow and patient way out of the city centre, traffic still heavy in the early evening and another powdering of snow turning the roads into treacherous meringue, Chill's thoughts grew darker. Apocalyptic, even. This betrayal of Trend's mattered a great deal to him. Life was a drama and an adventure if you set about it the right way and accordingly there were drastic times, moments of momentousness, and you had to be ready to meet them with everything you'd got. Otherwise you were dead inside. When the adrenaline dried up you might as well lie down in your wooden box and say ta-ta. So there was excitement in Chill's mood but it was a grim excitement. It was the deeper thrill, the thrill of great enterprises coming to a head. The showdown between triumph and disaster.

He was ready. He was fired up. He was mad as hell. But he was not the least bit anxious.

Also he was thinking straight, which in all modesty he very much doubted anyone else would be in his position. Rabbit's squat was his destination, but he wasn't about to park out front like a flaming taxi, oh no. Instead he parked the van a couple of streets away. Thereby illustrating a little fact of modern life that his ever-lively mind registered as interesting, even now when he had so much to do. The street where he parked was pure double-income-no-kids territory. Victorian terraces picked up for a song and made over into an estate agent's wet dream. If there was a single house here without a garlic-crusher in the kitchen he would be very surprised. But walk a couple of hundred yards and you were in Scumbag Row where the only status symbols were mattresses in the front gardens. Round here there was no point in smashing the windows. The residents did that themselves, from inside. Dear oh dear. Here they were, citizens of the western world, and they had cardboard glazing. Something was wrong somewhere.

The squat, at any rate, was quite a des res for this neck of the woods, though the snow had drawn a tactful veil

FREEZING POINT

over the disembowelled twin-tub and the piles of beer cans in the front garden. Chill stopped and gave the street a once-over. Not exactly your Neighbourhood Watch type of area, but you never knew. It was his combination of caution and daring that made him, though he said it himself, such a fly character.

Now then. Curtains drawn at the front windows, lights in both. Chill didn't fancy the front. He fancied the back and there was a passage running along the side of the peeling old house that would lead him there, assuming he could get through the gate.

Locked though. Very security-conscious, these squatters. Might get all sorts wandering into their pad and they wouldn't want that. The gate was about six feet high. Chill took another look round and then hoisted himself up and clambered over it. Now if the droogs who lived here were the sort who kept Dobermans under the mistaken impression that it made them look less pathetic, then he was a goner. But he landed on the other side without any teeth in his leg. Luck was with him and he rode it, softshoeing it up to the back door and trying the handle and, when it yielded, waltzing right in.

Well, he had seen some ratty kitchens in his time but this took the biscuit. Even the cockroaches had moved out. It was a wonder the people who lived here weren't all racked up with botulism and maybe they were because there was no sign of anyone.

Chill's blood hummed in his ears and his heart, not normally his most excitable organ by any means, started thumping away like a party next door. He was taking one step at a time but with each step his goal was becoming plainer.

He knew better than to tiptoe or creep: that was a

fail-safe way of making a noise. He just walked unhurriedly down the passage. And when he came to the door of the front room and saw it was slightly ajar he simply listened a moment and then pushed it open with one gloved finger.

This, surely, was Rabbit's room – posters of sundry guitar-wielding persons and an actual guitar and, good grief, a traffic cone, they still thought that was the height of rebellion after all these years – and that henna-headed lump, surely, was Rabbit, malodorously sleeping something off on a mattress piled high with hospital blankets and dope-impregnated clothes. No heating in this place, of course. Bloody fascist police state trying to freeze us to death, et cetera et cetera: Chill's mouth filled with a yawn at the thought of it. He retreated and put a hand on the banister and *then* he saw something that really got the cardiac party swinging.

A coat, hanging on a peg in the hall. Some sort of weird ethnic effort that looked as if it had come off a dead Aztec. Chill knew that coat all right. He had seen it hanging in the hall of 43 Grenville Street enough.

Tackling stairs quietly was always the toughest proposition, especially when they were uncarpeted and wormy like these. Your best bet was a sort of flat-footed glide, pressing down with the ball of your foot as little as possible, and Chill thought he carried it off pretty well. He did have an advantage, though. There was music coming from a room at the top of the stairs and blow him down if he didn't recognize that music too.

The door of the room wasn't fully closed, for the simple reason that it had no handle. So it seemed silly, really, to knock. Especially when they were such old mates. Why not surprise him?

Why not indeed?

Chill slipped into the room. In like Flynn.

'Hiya, Trend,' he said.

4

'Sean, please, I want some water.'

It seemed an age since she had heard the reptiles coming home, and now that Sean had at last come down to the cellar he wasn't doing any of his normal duties. She had nothing to drink and the bucket needed emptying but all Sean was doing was pacing around the cellar muttering under his breath and shaking his head.

'Please, Sean. Can I have a drink of water?'

He wouldn't even look at her.

'Sean, I'm sorry, I'm just so thirsty. Please—'

'Shut up, will you . . .'

'Sean, what's the matter?'

'Shut *up*!'

His face was drained of colour and he was shaking. Alison felt a coldness in her bowels. Sean was only a simplistic sketch of a human being: his moods and expressions were very few and she had come to know them all.

This was something new.

'Listen, man . . .' He approached the bed, then veered off, shaking his head. 'Listen, I got to do it. That's all there is to it, right, it's just the way it is.' He looked at her as if she were throwing a tantrum and he were desperately asking her to be reasonable.

'What? I don't know what you're talking about. Sean . . .?'

He had sloped away from her again, stood hunched

with his back to her, head wagging incessantly. And then all at once he came rushing at her and she saw a knife raised high and then stabbing down at her and, screaming, she put out a hand, shielding, and it gushed blood. And she was screaming no no with her last breath surely her last breath. But though the knife was up in the air again and his face was looming down the knife didn't descend and instead Sean was yelling.

'I've got to do it! Don't you see, I've got to do it, now don't – don't give me any hassle, because oh God I've got to . . .' His eyes took in the blood, expressed blood in their widening horror and the raised knife

kitchen knife knife for meat

wobbled and he took a step backward moaning, 'Look, I'm not supposed to make any mess, come on, you've got to help me here, I'll do it quick, man, just—'

'Don't, Sean, don't,' fire words from burned throat.

'I've got to, Chill said,' and then at that word *Chill* there was a nerving in his body and she saw the lunge in his eyes an instant before he made it.

And then his hand pressed down on her forehead and the bridge of her nose holding her and he was going to cut her throat and this was real, this was no new refinement of torture that would end with devil's laughter it was real and she screamed back the blade with the words: 'I'll do it! I'll do it myself!'

'Nah . . . nah . . . you won't, you won't do it . . .'

But he did not slash and kill, he suspended the knife and he left a space for her to plead and promise and she did it because the world had narrowed to it.

'I'll do it, Sean . . . I'll do it myself, I promise, let me do it myself,' and that worked, that kept the knife just at bay and then things breaking inside her made her cry out, 'Why, why have I got to die?' and that was bad because the knife flailed again.

'You've got to, man, that's it, you've had it, I'm doing it,' and the knife, no gleam now, dark with blood, down in a jerky scramble and cutting through the flesh of her upraised forearm, apple-deep, and her voice like a metallic barking as she writhed, 'Sean it hurts oh God Sean it hurts—'

A grunt from him, arm swinging up.

'I'll do it Sean let me do it *I swear to God I'll do it* . . .'

Sweating, grunting, hesitating. 'It's still going to hurt, man, it's still going to hurt—'

'No. No.' The blood on her was so warm. 'No, something else. Let me . . . something else.' So warm, and she was like an animal, throaty, bloody. 'I'll take pills, give me pills, let me do it so – there's – no pain . . .'

He stared at the blood and the spastic sobs and he was contorted and impatient, a man with the dirty end of the stick.

'Oh God . . . all right . . . but you've got to, you've got to . . .'

He went running off with a patter of blood drops and Alison asked herself if she would have to die and her self would not answer. All it said was, 'The spoon', and though she did not fully understand because her mind was fogged with sobs and blood she slid the spoon out of its niche in the mattress and she held it, covered, in her left hand, and then Sean reappeared through the fog.

'All right then,' he said. 'But you've got to do it.' He still clutched the knife in his right hand. In the other was the bottle of prescription painkillers, three-quarters full. 'Sit up.'

She obeyed, not sobbing now. Not anything.

He unscrewed the cap and shook out the tablets on the blanket beside her. Squatted down on his haunches with a creak of boots, watching her, a faint frown between his thin eyebrows.

'Hurry up, or I'll do it.'

The world had narrowed down to this and there was no more. Alison Holdenby, nineteen years old, sentenced to death, picked up the first of the tablets and swallowed it.

5

'How'd you find me?'

'Oh, come on, Trend. It wasn't that hard.'

Ian Christopher Elderkin, a.k.a. Chill, smiles in a friendly fashion as he says this, and takes a couple of steps into the room. The walls of the room are painted black, the skirting boards bright yellow. An unshaded light bulb hangs from the ceiling. A bedsheet is tacked up at the window. An oddly shaped piece of carpet, like a piece of a giant jigsaw, covers roughly half the floorboards. Apart from Trend's bags and his boombox and a heap of tapes there is only an old sagging sponge sofabed in the room, and Trend is sitting on it. His face is a closed and sullen one, not made for fear, but there is fear in it now.

'How'd you get in?'

'Blimey, what is this, twenty questions?' Chill claps his gloved hands together and blows out a white breath. 'Bloody hell, it's as cold as the Tin Man's willie in here. Haven't you got a fire or anything?'

Trend stares at him balefully, motionless.

'It's a lot warmer at Grenville Street,' Chill says winking.

Trend glances at the door behind him and his throat works, swallowing.

'Dear oh lor,' says Chill breezily, 'what's the matter with you? You look like you've seen a ghost.'

'Chill,' Trend says, and suddenly he is gabbling, the words tumbling over one another, 'I couldn't hack it any more, I just couldn't, them finding Zoe and everything I just couldn't I had to get out I had to get away and get my head straight that's all that's all it was—'

'Whoa, whoa,' says Chill, holding up his hands. 'What's all this? Eh? Anybody'd think I was accusing you of something. I mean what have I said?'

Trend swallows. Swallows again. It's as if he can't stop.

'Now just calm down. I thought you were learning to be cool, Trend mate, I really did, and now look at you. Listen, we're mates, aren't we?' Chill's eyes seem exceptionally blue and fresh in this black room. 'Well, aren't we?'

Trend nods.

'Well, then. We can talk about it like mates then, surely. Which is basically what I came here for. Look, I'll be honest, when I got home and found you'd gone I must admit I was worried. That doesn't mean I don't trust you, it's just . . . well, put yourself in my shoes. You'd be worried too, wouldn't you?'

'You don't have to be worried, Chill. Honest.'

'Well, that's what I came to find out. I mean, old mates like us, of course I should know you wouldn't say anything, but . . . oh, I don't know, I was in a panic what with one thing and another and I just . . .' Chill shrugs and smiles ruefully. 'Just had to hear it from your own mouth, that's all.'

'I haven't said anything, Chill. I swear I haven't said a

word to anybody and I promise, I swear on my life that I won't. Not ever. I'll never tell—'

'All right.' Chill stops him with a wave of his hand. 'That's all I want to hear, Trend my old mate. If I've got your promise – and listen, I am serious about this – if I've got your solemn promise that you'll keep your mouth shut no matter what happens, then—'

'I promise.' Trend's voice is guttural with urgency, and he rubs his hands nervously back and forth across his thighs. 'Chill, I promise you.'

'No kidding?' Chill cocks his head, a little roguish.

'No kidding.'

'All right then.' Chill lets out a long breath and closes his eyes for a moment. When he opens them again his look is bright. 'Well, I've got to admit, you did have me worried there for a while.'

'I didn't mean to . . . you know . . . I just . . .'

'Nah, no worries, mate. Come on. Let's have a joint on it.'

He produces the joint, ready-made, from a pocket inside his coat. Looks at Trend.

'Don't say you're going to turn down a spot of blow? Now that *would* be a first.'

Trend shakes his head, eyes wide.

'Gonna say. I'm well ready for a smoke myself, the day I've had. All right if I park my bum down here?' In a twinkling Chill is sitting on the sofabed close beside Trend, lighting up the joint. 'Coh. Nice one. Here you go.'

He passes the joint over and Trend, after a fractional hesitation, accepts it and takes a toke.

'Must say I'm not completely sold on the décor in this place, but each to his own I suppose . . . Nah, you stay with it, mate—' as Trend offers the joint back. 'Depress me, this room would. Mind you, it's striking, I'll say that for it. You know, you could do up your room at home like this, if you wanted to come back.'

Trend shakes his head and draws deep on the joint.

'The offer's there, you know, Trend. Just because you did a runner on us doesn't mean you can't come back.'

'Nah. No way.'

'Well...' Chill stretches out his legs, 'if your mind's made up.'

'Yeah, it is.' The joint is a strong one and its effect is visible on Trend, who lounges back on the sofabed, his eyes half closed. 'I'm out of it, Chill.' He lets out a giggle. 'I mean not out of it in that way, I mean... you know. I'm out of all that. Just going to go my own way.'

'Well, OK. If you say so.' Chill turns his head and smiles at Trend. Their faces are a few inches apart. 'You never did like having that girl around, did you? You know. Ali.'

Trend's face, with stoned suddenness, is a mask of solemnity.

'No,' he says huskily.

His voice gentle, Chill says, 'Because of me?' He lifts a hand and places it on Trend's shoulder. 'Hm?'

Trend nods, his eyes fixed on Chill's.

'I thought so. I had a feeling...' Chill shakes his head, with the faintest, softest of smiles. 'Hey listen, mate, that's cool. That's no big deal, I mean... you should have just said.'

Something kindles in Trend's stoned, slow-blinking eyes. His lips tremble.

'Really, mate,' Chill says. 'You should have just said. I've got no problem with that. No problem at all.' His other hand moves to Trend's thigh, rests there a moment, then slowly begins stroking upwards. 'I mean, if I'd known . . . But I didn't know, did I? I'm not a mind-reader.'

Trend sinks lower on the sofabed, his eyes on Chill's face, his eyes anywhere but on that hand stroking, stroking, moving upwards. Chill carries on talking but there is no sound from Trend. Only a quickened intensity in his breathing.

'Funny old world, eh, mate? You know, you can pride yourself on being sharp, you reckon nothing can take you by surprise, and then something pops up that's been there under your nose all the time and you never saw it.' Chill's voice is very soft now, the slow, shushing, reverberant voice of the midnight lover, of eye-glints in the pillowed dark. And now his hand is higher up, fiddling and unfastening. 'I can understand a lot of things now, my old duck. It's all a lot clearer now . . .' A mischievous smile as his hand delves. 'Hello, hello . . .'

Despite the cold of the room there is perspiration on Trend's brow, matting his fringe. His head lolls and his mouth falls open and he puts out an unsteady hand to touch Chill's shoulder. As if Chill is a vision.

And then his hand tightens on Chill's shoulder and his breathing becomes harsher and faster and though there are no words in it there is a sort of vocalization, as of something struggling to be expressed. But his eyes do not leave Chill's face, do not stray even for an instant to the curled hand steadily moving at his groin. It is as if they are in some high and perilous place and Chill has told him not to look down.

Only when at last Trend's hand clutches convulsively at Chill's shoulder and his supine body flexes and shudders does he add words to the passionate breathing.

'Chill . . . oh God . . . I'll never tell, I swear I'll never tell . . .'

'No.' Chill smiles and his hand uncurls and relinquishes and moves to the pocket of his coat. There is pleasure in his face as he looks down at Trend's head lolling against his shoulder, but it is not exactly a sensual pleasure. It is that high, rarefied glee, an emotional frequency beyond the range of normal human perception: it is a sublime amusement at this last, most devilish piece of manipulation.

'No,' says Chill, holding Trend's lolling head, and the motion with which he draws out the knife and slashes Trend's throat is no less smooth and inexitable than any movement he has made since entering this black room, 'no, mate, you never will'.

6

Things come around again, Sarah thought as she parked her car in front of Jane's house. Things come around, and nothing ever dies.

A memory of her schooldays came to her. Hockey. The school had just made the transition from girls' grammar to comprehensive co-ed when she joined it, and there was a hangover from the old regime in its emphasis on character-building games. She had loathed hockey from the depths of her soul and every moment she was forced to participate in it was torment to her. And when she had left school and entered the real world where no one played hockey unless they were weird enough to want to, the thought had often come to her that nothing in adult life could ever be as bad as it seemed, simply because it did not include hockey. The worst moments of the worst days could always be lightened by thinking, *Well, it's better than hockey anyhow.* And it was much the same with the events of five years ago. They too became a touchstone, a measure of proportion. Not having to park her car in this street any more, not having to smell Jane's subtle perfume any more, not having to subject her thoughts and feelings to an endless laboratory-rat scrutiny – that absence alone had constituted a positive pleasure over the last five years. All sorts of bad things could happen, but at least *that* was over.

And now here she was again.

Nothing ever died.

Sarah tossed her cigarette out of the car, picked up her bag, briefly considered driving away again and calling Jane with an excuse. But Jane might already have seen her car from the window. With a sigh, Sarah got out.

The snowfall was freezing over rapidly in the clear black evening, and the narrow street had been denatured by it, stilled and muffled and swathed to the point where it no longer seemed like outdoors except for the cars parked along its vanished kerbs. The cars reflected the social makeover that the street had undergone: Citroëns and Volvos predominated. Probably that was why she gave a second glance to the blue Transit van parked directly across the street from her.

The third glance was different.

Icicles of memory, slipping through her fingers. But this time... this time she gripped them and ten seconds later she was running as fast as the frozen pavement would allow her to the phone box on the corner.

Her chilled fingers fumbled for change. The glass sides of the booth were misted over in a moment and she wiped impatiently, making a hole so that she could see the van.

There it was. No crust of snow on it, so it had been parked there fairly recently. It was the van. She knew it. Without being able to pinpoint any one feature that confirmed it for her, Sarah knew with her brain and her body and everything that was her that the van she had seen at the Arena was parked a few yards away from her.

No answer from Routh's home number. Croft Wood picked up on the third ring.

'Hello? I want to speak to Detective Sergeant Routh, please.'

'I'm sorry, he's not in at the moment. This is DC Martindale, can I help at all?'

Martindale, the master of supercilious flannel. She closed her eyes a moment.

'I really need to speak to Sergeant Routh. Is he really not there? My name's Sarah Winter.'

The moment's silence on the other end might as well have been the loudest of groans.

'I'm sorry, Miss Winter, but as I said Sergeant Routh isn't in just now. Can I take a message at all?'

Sarah wiped again at the condensation on the glass, squinting out. 'Yes. Please. It's urgent. Tell him I've spotted the van. I'm in Henry Street, off Stamford Road, and the van is parked here, it's empty. It's a light blue Transit.' She gave him the registration number. 'Have you got that?'

'. . . PGE. Yes, Miss Winter. Is that everything?'

Images of DC Martindale pulling faces down the phone, not writing anything down.

'Will you make sure Sergeant Routh gets that message? Tell him I'm keeping the van in sight, and—'

A man in a short dark coat and leather gloves was

approaching the van. His hair was buttery under the lamplight. He stopped, took out keys.

Unlocked the van door.

Icicles of memory...

'Miss Winter?'

'I've got to go. Just give that message to Sergeant Routh – ' She cut herself off, clattering down the receiver, flinging out of the booth, and now hurrying back down the street to her car, hearing the cough of the van's engine, started already, away any moment. Clambering into her car, panting a little, she glimpsed the fair head turning in the driver's seat of the van as he reversed and carefully edged it out of its parking space.

Her own engine spluttered, died, then caught at last as the van was pulling away down the street. Tyres skidding a little, Sarah's car jerked out after it, Jane forgotten, everything forgotten but the van and the man inside it, last seen in a glittering scramble of confusion, last seen with a girl with red hair. And this time, not to be lost.

7

It all depended on knowledge.

There was the knowledge of Sean's fanatical loyalty to Chill, which meant that he would kill her as he had been told if she did not do it herself with the tablets. That knowledge was absolutely certain.

And then there was the knowledge of Sean's stupidity. Its shape and its extent, and its limits. That was less certain. But it was all she had.

'C'mon. C'mon, man, hurry up.'

He was still squatting by the bed, watching her. He had watched her dry-swallow each tablet with as much anxious attention as if they were going to make her better instead of kill her. She had swallowed more than half the contents of the bottle and now her hand, bleeding and clumsy with pain, hesitated over the remainder of the tablets that lay on the blanket beside her.

'Take 'em!' Sean saw the hesitation and it drove him into a sort of suppressed frenzy. He grabbed one of the tablets and thrust it towards her face. 'For crying out loud, take 'em, man!'

Alison took the tablet from his fingers, blinked at him, then slowly placed it between her lips. Gulped it down. Her gullet hurt from the dry-swallowing.

Too soon to try it yet? Would he be fooled? And yet there was no margin for error. If she left it too late it would be just that: too late. The flame in this darkness that was Alison Holdenby would go out, for ever.

It all depended.

'C'mon.' He was quivering, his smooth unfinished face contorted, and rubbing his hands feverishly up and down his legs. In order to do this, he had placed the knife on the floor just beside him. 'C'mon, hurry up, man, I told you...'

Alison's head inclined slowly back against the pillow. She blinked and blinked again, her eyes on the ceiling of the cellar, constant sky to her damned world. Her hand groped weakly, found another tablet. She let out a long thick breath, her eyelids fluttering. She let the tablet fall from her fingers.

It all depended, depended, depended... She could see it all literally depending, a vastness hanging on a thread, turning and swinging. She blinked again. She did not need to feign the dizziness and torpor: they were creeping over her steadily, and there was no telling how far behind them unconsciousness might be. No margin for error. It all depended . . .

She made a rattling noise in her throat, closed her eyes, and prayed that the real would not overtake the sham.

There were seconds of silence, each one a drop of water in a black pool. It was not a matter of holding her breath. Alison simply did not breathe. She made herself impervious to air, lungless, a thing of stone immemorially carved here.

A creak of boots came first, and then an alteration in the light that filtered her closed lids told her that Sean was leaning over her.

'Ali?'

So hard not to twitch the eyelids. Bedtime rows with Martin, back in the other world, remember, somehow you could always tell when someone was only pretending to sleep . . .

It all depended . . .

'Alison?'

No breath. A thing of stone, head flung back, one chained, knife-slashed hand amongst the tablets, the other loosely curled by its face.

'Alison?'

There was a faint pressure on the mattress by her side, as if he had leaned his hand against it. She could smell him. She remembered the smell when it had overwhelmed her, the time of the birthday cake and the laughter.

He was leaning over her.

A thing of stone.

'Alison . . .?'

She felt his breath on her face. When she opened her eyes she stared full into his, round blobs of surprise, and a second later when she stabbed the sharpened spoon deep into his neck the eyes hardly changed at all, only widened further, amazement, sheer amazement at what she had done to him. Then he fell across her, putting up a hand to his neck just as if a bee had stung him, and it seemed the sheer fact of the spike embedded in his flesh started him screaming rather than the blood or the pain. And though the screams were beautiful to her and he owed her more screams than hell had ever heard she cut them off. Grabbing him by the hair with her left hand, she jerked his head up and pulled the steel chain that bound her right hand taught across his throat and as she tightened it and tightened it, gripping his hair and feeling him flipping like a caught fish, Alison found herself screaming too. A weird ululation, a warrior's cry echoed round the cellar as she throttled him.

The cry stopped. Sean lay across her. He was making bubbling, gargling noises in his throat but he wasn't moving any more. Alison ferreted her hand underneath his body, found the keys on his belt. She wanted to weep at the feel of them. She knew this was a bad sign because she had no time to weep. She had no time for anything.

The key-ring would not come off the belt. Her lacerated, deadened hand might have been a pig's trotter. She fumbled and fumbled and the rhythm of the fumbling became hypnotic and she wondered whether she should lie back and have a sleep. Then she jerked herself back from the brink and shouted to wake herself up.

'Come *on* . . . come *on* . . .'

The echoes came flatly: everything seemed muffled. Alison's primitive hand worked and worked and suddenly did something right. The clasp of the key-ring opened its jaws to the loop of his waistband and she turned and turned it, it seemed to go on for ever, turning and turning...

The key-ring came off and the keys were in her hand. She bit back another sob, brought the keys up close to her eyes, tried to focus on them. Which was the one that fitted the cuffs? It must be a small one, but she couldn't distinguish it when they all kept spinning round and round like that.

'Come *on*... come *on*...'

She gave the keys a shake and the heavier ones jangled to the bottom of the ring and there was the little steel key, right under her thumb.

She gave a heave that seemed to cost her lifetimes of effort, to drain her of every last drop of strength she would ever have, and rolled Sean off the bed on to the floor. He fell on his face, rump sticking up, boots splayed. His tongue was sticking out and he had a frothy muzzle of blood. And he was spinning round and round like a breakdancer, how was he doing that...?

No. She shook her head. It was the pills, it was the pills, she had only the pills to fight now, 'Come *on*, come *on*...'

She unlocked the first cuff easily enough. But the joy of having one hand free sent her off into a dreamy world of satisfaction and when she jerked her head up she found she was kneeling on the floor with her head on the pillow and her mouth dribbling and one hand still chained to the bed.

She slapped her own cheeks violently. She felt the slap and it wakened her, but it didn't hurt. Her whimsical shape-changing hands obeyed her long enough for her to unlock the second cuff and then Alison was lurching across the cellar towards the steps. She was thinking that

Freezing Point

she wanted to give Sean just one good kick before she went, but there was no chance with these legs of hers. They didn't have any bones, they were just tentacles, flopping around everywhere, and though they had somehow got her to the foot of the steps, flung her against the foot of the steps indeed, she didn't see how they were ever going to get her up there. Look at the way they mounted up, so many of them, steps in a Disney castle . . . Surely it would be better to lie here a moment and sleep and then . . .

She felt herself slapping her own face again, though her hand seemed to come at her in slow motion.

'Come *on* . . .'

Alison crawled up the steps out of the cellar like a rock-climber negotiating a sheer cliff-face. It took a few minutes: several years. When she pushed open the cellar door and fell out into the passage she was screaming that jungle scream again, but it only sounded to her ears like a gnat's wail, thin and remote.

The house which she had expended so much mental energy trying to picture swam disregarded around her. She saw only a passage diminishing in incredible perspective to a door and she set her weird octopus body towards it because all that mattered was to get out of this house, the others might come in at any moment and then all would be lost, just get out get out . . .

The door opened into a bizarre wonderland which her cottony brain registered after several moments as a kitchen. Alison wobbled about in it, seeing coffee jars and saucepans and dishcloths doing comical dances around her. She wondered what she was doing here. Then faintness hit her, not in a soft wave but like some thunderous fist in the small of her back, and she swayed towards the sink. A dual function, the sink. Water. Water to wake her, also hold on to the edge of the sink, hold herself upright. Funny wacky hands just not able to hold on, though, cold steel edge of sink turning to putty and Alison slithering down, reaching out one misshapen paw to the window above the sink and clutching a fistful of net curtain, that wouldn't hold her though, twang of curtain wire coming away and Alison sinking, falling, away.

8

Well, he had taken it one step at a time and the steps had certainly led all the way. Chill had always believed in going with the flow and here was his belief well and truly vindicated because it was hard to see how things could have gone better. Trend's mouth had been shut permanently and Chill's honour had been satisfied.

And really there had been no alternative. Even if Trend had agreed to come back to Grenville Street and rejoin the Musketeers, how could Chill ever trust him not to do a runner again? As for promising never to tell, that was easy for Trend to say, and Chill would have had to have been a fool to have believed it for a second. It was obvious from the moment Trend did a runner that it only needed the right opportunity for him to, as the old gangster movies said, sing like a bird.

Besides, this one had been personal. Trend had tried to do the dirty on his old mate Chill and as anyone who knew the said old mate would tell you, he didn't stand for that.

Best of all, no one knew he had even been there. This Rabbit effort had slept the sleep of the hopeless the whole time and there were certainly no signs of forced entry or a struggle in the old bughutch. Hopefully leaving poor old Trend there with his pecker hanging out et cetera would make it look like a renty sort of affair. Drugged-up homo slain in squalid sex squat sort of thing. They might even pin it on Rabbit. Of course there were bound to be a few questions coming his way but by that time the cellar should be clear and he would have his story straight with Sean and nothing would stick. Maybe, anyway. Chill was rather surprised to find that maybe was enough for him. This was definitely the biggest risk he had ever taken but he'd be beggared if it wasn't the biggest thrill too.

A new sort of thrill, in fact. To get a bit mystical and airy-fairy about it, he'd moved on to a higher plane today. He was living as he was meant to live, living to the full, going all the way. Changing body into soul. He felt proud and a bit humble too, as if he'd stood in the presence of God and managed to look him right in the face.

Also, he felt cool. He felt cool as he drove away from Henry Street and he was still feeling cool five minutes later when he knew he was being followed.

It was a car and it was being driven by a woman. Now it might be plain-clothes filth or it might be some non-constabulary nosy parker taking an unhealthy interest. Whichever it was, it was seriously dodgy. Depending on how long she had been following him, it might even be terminally dodgy, though he was almost certain he hadn't been followed on the way to his appointment with Trendy-boots because he'd been very, very careful. But one thing was for sure. He wasn't going to head for Grenville Street, not with whatsherface on his tail. He didn't want any nosy nurks around that particular neck of the woods just now, thank you very much, whether Sean had finished his little job or not. So when he came to the ring road junction he hit the west route, in the opposite direction from Grenville Street, and once on the parkway he put his foot down and cordially invited the van to show him what it could do.

Which, alas, turned out to be not a great deal with the roads the way they were. There was a limit to how far you could push even a chunky number like this when the tarmac was somewhere underneath a mess of half-frozen slush and every other driver was understandably reluctant to end up in a body cast. She slipped in behind him and there wasn't a damned thing Chill could do about it. Getting a good look at her would have eased his frustration *un peu* but though he kept checking the mirror the headlights just made a female shadow out of her.

Well, he wasn't tired, and it would be interesting to see how long she could keep it up. He was game for a wild-goose chase if she was. Chill clicked the radio on and gently pressed the accelerator.

Fifteen minutes and five roundabouts later, Chill found himself getting the teeniest bit miffed. He didn't know what she hoped to prove by tailing him round the city's much-admired ring road system, but he was certainly finding that sodium lamps and dwarf trees could pall after a time in point of scenic interest. He was going to have to head somewhere. Somewhere that wasn't Grenville Street but somewhere he would have a legitimate reason to go to if it turned out that she was a female plod acting on a hunch.

And once again, it was cool and he was cool. He knew the very place.

Chill turned at the next junction, where a sign pointed to the Longthorpe Industrial Estate.

9

'I tell you there is somebody in there, a girl and she needs help!' shrieked old Mrs Dhanecha.

'How do you know?' Ram had not been long home from work and had found Trupti with her head in a tea towel, Kishen crying, Arun and Prakash fighting and his mother coming at him with some new cock-and-bull story about next door. He was tetchy, as tetchy as he dared to be. 'How do you know this? Did your bloody rats tell you?'

'I saw! I saw from the boys' room. You can see right down into their kitchen from there and I saw her, she was sick, she was falling—'

'What were you doing in the boys' room peeping into next door's kitchen?'

'Ai, don't stand there asking stupid questions, come with me, come next door with me now and see.'

'Amma, I'm tired of all this. I don't care what you saw or didn't see next door because I've had enough of it. God knows why, but you've got that house on the brain and I'm just about—'

'Ram!'

It was Trupti, taking her face out of the tea towel and advancing on him with quite a militant spring in her step.

'Ram, do as your mother says,' Trupti said.

Ram threw up his hands. 'You as well? Is it catching? Is everybody in this house going mad?'

'Do as your mother says, Ram. Go next door and see what's wrong.' Trupti was firm. Old Mrs Dhanecha eyed her daughter-in-law speculatively.

'Don't tell me you believe this too?' Ram said.

'Why not? Women see things. Men can't see what's

right under their noses,' Trupti said. She flapped the tea towel at him. 'Go, go!'

'Well,' old Mrs Dhanecha said, hitching up her chin, 'you hear what Trupti says. Come on.'

Ram went, old Mrs Dhanecha scuttling along behind him. He had raised his hand to knock on the front door of Number 43 a third time when his mother caught his arm.

'The back, the back,' she said. 'Quickly.'

An old ash-path ran along the foot of the back gardens at Grenville Street. The gate for Number 43 was only a low wicket-gate rotting on its hinges, and when old Mrs Dhanecha ordered Ram to kick it down he did so after no more than a single moment of surprise. And he seemed pleased when he had done it.

Old Mrs Dhanecha beetled ahead of him down the garden path. When he caught up with her she was pressing her face to the kitchen window.

'See?' she cried. 'She was here. She fell, she pulled down the curtain, there, see? Hai, in there!' She began banging on the glass and shouting. 'Anybody there? Hello? We've come to help you! Hello . . .?' She looked up at Ram, troubled. 'What do you think, son? Should we call the police?'

Ram cupped his hands round his face and peered in at the lighted kitchen. Then he shook his head and took his mother's arm.

'No, Amma. Stand back here. Stand well back.' He studied the littered path around the dustbin, stooped.

'Turn away, Amma.' He weighed the broken piece of paving slab in his hand a moment, then smashed it through the window.

10

The SIO had called the first office meeting of detectives on the Zoe Bayliss case right at the end of a hard working day and it had been a depressing experience. The Super had conducted a not very smooth press conference earlier and the experience had put him in a sour frame of mind. While not going so far as to demand why his officers had not got him a collar already, he picked holes in everything that had been done and gave Routh a particular dressing down for his supervision of the crime scene. Twenty uniforms combing the place and not a scrap, what was going on? Routh refrained from correcting his superior's rather inexact use of language and pointing out that the Huntley gravesite was almost certainly not the crime scene but only where the perp had dumped her and that therefore they would be lucky to get doodley-squat out of it. He thought that would be unwise.

When the meeting broke up and everyone slunk away Routh was ready for nothing more than a cold drink and a hot bath, or maybe just the cold drink. But when he looked into the office for his coat he found Martindale waiting for him.

Routh did not much like DC Martindale, regarding him as too smugly efficient to be true. Also, Martindale hadn't been put on the Bayliss case and Routh could see that it rankled. He could see why, too. All in all, it was awkward being around the man and he wanted to get away. But Martindale wasn't having it.

'Message for you, sir. Came in about twenty minutes ago. I said you were out.'

'Urgent?' Routh put on his coat.

'I can't comment, sir. The lady seemed to think so.'

Routh supposed Martindale had every right to display this in-your-face correctness. He was as good a copper as anyone on the Bayliss case and he was answering telephones.

It was just that he was so smarmy.

'Which lady was that?'

'The, er... Miss Winter. The lady who kept, um, feeling the need to give us information.'

Routh ignored that. 'Well?'

'She said to tell you she was at Henry Street and she had spotted "the van", to use her expression. Light blue Transit. Here's the registration number. I hope that makes sense to you, sir.'

Routh grunted. He felt much too weary for this.

'Anyway, I took the liberty of having the registration number checked through the VOI. And it is actually a genuine number.' Martindale did not make a meal of his surprise at this: just touched on it.

'Local?'

'Yes, sir,' Martindale handed him a print-out. 'Those are the details. I don't know whether they're of any use to you.'

Routh glanced at the vehicle owner's name and address. 'Elderkin, I. C., Mr, 25/5/65, 43 Grenville Street...'

Oh, he was too weary for this. There must be scores of vans like that in this city alone. Then he looked up to see the faintest of smirks on DC Martindale's face and something shifted inside him.

'Yes, very useful.' He put the print-out in his pocket. 'Thanks.'

On the way out of the building he wavered again. A raging harridan in an unseasonal boob-tube decorated with sick was just being dragged in, the night was dark and bitter, and he was off duty: he didn't want to be a copper any more, not just for the moment, thanks.

And then he remembered telling Sarah that he wasn't strictly doing this as a copper anyway.

As what then? A friend?

Yes, all right. As a favour to a friend, and also – he had to admit it – because it might put an end to this business once and for all, he decided that he would drive over to 43 Grenville Street and see if Mr I. C. Elderkin knew Miss A. Holdenby and all the rest of it. Just as a favour. And *then* he would have that cold drink.

His mind was dwelling on the cold drink, in fact, far more than on the favour when he turned into Grenville Street. But he forgot all about cold drinks when he saw the blue lights and the ambulance and the cruiser and he didn't need to count the houses to know which was Number 43.

11

Sarah didn't know the part of the city her quarry had entered now. It was a huge bleak place of industrial units and warehouses, buildings reduced to the absolutely functional, their blank brick walls coldly floodlit and giving no indication of what went on behind them. High wire fences and security barriers loomed on all sides. It was astonishing that any part of a modern city could be so completely deserted. No one lived here and it seemed that no one passed through here, certainly not at this time. She saw some lighted windows, and a few corralled parked cars, but there was no traffic. It was just her car, and the van ahead of her.

He must know she was following him, and she

supposed she ought to trust to the same intuition that had made her take up this quest in the first place and be careful. But she had gone past the point where being careful or not careful had any meaning. He could have been leading her to the edge of the world and she would still have followed.

Up ahead the van made a sudden turn into what looked like a service road. Sarah slowed her pace. Out here the snowfall was still crisp across much of the road, except where a juggernaut had ploughed two deep and dirty furrows through it.

If that road didn't connect anywhere, he would have to stop. She slowed to a crawl at the turning, wondering if there was a phone box anywhere: she might need to call Routh again.

The van was turning in at an open gateway where the service road ended. Some sort of small factory? She couldn't see any security from here.

Sarah hesitated a moment, then got out of the car, unwilling to subject it to unchartered conditions ahead. The main thing was not to lose him.

She began walking down the service road. There was no pavement out here, where the pedestrian was a trespasser, and twice she nearly turned her ankle in the pot-holed snow. The icy glitter, tinted with orange by the sodium lamps, made her eyes ache. A desolate silence seemed barely touched by the crunching of her boots.

At the gateway she hesitated. She saw three sides of a quadrangle of identical flat-roofed single-storey buildings with steel doors: garages or lockups. Nothing else but an expanse of frosted tarmac. No cars. No people.

Just the van, parked over in the left-hand corner, its lights off.

A high wire fence ran directly behind the rear of the lockups on two sides of the quadrangle, sealing the place off. But between the right-hand row and the fence there was a gap of scrubby wasteland. She might get closer that way, without being seen.

She darted, cutting across the corner of the quadrangle, out in the open for a handful of seconds and then into the scrubby shadows behind the lockups. She caught her breath for a moment and then began picking her way along, one hand inching along the wall, her feet tense and uncertain in the gritty frozen debris, untouched since the beginning of the unending winter. The three rows of lockups weren't joined at the corners, she was sure of that, and if she could get round to the gap...

She gasped in sudden pain as her pupils contracted. A flashlight was shining full in her eyes.

'Can I help you at all?'

The beam of the flashlight lowered, and brought into view the face of the young man. Blond, cheery, boyish, and puzzled-looking.

Slippery shards of memory... something she had noticed at the Arena and forgotten till now. He was noticeably of less than average height. If she had had to give a description, she would have said he was average-to-tall.

And with that simple realization, and with this brisk young man standing where he plainly had business to be and where she had none, Sarah felt her mind spinning helplessly backward.

Mr Peter Foley... repeat the name to yourself, Sarah...
Remember the normality jigsaw, Sarah...

'Are you looking for someone?' the young man asked, helping her out with a smile.

Just the perpetrator of some nameless crime that probably never happened at all. That wouldn't be you, by any chance?

Sarah Winter, the fearless hunter of innocent strangers.

Her mind spun, retreating. Her body retreated too, two clumsy steps. The young man did not move.

'No, no,' she said. 'No, I just . . . I've got myself terribly lost, I'm afraid, and I-I couldn't find a single person to ask, and so I . . . I just need pointing to the ring road, if you could . . .'

'Sure, no problem. It's a right maze round here, isn't it?' The young man's smile broadened, genial yet intimate. The skin at the corners of his eyes crinkled readily. 'Where's your car?'

'Just – just at the top of the service road.'

'Right. From here you want to go left, then left again where you see the sign for the Co-op depot. Then it's right . . .'

The young man had a pair of gloves tucked under his right arm, and when he lifted it to point one of them fell to the ground. Sarah, with overcompensating helpfulness, stooped for it first. And so saw the blood first, leaking into the snow, a scream of colour in the silent monochrome.

When she turned to run he grabbed hold of her by the hair and had her for two seconds before she pulled away leaving a fistful of it behind. She should have headed straight for the gateway but in her terror she lost her bearings and found herself running straight at the lock-ups. Realizing, she banked and slithered and fell on one knee with an explosion of pain. When she looked up he was coming at her from the gateway side, cutting off her escape.

She slithered again trying to scramble up and that saved her. The swinging blow he aimed at her head with the flashlight only caught her shoulder and threw him off balance. Scuttling backwards crabwise she managed a kick at his groin and heard him grunt and then she was on her feet and making for the high wire fence.

It must have been fifteen foot high and the wire links cut like blades even through her gloves. The whole thing shook crazily and her muscles screeched and Sarah knew she couldn't climb it, not ever. Then a hand gripped her ankle and pulled, tugged, a vicious steely tugging, come here bitch tugging. She kicked out with a jerk, freeing herself, and felt her boot heel make soft terrible contact. A glance over her shoulder: he was roaring and clutching his left eye. And then, still roaring, he swarmed up after her, his left eye screwed dreadfully shut, a puckered plum.

The fence rattled and juddered more violently than ever with the two of them climbing it and when she came gasping to the top she was convinced for a moment that the whole thing was going to give way. It was perhaps that which gave her the impetus to jump the whole fifteen feet to the other side: it was certainly the drifted snow at the bottom of the fence that stopped her bones breaking.

Still the jarring impact was enough to leave her winded and staggering. She wasn't moving fast, not fast at all, not fast enough to outrun him, and she had no idea where she was going. All she could see was the long blank wall of a factory, offering no doors, offering no hiding-places, offering nothing, and seeming to go on for ever...

She skidded round the corner of the building, her breath a live coal in her throat. Another expanse of blank wall terminating in another high fence. She made for the only other thing she could see.

It was the flatbed from an articulated lorry, half loaded

with used Calor Gas canisters. Sarah ducked her head and scrambled underneath it.

It was dark under there and smelled of oil and rubber. She wriggled further in like a frozen snake and hunched herself behind one of the vast wheels.

His boots, crunching and swift and emphatic, drew near to her and then stopped. She could see him from the knee down, six feet away from her. She could hear his breath. He was breathing hard, but not panting. He was still for several seconds, then began walking, steadily and almost casually, the length of the flatbed. Ten feet along he suddenly fell into a crouch and she saw his blond head thrust under the flatbed, looking for her. Looking for her with his one eye. Something else was looking for her too. The smiling young man had a knife and his neat square thumb was gently rubbing the haft.

She huddled herself against the wheel and held back a sob of fear. Then his head withdrew and the boots resumed their crunching progress. Up to the other end, and round. He was coming down the other side.

He would see her. She had no doubt he would kill her if he could. She had no doubt he had killed the girl with red hair.

The boots crunched past the wheel at the opposite corner of the flatbed.

Sarah moved, a frantic spider now, low and scuttling, round the wheel and out and then reaching up at once to grasp the edge of the flatbed. She swung herself up, no gymnast, boots scrabbling at the giant tread of the tyre and a starburst of pain as she knocked her knee against the edge, the knee she had fallen on. Head swimming and teeth biting down on her lip to keep the cry in and then she was up, in amongst the rusting platoon of gas canisters, and she crawled a writhing way between them to the other side, all animal now, a creeping thing, humanity set aside by older and darker powers.

Head low, she squinted between the canisters. A blond head came into view. He was walking slowly along beneath her, stooping a little, studying the shadows underneath the flatbed.

He stopped, licking his lips. Sarah laid her hands against the icy metal of the nearest canister and commanded her thundering heart to silence.

Suddenly he dropped into a crouch, thrusting his head under. She heard him say with jaunty triumph 'Boo!' and then she was up, pushing the canisters, throwing her whole weight behind them. Her boots scrabbled for purchase for a moment and then she was thrusting forward and the canisters were shunting along like some crowded production line and over, over the edge with a rattling booming din and she almost with them, stopping herself just in time and clinging to the side of the flatbed and just in time too to see him go under them, a flash of one blue eye as he flung his hands over his head and then more blueness raining down on him, tubby blue shapes like giant skittles tumbling grotesquely balletic through the air and striking him, down, down to his knees, down flat, thudding and booming, down.

12

When Routh and his uniformed backup came to the industrial estate Sarah was still sitting on the edge of the flatbed, her legs dangling, and she did not know how long she had been there. Nor would she get down, even after the ambulance had come and carefully picked the broken man out from among the gas canisters and put him, just breathing, on to a stretcher and taken him away from her sight. In the end the only thing Routh could do was get up beside her and after looking at her for a moment he changed his mind about putting his arm round her and instead took her hand and held it.

Sarah stirred but did not look at him.

'Is he dead?'

'No.' He cleared his throat. 'We found her. Alison Holdenby. At his house. He'd been keeping her there. He'd . . . done things to her. There was another guy in on it, she'd fought him off, tried to get out. He was in a bit of a mess, but he was coherent. I tried to talk to him before they took him away, but he wouldn't say anything. I'm no grass and all that crap. The next-door neighbours got suspicious and alerted us.'

Sarah gazed deep at the weave of her jeans. 'How did she die?'

'She didn't. She's alive. They've taken her to hospital.'

The tears were slow, painful, and halting, like the first drops of a thaw after an age of ice. They trickled down her face and fell at last, one by one, from her lips and jaw and Routh watched them fall.

'How . . .' She lifted a hand, but let it drop again, did not wipe them. Instead she looked at him. 'How did you find me?'

'The neighbour. When I said we needed to find Elderkin and his van the neighbour remembered him saying he had a lockup out at Longthorpe. It was our best shot.'

'How long had she . . . Alison been there?'

'We don't know yet. But it looks like . . . it looks as if . . .'

He couldn't finish it. She answered the pressure of his

hand, knowing that he was the one needing reassurance now.

13

The ward seemed to be filled from one end to the other with daffodils. Sarah looked with vague dismay at the bunch she carried in her hand, then shrugged and carried on walking. Bright bars of sunlight lay across the scrubbed floor and she could feel the moments of warmth as she passed through them.

When the nurse showed her into the room Sarah stood for a moment, timidly, a long way from the bed. All at once she felt absurdly shy.

After all, she didn't know this person at all.

'Hello.'

The girl in the bed had spoken first. Sarah jolted herself into movement, and approached the bed.

'Hello. I'm Sarah Winter.'

'Hi. They said you were coming.'

'Good, good ... Didn't want to spring a, you know, surprise on you.' Sarah chuckled nervously, then looked at the flowers she was carrying. 'More daffs, I'm afraid.'

'They're lovely. Thanks ever so much. Please, have a seat.'

Sarah sat down. She looked for a moment at the girl in the bed, thin and pale, her auburn hair neatly brushed, her dark eyes here but not here: then looked around the room.

'Goodness,' she said, 'your own private ward.'

'I know,' the girl said, with a trace of a rueful smile. 'It's a bit boring in here, specially now I'm feeling better. But the press kept trying to get at me so they had to hide me away. Ordeal in the house of horror and all that.' She made an involuntary noise that she tried unsuccessfully to turn into a cough.

Sarah's unaccountable shyness deepened. Suddenly it seemed impossible that she would ever think of something to say. She talked for a living and now she couldn't find a single word.

The silence stretched to snapping point and Sarah burst out desperately, with a gesture at the window, 'Isn't it nice to see the sun again?'

And then she knew that that was the worst, most tasteless, most inappropriate thing she could possibly have said. Her face flamed and looking down at the girl's white hand lying on the coverlet she murmured, 'I'm sorry – what am I . . . I'm so sorry . . .'

'It's all right.' The girl shifted in the bed and then her hand reached out, simply and openly, and after a moment Sarah took it.

'Shall we start again?' Sarah said.

The girl smiled. 'All right. Hello, Sarah.'

'Hello, Alison.'

And then they were both smiling and the silence didn't matter. There were no words because there were no words.